Forge Books by Heather Webber

Midnight at the Blackbird Café
South of the Buttonwood Tree
The Lights of Sugarberry Cove

THE LIGH
SUGARBERI

THE LIGHTS *of* SUGARBERRY COVE

Heather Webber

A TOM DOHERTY ASSOCIATES BOOK
New York

This is a work of fiction. All of the characters, organizations, and events portrayed in this novel are either products of the author's imagination or are used fictitiously.

THE LIGHTS OF SUGARBERRY COVE

A Forge Book
Published by Tom Doherty Associates
120 Broadway
New York, NY 10271

www.tor-forge.com

Forge® is a registered trademark of Macmillan Publishing Group, LLC.

Library of Congress Cataloging-in-Publication Data

Names: Webber, Heather S., author.
Title: The lights of Sugarberry Cove / Heather Webber.
Description: First edition. | New York : Forge, a Tom Doherty Associates Book, 2021. | Identifiers: LCCN 2021009112 (print) | LCCN 2021009113 (ebook) | ISBN 9781250774620 (hardcover) | ISBN 9781250774637 (ebook)
Classification: LCC PS3623.E393 L54 2021 (print) | LCC PS3623.E393 (ebook) | DDC 813/.6—dc23
LC record available at https://lccn.loc.gov/2021009112
LC ebook record available at https://lccn.loc.gov/2021009113

Our books may be purchased in bulk for promotional, educational, or business use. Please contact your local bookseller or the Macmillan Corporate and Premium Sales Department at 1-800-221-7945, extension 5442, or by email at MacmillanSpecialMarkets@macmillan.com.

First Edition: July 2021

Printed in the United States of America

0 9 8 7 6 5 4 3 2 1

To all those who believe in life's magic.
May you always continue to see it.

THE LIGHTS OF SUGARBERRY COVE

Chapter 1

Sadie

"Whereabouts are you from, Sadie?" Mrs. Iona Teakes asked as she deftly chopped pecans on a wooden cutting board in her sun-steeped kitchen, the summery afternoon light spilling through a bay window overlooking the Coosa River.

Across the yawning stretch of water, the main street of a small town fluttered with activity as people went about their day. Before coming to Mrs. Teakes's charming home, I'd stopped for lunch at the local burger place, not only for something to appease my grumbling stomach but to also get a feel for the town. Its people. Its mood. Its potential. Its heartbeat.

I'd been looking for a place to call my home for so long now that I was beginning to think I'd never find it.

But Wetumpka, Alabama, had promise.

A revitalization initiative was in full swing, and the heart of the community was evident in the rebuilding that had taken place in the years since a tornado swept through uprooting trees, buildings, lives. Heart was my number one requirement when it came to a hometown.

"I was born and raised about an hour and a half north of here. In Shelby County."

Curiosity burned in Mrs. Teakes's watery eyes as her gaze shifted to my hair, then away again, but she was much too polite to ask any prying questions, for which I was grateful. I'd rather not talk about myself at all, but especially not about my hair and the circumstances of how it had come to be this particular color.

My mama has often said my glittering silver tresses reminded her of starlight, as though all the stars in Alabama had fallen directly onto my head, leaving me with a sparkly crown, a stunning glow. Time and again, I'd pointed out that Alabama's famous fallen stars had been meteorites, and if they'd crashed onto my head, I'd be dead. But Mama always argued the fact that I *had* died the night my hair turned color, and who was to say it hadn't been the *stars* that had caused my brief death?

It hadn't been the stars. It had been a watery accident. But Mama wasn't one for accepting small truths, favoring bold exaggerations instead.

Stars bested water, plain and simple.

I'd drowned that summer night nearly eight years ago in Lake Laurel, at just eighteen years old. But I'd been saved. Brought back to life. Brought back to a *new* life. To a new normal. All these years later, I hadn't quite figured out who this new Sadie Way Scott was exactly. Or why I had been saved. No matter how far I ran away from my hometown of Sugarberry Cove, Alabama, that particular *why* haunted me, following my every move, because there had been a reason. I felt it, deep down, like a pulsing bubble of pressure that kept me searching, seeking.

"Is there anything I can do to help, Mrs. Teakes?" I needed a diversion from my thoughts or else I was bound to fall into a deep mudhole of self-pity. I'd already set up my cameras, three in all, to frame specific shots of the homey kitchen that breathed vintage charm, which was easy to do since it hadn't been updated in at least sixty years, possibly more. The room was painted a cheerful blue, and the scent of vanilla floated in the air, as if being exhaled by the colorful floral wallpaper that served as a backsplash. The bulbous white fridge, covered in family photos, postcards, and old newspaper clippings, hummed loudly, its long chrome handle gleaming. The wide stove with side-by-side ovens had two storage drawers at the bottom, and I could only imagine the stories it could tell of the meals it had cooked.

But those stories would have to wait. The focus of today's video was on a dish served cold. Several small glass bowls were lined up along the ceramic tile countertop, each filled with a different ingredient. Shredded coconut. Mandarin oranges. Sour cream. Maraschino cherries. Pineapple chunks. Mini marshmallows. Once the food prep was complete, I'd be the one asking all the questions for the sake of the video, which would be posted the following week on my YouTube channel, A Southern Hankerin'.

The videos were about more than Southern cooking. At their heart were human-interest pieces featuring people across the South willing to share a family recipe and the story behind it. Last week, I'd had an in-depth preliminary phone interview with Mrs. Teakes, and today, I'd film her while she told me how, in the late 1960s, she'd captured the heart of her late husband with her recipe for ambrosia salad.

During the interview I'd be sure to mention how the South proudly labeled some desserts as salad. To those who lived here, this came as no surprise. After all, this was the land where mac and cheese was considered a vegetable. But my audience wasn't limited to the South. I had viewership that spanned the globe, a fact that amazed me—though it shouldn't. People tuned in for the heartwarming, relatable stories, which were needed in the world more now than ever.

Mrs. Teakes set down her knife and flexed age-spotted hands. Intelligent brown eyes, framed in an abundance of delicate wrinkles, assessed while their softness begged for more information. "Not much left to do, only these pecans to finish chopping. Whereabouts in Shelby County?"

I fussed with a camera setting that needed no adjustment. "Sugarberry Cove."

The river water below Mrs. Teakes's kitchen churned with happiness, white-crested rapids pushing and pulling and racing. Farther down the river, the water calmed, gradually stretching into stillness near a bridge with five arches that created circular reflections on the water's suddenly smooth, glassy surface.

Still waters that reminded me of what used to be my home.

"On Lake Laurel? How wonderful! I've been several times for the water lantern festival. A lovely little town. So enchanting. Do you still live there?"

Much like the rapids, my stomach churned as I glanced at the clock on the countertop microwave, wishing time away. My gaze shifted to a tarnished brass teakettle that rested on a stove eye, then to two teacups that dangled on hooks under a golden oak cabinet, one cup having MR. stenciled on it, the other MRS. The former looked pristine in condition, the latter well used, well loved, with its tea-darkened interior and chipped handle. Hung askew on the wall by the fridge was a framed, stained cross-stitched cloth with the words HOME IS WHERE YOUR HEART IS.

Old wounds ached at the simple words, and I turned to look out the window instead of at the phrase that haunted. Mocked.

"No, ma'am, but I still have family up that way. My older sister, her husband, and their little boy live up there. And my mother owns a bed-and-breakfast cottage on the lake and my great-uncle, who's more like a granddaddy to me, lives and works at the cottage, too." I bit my lip to keep from saying any more, from spilling my heart onto the cutting board next to the pecans. Why was I revealing so much?

But I knew why.

The water.

I missed Sugarberry Cove.

I missed my *old* home.

The home, the family that I'd had before the watery accident that had changed everything and everyone. Most especially me.

Mrs. Teakes picked up the knife once more. "Where *do* you live, Sadie?"

I turned my back to the window and on old memories. "Here and there and everywhere. I travel a lot, and I'm still looking for the right place to settle down. This seems like a nice area. Wetumpka, I mean."

"Indeed it is. I grew up here, and I wholeheartedly recommend it." She chopped another pecan, the sharp knife slicing nutty, brown flesh into small, pale pieces. "The water lantern festival is coming up soon, if memory serves. The weekend after next? Will you go back for that? Such a special event."

"No, ma'am." Truly, it was the last place on earth I wanted to be.

Setting the knife down again, she faced me. Slim, graceful fingers fiddled with the top button of her pale-blue cardigan as she said, "No? The lady of the lake, Lady Laurel, might be especially generous this year, granting multiple wishes. You don't have any wishes to set afloat?"

The lanterns at the festival carried wishes across the lake, which came true only if Lady Laurel pulled the floating vessel from the surface of the dark water to fill her underwater home with the glowing light created by pure, heartfelt wishes.

Deep lines fanned across her cheeks as Mrs. Teakes smiled, and the warmth in her eyes pulled at my heartstrings, making me want to tell her the whole story, start to finish, about how sometimes during the water lantern festival it was important to be very careful what you wished for.

"The festival will make do without my wishes." Faking a smile, I picked up the knife to finish chopping the pecans, etiquette be damned. The sooner I could stop talking about myself, the better.

Mrs. Teakes's gaze slowly drifted to my hair again. "I've heard told several stories of Lady Laurel's kindness, not always having to do with the lanterns. There've been rescues, haven't there? Boaters? Swimmers? Didn't she save a young woman once from drowning?"

The glimmer in her eyes made me suspect she already knew why my hair was this color. There had been a flurry of media interest after my accident, but it had died down fairly quickly, thankfully. I'd hated the attention. Everyone stared. Whispered. The doctors had been mystified by my hair but ultimately chalked up the startling change in color to a traumatic shock reaction. These days the looks my hair garnered were a sight easier to deal with because most people assumed I purposely dyed it this color. To be edgy or artsy or as a *brand*, to set myself apart from a zillion other online creators. But back home in Sugarberry Cove, everybody knew its true source: lake magic.

I'd been saved by Lady Laurel, the lady of the lake.

There were many days I cursed the wish I made the night I'd fallen into the water, the wish that had ultimately caused my accident and its aftermath. I'd love nothing more than to go back in time to make a different choice. But there was no going back to what used to be. It was gone, left behind in the lake after I'd been pulled out, floating away on a water lantern carrying a wish that had changed life as I knew it.

In a span of a few short weeks, I'd died, been brought back to life, dropped out of college, shattered people's belief in me, suffered crushing heartbreak, and began drifting around the state in search of odd jobs to keep afloat until I eventually started making videos to tell other people's stories. Now I lived out of a suitcase as I traveled the South for A Southern Hankerin'.

Why had I been saved?

Using the blade of the knife to sweep pecans from the chopping board into a glass bowl, I barely noticed as the knife bit painlessly into the side of my thumb. A spot of red blossomed instantly.

I quickly folded my fingers over the wound, pressing tightly.

Mrs. Teakes gasped and set her hand on my arm. "Oh dear. I'll fetch a bandage."

"No need. It's only a nick, and I'm a quick healer." An understatement, to be sure. "It didn't even hurt."

"Nonsense. I'll be just a moment."

As Mrs. Teakes hurried out of the room, an incoming text message vibrated the phone in the back pocket of my jeans. I pulled the phone free and saw the message was from my sister, Leala Clare.

Sadie Way, you need to come home. Mother's okay but had a minor heart attack. She's at Shelby Baptist.

My stomach lurched into my throat, and my hands shook as I stared at the screen. At first I was disbelieving that my sister would *text* me this news, but then I remembered I'd asked her to always text before calling in case I was filming. And even in the face of something so important, she hadn't ignored my request. Leala was nothing if not a rule follower.

"Sadie, are you all right? You've gone ghostly white."

Mrs. Teakes stood before me, concern flaring in her eyes, bandage in hand.

"I'm okay, but I'm sorry, I need to go. There's been an emergency." I quickly gathered my cameras and notes. As I headed out the door, I said, "I'll call to reschedule our interview."

"Anytime, dear. Anytime."

A few minutes later, I turned down the jazz playing on the car radio and backed carefully out of the narrow asphalt driveway. Mrs. Teakes stood on the front porch, waving, the bandage fluttering in her hand like a tiny white flag. My gaze dropped to my thumb on the steering wheel, to the spot where the knife had pierced. The wound had already disappeared, the skin as smooth as it had been before being sliced.

As I headed north toward the home I'd barely seen in years, I couldn't help but wish that my emotional wounds could be so easily healed as well.

Chapter 2

Leala

"Stay true to yourself," I said to the bathroom mirror, trying not to notice the panic-induced storm clouds gathering in my gray eyes. I carefully placed a small bottle of shampoo into a clear sleeve of a toiletry bag and turned the container so the label faced outward. I did the same for bottles of conditioner, moisturizer, eye drops, sunscreen, and hair spray.

"You'll be fine, Leala Clare," Connor said from the bedroom, his deep voice loaded with impatience. "You'll be there only a few days."

He barely tolerated my affirmations, which I'd adopted not long after I started practicing yoga, six months after Tucker's rough birth. Often, the simple phrases were the only things that got me through the days when I started questioning decisions I'd once been so sure about.

"Do I need to mention," he added, "how much you sound like your mother when you do that?"

I poked my head out the bathroom doorway so he could see the dirty look I was shooting him. "Are you trying to pick a fight?"

Without looking my way, he shrugged. "I'm just saying."

Early morning summer sunlight filtered through the curtains, casting the master bedroom in a soothing orange haze, and I took a deep breath and tried desperately to find some inner peace. Or any peace at all. I was on edge. A nervous wreck. I nibbled a thumbnail, then forced myself to drop my hand. It had been years since I'd bitten my nails.

Connor sat in the king-size bed in a tight-fitting white T-shirt and blue boxer briefs, his back against the tufted headboard, his laptop balanced on a pillow on his lap. Thick brown hair stood in disarray, as it did every morning until he showered. He was a fitful sleeper, and the tossing and turning gave him extreme bedhead.

"Well, stop saying it, please." I was nothing like my mother. She was an F5 tornado while I was a light breeze.

He turned his head slightly to give me a brief smile, then glanced back at his computer screen. Stifling the urge to cross the room to smooth his unruly hair into place, which he'd hate, I tightened the sash of my robe and instead headed for my nightstand, where I picked up two romance novels. I carried them to the upholstered bench at the foot of the bed where an open weekender was waiting to be packed, and said, "I need all the pep talks I can get to survive the next few days without losing my composure. Or my mind."

Or myself.

I'd worked too hard on all three to lose sight of them now.

I placed a pair of pajamas into the bag. "You know how my mother brings out the worst in me."

Mother's heart attack had been treated with what the cardiologist had called "clot-busting" drugs to clear the 60 percent blockage in her artery, and I'd been grateful no major surgery was needed. After recuperating for two days in the hospital, she was to be discharged early this afternoon, and Sadie and I had agreed to spend the weekend with her—mostly to give our great-uncle Camp a well-deserved break and to make sure Mother rested as the doctor had prescribed, because Susannah Scott rarely did what she was told.

Saying nothing, Connor continued to peck at the computer's keyboard. Deep worry lines creased the skin between his blue eyes as he concentrated on the screen. At thirty years old, he was a senior associate at a big law firm in Birmingham, trying to make partner this year, and his work consumed his every waking moment. Or at least it seemed that way.

I picked off a loose, long blond hair from the arm of my robe. My hair tended to shed when I was stressed, and after these last few days of dealing with my mother and seeing Sadie, I was surprised I wasn't yet bald.

The last time I'd seen my little sister had been at Easter brunch four months ago, here at my house. The stretches between her visits were growing more and more distant. If not for Mother's cardiac situation, Sadie might not have come around again until Thanksgiving.

Even though we were four years apart in age, we'd once been so close. Thick as thieves, tied at the hip. We'd done everything together growing up, mostly because Mother had designated me

Sadie's keeper while Mother was busy with the cottage or with her (now ex) boyfriend, our neighbor Buzzy Hale—which had felt like always. I'd hated the forced responsibility but loved Sadie enough to accept it without much argument, because for one, I wasn't much of an arguer. And two, if not me, then who'd watch over Sadie, keep her safe? Certainly not Mother. She had a proven track record of being negligent.

As Sadie and I had grown older and Mother and Buzzy's public displays of affection intensified, we'd take off to escape the embarrassment of it all. We'd go swimming or biking or spend long hours at the library, giggling as we read romance novels hidden behind *Teen* magazines. We'd drifted apart some when I went to college, but we still managed to make time for each other. Weekend spa dates. Movies. Long lunches.

Then, the accident happened and nothing had ever been the same. At the thought of that lantern-lit night, guilt twined through my stomach, making it ache. I pressed a hand to my belly and said, "As much as I hate to be away for three nights, this weekend will be a good time to have another heart-to-heart with Sadie about moving back to Sugarberry Cove for good. I can't remember the last time we spent more than a few hours together."

Connor didn't look up from his computer. "You'll be wasting your breath. Sadie doesn't want to move back. She's made that quite clear."

It was true that every time I brought up the subject, Sadie shut down the conversation quickly. "Maybe this time will be different, since she'll be *here*, in Sugarberry Cove." Right now, she was staying at a hotel close to the hospital. I'd asked her to stay with me, but she'd declined, saying she wanted to be near Mother. "I know the lake is a painful reminder of what she went through, but staying away isn't helping her any."

Of course, Sadie never blamed the lake outright for her desertion, instead claiming she simply loved to travel and that her career was on the road—but I wasn't buying it. She was escaping—just like we used to do when Mother and Buzzy got too touchy-feely with each other. Sadie's job was nothing but a front. She had dubbed herself a "content creator," and I couldn't help but roll my eyes even thinking about the title. I truly didn't even know how she was making ends meet.

If she wanted to see what hard work really looked like, she

should spend some time with Connor. He'd had a hardscrabble upbringing, earned a hardship scholarship to college, and was top of his class in law school down in New Orleans, where we'd lived for three years before moving back here, to my hometown.

But I knew better than anyone that Sadie would hate spending time with Connor more than being back in Sugarberry Cove, a place she'd once loved with her whole heart, near family and old friends, all of whom had become virtual strangers.

I plucked another long hair off my sleeve. "Since Sadie will be staying at the cottage, she won't be able to hide from her fears. Three days isn't a lot of time, but maybe with being so close to the water, she'll finally be able to start healing. That's all she needs. A *start.* Don't you think? Every day is a chance at a new beginning."

"Mm," Connor grumbled.

He'd obviously tuned me out. Sometimes I wanted to get rid of our internet altogether. There was something to be said for unplugging once in a while. Suddenly irritated by his distraction, I picked up a pile of three blouses from my side of the bed and tossed them into the open weekender, having instant regrets as soon as they landed in a loose heap. I quickly refolded the shirts into a neat stack. "Maybe I should take Tucker with me this weekend after all."

At this, Connor finally glanced up. "A two-year-old at the hospital? And underfoot at the cottage while your mother convalesces? You think that's a good idea?"

His tone stated that this was a ridiculous idea, and maybe it was. But I liked it better than Tucker staying here with a distracted Connor.

"A cottage under renovation, at that," Connor added.

Truthfully, the renovations were the least of my worries, as they were confined to two guest rooms on the first floor that had been damaged by water from a burst pipe. The restoration work was almost done, due to be completed just in time for the water lantern festival.

I said, "It's not ideal, but you're busy with work."

"We've been through this. I took today off, didn't I?"

We had been through it. I'd insisted Tucker come with me. Connor insisted Tucker stay home, away from hospitals and illnesses and recuperations. It wasn't as if I wanted Tucker exposed to the hospital and its germs, either. And I certainly didn't want Tucker exposed to my mother's quirks for any great length of time. Except for our monthly dinners, I managed to keep our visits quick. In and out in less than half an hour.

But at the cottage, at least Tucker would be with me, where I could keep a close eye on him. I'd even offered Connor a compromise—dinner at the cottage tomorrow night—but he had dismissed it straight off, saying he wanted the weekend alone with Tucker. Which on the surface was all well and good, but underneath there was one big flaw with his plan: Connor's inability to unplug from work.

"We both know that a vacation day isn't really time off," I said. "You'll be on call. You'll check your email. You'll be easily distracted. Like you are now." In truth, I could do naked cartwheels in front of him, and he probably wouldn't look up from his computer long enough to notice. Or care.

I wasn't sure which was worse.

Drawing in a deep breath, I glanced around at the big master bedroom with its vaulted ceiling, so cavernous that it sometimes made me feel small and lost. I had a successful husband, a beautiful little boy, and a fancy house that was so big we'd hired a service to help clean it. I should be happy. Content. Especially since I'd worked so very hard on being happy and content.

Yet . . . I felt restless in the one place where I should feel most comfortable: home.

And truly, I should be thankful for Connor's job. His hard work had allowed me to quit my job as a healthcare accountant to stay home full-time, something I'd always wanted to do once we had a child. Or thought I wanted. I shook my head, not wanting to go *there* right now.

But instead of thankful, I was resentful. Because somewhere along the line I'd lost Connor. The man I'd fallen in love with. The man who'd shared my hopes and dreams. And sure, those dreams had shifted over the years, blurred, and changed course due to unexpected bumps in the road, but the grand plan, the happy, close-knit family part, had never altered.

But somehow, over the eight years we'd been married, he'd lost sight of what we'd always wanted, too engrossed in billable hours to see that he was slowly erasing himself from our lives. I didn't know how to bring him back to us, to make him understand all he was losing by working all the time. Somehow Connor Keesling, the man I loved with my whole heart, had become the thing I despised most in the world.

A workaholic.

Uneasy, I shifted my weight and added two pairs of shorts and yoga pants and a yoga mat to the bag. "It takes only a moment for a two-year-old to wander away or find trouble. Not even a moment. A split second. If you're glued to your phone or laptop all weekend . . ."

I couldn't even finish the sentence as all the what-ifs flew through my head, flashes of the worst-case scenarios that often gave me insomnia and nightmares.

I knew how fast a world could be turned inside out.

I tried not to think of my daddy's accident often, but every once in a while it sprang unbidden into my mind. One wrong step on a tall ladder, a long fall, and he was gone. I'd been only five years old, Sadie just one. I was grateful to still have memories of him, but Sadie only knew him through photos and stories shared time and again, because they were the only way we had to keep him alive, at least in our minds.

"Leala, I promise you I won't be working. Don't you understand? I'm looking forward to a little father-son bonding. We'll be fine, just us boys."

I blinked tears away and almost laughed. Did I understand? Of course I did. Better than he did.

I wished . . . No. Not wished. I *hated* wishes. I *wanted* to trust him to not break his promise. I also wanted him to have time with Tucker and to know our son like I did—and for Tucker to know Connor. It was one of my deepest desires. Maybe if they had this time together, Connor would come to understand all he was missing. Money and a big house were nice, but they weren't your son's chubby arms squeezing you tightly at bedtime. They weren't his little voice saying, "Luh you," because he couldn't pronounce the *v* in *love.*

But the thought of leaving them together made me ache with fear.

Connor glanced up and, with a heavy sigh, set the computer aside, stood up, and walked over to me. Gently pulling me into a hug, he rested his chin on the top of my head. "We'll be fine, Leala. You're acting like I'm not capable of taking care of my own child."

I bit back a sharp confirmation. Connor was barely home other than to sleep. He worked eighty-hour weeks, and when he was home, he was always on call. He'd missed so much already. First words and steps and all the everyday little things that made me laugh, like how Tucker chirped back at the birds outside the window as if having a meaningful conversation and how he chased his shadow on a sunny day.

Connor didn't know Tucker the way I did.

He couldn't take care of him the way I could or keep him safe.

Connor kissed the top of my head. "Tucker and I are going to be fine. And so will you. So it's settled?"

I pressed my eyes closed and nodded, hoping I wasn't making yet another choice I'd come to question later on. To regret. Lord, some days the regrets felt like they were suffocating me. I wrapped my arms tighter around Connor, suddenly not wanting to let him go.

It had been so long since he'd held me for any length of time, and my body reacted, aching for more of his touch. I glanced at the clock, then tipped an ear to the silent baby monitor. Tucker usually woke around seven thirty, an hour from now.

Emboldened, I slid my hand under Connor's shirt and slowly skimmed it up to his chest. His breath caught, and he smiled down at me, and for a moment, a blissful second, it felt as though we had no problems at all. It was just us, Leala and Connor, with our all-consuming love and an old, familiar white-hot passion that instantly flared to life from the cold, gray ash it had faded to over the years. As he slipped his hand inside my robe, his thumb resting near the top of the long raised scar on my stomach, his phone on the nightstand dinged with a notification, and he froze.

"Leave it," I said, holding his warm hand against my skin. It was six thirty in the morning. Whatever it was could wait. These kinds of loving moments between us were so few and far between of late that surely right here and now with me was more important than whatever message had come in.

There was a slight hesitation before he made his decision. "I can't. I'm sorry." He pulled away and stretched across the bed to grab his phone. The warm spot on my skin where his hand had rested instantly chilled, and I turned to hide the wash of tears in my eyes. I tightened my robe and tossed the rest of my clothes into the weekender, neatness and organization be damned. I hurried back to the bathroom, closed the door behind me, and finished packing my toiletries, throwing makeup and hair brushes into the bag without care. Suddenly I wanted to get away from Connor for a while. To get away from the anger that flared a bright, hot red, obliterating any and all flickering white passions. I glanced in the mirror, and unable to find any affirmations for this moment, I quickly looked away, unable to bear the pain I saw in the reflection.

I missed my husband.

I hung my robe on the back of the door and tried to ignore the doubt that came flooding in full force, nearly knocking me over. If Connor couldn't put his phone down for me, he surely wouldn't if Tucker needed him, promise or no. I took a deep, steadying breath and heard Connor's voice in my head, telling me how he wanted this weekend to bond with Tucker. I let it replay over and over again, reminding myself that I wanted them to bond too. I needed to trust Connor. Dear God, I didn't know how I was going to do it, but I loved him enough to *try*.

Before I changed my mind about leaving altogether, I dressed quickly. I'd originally planned to have breakfast with Tucker before leaving, but I decided to go now. Right now. I'd sneak into Tuck's room, give him kisses, and be on my way. It was probably better this way, anyhow, without a long, drawn-out goodbye.

Toiletry bag in hand, I opened the door. "Tucker likes his bananas cut up, not whole."

I couldn't even look at Connor straight on while I zipped the weekender bag and slipped on my shoes, but out of the corner of my eye, I could see that he sat on the edge of his side of the bed.

"Leala Clare . . ."

I ignored the plea in his voice.

"And he won't go to sleep without a book and his plushie, Moo the cow."

There was a long pause before he said, "I know."

"He hates bath time. You'll need to bribe him with bubbles." I headed for the door, bag in hand, pieces of my heart trailing behind me like broken glass.

"Leala."

Tears clouded my eyes as I set a hand on the doorknob. Bracing myself against waves of pain, I pulled open the door and walked out. I'd predicted this to be a hellacious weekend but hadn't expected my misery to begin before I even left home.

Chapter 3

Sadie

"If I'd have known all it would take was me dying to get my girls together at the cottage for an extended visit, I'd have done it long ago."

The cottage. Not *home*.

This said everything about how my sister and I had been raised up. Sugarberry Cottage had always been Mama's first priority. Leala and I had often felt like afterthoughts while Mama had dedicated most of her time and energy to the cottage's upkeep and guests. Yet, when I had walked through the wide front door earlier, I hadn't been able to deny the emotion that had washed over me, a brief swallow-me-whole sense of belonging, of love, for this old house. This was where I'd been born and raised, and my homesickness was undeniable.

On the third floor of the house, the air-conditioning hummed and a ceiling fan stirred the tepid air—in the summertime it was never truly cool up here. Off a short hallway, Mama's bedroom was as colorful and dramatic as she was, loud and proud, with its vivid teal walls and tangerine-colored drapes, which bracketed three side-by-side windows that overlooked the lake. The bedroom's vibrancy should've been too much, an overload of senses that would have most people squinting at its brightness or turning away, but instead it was somehow comforting in its all-encompassing radiance.

Like the rest of the house, this room showed some wear, but in a cozy kind of way, a sharp contrast to the disconcerting whispers of neglect I'd noticed downstairs. This space felt lived in. *Loved*.

"Mother," Leala Clare said sternly as she flew about the queen-size bed, throwing back a bold floral quilt, tugging sheets, and fluffing pillows like a small bird prepping a nest. "Joking about death isn't the least bit funny. *You didn't die*."

"Lighten up, LC." Mama produced a tight smile, her usually rosy cheeks unnaturally pale, and her blue eyes dull. "You've become so tightly wound that even the curls on your head have straightened out."

Color climbed Leala's neck as she ran long fingers through straight blond hair, then picked off a loose strand that had landed on the cap sleeve of her white blouse. "I flat ironed it. It helps stop the frizz." She pasted on a fake smile. "I'd be happy to loan you my flat iron, *Mother*, if you're wanting to give it a try."

Pick, pick, pick.

The two of them were like to make me crazy. Mama hated being called Mother, something Leala had adopted after starting college, and Leala hated being called LC, a childhood nickname she'd abandoned about the same time.

"No thank you," Mama said, sweeter than artificial sugar. "I'm not embarrassed by the things that make me unique. Might I remind you that beauty is found within, LC? I choose to stay true to myself." She patted her hair, and it sprang up again the moment she lifted her hand, like a Jack released from its box. Short, graying brown curls corkscrewed about her head like she'd recently stuck both hands in a light socket.

At the words, Leala frowned deeply. "And *I* do visit."

I held back a sigh at Leala's inability to leave well enough alone. She was forever picking at old wounds with not only her need to be right but also her longing for recognition for always doing the *right* thing. The proper thing. And, well, to simply be *recognized*. Mama hadn't exactly been a hands-on mother.

With my arm curved around her back, I guided Mama across the wide-plank white pine floor toward her bed while trying my best to avoid my sister's dangling bait, which I'd become an expert at dodging these past eight years. Worried about my happiness and my distance from family, she'd made no secret of wanting me to move back to Sugarberry Cove. She believed, and I had let her, that I'd been avoiding coming home because of some sort of traumatic response to the lake. That I was scared of it, or that it made me relive the night I'd drowned. All of which couldn't be further from the truth but was easier to use as an excuse for the complicated reasons I stayed away.

Through a crack in the tangerine curtains, I watched the shimmery waters of Lake Laurel pulse against the seawall behind the cottage. I had always been drawn to the lake, like a child reaching for her mother, knowing she'd be embraced wholeheartedly. Well, some children and some mothers. Around here if I'd wanted a hug, I went to Leala or Uncle Camp, my daddy's uncle, who was as close to a granddad as Leala and I have ever known. My mama wasn't one for tender affection. At least not with Leala and me. At least, according to Leala, not since Daddy had died.

No, the lake certainly was not at fault for why I'd stayed away. I loved the lake with my whole heart. In fact, I was going to have to do my best to avoid the water, especially swimming in it, if I was going to be able to leave it behind on Monday morning. It held the power to keep me here, a place I most definitely did not want to stay.

For one, my life was on the road. Then there was the guilt and shame that went hand in hand with being home. Then last, but certainly not least, there was Will Lockhart. Thinking of running into him made me want to hop in my car and drive as far as a tank of gas would take me.

"Ah, yes, and your visits are such a delight, LC!" Mama exclaimed, slightly out of breath. "Your arrival always comes with the air of a death-row prisoner being summoned to her final meal."

The climb upstairs had been arduous for Mama, but it was one she'd insisted on, having refused to convalesce in one of the three empty second-floor guest rooms. And when Susannah Scott made a decision, it was near to impossible to change her stubborn mind. I'd learned a long time ago when to pick my battles.

Mama used my arm for balance, and I could practically feel exhaustion buzzing through her dry skin as she slowly lowered onto the edge of the mattress. A dark bruise marred the underside of her arm, where an IV had been in place for the last two days.

"But," Mama went on, "you do bring Tucker with you, the little darlin', who's a ray of sunshine amidst the gloom, so we make do, don't we? Where is he, by the way?"

"Home," Leala said. The word was punctuated with pent-up frustration. "With Connor for the weekend."

Mama's eyebrows rose. "Is that so? Three whole nights without Tuck? You'll have separation anxiety by midnight, you poor thing. I have sleeping pills if you need them. You're more than welcome to poke around my medicine cabinet."

Leala's jaw tightened but she didn't snap back, which was a feat of strength if ever I saw one. She might be a bit of an overprotective, overly attached mother, but only because our mother had been the complete opposite and Leala was overcompensating, wanting to break the cycle.

Above the queen-size wrought iron bed hung a large square canvas drenched in a riot of jewel-toned colors. The painting was of a mandala in an elaborate lotus flower design that Mama had created and framed not long after my accident. If one studied it carefully, the center of the flower, its innermost petal from where all the others unfolded, was made of three distorted hearts, so twisted they were barely discernable. They represented Mama, Leala, and me, and I didn't have to think too hard as to why Mama had painted them all bent out of shape . . . or why she had omitted Daddy's heart from our family core; he'd been gone for so long now.

Mama heaved a sigh as she leaned back against the pillows. "It's a damn shame," she said, reaching up to fluff her hair, "that upon *my* dying I wasn't gifted a lovely head of starlight like our Sadie Way received after the one time *she* died. But then again, I wasn't saved by the lady of the lake like she was. For shame. It was only Dr. Barnhill after I mentioned a little heartburn at my checkup."

I flicked a glance at my sister at the mention of my hair, but she wasn't paying any attention to me. Leala Clare hated my hair color and had been the first one to try to dye it—only for the dye to slip off the strands like they'd been coated in oil beforehand. Mama, on the other hand, adored the silver color and whenever given the chance, proudly called attention to my head like a carnival barker pitching a new addition to the freak show. Since dyeing hadn't worked, shaving it had been a lesson in humility, and wigs were too hot and itchy, I had no choice but to accept that my sparkly hair was simply a part of who I was now. Which didn't mean I wasn't embarrassed by it occasionally—I was. Especially when people stared.

Mama yawned loudly, then smiled at us. "Having you both here with me for the weekend was definitely worth dying for."

Leala pressed her lips together and her chest puffed up with everything she'd been holding in for a while. Years maybe. Possibly decades. "No. One. Died. *Yet.*"

I bit back a smile. It had been a good long while since I'd seen Leala's fiery side.

She pulled a notepad from her purse and said between clenched teeth, "You should get some rest, Mother. The cardiologist told us that sleep is of utmost importance for your recovery. I'm going to head over to Lockhart's General Store to pick up your prescriptions. Is there anything else you need?"

"I *almost* died. It counts," Mama said. "A heart attack is nothing to sneeze at, LC."

Leala's nostrils flared briefly before she bent her head to scribble something on the notepad with the force of a sculptor chiseling rock. The paper tore, but she didn't seem to notice, and when she looked up again, she'd slipped on a tranquil mask, her features schooled into pleasantness.

As Mama rattled off an assorted list of sundries to be collected, including a sudoku puzzle book, a box of tissues, a bag of Twizzlers, a bottle of Diet Coke, and a romance novel, I walked over to the velvet-padded bench beneath the sill of a wide dormer window and sat down. A stack of paperback books teetered on the far end of the bench, all the spines broken, the pages dog-eared. As eccentric as Mama was, it was no wonder she had titles ranging from romance to political nonfiction, but most of the books were travel guides. Paris, Spain, Romania, Japan. All places she'd never seen in person.

The window seat offered a glimpse of the downtown promenade called the Landing, the heart of Sugarberry Cove. Currently the streets were flooded with summer vacationers. I could practically feel its pulse, strong and steady, as people flowed in and out of the shops. My gaze skipped around, from one storefront to another, lingering on Lockhart's for a moment longer than necessary before flitting away.

As much as I wanted to venture into town, it was best to stay put. I certainly didn't want to dredge up old, painful memories by reminiscing with those I hadn't seen in eight years. Because even though I now had a successful career, I still felt like I'd let down the people of this community and their expectations of me.

Once upon a time, I'd dreamed of being a writer. A great storyteller. I'd always loved stories. Stories of any kind, as long as I *felt* them. I told anyone who'd listen that I was going to write a Great American Novel one day. Buoyed by the encouragement from the people in Sugarberry Cove who believed in me, my potential, I'd been ready to learn anything and everything to set that dream in motion, and I couldn't wait to go off to college as an English major.

Only to find out I hated college. I felt muted on campus. Alone.

My creativity plummeted. On day three I knew it wasn't for me, but it was Will Lockhart who'd told me to give it time, give it a chance. So I did. But then two weeks after move-in day, I'd gone back home for the water lantern festival, a tradition I wouldn't have missed for the world, and had fallen into the lake. Immediately townsfolk were convinced I'd been saved because I was destined for greatness. They'd expected me to go back to college and do great things with my writing talent.

But I hadn't been destined for greatness. I was just Sadie Way Scott, and I still didn't know why I'd been saved.

Outside, a dust-covered sedan drove up the long driveway, past the enormous sugarberry tree that Sugarberry Cottage was named for, its branches dripping with fruit due to ripen soon. The car parked in between my hatchback and Mama's truck in one of the eight designated spots along a hedge of mountain laurel. Two women emerged from the car, one older and one in her teens.

I smiled, immediately recognizing Claudette "Teddy" Aldridge, her bottle-blond hair teased sky-high. Seven years older than my mother, sixty-year-old Teddy felt like a favorite old aunt we saw only once a year. I didn't recognize the young woman, however, and to my knowledge, Teddy had never before brought a guest on her visits.

I was soon enveloped in a sweet cloud of vanilla-scented perfume as Leala rushed over at the sound of the car door closing.

She kneeled next to me on the bench. "Why is Teddy here? With luggage?" She squinted. "And a dog?"

A dog? I looked out. Sure enough, a small fluffy dog pranced around the younger woman's feet.

Mama yawned. "Surely you remember Teddy stays here every August. This year she's bringing along her grandniece, Bree."

"But there's a dog," Leala repeated. "The cottage doesn't allow pets."

"Sure it does," Mama said. "Don't be silly!"

Leala set her hands on her hips. "Since when?"

If Mama heard the hurt in Leala's tone, she did a good job of ignoring it. I couldn't count the times Leala had begged for a pet while we were growing up only to be denied.

Mama smirked and gave a half shrug. "Why, since Teddy adopted a dog, of course! The cottage now allows small dogs, ones that weigh less than fifteen pounds."

As I watched the dog sniff the hedge, the new pet rule suddenly made a lot more sense. Mama and Teddy had become close friends during the twenty-five years she'd been coming to Sugarberry Cottage. I doubted anyone else would've prompted such a big amendment to Mama's no-pet policy.

I watched Uncle Camp hobble down the front walk, and his high forehead, dotted with perspiration, glinted in the sunlight as he bellowed out a welcome to Teddy that carried easily through the double-paned window.

When I arrived at the hospital on Wednesday, Uncle Camp had been the one to meet me at the door, and I think I hugged him for a whole five minutes. No one comforted like him, which was quite a feat for a dedicated bachelor who had no children of his own.

"Why didn't you have Uncle Camp cancel the reservations?" Leala asked. "There are renovations going on. Plus, you need to rest! Teddy would've understood."

"Why would I cancel?" Mama blinked slowly as if it was a chore to keep her eyes open. "You know our summer season carries us through the year. The guests have been made aware of the renovations and most chose to keep the reservations in spite of a little hammering. Thank the Lord above. We need all the guests we can get right now, since we have two rooms out of commission. As it is, up until yesterday I had an empty room for this weekend, which is unheard of. Fortunately, Camp was here to take the call."

It *was* unheard of. I'd never known the cottage to have weekend vacancies during the summer months. The lake was a vacation hot spot for water lovers, and by the streams of people on the Landing, it didn't seem as though a lack of tourists was the issue.

Mama added over a wide yawn, "LC, you should really go down and greet our guests right and proper. Be a good host and help Camp get Teddy settled."

Leala's gray eyes widened and her jaw fell. Color infused her face, her hands fisted, and without another word, she flew out of the room like she was being chased by the devil himself.

Not a second later, Mama's soft snores filled the air. I rose from the window bench, walked over to the bed, and pulled the light blanket up to tuck her in. Stepping back, I watched her sleep for a moment, comforted by the steady rise and fall of her chest. My gaze lifted to the colorful mandala and those twisted hearts.

So caught up in their battle of iron wills, neither Mama nor Leala seemed to notice that I hadn't said a single word this whole time. It was almost as if I hadn't even been here at all. Which was fine by me. If I could just keep this trend going for the next three days, it would make it so much easier to leave again.

But not any less painful.

Chapter 4

Sadie

Voices floated up the turned staircase as I headed down, wanting nothing more than to turn around and go straight to the small bedroom on the third floor that I'd shared with Leala while growing up. The one we'd share again this weekend.

After days of hospital noise and family drama and worry, I longed for peace and quiet. For time to just *be*. But I couldn't let Leala do the lion's share of work when it came to the cottage—it wouldn't be fair. Besides, I had always enjoyed helping Mama run the place. I loved talking with the guests, cooking big breakfasts, and I never even minded the cleaning, though I had to admit some guests would have been better off staying in a barn.

And then there was Teddy, who was brimming with life and love. She had a way about her that made you feel like you were the most important person in the world. A lifelong waitress, she changed jobs as often as her hair color, searching for the perfect fit but never seemingly finding it. These past few years she'd been waiting tables at a diner near Fort Payne, and I always stopped by to see her when I traveled through the area.

On the lowest landing, sunlight struggled through the panes of an arched window, the dirty glass nearly opaque. The house had always had a shabby chic feel to it, but now it just felt shabby. Earlier in the entryway, I'd been glad to see a PARDON OUR DUST sign sitting on the secretary desk Mama used for reception purposes, but my joy had been short-lived when I learned the work was limited to two first-floor guest rooms damaged by a burst pipe. The torn wallpaper, scuffed paint, and outdated furniture throughout the rest of the cottage would unfortunately remain long after the construction crew left.

Thinking back, I tried to remember if the cottage had always been in such sad shape with its general feeling of malaise or if it had happened since I'd been gone. I didn't remember any disrepair, but at eighteen I might not have noticed. My mind had been elsewhere. On starting college. On Leala's wedding. On Will Lockhart.

With that last thought, my cheeks flamed with embarrassed heat, and I angrily banished old memories.

Through the grimy window I saw Uncle Camp was still outside, standing with Teddy's grandniece as he loaded a luggage cart. The dog, a small cream and light-brown fluff ball, happily sniffed the bushes.

According to Mama, it had always been my daddy's dream to turn his family's small summer lake cottage into a B and B. So when he inherited this place, he immediately enlisted his uncle Camp, a master carpenter who lived down in Montgomery, to help make that dream a reality. Uncle Camp had planned only to stick around in Sugarberry Cove until construction was finished but ended up staying on as a hired hand, claiming he'd found unexpected happiness here on the lake with the only family he had left, as Daddy's side of the family, with the exception of a few distant cousins, had all but reached the end of its line.

After Daddy died, Uncle Camp took over the roles of property manager and primary breakfast-maker here at Sugarberry Cottage, and even though he was now well into his seventies, he scoffed at the idea of retirement. Loyal and steadfast, he was the glue that had held this place together on a daily basis.

In the wide entryway, Leala and Teddy were chatting about Tucker, and how he was spending the weekend with Connor. "Just the guys," Leala said, and I wondered if Teddy picked up the tightness in Leala's voice, something that was quite evident to me.

Taking a deep breath, I forced myself down the remaining six steps. The runner was threadbare, the pine treads in need of refinishing. The wallpaper along the inner stairwell peeled at the seams, and there were sections that time had completely worn away, leaving behind bald spots. A strong floral scent hovered in the air from the dozen get-well-soon flower arrangements that had arrived over the last few days and were now scattered throughout the cottage. No doubt about it, Mama was a beloved fixture around these parts.

Just beyond the foot of the stairs, a hallway branched to the right, off of which were the two guest rooms under construction, Uncle Camp's suite, Mama's office, the laundry room, and a small powder room. The open kitchen was straight ahead, big with plenty of storage but dreadfully outdated.

The wide entryway spilled into the great room, with its high-beamed ceilings, and that opened to my favorite space. We called it the back porch, but it was actually a four-season room with a vaulted ceiling and tall windows that gave a dazzling view of the lake. Light flooded in through those windows, breathing life into the house, keeping it alive and feeling hopeful.

As I neared the bottom step, the wood creaked under my feet, and Teddy turned at the sound. Joy lit her eyes and her hand flew to cover her mouth as she stifled a squeal. Without missing a beat, she rushed over to me and held out her arms as I stepped off the bottom stair. I willingly went into her hug, old memories stirring at the familiar scent of her, a hint of Chanel N°5, a whisper of lavender bath powder, and a trace of cigarette smoke. Memories of us playing checkers or gin rummy on rainy days or flying kites or walking into town to browse the shelves at the Crow's Nest, the local bookshop. Welcome memories, warm and comforting.

Bleached blond hair was coiled high atop her head and held in place with a tortoiseshell hairpin. She stood slightly taller than my five foot four and was curvier than I was through her chest and hips. Her peaches-and-cream skin had been sunbaked to a deep brown and her large eyes dominated a small face dotted with a button nose and tiny mouth. She wore a full face of makeup, heavy on the mascara but light on the red lipstick. Wrinkles pulled at the corners of her eyes and lips, especially when she smiled, but the rest of her face remained largely unlined, her skin smooth and glowing, despite her affinity for cigarettes. She'd tried to quit smoking at least twice a year for a good fifteen years now but had never quite been able to kick the habit completely.

"Oh my gracious! Let me look at you, Sadie Way. It's been too long." After releasing me, she held me at arm's length and studied me, silvery top to toe. "It is so good to see you here at home."

I fought the urge to run a hand over my thick hair, to tuck it behind my ear or under a hat, all while my heart tripped at the word *home*. I swallowed a rush of emotion and the uneasy feeling she could see right through me, past my anxieties and straight to my lonely heart that ached to stay here at the lake forever. "It's good to see you, Teddy. I've missed you."

"Same here, sugar." Teddy sighed dramatically. "You must be fighting off suitors, left and right, you gorgeous, young thing. You must tell me about them. All of them. I don't mind the details. Don't be stingy. I need to live vicariously through others."

I laughed, thinking she'd be sorely disappointed if she knew the truth. I had a nonexistent love life. I'd tried casual dating and hated it. And life on the road and attempts at long-term commitments had been a disaster. It was easiest just to avoid dating altogether. "Nothing to tell, Teddy."

Her pile of hair wobbled as she shook her head. "That's a damn shame."

"Agreed," Leala added.

Leala was forever harping about my lifestyle and would love for me to find a nice guy to settle down with, preferably here in Sugarberry Cove near her, in a house with a picket fence, a couple of pets, and, of course, babies. Lots of babies. She was worse than any overbearing mama out there.

"You'll have to settle for details from Leala," I said.

The light didn't quite reach Leala's eyes as she smiled. "I'm a boring old married lady now."

Leala wouldn't have told, no matter what. She wasn't a kiss-and-tell kind of person. But as she spoke, I noticed tightness in her tone again, and it made me look at her more closely. Sadness lurked in her eyes, and suddenly I was worried that she might be dealing with trouble at home. I wanted to ask but knew she would brush off any questions. She'd always tried to hide her pain, even when we were little. She was forever having her tender heart broken—mostly by Mama—so over the years she'd built a high wall around her heart to protect it, but those walls didn't seem to be helping her now. I wished it were easier to talk to her, or for her to open up. We'd been close once, but then she went off to college, met Connor, and forgot I existed until the night I drowned.

Teddy laughed, a joyous, throaty sound. "The grass is always greener, ain't it? I wouldn't mind being married—I'm just sayin'." She walked back to the reception desk and pulled a credit card from a slim billfold. "You need to catch me up on A Southern Hankerin', Sadie. You know I'm a big fan. That video you did on the young woman from Atlanta and AuntMama's scrambled egg recipe? Oh my heart! I cried for hours."

Leala's eyebrows dipped low, and there was a hint of disapproval on a pinched face as she placed the credit card on an old-fashioned imprinter and slid the bar across carbon paper. "AuntMama? Is that really someone's name?"

Teddy nodded. "It's all explained in the video. I don't know how you missed it, but you must go back and watch it. You won't be sorry you did."

Leala passed the carbon paper across the counter for Teddy to sign. "Hmm, yes. I'll do that."

She said it in a way that told me she wasn't going to do anything of the kind, and I tried not to be offended. She didn't understand my career, since my job wasn't remotely close to traditional nine-to-five work. Leala, who used to be a healthcare accountant before she had Tucker, was as by the book as people came. Numbers made sense to her—creativity did not. To her, I was wasting my time, whiling away life making fun little videos. And while I had to admit mine wasn't the most conventional of careers, it *was* a career. One tougher than it looked. I worked hard to make sure the stories I shared were memorable, heartfelt, and comforting.

Teddy signed and pushed the paper back toward Leala. "Not that I don't love seeing you both, because I do, Lord knows I do, but what're you both doing here? And . . . what're all these flowers for? Oh good heavens, did someone die? Please tell me no one died."

"No one died," Leala said in a slightly less bitter tone than she'd used with Mama a few moments ago. Metal clanked together as she grabbed two keys from a drawer in the desk. "Mother's a bit under the weather, and Sadie and I are here to make sure she rests this weekend."

Teddy gasped. "Under the weather? It must be serious for you *both* to be here."

She emphasized the word both, and I knew she meant me. *My* presence. Guilt swelled, making me suddenly question the choice I'd made to stay away.

Leala said, "Mother's been dealing with a cardiac situation these past couple of days."

"Situation?" Teddy pressed a hand to her chest. "What does that mean precisely?"

Since Leala was insistent on downplaying the matter, I spoke up. "Mama's fine, just fine, but she had a minor heart attack on Wednesday. She came home from the hospital today. She's upstairs, napping."

"Oh my word! Susannah? A heart attack? It doesn't seem possible. This is shocking. I'm shocked. Is she taking visitors?"

Leala glanced upward with a look of resignation. "I'm not sure we could stop her—you know how she is. But the doctor wants her to rest as much as possible."

"Of course. And I'll do whatever I can to help out around here," Teddy said. "Just say the word."

"That's real kind of you," Leala said, "but you're on vacation. It's your time to rest and relax. Uncle Camp, Sadie, and I can handle everything until Mama's on her feet again, which you know won't be long."

It *had* been kind of Teddy to offer, especially since she saved her pennies all year to be able to afford this vacation—and loved being catered to, rather than being the one doing the catering. But the offer hadn't been surprising. That was Teddy's nature—to jump in and lend a hand when need be.

Voices carried in as Uncle Camp and Teddy's grandniece strolled up the ramp on the side of the front porch, talking about the kayaks, canoes, and stand-up paddleboards the cottage had available.

Teddy whispered, "Here comes Bree. She's from up in Indiana, the granddaughter of my sister, Bernice, God rest her soul. Bree's been staying with me this summer but heads back north in just two weeks. She's terribly shy until she gets to know you, so be forewarned. She just turned eighteen last month and has already known so much tragedy. Only last year her m—" She abruptly cut herself off. "Bree! Come meet Sadie Way and Leala Clare. Ladies, this is Bree Bynum, my grandniece."

The small brown-and-cream dog raced through the door ahead of the young woman, who approached slowly, her small steps so light her footfalls didn't make a sound on the pine floorboards. As Teddy finished the introductions, Bree kept her head down, her brown hair hanging nearly to her waist. She didn't offer to shake hands and only murmured her hellos.

Teddy gave a small, sad smile as she watched Bree and then redirected her attention to the dog. "And this furry little imp is Nigel. Don't be fooled by his prim-and-proper name. He's a scamp."

As he sniffed my shoes, I bent to pat his head. His coloring oddly reminded me of a snickerdoodle, blondish with a touch of cinnamon. "Nigel is adorable."

Leala bent down, too, and Nigel licked her chin. She laughed, and a small spark of happiness zipped through me at the sound. Leala had been so serious lately—more serious than normal, and it was nice to see a genuine moment of joy.

When I stood up again, I noticed that Bree's gaze lifted along with me, her eyes focused on my hair. For once I was grateful for the attention, because she hadn't seen the shock in my eyes when I saw the thin scars that zigged, then zagged across her left cheek. They looked to be fairly recent wounds, glowing slightly red against her fair skin. There was another smaller scar on her forehead that looked to be about the same age as the others.

Swallowing hard, I tried not to stare . . . or wonder at how the scars had come to be. Tragedy, Teddy had said, and my heart suddenly hurt for her.

Uncle Camp gave a gentle cough and scratched the snow-white beard that covered a deep dimple in his chin. Unruly salt-and-pepper eyebrows slid upward, and his forehead wrinkled as he said, "Are Miss Teddy, Miss Bree, and the little imp staying in rooms four and five?"

Uncle Camp's genial smile hid any questions he had of the scars as well, but he was exceedingly good at keeping his thoughts to himself and always had been. It was part of his kind, levelheaded nature.

Leala was pale as she looked away from Bree, nodded, and handed him the keys. "I can help with the bags, Uncle Camp."

"I've got them just fine; don't you worry none, darlin'." Gray-blue eyes twinkled, and he wiped his bald head with a red bandana before picking up two of the suitcases.

Nigel tried to follow him up the stairs, but his leash stretched only so far, so he circled back and sat at Bree's feet, his tiny pink tongue lolling. Bree still hadn't torn her gaze from my head, and I tried not to fidget under the scrutiny. Now that the shock of seeing her scars had waned, I noticed she had the same green-colored eyes as Teddy, but that was where their similarity ended. Bree had wide-set eyes, thick eyebrows, a long thin nose, high cheekbones dotted with pale freckles, and full lips. She wasn't wearing a lick of makeup other than some lip balm, and there was a depth of sadness hovering in the shadows of her eyes.

Finally, she said to me, "Your hair. It's *awesome*. Is that glitter?"

Teddy smiled as she, too, turned her attention on me. "That's not glitter. It's lake magic."

Bree's dark eyebrows dipped together as she frowned. "But seriously."

Leala said, "Our mother says it's starlight. Whatever it is, I think it's gorgeous."

There was no snark in the comment, which made me look her way. She was staring at me with a pensive look on her face.

Bree looked like she wanted to touch my ponytail. "It's just so different. How do you get it that way?"

Heat climbed my throat. "I can't take any credit for it. It's unnaturally natural."

Bree shifted her attention from my hair to my face. "I don't know what that means."

I let out a weary sigh. "It's a long story."

She seemed to recognize that I didn't want to talk about it. "Well, it's the prettiest hair I've ever seen."

"Thanks." My cheeks burned with embarrassment.

Leala finally took mercy on me and said to our guests, "Let me show you to your rooms, get you settled. Do you need help with reservations for dinner in town?"

Teddy adjusted the strap of her backpack purse. "Leala, if you can get us into Anna Ruth's, I'll love you forever. Forever and ever. Bree, Anna Ruth's has some of the best mac and cheese you've ever tasted, besides your mama's, but nothing compares to that. You have to try it."

Bree shifted on her feet. "All right, but can we get it to go?"

Teddy shook her head. "Nope. It has to be fresh from the oven, piping hot. You've got to trust me on this. That mac and cheese is heaven on earth."

Bree didn't look swayed, and my heart hurt for her. I knew what it was like to have people stare at my hair in restaurants. Openly. Rudely. I could only imagine the rubbernecking when it came to her scars, never mind the questions that she probably faced day in and day out.

As her head dropped again, Bree's hair fell forward, hiding her face. "You know, I'm not really hungry after all. Maybe we can do mac and cheese another day. I'm . . . tired." Nigel rose up to put his paws on her leg.

Teddy sighed softly, sympathetically, apparently realizing this conversation wasn't about hunger at all.

Unable to tolerate the ballooning emotions, I quickly said, "I was going to make homemade pizza for dinner tonight." A lie, but no one needed to know that. "There will be plenty for everyone if you just want to stay here at the cottage and rest up. Travel days can be exhausting. What do you say?"

Surprisingly, it was Leala who chimed in first. "I think it's a great idea. We can even eat outside, if you want. It looks like it's going to be a gorgeous night, and there's a great lake view from the patio."

Bree's chin came up a notch. "I like pizza."

Teddy threw her hands in the air and laughed. "I know when I'm outnumbered. Pizza it is." She put an arm around Bree and glanced at Leala. "I don't suppose Susannah's overcome her Luddite tendencies and installed Wi-Fi since the last time I was here?"

"I'm sorry." Leala shook her head. "No Wi-Fi. No internet at all. We have good cell coverage if you have a generous data plan, and the library has free Wi-Fi, as do a few of the shops in town."

At this news, I stifled a groan. I had planned to upload a Southern Hankerin' video this weekend after I finished its editing, and Mama not having internet was going to throw off my schedule. She'd always shied away from technology, preferring a simpler way of life.

"I can hear Susannah now," Teddy said, and mimicked, "'Unplugging is good for the soul. Turn off to tune in.'"

Leala looked strangely pained at the spot-on imitation as she guided them toward the stairs. "She's certainly set in her ways."

As Teddy, Bree, and Nigel headed up the steps, Leala lingered behind a moment and pulled the list she'd written earlier in Mama's room out of her pocket and held it out to me. "While I get Teddy and Bree settled, can you run to Lockhart's real quick? The store's open till nine, but the pharmacy closes at five."

I did not want to go into town and most definitely did not want to go to Lockhart's. Not now, not ever again. "How about I get them settled and you run to Lockhart's?"

"Sadie."

"Leala."

As she stared me down, I took a long look into her eyes and saw tears gathering along the lashes. I snatched the list and curled it in my fist. "Fine."

Her shoulders slumped with relief. "Thank you. And could you get me a pint of ice cream while you're there? Something chocolatey with extra chocolate."

"Everything okay with you, Leala?" I asked, hoping she'd open up.

"Just stressed. With Mother, you know."

"Only Mother? Not, by any chance, Connor?"

She stiffened and wouldn't look me in the eye. "We're fine."

So her marriage *was* in trouble. *Dang.* Hindsight had greatly softened the hard feelings I'd once had toward Connor, and I was now truly embarrassed by the way I'd treated him when I was a teenager. Through the years, whenever we were all together, it was easy to see the love he and Leala shared, so I wondered now what was causing her heartache and wished again that she was easier to talk to.

I ran a finger over a hole in the list, where earlier her pen had gouged the paper. "You never were a very good liar."

"The pharmacy closes in twenty minutes." Spinning around, she started up the steps, rushing to catch up to Teddy and Bree, who'd already disappeared down the second-floor hallway.

I called after her. "It was vanilla ice cream you wanted, right?"

She paused for a moment, then slowly turned around with a flash of a genuine smile on her face before continuing on her way.

I watched her climb and decided I'd go to every store in town if I had to in order to find triple-fudge ice cream. Because suddenly I wanted nothing more than to see Leala smile. Or maybe even hear her laugh again.

A master of disguise I wasn't, but I thought I'd done a fair job of hiding my hair beneath one of Mama's floppy sun hats. Between that and an oversized pair of sunglasses, I was as anonymous as I could be in my old hometown.

Late afternoon sun blazed like fire onto a dark ribbon of asphalt, lifting iridescent waves into the thick air as I biked into town, borrowing one of the Schwinns Mama kept on hand for the guests. The bike was brilliant blue with a fraying, dingy white wicker basket, and I'd had to fill flat tires with air before I left. As I steered toward the shops, I couldn't ignore the thought that something was terribly wrong at the cottage. Yes, the décor was out of date and shabby, but it wasn't like Mama and Uncle Camp to ignore small jobs like filling bike tires and keeping windows clean. It was obvious the cottage's upkeep had become too much for them.

Because of Mama's heart attack, it seemed like a good time to hire on more help, though I knew any conversation about the cottage would have to be broached carefully. Mama was fiercely independent, hated asking for help, refused handouts, and was committed to doing as much as she could with as little help as possible.

I kept to the boundaries of the bike lane and used the crosswalks at the traffic circle, catching a glimpse of the shimmery lake on my left, down a narrow lane that led to the public beach and marina. I glanced quickly away from the water before I made a detour for an up-close-and-personal look and continued along on Hawker Street, named for the vendors who hawked wares to visiting beachgoers before the town had been built up.

The cove along this shoreline had long been a vacation spot, with its picturesque location, clear water, and sandy beach, but it wasn't until the 1960s that people had started building here, putting up small summer cottages and camps. Later, most of those places were either remodeled or knocked down and spacious lake homes went up. The town was born. A business district rose up around the cove and fully embraced its lakeside location. Brick facades had been painted beachy soft blues, creams, and light greens, but they'd been sandblasted for a rustic, cozy effect.

Shops and restaurants lined both sides of the street, most with wide pastel awnings shading window displays and doors. Despite the heat, the Landing was chock-full of tourists who meandered from shop to shop, all slightly pink in the cheeks and their arms full of bags. It was easy to spot the people who weren't originally from the South, the ones wilting in the heat like drooping sunflowers. Cars rolled slowly past, and bits of music floated from open windows. Every slanted parking spot was full and the town hummed with an undercurrent of happiness. Sugarberry Cove had a lived-in, loved look about it, welcoming and comfortable.

I rolled to a stop in front of Lockhart's and parked the bike in a rack on the left side of double wooden doors propped open with small doorstops in the shape of a loon. Coolness and the sweet scent of waffle cones invited me inside. I picked up a wooden hand basket and hurried toward the pharmacy counter at the back of the shop before it closed up for the day, praying the whole way that no Lockhart was on duty. Especially Will.

Will Lockhart and I had known each other our whole lives, being the same age and in the same schools, but we really hadn't become friends until tenth-grade chemistry class when we were paired as lab partners. On the first day of class, I'd tripped over my feet as I walked toward our lab bench, and Will had reached out to catch me. Our fingers had entwined, his dark, mine light, and our hands had fit together perfectly, two puzzle pieces finally joined together. "A Will and a Way," our chem teacher had joked when she took attendance, and it had suddenly felt as though we had been destined to be paired together. We were virtually inseparable after that, becoming best friends—and I'd been desperately in need of one after Leala all but abandoned me when she went to college. Then, a few years later, not long after a night at a lake surrounded by water lanterns, Will abandoned me, too, leaving me confused and heartbroken.

The last I knew, Will had been going to college to become a pharmacist and planned to eventually join his dad in their family business, here at Lockhart's. Now twenty-six, there was a good chance he'd be working today, and I wasn't sure what I'd do if he were.

Turning and running sounded like a fine idea until the image of Leala's sad eyes popped into my head. With renewed determination, I marched my way down the greeting card aisle toward the back of the store, past two employees doing more talking than working. A bit of their conversation floated after me, nearly making me stop in my tracks. Talk of how the Lockharts were currently enjoying a six-week European vacation to celebrate their thirtieth anniversary.

With that news, my anxiety crept up. If Will's dad was out of town, the chance that Will would be the pharmacist on duty was highly likely. I dragged my feet and desperately tried to shake the feeling that I was headed to the gallows. At the end of the aisle, I turned right and looked ahead, bracing for the worst only to see no one working at the pharmacy. Taking a fortifying breath, I tapped a bell on the counter, kept my fingers crossed, and waited for Will to appear.

"Well, hello there!" a cheerful voice boomed as a woman I didn't recognize stepped out from a storeroom. "How might I help you, miss? Are you picking up or dropping off?"

My shoulders relaxed, but as I finished up the transaction, collecting and paying for Mama's prescriptions, making small talk with the personable pharmacist, I couldn't help but question why it wasn't relief I felt at not seeing Will . . . but disappointment.

Chapter 5

Leala

"Psst."

From my spot in a rocking chair on the back porch, I didn't see anyone as I looked up from my phone, which glowed brightly with a photo of Tucker on his second birthday, his face covered in chocolate frosting.

It was a little past seven, right about the time when Tucker would normally be done with his bath. Soon it would be reading time, when he'd pull several books from the case in his room, and we'd curl up in the rocking recliner next to his bed until he started nodding off. Then he'd sleepily say his prayers, climb into bed, give kisses, and hug Moo like he never planned to let the stuffed cow go as he drifted off to sleep. Would Connor remember to kiss Moo good night, too?

I'd been holding off on calling because Tucker didn't quite understand cell phones or video calls, and I didn't want him to melt down over hearing my voice and not understanding why I wasn't there. But my resolve was wearing thin, especially since Connor hadn't sent any pictures or text messages. Not a single one, all day long. I gritted my teeth, thinking of how I sent Connor loads of pictures every day, to keep him involved in our daily lives even if he wasn't there. The least he could've done was return the favor.

"*Psst.* Leala, over here."

Glancing over my shoulder, I squinted through the sliding screen door to see Mother's ex-boyfriend, Buzzy Hale, waving as he stood beneath an arched arbor that served as a shortcut between his yard and the cottage's—yards otherwise divided by a white picket fence that ran the length of the property line. The fence and arbor were both covered in Alabama Crimson honeysuckle, the vines twisting and twining around pickets, rails, lattice—a little wild and a little tame, a fitting representation of Mama and Buzzy's past relationship. Vibrant crimson flowers normally bloomed in early spring, but it seemed every year a red flower would appear out of season and Buzzy would declare the bloom the result of lake magic blowing just the right way.

"Hey, Buzzy. You okay?" I called out.

He nodded and gestured me over. The slider's screen door squeaked dramatically as I opened it and stepped outside. Without the back porch's ceiling fans to stir the late-day heat, it settled around me like a weighted blanket, oddly comforting on such a hot evening.

I skirted two patio tables, cushioned Adirondack chairs, and a freestanding three-person canopied swing as I crossed the fieldstone courtyard and stepped onto thick grass. I noticed for the first time a small fenced-in area on this side of the house that had dog bones and toys within its confines. A doggy play yard. I stifled a groan of frustration, irritated beyond belief that Mother now allowed pets at the cottage. I'd lost count of how often I had begged her for a pet while I was growing up. Mostly I'd asked for a kitten. A sweet, cuddly kitten. But honestly, I'd have accepted any pet. A dog, a hamster, a turtle. Anything. Someone to love, and who'd love me unconditionally. But each of my pleas had been met with the same answer: No.

Let it go, let it go. I pulled in a deep breath through my nose, held it, then released it. Breathwork usually calmed me right down, but today I could still feel a thrum of exasperation humming under the surface of my skin. I had to *grow forward to go forward*, as one of my morning affirmations would say. Which was entirely easier said than done.

Buzzy waited patiently as I made my way over to him, and I hoped he couldn't read my thoughts. I didn't want to talk about my relationship with my mother, a topic he used to favor as he tried to make peace between us.

As I neared the arbor, I noticed the honeysuckle vines seemed to glow in the fading sunshine as light gently skimmed emerald-green leaves. "It's good to see you, Buzzy. I guess you heard about Mother."

Buzzy, a retired banker, had a pleasantly round face, thick silvery-blond hair, wore round black-rimmed glasses, and had an air of importance about him that contradicted his nickname, one he'd acquired as a teenager when caught smoking weed with a bunch of his marching band friends after a high school football game. Nicknames in the South tended to stick for life. I was glad to have broken the usage of mine, though there were a few around here who still called me LC—namely, my mother. I suspected she used it solely because she knew how much it bothered me. She was a contrary sort—at least with me. Oil and water, Buzzy had once said of us. To me it felt more like gasoline and a match.

"I did, I did. I'm glad she's out of the hospital."

I wasn't surprised he knew she was already home. In a town the size of Sugarberry Cove, word traveled like an electric current, sparking between houses, stores, ears, mouths.

"She's glad, too. You know how she can't abide being told what to do. I think it was just about killing her to be a nice, docile patient. She's doing quite well, considering."

Mother had come downstairs after her long nap looking remarkably refreshed for what she'd been through these last couple of days but moving a touch slower than her usual full steam ahead. Much to my dismay, instead of taking supper in bed, she had insisted on joining us on the patio and had scowled the whole time after Sadie served her a no-cheese flat-bread pizza with heart-healthy veggies. After we ate, Mother and Teddy took to the great room with a pitcher of sweet tea. Bree had gone to her room. Sadie, Uncle Camp, and I had cleaned the kitchen and they were still catching up with each other when I'd stepped outside to check my phone.

Buzzy cradled a ceramic bowl in his arm like a baby and said, "Susannah's iron will is her greatest strength and her biggest weakness."

There was no arguing the statement because it was true. I flicked the tip of a honeysuckle leaf just to watch it shimmer. "Hopefully she'll stick to the doctor's recommendations. She needs to make changes to her lifestyle and follow up with a cardiologist in the coming weeks, but she should make a full recovery given time." Relief flashed in his eyes before he blinked it away, and I added, "Do you want to come inside? Say hi? I'm sure she'd be happy to see you."

"I'm sure she wouldn't," he said with a grim smile.

Another knot of guilt tightened in my stomach, and I glanced at the lake. The water was calm, so like the night that Sadie had fallen off the dock and hadn't resurfaced for nearly ten minutes. The night my wish, the last one I'd ever made, had affected so many lives, one change leading to another, leading to another, like out-of-control dominoes.

That dock was gone now, replaced a few years ago with a newer model right around the same time the house got a new roof. My gaze lifted upward to the roofline. In my mind's eye I could see a rusty extension ladder leaning against the siding and my daddy lying on the ground, my mama kneeling over him, shouting for help. She was supposed to have been helping him by holding the ladder but had gotten distracted by something.

Swallowing hard, I forced myself to look away and face Buzzy, whose eyes shined with kindness, compassion, as if he'd caught a glimpse of my memories.

I flicked another leaf. I wanted to apologize to him but didn't want to explain why—how it was my fault he and Mother split up in the days following Sadie's accident because my wish had come true.

"I heard Sadie's home," he said, breaking the pained silence.

"She is. I'm hoping to convince her to stay awhile this time. She's been gone from these parts for far too long."

"That she has. Send her around so I can give her a proper hello. I've sure missed that girl."

Once again I wanted to invite him inside but knew he'd only turn me down. "I will. No doubt she'll be foraging for vegetables from your garden soon enough, so be prepared for the invasion. She still loves to cook."

Buzzy had an immense garden, a thing of beauty, lovingly tended. He had graciously allowed Sadie and me free rein of his yard when we were younger, permitting us to pick anything we wanted, welcoming us with open arms and heart, treating us as if we were family. His cozy bungalow had been a second home, sometimes more comforting to us than our own. He was a good man. One of the best, and we'd been blessed to have him as part of our lives.

"It comes across on A Southern Hankerin'," he said. "Such darn good stories she shares. I learn something every time I watch and not always about food. Tell her she's welcome anytime."

I yanked a leaf from the vine and rubbed it between my fingers. The shine vanished instantly, the leaf now dull and plain. Why was everyone so impressed with Sadie's little videos? All this praise was only going to feed her ego. At this rate she was never going to stop traveling to settle down. She was just going to keep running away from her fears, away from family, away from everyone who loved her.

A melancholy wail filled the air, and Buzzy and I turned toward the lake. A lone loon floated across the glossy surface, her body barely creating ripples in the water. She was beautiful, absolutely stunning. A muted black with a long, graceful white neck, a grayish pattern on her back, long beak, and those brilliant red eyes that seemed to sparkle even in the waning light. Birders not familiar with the lake might label her a common loon, rare to be seen in Alabama this time of year, but she wasn't common. Not by a long shot. Every day for as long as I could remember, she floated by at dawn and dusk, calling for her mate, and tonight the haunting sound echoed across the lawn and through my soul.

Buzzy and I watched in reverent silence until the bird floated around a bend in his seawall, near the spot where two water oaks had entwined over the years to form a single tree. She faded from sight, but I knew she'd continue swimming toward the cove where the public beach was located until disappearing along with the sun until it rose again.

"Here." His voice was hushed as the loon continued to cry in the distance. "Take this."

He thrust the bowl into my hands. It was full of the most beautiful raspberries I'd ever seen, plump and a stunning reddish pink. "These are gorgeous."

"They're Sus's favorite and heart-healthy. Don't tell her where you got them or she might chuck them into the lake."

"Buzzy, you know she wouldn't do that."

He lifted a thick eyebrow.

Okay, maybe she would. Mother *was* a bit unpredictable.

A bee inspected the honeysuckle, dipping in and out of sight. "It's been eight years. Maybe it's time to mend some fences?"

Surely my wish held no power all these years later. What was broken could be fixed. Everything could be repaired, given time and a little forgiveness. At least I hoped so.

He glanced toward the water. "You're as sweet as your mother's mint tea, but sometimes it's best to let things go and move on."

I held up the bowl. "These raspberries don't say moving on to me."

"I said it's best, not that I've been able to do it. You take care, Leala Clare."

With a wave and a smile, he turned and headed back toward his house. I stood there a moment, hugging that bowl, until I heard a noise behind me.

Sadie stood on the back porch, a cell phone glowing at her ear. I heard her say, "Hi, Mrs. Teakes; it's Sadie Scott. If you could give me a call back, I'd appreciate it. I'd like to come back on Monday if that's all right with you. Just let me know."

Monday. I had so little time to convince Sadie to stay, to remind her how much she loved Sugarberry Cove and that she was happiest here in her hometown. It suddenly seemed an impossible mission, especially since she was as stubborn as Mother.

The sun sank lower in the sky, coloring the lake in bold oranges and pinks as I crossed the stretch of yard toward the back porch. The screen door squeaked as I came inside, and I made a mental note to oil the track first thing tomorrow.

Sliding her phone into her back pocket, Sadie nodded to the bowl. "What have you got there?"

"Contraband." I set the bowl on a side table and quickly told her about my conversation with Buzzy. "Don't tell Mother."

Sadie turned a rocker so her back was to the lake when she sat down. "My lips are sealed."

I sat in the chair next to hers. "Buzzy pretty much invited you to plunder his garden. He said to come on over anytime. Standing invitation. He's missed you."

The fans stirred the loose hair that fell around her face, framing it in sparkles. At supper, she'd kept her back to the water as well. The key to her staying in Sugarberry Cove definitely went hand in hand with her making peace with the lake.

"I've missed him, too," she said with a smile aimed toward his yard. "A lot."

"You know, if you moved back here, you wouldn't miss him so much."

Her brows dipped low as she scowled, and I smiled innocently and rocked slowly, watching colors fade in the sky as the sun sank, its last beams glittering on the lake's surface. And dang if those sparkles didn't look just like the shiny glimmers in Sadie's hair.

"Did you run into any familiar faces at the pharmacy earlier?"

I asked, hoping that reconnecting with the community she loved would help my cause.

"No, thank goodness."

"Thank goodness?" My eyebrows lifted in question. "Why?"

"It's just . . ."

"What?"

Lifting a shoulder in a half shrug, she said, "People were so disappointed when I dropped out of college. I don't really want to revisit those memories."

I rocked slowly, letting her words settle. After her accident, she'd gone back to college but dropped out less than a week later. It had been a huge shock to those who knew Sadie well. The ones who expected her to get her English degree, then an MFA, and change the world with her storytelling. The accident had changed her. She'd been so withdrawn and people had been worried, concerned for her well-being.

But perhaps now, looking back, there had been some disappointment, too. Disappointment that she'd given up so easily. That she'd quit. At least, I suddenly realized, there had been disappointment on my part. With that thought, my stomach ached with remorse.

"Do you regret dropping out of college?" I asked, trying to keep my voice even, my emotions hidden.

"Not even a little." She picked at the frayed edge of her denim shorts. "I hated school. I hated it even before the accident, but afterward it was unbearable."

I hadn't known that. "You hated it? You never told me."

Lifting a dark eyebrow, she said, "You weren't exactly available."

"I'm always available for you, Sadie Way." She'd only been in college for two weeks before the accident, and it was on the tip of my tongue to ask if she'd given it enough of a chance, given herself time to acclimate, before I squashed the question. She'd just said she had no regrets of quitting, and I needed to listen. To hear her.

She stared at me with big blue eyes full of disbelief, as if she couldn't believe what she'd just heard, and said, "College was a hundred times worse after the accident. I went back to stares and prying questions, and I came to the realization that life was too dang short to spend four years hating it. So I came home, hoping for some sort of normalcy, only to find the people here staring and voicing their dismay that I'd dropped out."

I took a deep breath, trying to find the right words. "I only saw people who were worried about you, Sadie Way. Because they love you. They still do. Whenever I'm in town, I'm always asked how you're doing, when you're coming back. I'm not the only one who wants you to come home for good. You belong here. Always have."

She wrapped her arms around her legs and shook her head.

"What about Will?" I asked, knowing I was pushing my luck. She had clearly entered her stubborn mode, but I only had two more days to work on getting her to reconsider her stance on this town.

Sadie looked over at me and snapped, "What about him?"

Whoa. I'd obviously hit a sore spot. I held up my hands to ward off the fury in her voice. "I was just wondering. You two were so close once. I thought you might like to reach out to him, catch up some."

"Will cut me out of his life after I left town," she said, her voice shaking slightly with raw emotion, "so I certainly won't be reaching out to him."

I was starting to get upset, too. This was something else she hadn't told me, and it hurt like a knife in the heart that I hadn't known. She and Will had been best friends, and it was obvious to anyone who saw them together that there was more lurking under the surface if either of them would have given it a chance.

Why hadn't she told me what happened? Why had she thought I was unavailable? Sure, I'd been busy with the wedding and planning my and Connor's move to New Orleans so he could attend law school, but she was my little sister. I'd always make time for her.

The silence between us stretched, open and aching, the only noise the cheery birdsong that seemed to mock this dark moment and the lap of the lake against the seawall, which suddenly sounded mournful.

I couldn't take the quiet any longer, so I said, "Who's Mrs. Teakes? I heard you on the phone earlier."

Sadie seemed to recognize the life preserver I'd thrown and grabbed hold. "She's a darling woman, lives down in Wetumpka. I was at her house to film a piece for A Southern Hankerin' on making ambrosia when I got your text about Mama's heart attack."

"Everyone knows how to make ambrosia."

Sadie studied me for a long moment before saying, "You don't watch my videos, do you? Any of them."

I shifted, uncomfortable. "I mean, I used to. The early ones. They were okay. As you know, I'm not much of a cook, so the videos kind of aren't my thing. Plus, I don't really spend much time online. Only to pay my bills and check email."

In truth, I'd only watched the first video. It was enough. Not because it had been an amateurish cooking show but because it physically pained me to watch Sadie. Not only because I missed her, but because of her hair. That sparkling silvery hair that reminded me every time I saw it how my selfishness caused her to look the way she did. And was why she had died on a long ago summer night.

It had taken a lot of time, and a lot of self-reflection, to view her hair without guilt, to see it more as a symbol of her survival. Her hair was a beautiful reminder that she was still here with us.

"That's a lame excuse and you know it. Even Mama watches my videos, and she doesn't even have internet. She watches them on Uncle Camp's cell phone."

The knife in my heart twisted, and I suspected it had been an intentional wound, comparing me to Mother.

"You should probably watch one of the more recent ones sometime," she added.

"Mm." I pulled out my phone to see if I'd missed any calls or messages from Connor. I hadn't. I glanced toward the wide opening leading into the great room and didn't hear any voices. "Are Mother and Teddy still catching up?"

Always the peacemaker, she accepted the change of subject for what it was. "Mama fell asleep while they were talking, so Teddy helped me get her back upstairs and ready for bed. Hopefully she'll sleep through the night."

"There's no way we're going to be able to make her rest this weekend, is there?"

"Not even the slightest chance." Silence yawned and stretched between us before Sadie stood up. "I think I'm going to get some ice cream now. You want some?"

"Definitely."

I followed her to the kitchen. Like everywhere else in the house, the kitchen was tired. The cabinets were outdated; the appliances, too. The wood floors needed refinishing. Wallpaper peeled like it was trying to remove itself to save anyone else the trouble.

Sadie opened a drawer to grab spoons and the handle fell off in her hand. She held up the round knob. "This place is falling apart."

I settled onto one of the three stools lined up in front of the peninsula. "It's happened so gradually that I really hadn't seen it before now. Or maybe I just wasn't looking hard enough."

She closed the drawer with her hip and slid a pint of ice cream and a spoon across to me. "I can't believe there's no Wi-Fi. Do you think that's why Mama's not getting her usual occupancy?"

I plunged the spoon into the ice cream. "Maybe."

"I stay in a lot of B and Bs and I can tell you right now I wouldn't stay here. Not twice, at least. We should talk to her. Maybe convince her to expand the renovations. At least to the entryway. First impressions and all that. At the very least, we need to talk her into upgrading her technology. How is she even handling the accounting books? An old-school ledger? An abacus?"

I smiled at the thought. "She doesn't even own a cell phone, Sadie. Nothing we say to her will go over well. She's stubborn and hates change."

"She can't be blind to the disrepair."

"People see what they want to see. Always have, always will." Mother had always been able to turn a blind eye or a deaf ear to the things in life that made her uncomfortable, things like talking about Daddy's death.

"All I see is that this wallpaper is older than I am. Mama has to know it's not good for business." She held up a wait-a-sec finger, pulled out her phone, and a moment later winced. "Her Tripadvisor ratings in the past year are worrisome. Mostly two and three stars. Praise for Mama's outstanding hospitality and the hearty breakfasts, but the cottage is being skewered for its dated décor and lack of Wi-Fi."

I skirted the peninsula and looked over her shoulder. "She doesn't have internet, so there's no way she's seen these reviews."

Sadie spoke around the ice cream she'd just spooned into her mouth. "Since we're here for a couple of days, maybe we should give the cottage a little makeover. Some paint at least."

"Do you really think Mother will let us paint anything? You

know how she likes to do everything herself. She'll see our help as charity and block it straight off the bat."

Light sparkled in Sadie's eyes as she said, "I have an idea." She practically skipped over to the bottom of the stairs and eyed the wall.

Pushing my ice cream aside, I reluctantly followed her. "What're you doing?"

"Strategizing." She flashed a smile before reaching out to take hold of a loose wallpaper seam on the wall leading up to the turn in the staircase, a small landing that housed a very dirty window and a bench with a built-in bookcase beneath it. Then she pulled, and a strip of wallpaper ripped off the wall, leaving behind its fuzzy backing.

My jaw dropped. "What are you doing?"

She grinned. "Sometimes, Leala, it's better to ask forgiveness than permission."

Chapter 6

Sadie

Even though I'd been up late baking and prepping for the breakfast service, I woke at the crack of dawn. There was a lot to do today between taking care of the guests and the cottage, removing the rest of the wallpaper, and also getting my own work done. I had emails to sort through and an episode of A Southern Hankerin' to edit. I crept carefully around the room trying not to stir Leala before realizing in the soft light of the breaking morning that she wasn't in her bed.

I switched on a lamp. Her twin bed was neatly made, with its thin cotton quilt folded at the foot of the bed and the down pillows plumped against the white iron headboard. A pink blanket was tucked in tightly, and the corners of the pillowcases had been pulled taut.

After rummaging through the battered suitcase I'd carried from town to town over the years, I pulled out a pair of knee-length denim shorts with folded hems and a fuchsia short-sleeve T-shirt. I brushed my hair and set about braiding it, and the sparkles danced in the mirror over the dresser.

It was a little surreal to be back in my old room, especially since nothing had changed from the day I moved out—not one little thing. My side of the room was an explosion of organized chaos. Old posters hung at angles. My bed was a riot of color, from the patterned quilt to the mismatched sheets and blanket. Some of the books in my case were laid horizontally, others stood vertically. Books that reminded me that I once wanted to be a writer more than anything else in the world. The thesauruses, the *Chicago Manual of Style*, the books on how to develop a writing voice. It all seemed a lifetime ago, a blurry memory just out of reach. The desire to write still lurked somewhere deep within me, but my creativity had waned after my accident and hadn't returned. Maybe one day it would come back, but until then, I was happy sharing other people's stories. I loved my job and couldn't imagine life without it now, which was a good reminder that sometimes the first paths we take aren't the right ones.

I tied off my braid and crossed the room for my shoes. Leala's side of the room was a study in perfection. Her books were organized alphabetically. Her posters hung levelly. She'd always preferred neat and tidy, and I had the feeling it was because it was something she could control while living in a home that was wildly unpredictable.

A fishbowl filled with Leala's pet rocks sat on her side of the bench we used as a shared nightstand, and I picked one up from the top of the pile, rubbing my finger over the smooth stone that had a painted cat face on it, complete with inverted V-shaped ears. Then I smiled at the sight of the paperback she'd been reading before bed last night—Mama had the same book on the window bench in her room, except where Mama's book's spine was broken, the pages dog-eared, Leala's was pristine in condition, appearing to never have been cracked open.

Pipes squeaked, and I tipped my head. The water was running in Mama's bathroom shower. I glanced at the clock. Not even six yet. I hurried to Mama's room. Her door was ajar, and I pushed it fully open to find her bed already made as well—not as neatly as Leala's but not as haphazardly as mine.

Mama was singing in the shower—"Shallow, allllow, allllow, allllow"—and I smiled despite the fact that she should be in bed.

I gently knocked on the bathroom door and opened it a crack. I stuck my mouth in the gap. "Mama?"

"Don't you just love that song?"

Steam floated out, swirling around me in billowy plumes. "You should be in bed."

"No, I needed to wash up. I stunk like a hospital."

"You should've at least let Leala or me help you."

"I'm not an invalid, Sadie Way. I can take a shower."

I breathed deeply through my nose. Again I had to choose my battles, because I knew about the stairwell wallpaper and she did not. Yet.

"Give me fifteen minutes," I said, "and I'll bring up a breakfast tray. How's an egg white omelet sound?"

"Dreadful."

"Mama, the doctor said—"

"Alllow, allow, allow!" she sang loudly, not even getting the lyrics right.

Downstairs, Nigel started barking. I groaned. "I'll be right back."

I closed the door firmly behind me, turned down the covers of her bed to encourage her to get back into it, and quietly made my way down to the kitchen, resisting the urge to tear off another panel of wallpaper along the way.

The lights were on throughout the main level and the coffee pot dripped its liquid magic, delightfully scenting the air with all the hope that came with a new day. A few of the back porch windows were open, letting in a gentle breeze. Birds sang, bugs hummed, and somewhere in the distance a boat motor buzzed dully.

I glanced out the wide window above the kitchen sink as I washed my hands. Dawn was breaking open over the lake, spilling soft gray light onto the water—and illuminating Leala, who stood on one leg at the end of the dock. The other leg was pulled up behind her, held high by her right hand. Her left arm was stretched forward. She looked like a ballerina as she executed the yoga pose, and I couldn't help staring. Leala was the last person in the world I would have thought to practice yoga. She was so buttoned-up, a planner and organizer. She'd had her life mapped out since she was a young girl, dreaming of everything and anything that was different from what she already had. Yoga was all about living, being, in the moment. Yet, there she was. And by the looks of her, she wasn't a novice.

I dried my hands and reached for the coffee pot as Uncle Camp shuffled into the kitchen, already dressed for the day. He smelled like soap and kindness and love. The ceiling lights reflected off his bald head as he planted an exaggerated, noisy kiss on my temple, his soft whiskers tickling my cheek. "Just like old times seeing you standing there. We sure have missed you around these parts."

"I've missed you, too," I said honestly as I added a splash of cream and a pinch of sugar to my mug. Uncle Camp and I regularly kept in touch through text messages, mostly silly memes. But being here with him in person was just one more thing that reminded me of how much I missed home.

As I poured coffee into a mug for him, adding a spoonful of sorghum syrup to it, a reedy wail filled the air, and we both turned toward the window as the loon trilled her morning plea. The bird looked spectral on the eerily gray water as she glided along, her call echoing in the quiet morning.

I stared at the ripples she made in the water, thinking back to my accident. I had very few memories of that night beyond tripping over my own feet and falling. I didn't remember hitting my head on a pylon. Or tumbling off the dock into the water. I didn't remember being lost beneath the surface for ten long minutes. But I remembered the lights. There had been twinkling orbs floating around me, swirling, wrapping me in what felt like a warm hug. And then there was the feeling of air in my lungs. Life. My mind was blank from that point on until I woke up in the hospital the next morning.

After the bird floated past, Uncle Camp said, "Did I hear Susannah singing earlier?"

I set down my mug and crossed to the fridge for eggs. "I think the whole street did. I'm going to try to get her to eat something healthy and stay in bed all day, resting, reading, watching reality TV. You know she can't resist all those Housewives shows." Which was probably the only reason the cottage had a good cable package. "Are you hungry? I'm fixin' Mama an omelet. Happy to make one for you, too."

"Thank you kindly, but I already ate." From the counter he picked up the drawer pull that I'd forgotten to replace last night and held it up, a question in his eyes. "Don't suppose this is related to the missin' wallpaper in the stairwell?"

I blinked as innocently as I could manage. "The knob plumb fell off the drawer when I opened it last night."

Using a screwdriver from his Swiss Army knife drawn from his pocket, he easily reattached the drawer pull. "And the wallpaper?"

"It plumb fell off the wall when I pulled on it."

Humor filled his eyes—eyes so like my daddy's. "You hopin' your mama stays in bed to rest or to not kill you for messin' with her walls?"

I broke an egg, separating the yolk from the whites using my fingers. "Mostly the first. Partly the second. Leala and I plan to redo the stairway and entryway this weekend. Well, I am. Leala thinks I've done lost my mind. But hopefully once she's over her shock she'll lend a hand."

"The contractor will be by 'bout nine." Uncle Camp's wiry

salt-and-pepper eyebrows dipped low. "You should talk to him about finishing the job for you."

I'd taken a moment last night to inspect the two guest rooms under construction and had been impressed with the work being done. The rooms, both of which had double doors that opened into the backyard, were bound to be highly desirable among guests. The work seemed close to completion with the walls having already been repaired and primed, and the bathrooms had received a complete overhaul, with new walk-in showers. Flooring and fixtures were still needed, but it seemed reasonable that the rooms would be rentable by next weekend.

I finished cracking the rest of the eggs, then washed my hands and dried them. "You don't trust Leala and me to do it right?"

Uncle Camp smiled. "All I'm sayin' is no one's a tougher critic than your mama. Don't you remember the one time she made the house painter redo the job three times?"

I remembered. I also recalled how she'd done it so sweetly—and always with a baked good in hand—that the house painter hadn't seemed to mind. Mama had a natural way with strangers that was nothing short of a gift. Her enthusiasm for life was charming, and people were always charmed.

Uncle Camp pulled a sauté pan from a cabinet. "All I'm saying is that it might be best to let someone else carry the weight of her expectations."

I noticed a slight tremor in his hand as he set the pan on the stovetop. He'd turned seventy-six earlier this year and was just as active as I'd always known him to be—he just moved more slowly now. I didn't even want to think about the day he would no longer be around, this man I loved so much, who was the last connection to my father and the Scott side of the family. Though Uncle Camp had done a good job through the years of teaching us our family history, I felt like there was always more to learn. Especially about Uncle Camp himself.

I only knew bullet points of his life, mere glimpses, culled together through the years. Whenever I'd asked about his life before living with us, he always joked that it had begun only after he moved into the cottage, but I always sensed a serious, almost somber, nature lurking deep within him, hidden by a quick smile, a bad joke, or an offer of something to eat.

Uncle Camp had been in the military during the early days of the Vietnam War but never, ever spoke of it, and Mama always warned us not to bug him about it, because according to her, no one in the Scott family liked talking about their tragedies.

Apparently, I'd inherited that particular trait, too, because I'd rather talk about anything other than my accident.

After his time as a soldier, Uncle Camp found his way back home to Alabama and took up carpentry, which eventually landed him here at the lake. And I quite honestly wasn't sure what we would have done without him. Any of us.

"Has Mama talked at all about doing a bigger renovation or hiring on any help?" I asked.

"It comes up from time to time."

"Then goes away again?" The pipes squeaked, a sure sign that Mama had just shut off the shower. I had to hurry. I gathered an onion, mushrooms, spinach, and Swiss cheese.

He took a sip of his coffee and shrugged. "Susannah doesn't like change. And big renovations will hurt business, and that's hurting enough already."

I chopped the onion, sliced the mushrooms, then turned the knob on the stove. A blue flame jumped to life beneath the pan. I adjusted the flame, then bypassed the butter to use spray oil to coat the bottom of the pan. I sautéed the veggies, then added the egg whites to the mix. "How bad is it?"

"Can't say for sure. Susannah handles all that, but it hasn't escaped my notice that we've had many empty rooms this year."

Stress from worrying about occupancy probably hadn't helped Mama's heart issues. But in order to bump up occupancy, changes needed to happen. That much was obvious from the reviews I'd read last night. As the eggs cooked, I grabbed a breakfast tray. "I'm going to do my best to help out while I'm here. I can take down wallpaper, paint, clean windows."

With an unwavering gaze, he watched me over the rim of his mug. "Ain't but twenty-four hours in a day, Sadie. Perhaps you should consider extending your stay if you're all fired up to lend a hand around here."

He played dirty. "I can't stay. I'm heading down to Wetumpka on Monday." Or at least I hoped I would be—I still hadn't heard back from Mrs. Teakes on whether that day worked for her. I was already looking forward to being back in her charming kitchen, making ambrosia and hearing about her late husband, Whit, who'd knocked her off her feet at a church picnic in the late 1960s. Literally off her feet—he'd bumped into her, and she'd fallen onto the grass . . . and for him.

Uncle Camp took a leisurely sip of coffee. "If you say so."

His hand was shaking again. I nodded to it. "Is your hand okay?"

Those out-of-control eyebrows of his dipped low as he gave his fingers a wry look. "Oh, that. It's just the wobbles."

"The wobbles?"

"Comes on in old age. Ain't nothing to be done for it, unless you've got a fountain of youth around here someplace."

I smirked. "Is *wobbles* the technical term for the diagnosis?"

His eyes twinkled. "Of course it is. It's written plain as can be in the medical journal, printed right after *the wiggles*. But that affliction affects toddlers mostly."

A vision of Tucker wiggling with excitement over his Easter basket popped into my head and I smiled. I turned the omelet out of the pan and onto a plate. I filled a ramekin with the raspberries Buzzy had sent over and set it on the breakfast tray. "Have you seen a doctor about the wobbles?"

"Don't go worrying about me, Sadie Way. Just had my checkup with Dr. Barnhill not two months ago. I'm fit as a wobbly fiddle."

I was going to worry no matter what. Over the years he'd filled in as a parent more often than I could count, especially giving of his time and attention—two things Mama rarely spared for us girls. I loved him with my whole heart. "But not a wiggly one."

He laughed as he rinsed his mug and put it in the dishwasher. "You always were a quick learner. Me and my wobbles get by just fine. Life's about adjusting. Gettin' old isn't for the faint of heart, but it is for the lucky. No question, I'm a lucky man. It's a gift to be alive."

The lucky. Old age was a privilege not granted to all. My daddy had been only thirty when he passed away after falling off a ladder here at the cottage—he'd been only four years older than I was now. Why had he died so young, yet I'd been allowed to live when I fell in the lake? Both had been accidents.

Why had I been saved?

Uncle Camp crossed the hall to adjust the thermostat for the day, and said, "Thanks for covering the kitchen this weekend. It's a rare day I get a break from cooking breakfast."

Since Leala didn't like to cook, we'd made a pact. I'd cook and she'd do the dishes while we were here, to give Uncle Camp a rest along with Mama.

With his big hand he cupped his ear. "I hear weeds callin' my name—they're easier to pull when the dew is fresh. If you need me, I'll be—"

It was the sound of footsteps on the stairs that cut him off. I wiped my hands on a dish towel and hoped to the stars above it was Bree or Teddy on their way down, but those hopes were dashed when I heard humming. Mama soon appeared on the landing, and I braced myself for the incoming wallpaper storm.

"What a gorgeous morning," she said, pausing to look out the window.

Sunlight seeped through the filthy glass to illuminate her face. Her coloring was nearly back to normal. Her hair was combed and damp, her wild curls mere waves. I was disappointed to see she was dressed for the day in long shorts and a bright-yellow V-neck tunic top, embroidered at the collar with colorful flowers, and had on slip-on canvas shoes. She was treating this like just another day on the job when she should be resting, healing.

"Sure is." Uncle Camp headed for the back porch. "Was just about to head out to do some weeding."

I grabbed his arm, yanking him to a stop. "You sure you don't want an omelet, Uncle Camp? Or a scone. Yes, a scone! They're raspberry with vanilla glaze. I made them last night."

He tried to wriggle free. "Not hungry, darlin'."

"Another cup of coffee, then?"

With a grin, he said under his breath, "*Bawk, bawk.*"

I stepped in even closer to him and kept a firm hold of his arm as I whispered, "Do you blame me?"

"No, ma'am," he whispered back. "Surely don't."

Mama slowly descended the remaining six steps. "Did you say raspberr—"

She abruptly stopped talking, her gaze on the wall, where the missing strip of wallpaper was glaringly obvious in the growing light of day. Her jaw dropped and she tentatively reached out to touch the wall that still had the fuzzy wallpaper backing attached, as if to make sure she wasn't hallucinating.

For a moment, I felt six years old again, wanting to blame the crime at hand on Leala Clare. I shook the thought away since those two had enough issues as is. Plus, Mama would never believe me. I was always the one getting into mischief and messes as a child, not Leala, who tended to follow rules like she'd been the one to write them. Besides, this had been my plot, my plan, and while I had deemed it brilliant last night, suddenly I was having second thoughts.

"I tripped," I blurted, lying through my teeth. "And when I reached for the wall to catch my balance, I caught an edge of the wallpaper, and it tore. Sorry, Mama. The paper was so ripped up that it couldn't be glued back on without it looking like a hot mess. But I promise I'll fix it right up. The whole entryway."

Shoulders stiff, I braced for hurricane-strength gusts and barely noticed Uncle Camp patting my hand that clutched his arm.

Mama continued to stare at the wall, silent as the grim reaper.

"Mama?" I questioned with a wince. "Are you mad?"

At the question, she reached out, grabbed hold of another loose seam of wallpaper, and yanked. The sucking sound echoed through the entryway and up the staircase.

Uncle Camp and I glanced at each other, wearing, I was quite sure, identical expressions of shock.

Finally Mama turned to face us, and I was surprised to see light in her eyes instead of flames. She smiled and said, "Depends on your definition of *mad*."

Chapter 7

Leala

It was past time to head back inside the cottage, shower, and get started with the morning chores, including breakfast service. But the longer I sat on the end of the dock, the longer I wanted to stay exactly where I was. I wasn't even sure how long I'd been out here. A half hour? An hour? Long enough to see the sun come up and the loon float by. And hopefully long enough to avoid Mother's hissy fit at seeing Sadie's wallpaper handiwork.

It was peaceful out here, just the way I liked it. Calm, despite the occasional noise from johnboats puttering by and the chirp of the birds, katydids, and frogs. I honestly didn't know how Sadie could stay away from the lake so long. Sometimes it felt like heaven on earth, and I deeply regretted that Connor and I hadn't bought a smaller place on the water so I could enjoy it day in and day out.

The water gently lapped the stone seawall, rhythmic and lulling, and for a moment I thought about napping on my yoga mat. I hadn't slept well at all last night, tossing and turning and checking my phone, despite finally receiving a picture from Connor of Tucker sound asleep in his bed with the caption GOOD DAY, GOOD NIGHT.

I had stared at the picture for a good long while, before I sent back a pink heart emoji. I longed to talk to Connor, because I missed him. At the same time, I wasn't ready, because I wasn't yet sure what to say to the man who'd become so distant. Yesterday had made it abundantly clear that my marriage couldn't survive in its current state. Something had to give.

Rolling my shoulders, I tried to ease the growing knots of tension that I'd just worked so hard to release. I picked up my phone from the mat next to me and called up the photo again. Asleep in his toddler bed, Tucker's cheeks were pink, his mouth slightly open, his face slack with the peace that came with deep sleep. His sunny-blond hair, cut shorter than usual for summertime, was in disarray, reminding me of Connor's hair when he woke up every morning. Moo was tucked in close to him.

At the ache in my chest, I took a deep breath and willed away the feelings of grief. Like I had lost something. Someone. I hadn't. Though, maybe in a way, I had. Even though Connor wasn't gone, the man I'd fallen in love with was. And with that thought, the ache deepened.

I focused on my breathwork as the sunshine warmed my back, and as much as I hated to leave this spot, it was time to head inside. As I stretched my legs, a dog barked from nearby. I glanced over my shoulder. Nigel raced full speed ahead toward me, his feet barely making any noise on the dock's wooden planks, Bree not far behind him. I hadn't heard them come out because I'd oiled the track of the sliding door early this morning. Now I wondered if it had been left squeaky on purpose, a bell of sorts to announce comings and goings.

Nigel pounced, and I laughed as he licked my face and threw himself against my body. I gave him a good belly rub as Bree jogged toward us.

"I'm so sorry!" Her hair had been pulled up in a messy bun and she wore baggy lounge pants and a tank top. No shoes. "He saw you down here and made a break for it as soon as I stepped outside. Hopped right out of my arms. Nigel, come here," she ordered in an exasperated tone.

If Nigel hadn't come running, I was quite sure Bree would've avoided talking with me altogether. At dinner last night she'd said little, answering any questions with short answers. I'd been able to capture only a fuzzy picture of her life. She was an only child. She was going into her senior year of high school but was being homeschooled. She had no plans for college at the moment. She liked dogs. And art. And pizza. She'd talked nothing of her scars. I had desperately wanted to ask about them and her family but had recalled Teddy's hushed voice in the entryway, whispering about Bree's tragic life, so I'd kept the questions to myself.

"He's no bother." Nigel lolled in front of me, clearly not planning to go anywhere, especially if I intended to keep giving him belly rubs. His soft brown eyes shined with happiness. Tucker would love Nigel. Eat him right up. Perhaps it was time to get a dog of our own. Or a cat. That fluffy kitten I'd always wanted. As

I stood up, Nigel put his paws on my knees. His tail wagged as I added, "But as much as I'd love to stay outside and play, I was just about to head inside to help with breakfast."

Just steps away, Bree's attention fell to my stomach, bare between my crop top and the yoga pants that sat low on my hips. Slowly, she lifted her gaze to meet mine.

"Emergency C-section," I said as I petted Nigel's head and answered the question Bree hadn't asked. "The doctor had to do a vertical incision to save my baby's life. And mine, too."

"You almost died?"

In my mind, I could still hear the flurry of activity in the surgery suite right before they put me under, scared and confused. I nodded. "I lost a lot of blood. And the wound didn't heal well, obviously." The thick, raised scar was an eight-inch-long purplish vertical line starting just above my belly button and ending at my pubic bone.

I recognized that in this moment I was talking too much, sharing something quite personal—which was completely out of my tight-lipped character. It's not like she'd even asked, for heaven's sake, but I felt the need to connect to this young woman who seemed so shy and sad. If my story helped her in any way, I'd share it with her a thousand times over.

Bree's hand lifted to her face, her fingertips grazing the thin lines crisscrossing her cheek. Then she looked at the lake, at the shimmery glow kissing the water's surface as the sun crept upward.

When she said nothing, I took a deep breath and overshared yet again by gently saying, "Everyone bears scars, inside and out. And behind every single one of those healed wounds is a story of strength and resilience and recovery. My scar is simply part of me, part of my story."

"But don't you hate when people stare?"

"I don't mind the staring too much. People are curious, that's all—kind of like how you were with Sadie's hair. The looks of pity bother me more, because I don't like people feeling sorry for me when they don't even know me or what I've been through."

Her face crumpled into a frown. "The pity is the worst."

"I just try to remind myself that pity usually comes from a good place, one of empathy and sympathy. When I see a look of pity now, I try to think of it as a look of caring instead. It makes it much more tolerable."

I hoped she'd open up to me as well, but instead of sharing the story of her scars, she said, "How old is your baby?"

I gave her a smile because I recognized that some wounds were still too raw to share. "He's two and a half. His name's Tucker. He's having bonding time with his dad this weekend, while I'm helping out here."

"That's too bad he didn't come with you. I love little kids. So honest. So innocent. And funny."

"Ridiculously funny." Had Connor realized that yet? Had he laughed at Tucker's silliness or rushed him through the day so he could check his email after Tuck was asleep?

Suddenly agitated, I grabbed my yoga mat, forgetting that my phone had been on it. As if in slow motion, I watched as the phone launched into the air and dropped into the water with a loud plop, disappearing below the surface before I could even think to dive in after it. I swore a blue streak in my head, clenched my fists, and tried to quell a rising panic.

It was just a phone, I told myself over and over, but my stomach ached at the loss. Of not being able to call up Tucker's sweet face with a swipe of a finger. Of having to deal with getting a replacement. And how was Connor going to reach me if there was an emergency? The knot in my stomach tightened, and the panic rose into my throat, tightening it.

"I can go in after it," Bree offered, peering over the edge of the dock. "I'm a good swimmer."

I took a deep, calming breath, and the knots loosened enough to talk without my voice shaking. I tried for a light tone to mask how upset I truly was because I didn't want Bree worrying about me. "That's real nice of you to offer, Bree, but this part of the lake is quite deep. The phone's likely twenty or thirty feet down by now, and I doubt it would survive being submerged anyway."

I forced my fists to relax. I'd call Connor from Mother's landline to let him know what happened and then figure out how to get a replacement as quick as possible. I threw one last look at the water, finished rolling my mat, and grabbed the lightweight cover-up I'd brought outside. I shrugged into it, tying its strings into a bow. I motioned for Bree to follow as I headed back to the cottage.

She gestured at the yoga mat. "Is yoga hard?"

Nigel raced ahead of us, circling back every couple of steps to make sure we were following. "Yoga's great in the way that you can adjust it to suit your skill level. It's up to you on how much you want to challenge yourself. You're more than welcome to join me out here tomorrow morning. I can show you a few of the poses."

"I'd like that," she said quietly.

My heart soared. "Then it's a date."

She gave me a shy smile just as Nigel darted for the honeysuckle hedge, barking and bouncing at something wiggling in the vines. I was 100 percent sure I didn't want to know what it was.

"Nigel!" Bree called, chasing after him. "Hush!" She scooped him up and carried him to the doggy play yard.

The scent of cooking bacon greeted me at the sliding door, beckoning me inside. But I froze in shock as I stepped into the great room. My mother was standing on the landing yanking wallpaper off the wall with wild abandon, passing the strips to Uncle Camp, who stuffed them into a trash bag.

Sadie spotted me, rushed over, and whispered, "She's been at it for nearly twenty minutes now."

"You didn't tell her to stop?"

"Of course I did. You can see how well it went over. At this point, I'm kind of hoping she tires herself out so she'll stay in bed the rest of the day."

It was a technique I used on Tucker regularly. The more active he was early in the day, the better he slept at night. It seemed all kinds of wrong to employ the method on Mother, however. "Was she angry?"

"Not even a little, which surprised the heck out of me. She seemed more shocked than anything. She tore one strip off, started laughing, and kept going. Every once in a while, she sings, 'In for a penny, in for a pound,' as she tears off another section. She won't let Uncle Camp help, either. He looks like he's plotting a dozen different ways to escape." A buzzer rang out. "That's the bacon."

She scooted around the peninsula and opened the oven to remove a foil-wrapped baking sheet covered in crispy bacon strips. I glanced at Uncle Camp, who stared longingly at the front door, his nearest means of escape. His gaze shifted, and he sent me a pleading look. I shrugged. I wasn't sure there was any stopping her at this point, and the last thing I wanted was to try to force her to quit. Mother didn't like being told what to do.

"Good Lord, Susannah!" Teddy exclaimed as she came down the stairs, one hand holding up the hem of her maxi dress so she wouldn't trip. "I was wondering what all the commotion was down here. Come on, come here," she summoned when she reached the landing. "Leave that be for now and let's get something sweet to eat and maybe a Bloody Mary to kick-start the day. A virgin one for you, of course, my dear Susannah, since we need to treat that heart with a little tender loving care for a while."

For a moment, Mother looked like she was going to argue but then let out a puff of breath that blew a curly strand of hair out of her eyes. Finally she looped an arm around Teddy's. "Now that you mention it, I am a bit parched."

"It's no wonder! Look at this place. You've done tore it up, piece by piece. It looks a sight better already, if you don't mind me saying so." They slowly came down the rest of the steps like debutantes descending into a ballroom.

Looking mighty relieved for the reprieve, Uncle Camp hurried as fast as he could toward the front door, the bag of wallpaper still in hand. "I'll be outside if anyone needs me."

Mother turned to him to say something but he was already gone. She chuckled. "He hasn't moved that fast in years."

Her cheeks were flushed, and I quickly beelined for the fridge, dropping my yoga mat in the corner by the door as I went by. My call to Connor could wait a few moments until there wasn't an audience. "I'll get your drinks ready. The breakfast starters are here on the counter."

Sadie had done a wonderful job of laying out the spread. A coffee-and-tea station anchored the end of the counter near the wall, with a pitcher of ice water and orange juice, along with glasses, and a floral-embroidered runner ran the rest of the length of the peninsula. A three-tiered stand was stacked with rectangular white ceramic trays—the top was filled with fresh fruit, the middle displayed mini raspberry scones with vanilla icing, and the bottom held six mini mason jars filled with berry parfaits, nestled in a bed of crushed ice. To the side, ramekins held crushed nuts and granola.

As I grabbed olives, Worcestershire sauce, Tabasco, and vegetable juice from the fridge, Bree and Nigel came back inside, and Nigel raced around to greet everyone, his skinny tail wagging.

Mother beamed at him and laughed as he flopped at her feet. I ignored a stab of resentment and set the Bloody Mary fixings on the prep island.

Teddy fussed with the filigree combs that held her teased hair away from her face and took a deep breath. "I smell the magic in the air this morning! I can *feel* it, too. The air is crackling with energy. This might finally be the year my water lantern wish will come true. True love at last."

Mother inhaled and rubbed her hands together. "All I smell is delicious bacon."

"Your omelet is waiting to be reheated, Mama," Sadie said as she cracked eggs into a batter bowl. "If you're wanting bacon, I can make you some turkey bacon."

"Hell no!" Mother tsked. "I don't want any turkey bacon. That's sacrilegious. Why do we even *have* turkey bacon?"

"I ordered it from the market yesterday." Sadie stood firm, shaking an egg in her direction. "It's heart-healthy."

Mother scowled and looked to be building up a good head of steam. I was grateful it wasn't directed my way for once as I added ice into a cocktail mixer.

"Here," Teddy said, intervening. She plucked a parfait from the tray and pressed it into Mother's hand. "Eat this. Put some of that crunchy stuff on top. Looks like it might mask any healthiness."

Thank heavens for Teddy. I hadn't been on board with the cottage hosting guests this weekend, but since Teddy was practically family, she was the perfect foil for Mother's pigheadedness. And even though she looked like she still wanted to argue, Mother didn't put the parfait back onto the tray. Under her breath, she muttered, "Turkey," with such disdain that I thought ham would be on the menu this coming Thanksgiving.

Bree fed Nigel a treat and said, "Wishes don't really come true at the lantern festival, do they?"

"Oh yes they do," Mother, Sadie, and I said at the same time.

We all glanced at each other and laughed, and the tension in the air fizzled.

Teddy set two mini scones and a banana onto a plate. "Thanks to Lady Laurel."

"But seriously," Bree said. "The lady of the lake? That's just a made-up story to get tourists to come to town."

Suddenly intent on her waffle batter, Sadie turned away from the conversation, as she did any time Lady Laurel was brought up. She resisted talking about her accident at every turn. Again, I was reminded of wounds still too raw to talk about and wanted nothing more than for her to finally heal.

"Not quite." I poured Tabasco sauce into the mixer. "Local legend says Lady Laurel was quite real, once upon a time. Laurel isn't her real name, though—that's been lost to time."

Mother's eyes lit. "Talk of Lake Laurel's magic—lake magic—goes back centuries! The lake itself is an impact crater, formed when a meteorite crashed to earth millions of years ago, or so the fancy scientists say. There've been tales passed through generations of how the water is rejuvenating and refreshing and even one or two tales of miraculous healings, and that's all before the lady of the lake even made an appearance."

Nigel wandered over to one of the overstuffed chairs next to the fireplace and hopped up onto the seat cushion, turned twice, and settled in for a nap, making himself right at home. Bree sat down on a stool, looking both enraptured and cynical. "When was that?"

"Some fifty, sixty years ago, give or take, when the lake was more of a summer destination and the town was just getting established. The story goes that on the last weekend in August, a young couple up here on their honeymoon went out on a rowboat at sunset. There was a terrible accident when a speedboat didn't see the rowboat. It was an awful crash, with the rowboat ending up split in half. The couple disappeared into the water, seemingly lost to the depths."

Goose bumps rose on my arms, as they always did when the legend was retold, especially by my mother, whose enthusiasm was contagious.

"Upon hearing of the accident, search boats were launched and people gathered to set lanterns along the shore, beacons of hope. Some set lanterns afloat, too, and all were lit with the fervent wish that the couple was still alive and would see the light and know people were looking for them. Well," Mother said, dragging out the word, "after a time the floating lanterns started disappearing, one by one. *Plop*, *plop*, *plop*, like they were being plucked straight off the water's surface, and the lights began glowing under the water! Not a few minutes later, the missing man was found alive by one of the search boats."

As Mother paused for dramatic effect, I shook the mixer and

started filling two tall glasses. I'd heard this story a thousand times, but Mother told it as if she were telling it for the first time ever. There was a renewed light in her eyes and a brightness to her spirit I hadn't seen in quite a while.

"The man claimed the love of his life, who had died instantly in the crash, used the wishes from the lanterns to turn into a loon that helped keep him afloat until he was rescued. No one believed him at first, thinking he'd been hallucinating, until the loon appeared crying for her mate. The lady of the lake legend was born. The following year on the last weekend in August, people lit water lanterns in tribute, writing wishes on the wood. Some of those lanterns disappeared—*plop*, *plop*, *plop*—and those wishes came true. Eventually, the festival turned into what it is now." Her voice dropped to a whisper. "And to this day, on the darkest of nights, you can see Lady Laurel's lights shining underwater."

Sitting straight, fully attentive, Bree rapped the countertop. "Wait, wait. Did they ever find the young woman's body?"

It was nice to see Bree coming out of her shy shell and being so involved in this conversation. The lake was already working its magic on her and she hadn't even been here twenty-four hours yet.

"Never did." Mother stared with consternation at the parfait in her hand. "But the loon still shows up at dusk and dawn every day, crying for her mate."

Bree wrinkled her nose. "You think the lady of the lake is a *loon*?"

"You'll never be able to tell me differently," Mother stated. "Even though the lantern festival has become known for wishes being granted, it's really a tribute to that young woman and the strength of her love. It's a love festival." She slowly grinned as what she'd said registered. "*Shoo*. That doesn't sound quite right, does it? This isn't any Woodstock. Let's try that again. The water lantern festival is about the power of love."

"How do we not know her name?" Bree asked. "Wasn't there a police report?"

Mother laughed. "We didn't have any local law enforcement back then. By the time the county sheriff showed up, the grieving man had disappeared."

"So all this could be made-up," Bree said, one eyebrow raised. "To keep the tourists coming. It's kind of a brilliant marketing plan."

Mother patted her on the shoulder. "You'll discover the truth for yourself soon enough—I assure you. Everyone does if they stay here for any length of time. Lady Laurel isn't shy about sharing her kindnesses."

Teddy dipped a spoon in the parfait. "And as for Lady Laurel being a loon, there are tales that she gets so lonely sometimes that she comes out of the lake to walk among us . . ."

Mother's eyes widened as she theatrically added, "Disguised as a *tourist*. One who gives out random acts of kindness as a thank-you to the people of Sugarberry Cove for the kind wishes that saved her mate."

"Have you ever seen her?" Bree asked, enrapt at this point, despite her misgivings.

"Sadly, no. The closest I came was once over at the Landing, she was giving out gold coins to strangers. I missed it by minutes, and I'm still a mite salty about it."

Bree squinted as if she wasn't buying a word of what she heard. "What does she look like?"

"That's up for debate." Mother sprinkled a generous helping of granola onto her parfait. "Her description changes depending on who you ask. You know, at one point, I thought Teddy was Lady Laurel in disguise. I convinced myself of it for a full year."

"No you did not," Teddy said with a deep, barking laugh.

"Oh, I did so," Mother admitted. "She just seemed a little too perfect. And she'd come into my life at a time when I needed a friend most of all. Her kindness saw me through some dark days."

I glanced at Sadie and found she was looking at me with a question in her eyes. I'd never heard any of this and apparently neither had she.

Teddy put her arm around Mother's shoulders. "You sweet, sweet delusional woman. If I were Lady Laurel and could become anyone I wanted, I'd have much better hair and a whole lot of money."

Mother laughed, and I couldn't help but smile, too. Teddy was light and love and fun, and Lady Laurel or not, I was glad she had found her way into our lives.

"What made you change your mind about Aunt Teddy?" Bree asked.

I was curious, too.

"Well," Mother said, "the illusion was shattered one night

when Teddy and I went out for drinks at a country bar up the road a piece."

By Mother's droll tone, I could already tell this was going to be a good story.

"Oh Lord," Teddy muttered.

"Teddy perhaps had a little too much to drink and practically served herself up on a silver platter to the house band's drummer. At one point I found them in a hallway, getting a little, shall we say, *handsy*." Mother smiled fondly at Teddy. "It just didn't seem the type of thing Lady Laurel would do."

"Aunt Teddy!" Bree said, her eyes wide.

Teddy shrugged. "I'm not sure how that incident ruled me out. I was being kind." She wiggled her eyebrows. "Really kind."

After a roar of laughter died down, Mother looked at Teddy and added, "We've had some good times over the years."

"Sure have," Teddy agreed.

Bree smiled at them, then said, "I still think the whole Lady Laurel thing sounds fishy." She reached for a mug and then the coffee pot. "I mean, where in the world would she get gold coins?"

"From the lake bed." Mother spooned a bite of parfait into her mouth. She looked for a moment like she was going to complain about the taste, then tipped her head as if saying it wasn't too bad, considering the healthiness of it all. "Rumors have swirled for years that Confederate soldiers on the run during the Civil War had buried a chest of gold coins in the sands of the cove to ease their load. By the time they came back for it, the lake had risen, swallowing the chest."

Bree took a sip of the coffee and pulled a long, sour face. "Whoa, this is strong."

"It's the chicory in it," Sadie said. She pushed the sugar jar across the counter. "Adding a little sweetness helps."

As Bree spooned sugar into her mug—one, two, three scoops—Mother said, "Lady Laurel's also been known to rescue people from the lake. Stranded boaters might get pushed to shore with sudden waves that come on out of nowhere. Once, during a water lantern festival, she saved our Sadie Way. She was underwater ten whole minutes before the lady of the lake intervened. Sadie's the only one that Lady Laurel has brought back from the dead."

With a spoon, Teddy scraped the bottom of her mason jar.

"That's why we think she has that silvery hair—it's from Lady Laurel's magic touch."

Mother huffed. "I still say it's starlight. The lake was made from a meteorite, after all. It's possible."

Bree gazed at Sadie's hair. "Wow."

"Oh, good Lord," Sadie whispered as she pulled the waffle iron from a cabinet.

To change the subject, I quickly set the glasses on the peninsula and said, "So, true love, Teddy? Do you wish for it every year?"

"Sure do." Teddy took a sip of her Bloody Mary and smiled. "Just right. Thanks, Leala. And though none of my wishes have come true just yet, I feel like this is the year. What are you going to wish for?"

I froze. I didn't want the questions that would come with why I didn't make wishes anymore, so I shrugged. "I don't know."

"Wait." Bree added cream to the coffee, too. "I thought wishes wouldn't come true if you talked about them."

"That's birthday wishes," Teddy said, heading for the dining table on the back porch, her plate and drink in hand. "These are lake wishes. Anything goes. What about you, Bree? What will you wish for?"

Bree's eyebrows pulled together. "I don't really think this is all real, but it probably can't hurt to make a wish."

Ah, little did she know. "Make sure it comes from a good place, unselfish and pure."

Sadie dropped the spatula and mumbled something under her breath as she tossed it into the sink.

Nigel's head came up, and he let out a yip as though complaining about being disturbed.

"Sorry, Nigel," Sadie said. "It slipped right out of my hand."

He hopped down from the chair and followed Teddy onto the back porch, suddenly curious about her plate of food as she said, "Get to thinking about it, Bree. Time's a-tickin'. The festival is just a week away."

Mother wiggled off her stool, took a sip of her drink, and frowned at me. "Surely a *little* vodka wouldn't have hurt, LC."

I sighed. "Firstly, your heart. Second, your medications. You can't mix them with alcohol."

Mother scowled at me, then walked away.

I heard Teddy ask, "I wonder if that drummer from the bar is still single . . ."

Smiling, I turned to face Sadie and let out a long breath. "How is it only seven in the morning?"

She nodded toward the coffee pot. "Lots to do today still. You might want to fortify yourself."

I poured a cup, filling it nearly to the brim. "I have a feeling I'm going to need all the caffeine I can get. Mother's likely to need more supervision than Tucker and that's saying something. At least Tucker listens to me. Most of the time. Speaking of, I need to call Connor." My brain whirred with potential emergencies until I forced it to pause as I told her how my phone had sunk in the lake.

"Here, use mine," she said as she slid her cell from the back pocket of her shorts and handed it over. I smiled at the background image on the screen. It was a picture of Sadie and me when we were little, our faces and hands covered in blackberry stains after raiding Buzzy's berry patch. The photo felt like it was taken forever ago, in a time when life seemed so simple. Sunshine, smiles, and my sister. It made me suddenly question why I'd always wanted something more when it was obvious that I'd had so much.

I pushed aside those troubling thoughts and clicked over to the phone's keypad. As I stared at the numbers, I suddenly drew a blank, unable to recall Connor's cell phone number. Finally, I realized I had never known it. I hadn't bothered to memorize it; I'd simply inputted the numbers into my phone and trusted that I'd always have my phone handy. Embarrassed, I gave a little laugh. "I just realized I don't know Connor's number by heart. Do you have it in your contacts?"

Waffles sizzled as Sadie wiped her hands on a dish towel. "I don't think so. Maybe Mama has it in her address book?"

It didn't surprise me that Sadie didn't have his number. They had never been anything close to friends. "I'll check."

I crossed the hall and opened the office door. The room, wedged into the space under the stairs, was the size of a narrow walk-in closet, six feet by twelve feet. Light filled the room from the lone window that faced the front yard, and I winced at the mess on Mother's oak desk. Stacks of papers, file folders, catalogs, and travel guides. There was no computer, but I was happy to see she had an accounting calculator and not an abacus. Fortunately her address book was where it always was—under the landline phone, which made me hope that there was some semblance of organization to her chaos. I flipped through the address book and found no number listed under Keesling at all. I checked *C* for Connor as well, because Mother's method of filing was whimsical at best, but there was no listing.

Again, not really a surprise. Mother wasn't a fan of Connor's, either, though she'd warmed considerably to him over the years. The first time I'd brought him home to meet my family had been a disaster. It was shortly after we'd started dating our junior year of college. Sadie had shot him dirty looks all night, while Mother shared every embarrassing story about me she could remember, starting with adventures in potty training. It was a miracle he'd stuck around long enough to fall in love with me. But he had. And to this day I still felt a stab of pain, of betrayal when I recalled Mother's reaction to the news that I had gotten engaged.

"LC," she'd said, "you're too young to tie yourself down. You're young and free! The world is wide-open to you. Go and explore it. You shouldn't settle. Not now, not ever."

To Sadie and me, Mother had always sung the praises of seeing the world, of being footloose and fancy-free. While Mother had never seemed outwardly unhappy with her life, I suspected she held resentments. It wasn't a life that she would have chosen if she hadn't gotten pregnant out of wedlock. Seven months and a quickie wedding later, I'd been born. Not too long after that, Daddy inherited this property and, with Uncle Camp's help, started rebuilding. A tiny two-room summer cottage soon became a three-story bed-and-breakfast. But in fulfilling Daddy's dream, Mother had given up hers, which was to travel. Her wings had been clipped by responsibility, especially after Daddy died. She'd thrown herself into being an innkeeper, tirelessly working day and night to make ends meet.

Back then, I'd tried desperately to get her to see my point of view. "I'm not settling, Mother. I love Connor. I can't imagine living a day without him by my side."

What Mother had never understood, not in my whole life, was that I didn't want footloose and fancy-free. I wanted stability. Routine. Affection. Love.

Mother had shaken her head fiercely. "You say that now, but you're making a mistake you'll regret one day. Mark my words."

Bitterness swelled at the memory alone. Even worse, I could

only imagine how she'd gloat if she found out Connor and I were currently having marital problems.

Drawing in a deep breath, I used Sadie's phone to send an email to Connor's work and home accounts—those addresses I remembered—to let him know about my phone. Then I called my cell phone provider to see what I needed to do about getting a new phone and was dismayed to learn that only after paying the deductible on my insurance plan would a replacement phone be mailed to me—in one to two business days.

After I hung up with the phone company, my gaze fell on a letter on Mother's desk, a bill visible atop a teetering stack of paper. It seemed Mother was a month behind on her electric bill and had been hit with late fees. I glanced at the date—the notice had arrived early last week and was coming due soon. If it wasn't paid in full, the cottage's electricity would be disconnected. I nibbled my thumbnail as a pit grew in my stomach.

Fighting the urge to snoop some more into Mother's finances, I walked out of the office, leaving the bill behind on the desk, along with a growing suspicion that the missed payment hadn't been an accidental oversight.

Chapter 8

Sadie

Leala and I had rock-paper-scissored for who scored the preferred job of cleaning the guest bedrooms over the cruddy job of scrubbing the connecting bathrooms.

I'd lost. Which was why I found myself on my knees, wearing yellow rubber gloves, and running a rag over the tiles in Bree's bathroom. For a teenager, she was especially neat, and I was beyond grateful.

"Should we ask her about it?" Leala asked, popping into the doorway, a dust mop in hand.

Even though the house was well soundproofed, we'd been discussing in hushed tones the bill Leala had found in Mama's office. We didn't want to take any chances Mama could hear us through the vents.

She had gone to her room after breakfast to freshen up, and when she didn't come back down after a time, I'd sneaked in to check on her. She'd been sound asleep in bed, HGTV providing white noise. I tiptoed back out and hoped she'd rest for a good, long while.

Bree and Teddy had borrowed a pair of bikes to venture into town, and Nigel had fit neatly into the basket on Bree's bike. My heart had squeezed a little when I saw that Bree had combed her hair forward and wore a bucket hat to shadow her face, which I knew likely had to do with sun protection for her tender scars, but it also served the purpose of helping her hide them.

The strange thing was, after less than a day with her, I didn't even notice the scars so much. Sure, I was still curious about how they had come to be, but when I looked at her now, I mostly saw her big green eyes and the sadness in them.

I said, "I'm leaning toward no. It will only rile Mama up if she thinks we were snooping. She needs to stay calm this weekend."

"But what if she's in financial trouble?"

I dunked my rag, squeezed it out. "She'd tell us."

"Would she? You know how proud she is."

Leala made a good point. I stood up, my knees aching. "Uncle Camp did mention this morning that occupancy was down, but he wasn't sure how big of a hit the cottage was taking because Mama doesn't talk money with him. And now that I think about it, when I went to tip the grocery delivery guy last night, the petty cash tin in the kitchen was empty."

Leala leaned against the doorjamb. "If she's having money trouble, I can sit down with her, help her with a budget. See where she can make cuts, save some money, like not washing the sheets every day for guests staying multiple days. Besides being environmentally unfriendly, it's costly."

Mama had yet to adopt any kind of green initiative for the cottage, which meant all linens and towels were laundered daily. I already had a big wicker basket loaded to bring downstairs to the laundry room.

She added, "We can also ditch the bottled water she leaves in every room and replace it with a pitcher of filtered water. She already has a dozen pitchers on hand. The startup cost is minimal."

These were good ideas. "Not changing the sheets every day would also be easier on her physically."

Leala snapped her fingers. "Maybe that's the way we should approach it—frame it around her health instead of her finances. We can sneak in other changes, like the water, while somehow making it seem like they were her idea."

"That could work." We had used this method a lot growing up—dropping hints and making comments that would lead Mama to think she'd been the one to come up with the idea originally. It was often the only way to get something we truly wanted, like the trip to Disney World when I was seven. Leala and I had set that trap for months, laying the groundwork by mentioning how busy Mama always was, and how a vacation would be nice during our January off-season, and how so-and-so had just gone to Florida after their parents had scored a vacation package deal.

Leala bit her thumbnail. "I might have to do a little more snooping, see how big of a hole she's in."

In shock, I gaped at her as I peeled off the gloves. "Leala Clare, you'd never! You're such a Goody Two-shoes you wouldn't even peek at your Christmas presents when we knew where Mama hid them."

She laughed. "People change, Sadie."

It was true—they did. I knew I'd changed these last eight years, closing myself off more and more as time went by. "Speaking of, since when do you do yoga?"

"Since Tucker was six months old. The doctor thought it would help with my healing. Stretch the muscles. Heal the mind."

I tipped my head. "The mind? Did you have postpartum depression?"

Tucker's birth had happened so fast, nearly two weeks before his due date, because Leala's blood pressure had skyrocketed. I'd been in Louisiana, and by the time I'd reached the hospital, he'd been nearly a day old. I hadn't stayed long, either, only a few days to help Leala get settled at home. I'd used the excuse of needing to get back to work—which had been true since I'd had interviews scheduled—but the real reason was the same as always. This town brought back bad memories that made me feel like a failure.

"You know I had a rough birth with Tucker, an emergency C-section," she said. "What you don't know is that I hemorrhaged on the operating table. I needed blood transfusions—seven units of blood. The doctors fought for hours to get the bleeding under control. In order to save me, they eventually had to do an emergency hysterectomy. It was a lot to absorb. To grieve. It still is, if I'm being perfectly honest. Connor and I had wanted a big family. Yoga helps keep me focused on what's important. I'm still here. Tucker is here. We're both healthy."

I rushed over and threw my arms around her. "Oh my God, Leala. Why didn't you tell me?"

She laughed at my sudden assault but accepted the hug. "I wasn't ready to share the ordeal. At first, I wanted the focus to be on Tucker and how wonderful it was that he was here. And I really didn't want to face the reality of what had happened. I didn't die that day, but a few of my dreams did. I needed time to process the trauma in order to focus on healing. Mentally and physically. I'm not going to lie—it took a while, and there are some days I still work on it. It's hard, painful work, but I knew I had to do it, because I didn't want to live with that misery for the rest of my life."

I didn't like talking about the night I fell into the lake, either, so I couldn't fault her for wanting to keep the hysterectomy to herself for a while, but it pained me to know Leala had gone through something so traumatic and I hadn't known. She was my only sister, and *I hadn't known* she'd almost died. "But it's been years since then."

"I'd have told you, but you weren't around, except for holidays. Talking about what had happened over Christmas dinner or Easter brunch wasn't going to happen."

I'd purposely chosen to live away from Sugarberry Cove—and my old life. I had no right to feel sorry for myself now, but I did. Trying not to let the hurt come through in my tone, I said, "I can't believe I didn't know this. That you've managed to keep it quiet all this time. That Mama doesn't talk about it every time there's a gathering."

Her faced clouded over. "Mother doesn't know."

My jaw dropped.

"I didn't tell her on purpose. I saw what she did to you after your accident, and I didn't want that kind of attention. Mother . . . dwells. What you water grows, Sadie." Her forehead furrowed. "I was lucky that I had Connor and that he gave me the support I needed because I don't think I could've done it alone. I'm just sorry you had to deal with your experience on your own. I'm sorry you're still dealing with it. Eight years is a long time to suffer, Sadie. I'm here for you if you need me, you know. If you want to talk. Or do yoga." She smiled and pressed her palms together. "*Om*. You should join me tomorrow morning on the dock. Bree will be there, too. Don't say no straight off. Just think about it, okay?"

Before I could say anything at all, the sound of a power saw echoed up the stairs. The contractor had obviously arrived, and I prayed Mama would sleep through the noise.

Leala looked at her watch. "We should get a move on. I'll check the room next door, make sure everything's ready for the guest arriving today, while you wrap up in here."

As I went about finishing my chores, I thought about our conversation and how dreams can shift. Life was about adjusting, Uncle Camp had said. It was true. Life tended to set up speed bumps that send us veering off in other directions. If we didn't make changes, shift gears, we'd crash and burn. My accident had been a speed bump. And I had the feeling this weekend was one, too.

Ten minutes later, I headed downstairs with an overflowing laundry basket. I'd just taken the turn in the staircase when a man walked into the entryway from the hallway, a pencil tucked behind one ear, a piece of wood trim in hand.

Will Lockhart.

My foot slipped and I fell down the last three steps, landing with a bone-jarring thud on the pine floor. I squished my eyes closed and wanted nothing more than to run out the back door, fling myself into the lake, sink to the bottom, and stay there. But knowing my luck, Lady Laurel would throw me back out again, so I could flop around on the dock in all my embarrassment.

The air shifted, and I knew Will was kneeling next to me as he asked, "Sadie! Are you okay?"

"Mm-hmm." I kept my eyes squished closed, so I didn't have to see him studying me, my hair. Upstairs, the vacuum shut off; then I heard hurried footsteps.

Leala's voice floated down. "What was that noise? Oh my gosh, Sadie. Are you okay? What happened?"

Before I could answer, Will spoke up. "She caught one glimpse of me and flung herself down the stairs."

Humor laced his words, but I didn't particularly find them amusing.

"Well," Leala said, "that makes perfect sense since Sadie always was tripping over herself to get your attention, wasn't she? Are you okay, Sadie?"

Mortified, I groaned. I popped one eye open to peer up at her hanging over the railing. "I'm fine. Just sitting here plotting how to kill you."

Leala laughed. "Yep, she's fine. I'm going back to vacuuming."

Her steps retreated, and I realized I was still clinging to the laundry basket for dear life. I loosened my grip and slowly looked over at Will.

The kindness in his light-brown gaze caught me off guard, mostly because the last time I'd seen him he'd barely been able to look at me at all. He smiled, took the basket out of my hands, and then held out a hand to help me up. "Welcome home, Sadie Way."

I stared at his hand for far too long before taking it. Our hands fit together perfectly, like always. His palm was rough, his ring finger bare, and I hated that I'd even looked. "Thanks."

It had been nearly eight years since I'd seen him last, but I'd have known him anywhere. That beautiful smile, so big it stretched nearly across his whole face. The high cheekbones and strong jawline. Those eyes that reminded me so much of the lake bottom when the sand was stirred up. The inexplicable pull toward him, impossible to ignore. He stood a head taller than me and had filled out with muscle across his shoulders, chest, and arms since I'd been gone. He'd been my best friend through most of high school, but by the time we'd graduated, my feelings for him had deepened. He'd been my first love. I thought he'd felt the same.

I'd been wrong.

Painfully wrong.

Looking away, I pulled my hand free.

The vacuum droned above our heads as he said, "You sure you're okay? That was quite a fall. You'll have bruises come tomorrow."

I wouldn't, actually. "Really, I'm fine. It didn't even hurt, but it did boost my resolve to get rid of that flimsy runner." I stared at the faded floral print accusingly, as if it had been the one at fault, not my distraction.

"The runner. Right," he said with a glint in his eyes. "No pain at all, you say?"

I held his steady gaze, unwavering under thick eyebrows. I knew what he was asking. He was the only one, other than the doctor who'd treated me at the hospital after my accident, who knew I couldn't feel physical pain.

After I had woken up in the hospital, the doctor had mentioned I might have lingering headaches because of the knock to my head. He'd politely listened when I explained I didn't have any pain and then told me it was a result of the painkillers I was on and to be grateful. It didn't take long to realize I couldn't feel any physical pain at all, and not only that, but I healed exceptionally quickly when injured. Like from blood draws. The nurses were baffled. When I brought it up the next time I saw the doctor, he wrote it off as a psychological side effect, essentially insinuating that it was all in my head.

It wasn't, but I hadn't had any explanation for it either and was left to wonder if my numbness was because after I'd died that night, not all of me had come alive again.

I never told anyone else of my theories . . . except for Will. Back then, I told him absolutely everything. Well, almost everything. I'd never shared the true strength of my feelings for him.

"Still?" he asked now, watching me with concern flickering in those beautiful eyes of his.

"I'm fine," I repeated, not wanting to talk about it. "Which is good. There's lots of work to get done around here."

He paused a beat, and I imagined he was waging an inner war on whether or not to push for more of an answer.

Finally he said, "Camp mentioned you wanted to spruce up the place while you were in town. Are you thinking to repaper the walls?"

Inwardly, I breathed a sigh of relief that he accepted my change of subject. "No, we're going to paint."

He ran a dark hand across his chin, over a one- or two-day-old beard, slightly thicker than a five o'clock shadow. His hair was cut short on the sides, slightly longer on top, the loose curls flopping playfully around his forehead. His T-shirt was printed with LOCKHART CONSTRUCTION CO., and I couldn't help noticing that he smelled of freshly cut wood, earthy, and oddly enticing.

Reaching out, he gently touched the wall. "Have you ever taken down wallpaper?"

"Before last night you mean? No."

He gave a soft laugh as if he knew exactly how the wallpaper had come down. I suspected Uncle Camp had filled him in. I wished he had filled *me* in. Why hadn't he told me Will was Mama's contractor? Suddenly I suspected the detail hadn't slipped his mind. He'd asked me a few times over the years if I kept in touch with Will, and I always dodged the questions, saying that it didn't matter, that it was in the past. Maybe this had been Uncle Camp's way of getting me to face my past head-on. Something I most definitely did not want to do.

Will said, "You could spend a bunch of money on a steamer or bottles of wallpaper remover, but a mix of warm water and fabric softener does the job just fine. Spray it on, let it set, then scrape. It'll be a right mess, though, so best to be prepared with tarps."

I watched him closely as he talked, and I stifled all the questions that sprang to mind. Not about the wallpaper, but about him. Last I knew, he'd been a biology major who was planning to follow his daddy's footsteps into pharmacology. How had he ended up with a construction company? What had he been doing these last eight years? Did he still live here in Sugarberry Cove? Why, oh why, had he broken my heart?

I reached for the laundry. "Thanks for the tips. I should get back to work."

He didn't let go of the basket. I gave another tug.

He still didn't release it. He simply looked at me, his gaze intent on mine. There was a plea in the depths of brown. "Sadie, I . . . um."

The vacuum fell silent. We both glanced at the stairs as Leala started down them. She took one look at us, then turned around and went back up the steps. I had little doubt that she was eavesdropping.

I tipped my head, waiting for him to say what he had to say, not entirely sure I wanted to hear it after I'd waited so very long to hear anything from him at all. The last time we were together was two weeks after my accident. I'd dropped out of school, had endured the looks of pity in the community, felt their disappointment in me, and knew I had to leave town, get away, find myself, find the reason I was still alive. When I told him, he'd been quiet, barely looking at me the whole time, but supportive. He'd promised to text and call often, which had been a balm to my hurting soul, because I knew out of everything, I'd miss him most of all. But his calls never came. And mine went unanswered. My texts, too. He completely ghosted me, leaving me grieving not only for the loss of my best friend, my first love, but for my old life altogether. I hadn't seen him or heard from him in eight years. Until today.

Giving his head a quick shake, he abruptly let go of the basket and picked up the piece of trim that he'd leaned against the banister at some point. "I should get back to work, too. It's good to see you, Sadie Way." He tapped the board against his palm, then added, "You've been missed."

With that he turned and started for the front door.

You've been missed? What did he mean by that? Missed by him?

Halfway out the door, he stopped suddenly, and I stiffened, bracing myself.

He turned around. "Do you want to get a drink tonight? Catch up a little?"

I gripped the laundry basket tighter, feeling the wicker digging into my fingers. There was a little flutter in my chest as I sorted all the reasons to say no, trying to decide which to use. There were easily a dozen. But then I saw that plea in his eyes again, floating on nothing but hope, and I wanted more than anything to say yes.

But the high emotional cost that would come with spending time with him and taking a trip down memory lane was too high a price to pay. I needed to keep my distance for my own peace of mind.

"Thanks for the offer, but between helping Mama and the wallpaper . . . I don't have any free time. I'm only here till Monday."

Disappointment fell across his face as he pressed his lips together. He gave a brisk nod and disappeared through the doorway.

Blinking away a sudden, unwanted wash of tears, I stood frozen, watching him once again walk out of my life, wondering how it was possible that it could still hurt when I'd spent only ten minutes with him, tops. Wondering why, for the millionth time, the lady of the lake had taken away my ability to feel physical pain but not emotional pain. Right now I'd give just about anything to trade.

"You can come down now," I said.

Leala barreled down the steps. "*You've been missed*? What was that supposed to mean? Was that his roundabout way of saying that *he* missed you?" She tsked loudly. "I never took Will Lockhart for a coward."

Sometimes I loved my sister more than I could ever put into words. I took a deep breath and one last look at the door before heading for the laundry room. "I'm not sure. But it doesn't really matter one way or another, does it? Nothing would've come of spending time with him but heartache. Plus, I'm leaving soon, so it's best not to stir up old troubles."

Come Monday morning, I would be on the road again, headed south, away from old memories, old pain, and everything and everyone I loved.

Including Will.

Chapter 9

Leala

"You missed a spot, LC," Mother said from behind me as I squeegeed a window on the back porch. Sadie and I had established a steady rhythm as we tackled all the windows on the first floor. With a rag, she wiped the window with a mixture of warm water, dish soap, and vinegar, and I followed behind her with the squeegee for a streak-free shine. It was amazingly effective, and between the two of us, the work had gone quickly.

Mother had woken from her nap on the wrong side of the bed, and as I was her favorite target, she'd been nitpicking my window-washing technique since she'd come downstairs and insisted on helping us. It was getting harder and harder not to snap back at her. Doing so would only lead to something that decidedly would not be *calm*. So for her heart's sake, I bit my tongue. Fortunately, Sadie and I were almost done, just one window left, because my tolerance was running on empty.

I swiped the offending streak, Mother *humphed* in satisfaction, and Sadie shot me a sympathetic look as she dunked her rag into the bucket, then wrung it out.

"When was the last time you washed windows, LC?" Mother asked as she ran a cloth over the windowsills.

With the window open, the cries of nearby blue jays floated in along with a wave of heat and humidity. The lake looked invitingly blue, and if I had any extra time, I'd have happily escaped in a kayak. But free time wasn't to be had. After we finished the windows, Sadie and I were going to start on the entryway makeover. Well, Sadie was—she'd tasked me with running into town to pick out paint swatches and supplies, and I couldn't wait to have a few minutes to myself, even if it was to run an errand. And while I was out, I planned to stop at home, since I'd yet to hear from Connor. At the thought of seeing Tucker, I worked faster.

"Doesn't your fancy cleaning lady do that for you now? I'm surprised you remember how," Mother added when I didn't answer straight off.

I gritted my teeth and told myself to let the comment go. *Just let it*—"It's probably been as long as it's been for you by the looks of these windows."

Sadie sighed, and I faced Mother, silently daring her to keep picking, when the doorbell rang, placing the care of her heart in her own hands, because I was done accepting her not-so-thinly-veiled insults.

"I'll get it!" Sadie said quickly, sounding a little too eager to get away from us.

"No." Mother set her rag on the sill. "I'll go."

As soon as she was out of earshot, Sadie whispered, "Holy hell. What is it between you two? It's so much worse than I remembered."

That was because it *was* worse. Sadie had always been our buffer, our peacemaker. Plus, it seemed the more I distanced myself from Mother, the testier she became. Being here, all of us together this weekend, had been bound to bring all our old hurts to the surface.

I glanced toward the front door—it looked like it was yet another flower delivery. "You know she's never forgiven me for wanting a life completely different from hers. She passive aggressively needles my lifestyle every chance she gets. I can't tell you the amount of times she comments, out of the blue, about people getting above their raising. It's obvious that she's talking about me."

What Mother hadn't realized was that I was trying to forget my raising. I tried every single day, yet the memories lingered. Of Mother being too busy to attend a school concert or celebration. Or too busy to tend to a scraped knee. Or too busy to tuck us in at night. The list was endless. I'd grown up promising myself that I'd never be someone who gave more attention to the strangers staying at her bed-and-breakfast than to her own children. The more Mother had left Sadie and me to our own devices growing up, the more I had dreamed of a different life for myself. One that put family first, above all else.

On the day he was born, I'd promised Tucker I'd never let him down, and that I'd always be there for him, and that I'd be the best mama in the whole wide world. And I'd done my best to keep that promise . . . even when the regrets about quitting my job had started creeping in.

Often lonely and overwhelmed, I was struggling with staying

home with him full-time, even though it was something I always thought I wanted. It hurt, that inner betrayal of my lifelong dreams.

"Have you ever thought about sitting down with her to talk about everything?" Sadie asked as she finished wiping the last window. "I mean really talk? A good heart-to-heart?"

My head was starting to ache as I put down the squeegee and started closing the windows we had opened. "Honestly, I'm worried it'd do more harm than good."

"I can mediate if you want."

I glanced at her and smiled. "It's best to let her heart heal first, don't you think? She's bound to get all wound up. Maybe at Christmastime . . ."

With a big smile on her face, Mother returned carrying a large vase of lilies. "Well, look at this arrangement. Isn't it lovely?"

"They are," Sadie said. "Who sent them to you?"

Mother set the vase on the table, poured herself a glass of cucumber water from the pitcher on a side table, and then sat down, her gaze holding steady on me. "Oh, they're not mine. They're for LC. Sorry, I read the note before realizing."

Of course she had. I plucked the card from the vase and read the message with Sadie peering over my shoulder.

33°44.034'N, 86° 32.424'W
Now and forever. I'm sorry.
—C

Warmth flowed through me, a sense of love and happiness all wrapped up in one. Carefully, I tucked the card back into the torn envelope and slid it into my pocket.

Mother was about to say something I was sure I didn't want to hear, but Sadie cut her off. "What are the coordinates, Leala?"

"It's where Connor proposed to me," I said, not wanting to share the whole story. It was too special to subject to any mocking, especially from Mother.

The coordinates marked the historical marker for the Cahaba Heart River up in Jefferson County. In a flash, I was back in time, a junior in college seeing Connor sitting in the school library, so intent on his books and notes that he didn't notice for fifteen minutes that I had taken a seat at the same table. Eventually, we got to talking and I found out he was writing a paper on Alabama's historical markers. That night he asked me out for coffee. And that weekend, I went for a drive with him to document one of the markers for his paper. We did the same thing the weekend after that and soon became inseparable. Toward the end of the school year, when his paper was coming due, he had only one more marker he wanted to document. The Cahaba Heart River marker, and the lilies were just about to bloom, too, so we planned to make a whole day of it with a picnic.

Cahaba lilies were something special. A stunningly beautiful white lily, they bloomed in the water every May in only a few of Alabama's rivers, because the flowers needed just the right environment to bloom, amid rocks and swift currents and full sunshine.

Connor had been incredibly nervous when we pulled onto the side of the road, and he started rambling about the river being the heart of Alabama but how *his* heart was with me, now and forever. He got down on one knee and pulled out the ring.

Thinking of it now made me feel warm and sappy, and though the lilies he'd sent weren't Cahaba lilies, all lilies had become our flower, the one that represented how we'd bloomed and found love despite our adversities.

Sadie tipped her head to the side and asked, "How come I don't know the story of how he proposed?"

I shrugged. "You never asked. No one asked. No one cared."

Sadie's eyes instantly filled with tears. "I'm so sorry, Leala. I like Connor—I do. Back then, I was just so mad that he was taking you away from me. You were always with him, and I never saw you anymore, and I just—I was jealous. I'm sorry."

Seeing her teary made me teary. I needed time to think about what she had said about being jealous, because it didn't make sense to me. It was the second time she'd mentioned it, though, and suddenly I had an uneasy feeling that maybe she was right.

"What's Connor in the doghouse for?" Mother asked, nodding to the flowers. "Why's he sorry?"

I certainly didn't want to hear her gloating, so there was no way, no how I was telling her the reason. "It's nothing we can't work out." I hoped.

Mother tipped her head and studied me so intently that I thought she could somehow see the truth anyway, as if it floated around me like a guilty haze. Her gaze softened. "I'm sure you will."

I searched for sarcasm and found none. I didn't know what to do with this unexpected kindness, or how to feel.

"Leala, why don't you head into town now to get the supplies at the hardware store?" Sadie said brightly, apparently wanting to end this conversation on a high note. "I'll finish cleaning up here."

"Town?" Mother set down the glass of water and stood up. "We'll all go! We can get some lunch while we're out. At the Dockside Café? Their fried catfish would hit the spot right about now."

"All of us?" Sadie said. "No, no. You need to rest and not eat fried foods and I need to—"

"Hush. You need to hush." Mother clapped her hands. "Finish up and let's get going. Uncle Camp can watch over the cottage."

Sadie shook her head. "We don't all need to go."

I snapped a look at her. Surely she wasn't going to suggest Mother and I go alone.

"I can stay here," she finished, throwing me to the wolves. "There's so much to do."

Oh hell no. I wasn't going alone with Mother. "I think you should come with us," I said, smiling sweetly.

It was her turn to give me a dirty look. "It's just—How many people does it take to pick out a paint color?"

Mother clapped her hands again. "That's enough, girls. We are *all* going into town."

"But," Sadie said.

Mother narrowed her eyes. "Are you going to argue with your mama who just had a heart attack and nearly died?"

I wanted to argue the "nearly died" part but recognized that it was to my benefit to take her side in this conversation.

Sadie looked helplessly at me. "Well, I mean . . ."

Mother coughed pathetically.

Picking at the end of her braid, Sadie pressed her lips together in a fine line of resignation.

"So it's settled, then. Good, good." Mother picked up her glass to take into the kitchen. "And oh, the cucumber water was delightful, Sadie. Adding the hint of thyme was a nice surprise. Quite refreshing."

Behind Mother's back, Sadie acted out a fisherman reeling in a big catch. "I like it, too, but people are so accustomed to bottled water. They don't know what they're missing out on."

"I just had a thought." Mother turned around and snapped her fingers.

I nearly laughed when Sadie's hands abruptly dropped to her sides, and suddenly it felt like we were little girls again, the two of us against the world. When had that changed? I thought back, trying to find an event, a date, something. And I suddenly realized it was when I met Connor. He'd consumed my life from the moment I saw him sitting at that library table, which had nothing to do with him and everything to do with me.

Sadie had been right. I'd all but abandoned her to chase after love, to chase after the dreams I harbored of a perfect family, and in doing so I managed to damage the most loving relationship I already had.

Mother hurried into the kitchen and started opening cabinets. "I could replace the bottled water in guest rooms with pitchers of water. Oh, I like that idea. I have a stash of quart-size pitchers around here somewhere."

Feeling queasy with guilt, I stepped in close to Sadie and kept my voice low. "That was impressive. Maybe you should talk to her about her finances."

"Finances are where you shine, not me." She picked up the bucket of water to dump out in the laundry room's utility sink. She brushed by me, then glanced over her shoulder. "And for what it's worth, Leala, I'm not sure what all is going on between you and Connor, but I know how much you love each other. That counts for something."

It counted for a lot. I glanced over my shoulder at the lilies on the table and thought of the apology in the note. For the first time in a long time, I felt a little flicker of hope.

Chapter 10

Leala

Sugarberry Cove's hardware store was located a block east of the Landing. Sadie, decked out in sunglasses and a big hat that hid her hair, had volunteered to drive Mother's truck, and I wasn't sure if the offer was in deference to Mother's health or because she was a notoriously bad driver, often running over curbs and shrubs and, once, a fire hydrant in front of the middle school. If it had been possible to die of embarrassment, I was certain I would have gone to glory on that particular day.

I'd expected a full-on argument from Mother about the driving arrangement, but she'd agreed peacefully, docile as could be. I should've known she had ulterior motives. The five-minute drive had taken nearly an hour, because Mother had made Sadie pull over every time Mother spotted someone she knew to chat about her near-death experience, the fact that both girls were home and taking care of her, and the surprising delight of adding cucumber and thyme—*thyme, of all things*—to plain old water. Sadie and I grinned and bore the slow torture. Especially Sadie, who put on the tightest smile imaginable each time Mother said, "And did you see our Sadie is back in town? Isn't she a sight for sore eyes? She's only staying a few days this time around, but with any luck she'll be back soon! She's got to get back on the road. You know about A Southern Hankerin', right? On that internet. Isn't it fabulous?" Then Sadie had to get out of the truck to give hugs, accept kisses, make small talk, and show that yes, she still had glittery silver hair, and no, she hadn't developed any special powers like being able to grant wishes like a genie.

When we pulled into the hardware store's parking lot, Mother hopped right out of the truck saying, "Was that Marlee Hoskins who just went inside? I must catch up to her to thank her for the flowers she sent over."

Leaving the door open in her wake, she speed-walked away like she hadn't just been laid up in the hospital for two and a half days with a bum heart.

This weekend was surely testing my patience. I missed Tucker. And Connor. I'd used Sadie's phone to send him another email, a thank-you for the lilies, and saw that he still hadn't responded to my emails about my sunken phone. Part of me wanted to ask Sadie and Mother to stop by my house on the way back to the cottage, but I really didn't want them there, seeing the tension between Connor and me. The thought alone hurt a little too much. I'd go later on. By myself.

Sadie shut off the engine, then dropped her head back against the headrest. "If you'd just kill me now, I'd appreciate it. I prefer something quick, but I'll take any form of death at the moment. Beggars can't be choosers."

With the passenger seat vacant, I moved over from my tight spot in the middle, putting space between the two of us. "Don't joke about death. It's not funny. And you know, if you came around more often, this wouldn't be so painful. There wouldn't be all these reunions to suffer through. And didn't I tell you people missed you? Surely you saw today that they have. And if they saw you all the time, they'd get used to your hair like it's perfectly normal, like I have. It's the exposure effect. That's when people start to accept, even form a fondness for something that they're repeatedly exposed to. It's like how I used to hate leggings. Hated, hated, absolutely *despised*. Then after a year or two of people wearing them, now I kind of love leggings." I shrugged. "Go figure."

Sadie turned her head, arched an eyebrow, and tightly said, "Fondness? When did yours come on for my hair? After you tried to dye it? Or suggested a wig?"

Guilt wound its way through my stomach. "I'm so sorry about that, Sadie. It was wrong of me. It's just that—"

"Girls!" Mother clapped from the store's entryway. "Get a move on!"

Oh, *now* she was in a hurry. And apparently she had also forgotten that Sadie and I were both adults. The clapping was a bit much. But in truth, Mother was a bit much. She always had been and she always would be.

Sadie shoved open her door, hopped out, then slammed the door closed. She took two steps, stopped, turned, and tossed the hat and sunglasses through the open window into the truck. "No point to those if Mama's around. Might as well let people get *exposed*."

"Sadie," I sighed. "It's not like that. Wait for me." I scrambled out of the truck. "Let's talk about this. I need to tell you something about the night you fell in the water—"

"No," she threw over her shoulder as she strode into the store.

I followed her inside, sagging briefly against a blast of welcome air-conditioning. Piped music played cheerfully, and the counter clerk greeted me with a hearty welcome. The store obviously wasn't the place to talk to Sadie about her accident, but it was past time I did so. Confession being good for the soul and all that.

"Sadie," Mother boomed, "come say hello to Marlee!"

Marlee, a bleached-blond, fortysomething neighbor who lived three houses down the road from the cottage, stared at Sadie's hair with a look of utter astonishment as she approached, and at Sadie's pained expression, I suddenly felt like crying.

And as Marlee said, "Sadie! So good to see you. Your hair is fabulous. Just fabulous. Does it give you any magical powers? Can I touch it?" a tear fell from the corner of my eye.

I swiped it away and marched over. "Hell no, you can't touch it, Marlee. Do you go around asking to touch everyone's hair? For God's sake, woman, how rude can you be? Show some manners and respect for personal space. No wonder Sadie doesn't like to come back to Sugarberry Cove. *Can I touch it?*" I mocked. "Good Lord. Come on, Sadie." I grabbed her arm and tugged her toward the paint section.

"Leala Clare!" Mother gasped. "Have you done lost your mind?"

"Not even a little," I stated over my shoulder.

As I dragged Sadie away, I could hear Marlee saying, "Well, I never! Talk about rude. Did you hear the way she spoke to me?"

"I don't know what got into her," Mother said.

Their voices faded, and once Sadie and I were in the safety of the paint aisle, Sadie exhaled deeply. "Thanks for that."

The scent of turpentine swirled in the air as I picked up a paint swatch, a pale-yellow square. "It needed to be said. And Marlee's one of the biggest gossips in town, so come supper time, all of Sugarberry Cove will know not to touch your hair."

Sadie took the swatch out of my hand and tucked it back into the display. She picked up a teal color. "Instead they'll be talking up a storm about you suddenly being touched in the head."

I dismissed the teal, picked up a cool silvery-blue swatch, and laughed. "I kind of don't mind. It'll give me a little freedom to act nutty around town."

Sadie nodded approvingly at the paint color. "You've never acted nutty a day in your life. Except just now."

Our gazes met, and she smiled, and I smiled, and my heart melted with love for my little sister. "That wasn't nutty. That was speaking the truth. Do you deal with that kind of thing all the time?"

"Mostly staring. The majority of people think I dye it like this on purpose. People who don't live around here. You do know Mama's going to eat you alive once she tears herself away from Marlee."

I knew. "I'll just hide behind you. You were looking for a quick death earlier, remember?"

She laughed, and for a moment all was right in the world. A young woman walked by, stopped, and spun around. "*Hey, y'all!* Oh my good gosh! I can't believe it. Sadie Scott! No one is going to believe I ran into you at a hardware store of all places."

Slightly confused, I glanced between the woman and Sadie, who was smiling and held out her hand. "What's your name?"

"I'm Ellie. Ellie Yeargan."

Ellie looked to be in her twenties and wore cutoff shorts, a loose tee that showed her swimsuit straps, and cute leather sandals. I didn't recognize her.

"It's nice to meet you, Ellie. This is my sister, Leala. She lives here in Sugarberry Cove. Are you here on vacation?"

"It's so great to meet you, Leala. Sadie's mentioned you a few times on A Southern Hankerin'! And yes, ma'am! Me and my family are staying over at Hearthills Campground and forgot to pack the tent stakes. That's why I'm here. I mean in the store." She sagged dramatically. "Would you mind taking a picture with me?"

Sadie laughed. "Not at all. The campground is real pretty, especially this time of year. Be sure to stop at Anna Ruth's for some mac and cheese while you're in town. It's some of the best you'll ever have."

"Yes, ma'am, I sure will." The woman pulled a phone from her purse and blinked at me. "Would you mind, Leala?"

I took the phone. "I don't mind at all." I wasn't quite sure what was happening, but I could take a picture, no problem.

"I keep tellin' my mama to write to you," Ellie gushed. "She has the best recipe for divinity. Truly heavenly. She craved it so much when she was pregnant with my older sister that she held off on going to the hospital so she could make a batch to take with her. She ended up deliverin' right there in the kitchen. My daddy made sure there was a store of divinity on hand before I was due. He's a man who learns from his mistakes."

"Say cheese," I said. They put their heads together and grinned.

Sadie took the phone from me and passed it to Ellie. "I love that story. If your mother's willing to share it, my contact information is on my channel—be sure to mention in the email that you met me here."

"She's a little camera shy, but if she ever changes her mind, I will definitely let you know." She took a step backward. "You've been so kind—thank you. I won't take up any more of your time. Oh gosh. I can't wait to get back and tell everyone." She started walking backward, toward the front door.

"Don't forget the stakes," I said.

Her mouth dropped open and she laughed. "I would've, too. Thank y'all!" With a wave, she hurried off and soon disappeared around a corner.

I turned to face Sadie head-on. "What in the world was that?"

Sadie lifted a shoulder in a shrug. "Apparently she's a fan of A Southern Hankerin'."

"A fan? You have fans? Like, you're famous?"

She laughed. "I wouldn't say famous. Just recognizable, thanks to my hair."

I was starting to get more curious about her videos, but checking them out would have to wait until I went home. I had no source of internet at the moment. "Does that happen often? That people stop and talk to you?"

"Every once in a while."

"She was so . . . effusive."

With a smile, Sadie said, "I've discovered during my travels that there are a lot more good, kind people out there than you can even imagine."

I was still trying to wrap my head around what just happened when we walked into the next aisle and Sadie suddenly came to a dead stop. Then I realized why.

Will Lockhart looked up from the package of sandpaper he

held, and surprise flashed across his eyes, followed by a tight smile.

"Hey," he said casually. Too casually. "I'm surprised you two are still here. Didn't you leave the cottage an hour ago? I thought you'd be at the Dockside by now."

It didn't escape my notice that he'd planned to be here when we weren't. "Our drive over was delayed due to Mother insisting on stopping to talk to everyone on the planet."

I noticed the little looks he threw at Sadie, who was looking at everything but him, and I felt the sparks of tension between them. The sparks of attraction. They had always been there, even back when they were in high school pretending to be only friends. Seemed time and distance had done nothing to dull that particular flame. I wasn't sure why Will had cut her off when she left town, but whatever it was between them wasn't finished. Not by a long shot. And even though Sadie said earlier that only heartache would come of them talking about the past, I thought she could be wrong about that. A whole lot could happen—or it could simply lead to closure. Something, it seemed to me, both of them needed.

"I'm sure folks are glad to see Susannah out and about. Scary times this past week. Need any help finding anything?" he asked with a look that begged me to say no.

"Sure!" I said enthusiastically. "Can you help Sadie pick out paintbrushes while I grab some tarps and tape?"

Sadie elbowed me, and I ignored it as he said, "Yeah, I can do that. They're over here. A good brush is really important."

She glared at me as she trailed after him, and I smiled.

I was trying to eavesdrop while deciding between ten varieties of painter's tape when Mother turned down the aisle. "Leala Clare Scott!" she angrily whispered when she spotted me.

"What do you think of this swatch?" I held it up, hoping to distract her from a full-blown hissy fit, a good possibility since she was easily distracted. I talked fast as I added, "Sadie and I like it. It'll look lovely with all the natural light in the entryway and be a perfect complement to the stain of the pine floors. Don't you think blue and brown pair so well together? And this color is so neutral you can really play up accent pieces. You can get new artwork and rugs and throw pillows, since I know you like more saturated colors. This shade kind of reminds me of Sadie, actually. The blue of her eyes. The silver of her beautiful hair. Can you even believe people like Marlee asking to touch her hair to see if it's magical? I wouldn't like people asking to touch my hair. Whatever happened to personal boundaries?"

All Mother's bluster deflated as she took the square swatch from my fingers. "It is a pretty shade, and it'll almost be like Sadie's still with us after she leaves again on her next adventure. Where is she anyway?"

"With Will, picking out paintbrushes." I nodded toward the far end of the long aisle.

Mother stiffened and frowned, then walked off, heading toward them, full speed ahead. "Will!" she said in a booming tone. "What a nice surprise seeing you here."

Taken aback by her odd reaction, I hurried after her. If I hadn't just witnessed her displeasure, I'd have believed that she was actually pleased to see him.

Sadie held up three paintbrushes of varying sizes and said drolly, "Will's teaching me the benefits of quality bristles."

Will nodded. "A good paintbrush is always worth spending a little more."

Mother gave a quick glance to the brushes before saying, "Looks like you have some good choices there, Sadie. Thank you so much, Will. Always so helpful."

"Yes, ma'am," he said. "I should find my sandpaper and be getting back to the cottage."

"Oh!" Mother waved a hand. "Take the rest of today off. Tomorrow, too. You've been working so hard. A little R & R goes a long way in refreshing a weary spirit. The guest rooms will still be there on Monday."

His brows dipped. "Are you sure? That will be cutting the deadline close, with you wanting those suites ready by the water lantern festival."

She laughed and gave him a playful swat. "I've learned this past week that it's important to take time off. Learn from my mistakes, Will. I have complete faith the rooms will be done on time. Come on, girls. Let's get that paint and go. See you soon, Will." She put her arm around Sadie's shoulders and steered her toward the paint counter.

"Yes, ma'am," he said as she walked away, then threw me a perplexed look.

I was as much in the dark as he was as to why she was acting so strangely. Mother had embraced Will from the moment Sadie had brought him into our lives ten years ago. More than once I'd suspected she loved him more than me. "Thanks for your help with the brushes, Will."

He nodded and I quick-footed it after Mother and Sadie. Before I could question her strange behavior, she said, "You girls finish up here, ring out, and I'll meet you in the truck. I'm feeling a mite worn-out, and I think getting off my feet will help."

With that, she headed for the exit.

As we waited for two gallons of paint to be mixed, Sadie looked me over. "She didn't eat you alive, I see."

"She didn't have a chance to because she got distracted by you and Will. Despite her cheerful demeanor, she wasn't pleased to see you two together. Does she know he broke your heart?"

Her forehead furrowed. "Really? And no, I never told anyone but you yesterday, though I suppose it's obvious something happened between us, since we haven't talked in eight years."

"She must've figured it out. Motherly intuition or something." Though, it had been a long, long time since I'd thought of her as motherly. "She's probably trying to protect you while you're home, keep you from experiencing any awkward situations. That explains why she gave him the rest of the weekend off, too."

Sadie laughed, and light filled her eyes. "Well, she's a little too late for that, though I appreciate the effort."

We collected our paint, picked out a few other supplies, then headed for the checkout counter, where I was glad to see no sign of Marlee. Sadie pulled a credit card from her pocket and I said, "Put that away. I've got this."

"This was all my idea. I'm happy to pay for it."

"Even so, I'll cover it."

The clerk glanced over at us and smiled but kept on ringing up products.

With her hands on her hips, Sadie said, "Leala, I'm paying for it."

"Sadie Way, no. You live out of your car, for heaven's sake. I'll cover it."

Sadie took a step back, then started laughing. "I don't actually live out of my car, you know. I stay in inns and B and Bs and hotels."

"And that adds up, doesn't it?"

She grinned. "You think I'm poor."

I squirmed. "Not poor, necessarily." Perhaps living paycheck to paycheck. Did she even get a paycheck? I wasn't sure how *creators* were paid.

With a big step backward and a grand flourish, she invited me to pay.

"Thank you." I'd sleep better knowing I wasn't taking food out of her mouth, so to speak.

She was still smiling when we left the store and set our bags into the back of the truck. Mother scooted to the middle seat as we settled into the cab. Sadie started the truck. "So, to the Dockside?"

"Actually, I'm tuckered out," Mother said. "Let's just go home instead."

We drove home in relative silence, and I was grateful for the quiet and for the fact that Mother hadn't asked Sadie to pull over once.

As soon as we parked in front of the cottage, Mother said, "I'm going to lie down for a while."

Sadie turned off the engine and worry darkened her eyes. "Are you feeling okay, Mama? Should I call Dr. Barnhill?"

Mother smiled and shook her head. "I'm fine. Just need to rest my eyes a few minutes." With that, she hopped out of the truck and headed inside.

We watched her walk into the house, then collected the supplies from the bed of the truck.

"Maybe I should call Dr. Barnhill anyway," Sadie said. "That exhaustion came on so suddenly."

"The cardiologist said to expect her to be tired. Let's see how she is after a rest, then make the call if we have to."

We walked inside and before we could even set the supplies down in the entryway, Uncle Camp came bustling toward us from the back porch. "So glad you two are back," he said quietly. "Today's guest arrived early. I checked her in and I've been keeping her company. Nice lady—she's out on the back porch with a glass of that weird water Sadie made."

"Hey," Sadie protested.

Giving her an I-tell-it-like-it-is look, he shrugged. "You might want to go give her a proper welcome."

I set the box down. "Thanks, Uncle Camp."

But before I even had a chance to stand back up, an older

woman wearing a lightweight pale-yellow cardigan and matching capri pants appeared in the doorway. “Oh dear. I hope my early arrival didn’t throw everyone into a tizzy.”

Sadie let out a small squeak of happiness. “Mrs. Teakes? What’re you doing here?”

Chapter 11

Sadie

"Of all the bed-and-breakfasts in all the world," Mama said as she sat in an armchair in the living room, her body angled to face Mrs. Teakes.

It had been a few hours since Mrs. Teakes arrived, and she sat on the sofa, an unopened book resting on her lap, a cup of hot tea in hand. She took a sip, then said, "While at my home in Wetumpka last week, Sadie mentioned Sugarberry Cove and I had the strangest feeling that I should visit again. I tried to ignore the impulse—I have no car. I hadn't made reservations months ahead of time. It seemed a dubious quest at best. One that might have been better to postpone a year." She waved a swirling, dismissive hand. "There were a million excuses to ignore my whim, but life is uncertain, is it not? One day you're here, then you're gone. You need to make the most out of life. Live it to its fullest. At my age, there might not be a next year, so I decided I'd find a way to make this trip work, even if I'm here only for this weekend. If I'm so lucky to be around next year, I'll plan another trip to see the water lantern festival."

If I'm so lucky. It reminded me of what Uncle Camp had said earlier about how getting old wasn't for the faint of heart—it was for the lucky. I rather wished he could've heard Mrs. Teakes, but he'd excused himself to work on taming the mountain laurel, and I could hear the drone of hedge trimmers coming from out front.

Rarely was the cottage full of people in the middle of the day, but this weekend was proving anything but ordinary. Teddy and Bree had returned from their foray into town slightly pink-cheeked from the heat but smiling. They were now playing cards at the game table in the corner, while Nigel slept at Bree's feet.

Leala and I stood on separate steps of the staircase, both armed with a spray bottle full of watered-down fabric softener and a scraper. The scraping was going surprisingly easily. "How did you get here, Mrs. Teakes?" I asked, not realizing she hadn't driven.

"Rideshare." She grinned. "A neighbor helped me figure out the app on my phone."

"A rideshare all the way from Wetumpka?" Mama picked up her glass of iced tea from the coffee table. "*Shoo.*"

Mama's energy had returned. She'd spent two hours in her room before reemerging for lunch and had hit it off with Mrs. Teakes right away. Of course, Mama seemed to hit it off with everyone. Her big personality didn't know a stranger.

"It was a pleasant drive," Mrs. Teakes said. "My driver was a lovely young man, with perhaps a touch of a lead foot." She took a sip of tea. "We arrived sooner than I expected."

Across the room, Teddy threw her cards on the table, then pushed a pile of poker chips toward Bree. "You're a cardsharp wrapped up in a sweet, pretty package, Bree Bynum. If we were playing for money, I'd be flat broke. Flatter broke, anyway."

"It's beginner's luck." Bree's face flushed when we all looked her way. "Or a little of that lake magic all y'all are always talking about."

"'All y'all'?" Leala repeated, smiling. "Did you hear that? One day in town and Bree's already talking like a native. You're a Southerner at heart, Bree. I can tell."

"We say 'y'all' in southern Indiana, too. But I do like it here in Sugarberry Cove," she said simply as she stacked her winnings.

I liked that she was talking more, opening up. She'd seemed so despondent last night that I'd been truly worried about her. But today she was chatting and smiling, and seeing it warmed my heart.

"It's a special place," Mrs. Teakes said, and everyone nodded in agreement.

It really was. It was why I'd had trouble finding a new hometown—nothing measured up.

Mrs. Teakes added, "I'll be going into town later on to purchase a lantern kit. Could I trouble one of you to set it afloat for me the night of the festival?"

The kits came with a two-tiered piece of wood, rice paper paneling, tall dowels to hold up the rice paper, a tea light candle, a marker, and an invisible-ink pen.

Mama said, "I'll happily do it, Mrs. Teakes. It's a shame you won't be here next weekend, but we're surely delighted to have you with us now." She raised her glass in a toast toward me. "Thanks for the free advertising, Sadie honey."

"It wasn't me, Mama." I zigzagged my scraper along the wall, lifting slimy shreds of wallpaper backing that I then dropped into a brown bag on the step below me. Leala, I noticed, was scraping in perfectly straight vertical rows. "I never mentioned the bed-and-breakfast by name."

Mrs. Teakes took another sip of tea. "That's true. I was just as surprised to see Sadie here as she was me."

"Then how did you find us?" Leala asked as she squirted another section of the wall.

"When I tried to get a reservation for the lantern festival next weekend, everything was booked solid, so I did the next best thing and decided to spend this weekend up here. Yours was the only place around with a vacancy. What luck!"

"Luck?" Mama laughed. "I think not. That's lake magic at work, Mrs. Teakes. Mark my words."

"I agree," Teddy said from her spot at the game table. "A sudden urge to visit, then a rare vacancy? Magic's in the air. I said so this morning."

"That you did, Teddy. But if you ask me, magic is always in the air here on the lake." Mama leaned in toward Mrs. Teakes. "Did Sadie happen to tell you about my near-death experience just last week? Had myself a heart attack," she added before Mrs. Teakes could answer. "It's just like you said—one day you're here, then you're gone. I'm fine, just fine, thank the good Lord above. But I could've been gone, just like that." She snapped her fingers.

"Oh Lord," Leala whispered and scraped faster. She glanced over at me, eyebrows drawn low.

Mama was forever oversharing. It was part of her charm . . . and also her worst trait.

"Our Sadie Way died once, too, just off the dock back there." Mama hooked a thumb over her shoulder toward the lake. "She drowned and the lady of the lake saved her."

"*Mama.*" I let out a long sigh.

Mrs. Teakes turned wide eyes my way, but I didn't see shock or pity in them, only warmth. I'd suspected she'd known the truth of my hair, and her reaction now only confirmed it.

Mama waved a hand. "All I'm saying is that it's a wonderment that we've had two near-death experiences in the family. That we're still here is something to be celebrated." She clapped her hands. "We should have a party."

"Two?" Bree chimed in. "You mean three. Three near deaths. Don't forget about Leala. She almost died, too. When she gave birth to her little boy."

The room fell silent and every head turned toward Leala. And when I heard her swear under her breath, I almost fell down the steps for the second time today because I'd never heard Leala swear in my whole life.

"What's this now?" Mama asked.

Leala spritzed the wall. "Just some issues in the operating room during my C-section. I lost a lot of blood and needed several transfusions."

She didn't mention the hysterectomy, so I certainly wasn't going to. I was curious how Bree had known all this, though, seeing as we had only met her last night.

Mama looked between Leala and Bree, back and forth, back and forth. "Why am I just hearing about this now?"

"Did I say something wrong?" Bree asked, her face screwed into a wince.

"No, you didn't," Leala finally said, giving her full attention to the room. "Not at all. It's not a secret. I just don't talk about it much. The nearly dying part, not the C-section part."

"Or at all, apparently," Mama added tightly.

"Sorry," Bree apologized. "I just thought . . . She's your mom . . . I told my mom everything."

My breath caught at the past tense. *Told* my mom. What had happened to her mother? I bit back a hundred questions and fought the urge to make her a cake and give her a big hug. We all looked at each other except for Mrs. Teakes, who stared into her tea. I felt terrible that she'd been dragged into our family drama.

"Well," Teddy finally said after an uncomfortable minute, "I haven't had a near-death experience yet and don't particularly care to have one, thank you very much. But did I ever tell y'all about the time I turned down a wedding proposal? It was the only one I ever had, too. Happened right here at this very bed-and-breakfast, out on the back lawn. I'm half-convinced I've been cursed in the love department since."

With this bit of gossip too juicy to ignore, Mama tore her

irritated gaze away from Leala. "When was this? Was it to that man"—Mama snapped her fingers—"Rusty. No. Rudy?"

Teddy nodded. "Rudy. This is some twenty-five years ago now—my first ever stay here at the cottage. Rudy and I had come to the cottage for a romantic getaway during the water lantern festival. All those lights were floating around, the stars were shining, and he got down on one knee . . . and it was all so perfect. Dreamlike, even. Yet for some reason I couldn't say yes. He packed up all his things and left that very night. I stayed. I stayed for two whole weeks, and Susannah let me cry on her shoulder and assured me everything would be just fine in time."

That was not the woman Leala and I knew, but she'd always treated us differently from our guests, giving them endless attention and us hardly any.

Mama was sitting on the edge of her seat. "I knew you two had broken up, but I thought you had a fight or something. I didn't know about a proposal. Hot dang."

"Why couldn't you say yes?" Bree asked.

"I didn't love him. I liked him. A lot. But it wasn't enough. I wanted love. True love. You'd think the lady of the lake would take pity on me by now." In an aside to Mrs. Teakes, she said, "I wish for love every darn year, and yet . . . nothing. But maybe that's because I had true love back then but didn't give it enough time. I let it walk away."

"Rudy wouldn't have walked away if he were your true love." Mama's tone was firm. "Or at the very least, he would've come back. So take that thought straight out of your head."

We all nodded, even Mrs. Teakes, which amused me.

"Well, I'm holding out hope this is my year. Mrs. Teakes, would you mind some company on your trip into town? I need to buy lantern kits for Bree and me, too. Maybe a few of them. Can't hurt to set a few extra wishes afloat." She grinned. "Do you have dinner plans? We can make a whole date of it."

"Please call me Iona. All of you." Mrs. Teakes set her cup down on a coaster. "I'd love some company and dinner sounds lovely, simply lovely. Would anyone else care to join us?"

Mama jumped up. "I would!"

I didn't bother trying to talk her out of it. Thankfully, Teddy would be there, keeping an eye on her and hopefully preventing an order of deep-fried anything.

Leala and I both declined the offer to head into town, and a half hour later, the cottage had cleared out. Even Uncle Camp had been roped by Iona into going along, and I smiled as he took the time to dress up a bit in a button-down shirt and nice jeans. His beard had been freshly trimmed, and there was a smile on his face when he left the cottage walking side by side with Iona, the two of them talking about the honeysuckle, convincing me that maybe there was magic in the air after all. I'd never seen Uncle Camp dress up to impress anyone before, and a bright spot of hope spun through me that maybe after all this time, love would be part of his story.

Mama, while getting ready to leave, had given Leala the cold shoulder, not so much as saying goodbye when she left. Leala had taken the snub in stride, and it made me wonder how many times in the past she'd shouldered Mama's displeasure to be seemingly impervious to it now.

Even if I had wanted to go—I didn't, but even if—I couldn't have. There was too much to do around here, beyond finishing the wall in preparation for painting tomorrow. There was laundry to fold and a breakfast to plan and editing to do. The video I had ready to upload was definitely going to have to wait until I checked into a hotel with Wi-Fi, but I had leeway where that was concerned. I posted weekly and always worked a week in advance, so I already had a video scheduled to go live on A Southern Hankerin' this coming week. It had taken me years to develop a schedule that worked for me, and I was reaping the benefits of it now, because it had allowed this unplanned stop in Sugarberry Cove without causing too much anxiety.

Leala sat on the landing, studying the job we'd done. "Please stop me from ever wallpapering anything."

The removal process was tedious but not difficult, and we were just about done with the task. "I like wallpaper. Modern stuff, at least. Done in moderation, it can be quite pretty."

She frowned.

I laughed.

"Can I borrow your phone again?" she asked, already holding out her hand.

I tossed it to her. She'd been using it to log into her email account. After a few seconds of pushing buttons, her frown deepened.

"Still no email from Connor?"

She glanced at the clock before handing the phone back to me. "No. I'm going to drive over there once we're done with this. I'm actually starting to worry at this point."

"I'm sure everything is fine, Leala. Is it possible he hasn't checked his email?"

She bit her thumbnail. "He did say he wouldn't check email, but I can't remember the last time he truly unplugged." She reached into a bucket to pick up a sponge. She wrung it out with more force than necessary, then went to work wiping down the wall, scrubbing off any last bits of wallpaper glue. "Work, work, work. It's like he's married to it and not me."

Ah, so it was his work that was coming between them. I didn't know much about Connor's job. Just that it was at a fancy law firm in Birmingham and that he must make a ton of money, considering their big house and fancy cars.

"Where did Connor grow up?" I asked, at first to distract her but then I realized I truly wanted to know.

"Down in Coffee County, poor as could be. His family had a small peanut farm that barely earned enough to put food on the table. It went bankrupt when Connor was in high school."

"Are his parents still around?"

"No. His mom died when he was in grade school. And his daddy died in a tractor accident his senior year of high school. Seeing how hard his parents had worked on the farm only to fail really motivated him to focus on his education to succeed in life. Thankfully, he landed a scholarship to college. He's worked incredibly hard to get where he is, for all he's achieved."

I vaguely recalled that he was an only child, but I had known nothing of his parents. How did I not know what a tragic childhood he'd had? Why hadn't I taken the time to get to know him better? If not before he and Leala married—since I'd still been angry that he was stealing her away from me—but after I realized how badly I'd behaved? I could blame it on not being around him much, twice a year, three times at most. But deep down, really deep, maybe I was still a little angry that he'd taken her away. Only . . . now I realized it hadn't been him at all. It had been Leala who'd removed herself from the family, the same way I'd removed myself from Sugarberry Cove.

To protect ourselves.

"He's truly the hardest worker I know," she said. Then she

sighed. "But success isn't always measured by money, Sadie. He barely knows Tucker. He barely knows me anymore."

"Do you still love him?"

She rolled a scrap of wallpaper between her fingers. "Of course, but I don't love that he's a workaholic."

I gave her a small smile. "You just said how hard he's worked to get where he is. So is he really the one who's changed? Or is it you?"

Her forehead furrowed as she took a moment to answer. "Maybe I have changed. But it's more complicated than that, Sadie. We had plans, dreams—"

She broke off when a knock sounded on the back porch door. Buzzy waved when he saw us looking his way, and I went to let him in. "Buzzy! It's so good to see you."

It was, too, so much so that my eyes welled with tears. He kept a tight grip on the bowl he was holding and gave me a big hug. Immediately the scent of him, a mix of pine-scented shampoo and a hint of sage, brought me back to my younger years and all the times he sat with me at the farmhouse table, helping me with my homework, especially with my math, which had never been my forte. Seemed all those genes had gone to Leala.

"Sadie Bear, I sure have missed you."

I smiled at the nickname. He'd given it to me after he caught me raiding his berry patch for the hundredth time. I finally let go of him and said, "Come on in. Would you like some sweet tea? Coffee?"

"Sweet tea would be great, thank you." As soon as he stepped inside, he set a bowl of raspberries onto the counter and pushed his glasses up his nose and looked at the entryway. "Whoa. What happened in here?"

I hurried to the fridge for the pitcher of tea and then grabbed a mason jar from the shelf.

"Hurricane Sadie," Leala said with a wan smile.

I filled the jar with ice cubes and poured the tea. "I'd say I'm more of a tropical storm. I'm only mildly destructive." I handed him the glass.

Buzzy laughed. "I sure have missed seeing you two together. Feels . . . right, if you know what I mean."

I glanced at Leala. I knew.

Leala smiled at me before saying, "It's been too long since

you've come by, Buzzy, and I'm glad you're here. But if you were looking to visit with Mother, she's not home right now."

"I know. I saw her walk by earlier with Camp and a few others." He took a sip of the tea. "This is tasty. Thank you."

He'd known she wasn't going to be here and had purposely avoided her. I often wondered what had happened to them, and if my wish eight years ago had played a role in their breakup. After all, it had happened around the same time, only a day or two after I fell in the water. And although my wish hadn't had anything to do with their relationship, I couldn't help thinking the two events were related somehow. As if one thing had led to another. A snowball effect.

Unable to suppress my curiosity, I said, "If you don't mind me asking, Buzzy, what all happened between you two? I really thought you were going to get married someday."

For a moment I didn't think he was going to answer, but then he said, "Let's just say that we had a fundamental difference of opinion. Neither of us would bend."

I had no doubt Mama's stubborn streak had struck again. "What kind of fundamental difference?"

He stared into his glass like he was seeking guidance from the ice cubes. "It had to do with love."

With love? I hadn't been expecting that answer.

Tension pulled on the corners of Leala's mouth as she stepped up beside me. "Maybe things have changed. People *do* change. Sometimes it's for the better."

"Maybe so," he said. "But then again, maybe not."

"Only one way to find out," I offered up.

"You need to talk to her," Leala added with an encouraging nod.

He laughed. "Why do I feel like I'm being double-teamed?"

"What?" I asked innocently. "Would Leala and I do that to you?"

We grinned at him. He rolled his eyes.

Leala turned to me. "Oh! I know. Earlier Mother was talking about having a party. How about tomorrow night we have a cookout?"

I opened my mouth to protest, and she held up a hand.

"It'll be a small gathering. A party is just the thing to break the ice between you two, Buzzy. That way talking to her isn't such a big thing. It can be casual. Just to see if there's anything still there that might be worth pursuing. What do you two say?"

I thought about Buzzy and Mama and how they'd once seemed inseparable. Sometimes literally since they weren't shy with their public displays of affection. He'd had a way of softening Mama's hard edges, and she'd had a way of making him shine. "Okay. I'm in."

We both faced Buzzy.

He took a long look at us and let out a little huff of defeat. "I never could say no to you two. All right. What can I bring?"

"I'd personally kill for your potato salad," Leala said. "It's been years since I've had it. I miss it almost as much as I've missed Sadie, and that's saying something."

My heart swelled and again I asked myself why it felt like I was punishing myself for staying away . . . rather than protecting myself.

Buzzy smiled. "No need to go to such drastic measures, LC. Potato salad it is." He glanced at his watch, then set his glass on the peninsula. "I should get going before everyone comes back. See you tomorrow."

As he headed out the back door, Leala said, "Why doesn't it bother me when he calls me LC?"

"I suspect it has more to do with Mama than the nickname itself."

She frowned, picked up his glass, and brought it to the sink.

My head came up as I heard a car door out front. I walked over to the front window.

"Hey, Leala?" I called out. "Doesn't look like you need to run home after all."

"Why's that?"

I pulled open the front door. "Connor is here."

Chapter 12

Leala

"Mama!" Tucker barreled up the steps and ran straight to me for a hug.

He threw chubby arms around my neck and laughed as I picked him up and covered his face in kisses. He leaned back, took my face in his hands, and said, "Hi!"

My heart melted. "Hi, buddy. I missed you."

I breathed in the scent of him, the baby shampoo and peanut butter and . . . Tucker. It wasn't a smell I could describe, but my heart knew it. It would know it anywhere. I wanted to hold on to him and never let him go.

He looked around and lifted his hands, palms up, in question. "Where Meemaw? Where Campy?"

I adored how Tucker called Uncle Camp *Campy*, mostly because it sounded like Grampy. Fitting, since Uncle Camp had been a grandfather figure to Sadie and me our whole lives, and now he was filling that role for my little boy, too. They were best buddies whenever they were together. And even though we didn't spend great periods of time with my mother, she had somehow managed to charm Tucker. He adored her, and I had to admit she was a different person when she was with him. Kinder. Gentler. Patient. As a grandmother, she was the *mother* I'd always wanted her to be.

"They're not here right now, but Auntie Sadie is. Say hi?" I pivoted toward the stairs so Sadie came into his view.

Tucker buried his face in my collarbone and shook his head.

"Hi, Tucker!" Sadie said in a high-pitched tone. "You've gotten so big. And you're the cutest boy I've ever seen."

Tucker took another peek at her, then buried his head again.

"Don't take it personally. He gets a little shy around people he doesn't know well." I regretted the words the moment I saw her flinch. "That didn't come out right. Sorry."

"It came out perfectly well." She bent to gather the tarps that had been covering the stairs. "It's true—he barely knows me."

"Well, it's not too late to change that," I said.

She glanced over at me, the plastic bunched in her arms, and nodded. "No, it's not."

Tucker wiggled and I set him down. "Moo?" he asked.

I looked outside. Connor was taking a bag out of the trunk of his car. Tucker's overnight bag. Moo was hanging out of one of the zipper pockets. "Daddy has him."

Why, though, was he carrying an overnight bag? Had he changed his mind about Tucker staying with me? So much for their bonding. Anger burned, low and hot in my stomach, as Connor came up the steps.

"Hey," he said when he saw me.

He gave me a lopsided smile, and at the sight of it, some of my anger fizzled. Until I saw the bag in his hand again. "What're you doing here?"

"Didn't you get my text?"

I shook my head. "Didn't you get my email?"

His eyebrows dropped into a deep V shape. "I haven't checked email since you left yesterday morning."

At that, all the anger drained out of me, evaporating nearly as quickly as it had come on. I rushed forward, throwing my arms around him. He hadn't checked either of his email accounts, home or work. He'd kept his promise.

"Hey now," he said, dropping the bag to wrap his arms around me.

I felt Tucker throw an arm around my leg and looked down to see him hugging both Connor's and my knees. I blinked away sudden tears.

Sadie coughed. "I'm just, uh, going to fold laundry. Hi, Connor."

"Hey, Sadie," he said.

Swallowing hard, I pulled away from him and explained about my phone. "What's with the bag?"

"Moo!" Tucker yelled and yanked his favorite stuffed animal free. I picked them both up, and Tucker wiggled again until I set him down. "Meemaw?" he asked.

"She'll be back soon, buddy." To distract him from asking for my mother, I asked, "Do you want a snack?"

With Moo tucked under his arm, he ran on stubby legs to the kitchen, and Connor lifted him onto a counter stool at the peninsula. As I made up a plate of leftover mini scones and raspberries,

I noticed the laundry room door was open a crack and smiled. It was only fair if Sadie was eavesdropping, seeing as how I'd done the same to her earlier.

Connor leaned a hip against the counter. "Round about noon, Tucker and I were eating lunch, and he was throwing the pieces of his sandwich on the floor, and I hadn't even cleaned up breakfast yet, or gotten dressed for the day, and"—he took a deep breath—"I don't know how you do it day in and day out."

A part of me liked that he'd been overwhelmed by daily life with a toddler, especially one who probably took full advantage of not having me there. But I also recognized that because Connor had never spent more than a few hours alone with Tucker, he had been destined for burnout. He didn't know our routines. He didn't know when Tucker was pushing his limits, testing his boundaries, and when he was just being a little boy set on adventure. Connor had missed so much.

"Is that why you came here?" I asked. "Because you were at wit's end from caring for Tuck?"

Connor flashed a shy smile. "I'm not going to lie, I was stressed out, but it's not why we're here." He scratched at stubble on his cheek—apparently he hadn't even found time to shave today.

"At lunchtime I just kept staring at your empty seat at the kitchen table. As much as I said I wanted this weekend for just Tucker and me, it just didn't feel right without you there, Leala. Life just isn't right without you there. And since you can't come home right now, I thought maybe Tucker and I could stay with you. Here, at the cottage. My bag is in the car."

I set the plate on the counter and Tucker grabbed a scone and shoved nearly the whole thing in his mouth. "Small bites, Tucker."

He was already reaching for another scone, and I couldn't help but smile as he tried to feed it to Moo. My gaze lifted to Connor's. "I want you to stay, I do. But—" From the corner of my eye, I saw the vase of lilies sitting on the dining table on the back porch. *Now and forever.* My heart hurt, and I closed my eyes against the ache.

"I know," he said quietly. "I realized today how often you must look at my empty seat at the table. How often Tucker sees it. And how did I not know that he doesn't like apples? Or that he hums when he brushes his teeth? Or that he calls bubbles 'boobies'?"

Despite myself, I smirked at the last one. I'd been trying to break Tucker of that particular phrasing for a while now. It didn't help that I laughed every time he said it.

"Leala, I know there has to be a change," Connor said. "Give me time to figure it out. Please. Just a little time."

I looked into his eyes, into that deep sea of blue, and saw a brief glimpse of the old him. It swayed my decision. "All right."

Slowly, he smiled and came around the counter. I willingly went into his arms, loving the feel of his hug. Loving him.

It was good to have the old Connor back.

The only question that remained was how long he would stay.

Sadie

"That one divorced not long after this episode first aired," Mama pointed out. "And that one, too. Those two hate each other but pretend to be friends. Oh, that one. She's a real piece of work. Manipulates her so-called friends to do her dirty work."

It was late, almost eleven, and I was bone tired. How Mama was still awake, I'd never understand. We sat in her bed, both of us propped up with pillows. She had a bowl of Tabasco-and-chipotle-flavored air-popped popcorn on her lap. I had salted and buttered popcorn and pretended not to notice when every so often she *accidentally* slipped her hand into my bowl instead of hers.

I'd given up my bed to Connor and had been planning to sleep on the living room couch but Mama wouldn't hear of it. I'd share her big bed and that was that. "Just like old times," she'd said.

But honestly, I couldn't remember a time I'd ever slept with her. Not when I was sick. Or hurt. Or scared. I'd always sneaked into bed with Leala during those times, and she'd groan but pat my back and take care of me. Love me.

"You do know this show is scripted, right?" We were watching one of the reality TV Housewives shows—and Mama was giving me a play-by-play.

She swatted playfully in my direction. "Hush your mouth. Ooh, that one there is richer than God. Probably sold her soul to the devil to get all that money." She crunched a piece of popcorn. "I might could sell mine for that kind of cash, too."

I jumped through the door she opened. "What would you do with that kind of money?"

"What wouldn't I do?" She laughed. "Give Camp a raise, first off. That man is a saint. Travel more, definitely. Get out and see the world." She launched into an off-key version of "A Whole New World" from *Aladdin*, complete with flourishing arm gestures, and I had to laugh before shushing her when Nigel started barking. He clearly had a discerning ear.

"What about the cottage?" I asked.

"With unlimited funds? I'd hire a live-in manager. Make it more of an investment property. Give the old gal the upgrades she needs."

Ah. So Mama wasn't blind to the renovations the cottage desperately needed, which made me even more worried about her having money troubles. I had to tread lightly. "Small updates don't cost too much. Paint and such. I'm sure you could sweet-talk Will into cutting you a deal." I was pretty sure she could sweet-talk anybody into anything.

"Maybe so, maybe so. But I prefer the free labor you and LC are giving me."

"Our free labor runs out this weekend."

"Then I should take advantage while I can, no?"

The way she dismissed Will's involvement made me think Leala had been right about her protecting me. I wasn't used to such loving gestures from Mama, and basked in the warmth of her caring enough to shelter my feelings.

She grabbed another handful of popcorn and washed it down with a sip of Diet Coke. The ice cubes rattled as she set her glass back on the nightstand. With a nod to the TV screen, she asked, "What would you do with that kind of money? Spread your wings? Take your show across the pond, so to speak?"

"My wings are happy staying in the South. And I'm not much of a spender. Leala would probably tell us both to invest it."

"Humph," she said.

"*Mama*."

Mama's irritation with Leala hadn't dissipated during her time away from the cottage for dinner. When she'd returned, she'd been downright gleeful at seeing Tucker and friendly with Connor, but she had continued to give Leala the cold shoulder. An ice-cold shoulder.

"Did you know LC almost died?" Mama asked, the words coming out in an annoyed flutter.

I poked around my bowl, looking for a piece of popcorn saturated with butter. "Found out today, same as you."

Mama tsked. "It ain't right, her not telling us. Her almost dying and not telling her own mother."

"Actually, it is her right not to tell us."

Mama sat upright. "Don't you go taking her side, Sadie Way Scott."

I gently pushed her back against the pillow. "Don't go getting riled up. You'll have yourself another heart attack."

"My heart's just fine."

"Is that so? If you ask me, the cardiac unit of a hospital seems an odd destination for a vacation."

She *humphed* again.

I sighed and tried to stay on point. "All I'm saying is that not everyone likes to share absolutely everything. Sometimes it's too painful to talk about—and keep talking about."

"You should be able to talk to family about anything. Especially your mama. Or your *mother* as the case may be."

She'd sneered the word *mother*, and I had to fight not to roll my eyes. "Maybe so. But I know if I had the choice, no one would know about my accident. I don't like thinking about it, let alone talking about it. Yet, eight years later and people do talk. Talk, talk, talk." I gave her a pointed glare.

She pursed her lips, then said, "Talking heals."

"Talking hurts."

"Hurting is how you know you're healing."

Then I must be healing right this minute, I decided, because this conversation had become seriously painful. "All right, then, why don't you tell me what happened between you and Buzzy? Why did you break up?"

"I don't want to talk about that."

I couldn't help myself. I laughed. Then Mama let out a snort of laughter, too. "Fine, Sadie. Your point is taken. Why would you even bring up Buzzy after all this time?"

"I saw him today. Gave him a big ol' bear hug."

She sat up again. "You did? When?"

"He came by while you were at dinner. He heard about your heart attack and brought you some raspberries from his garden."

She sniffed as if disinterested; however, her body language and the light in her eyes told a different story. "He did? Well. That was nice of him, wasn't it? I'll be sure to write him a thank-you note."

Leala and I had decided not to tell Mama of our cookout scheme so she wouldn't lose sleep tonight trying to take over the planning. We'd spring the idea of a party on her in the morning.

"Very nice," I echoed.

"Why didn't you tell me earlier he'd stopped by?"

I nearly choked on a piece of popcorn. "Plumb forgot, what with Connor and Tucker showing up."

"That was a surprise. LC could've gone home, you know. I'm fine."

"Yes, I heard."

"You were joking about the vacation, but hand to God, this is the most time I've had off since we took that trip to Disney when you girls were little. I've never felt so rested."

"You should take more time off."

She set her empty bowl on the nightstand. "And who'd run the cottage? Camp can't do it all alone."

"Shut it down for a couple of days."

"Then how would the bills get paid?"

At that, my worries about her financial troubles grew exponentially. Was it possible she didn't have enough in savings to take even a few days off? I took a deep breath and asked, "Mama, are you doing okay? Moneywise?"

"What?" She laughed.

A little too hard if you asked me.

"Of course I am," she added. "Don't you worry that pretty little head of yours. Now, see here"—she pointed to the screen—"what you don't know yet is that the blond is sleeping with the other blond's husband."

I didn't miss the quick change of subject. She was definitely having money problems. But just how bad was it? "You know Leala is really good with numbers and finances. I'm sure she'd be happy to sit down and help you with a budget."

"I don't need any help, especially not from LC."

"*Mama.*"

"Don't you 'Mama' me."

I put my bowl on the nightstand. "Sometimes I wonder if you even know how hard you are on her."

"Hard on her? That's ridiculous."

"It's not ridiculous. It's true. You should've heard yourself when she was cleaning the windows. What was with that? Why were you trying to shame her about having a housekeeper? Who cares?"

"Sadie, honey, you don't know what you're talking about."

I folded my arms. "I think I do. You should be proud of what she's accomplished and happy that she's happy with her life."

Mama lifted an eyebrow. "Is she happy, though?"

I bit back the "not with you" that was balancing precariously on the tip of my tongue. "*Why* are you so hard on her?"

"I'm tired," Mama announced as she raised the remote and silenced the TV. "And I'm done with this conversation. Go to sleep, Sadie." She swung her legs off the bed, went into the bathroom, and slammed the door behind her.

Downstairs, Nigel barked. Down the hall, Tucker started crying.

I glanced up at the mandala, with its three twisted hearts, pulled a pillow over my face, and screamed silently, wishing I were anywhere in the world but here.

Chapter 13

Sadie

Early the next morning I decided there wasn't enough coffee in the world to help me make it through the day ahead. It was half past six, and I'd been up for more than two hours and was on my third cup of coffee. Between Mama's snoring and the thoughts racing in my head, I'd slept little. I'd finally come downstairs to work on editing my latest episode of A Southern Hankerin', but concentrating was proving difficult. Especially after Leala had come down, then Teddy and Bree and Nigel, to partake in sunrise yoga.

I'd passed on the offer, and Leala had given me a disappointed frown that would no doubt be quite effective on Tucker one day. From my seat on the sofa, I could just barely see the end of the dock. Leala was helping Bree balance on one leg, and Teddy appeared to be naturally limber. Nigel seemed happy enough to sniff around the dock.

I'd been surprised he hadn't barked when the loon floated by, as I'd expected a big to-do. It was as if he, too, recognized that there was something special about the bird.

After watching the yoga class for a few minutes, I forced myself to return my focus to my computer screen. I preferred my videos to be ten to twelve minutes in length, though there had been a few exceptions to that personal rule. Two years ago, I'd made mud pies with a five-year-old girl, and that video had been only four minutes long. It was also one of my most viewed videos as she shared how to make just the right pie—*not too much water, not too much dirt, pat, pat, pat, just like this, just like that.* She'd topped the pie with rocks spread in a heart design, just the way her granny had taught her before the older woman went to live in the clouds.

The video I was editing now was of two burly twentysomething brothers with ruddy cheeks and shoulder-length hair from Olive Branch, Mississippi, who, along with me, were learning from their dad how to make his family-famous chili recipe, which included the big reveal of its secret ingredient. There was a lot of joking and teasing going on, and some playful gagging when the secret ingredient turned out to be pickle juice. There was also a healthy dose of poignancy, at least on my part, because I knew while filming something the sons didn't. Their dad had been recently diagnosed with ALS and wouldn't be able to make the recipe himself much longer. As I edited, I spliced into the kitchen scenes my one-on-one interview with the dad as he talked about watching his boys grow into men and his hopes and dreams for them, seamlessly blending the bittersweet scenes.

His voice cracked in my ear as I listened to the feed through my earbuds. "I want them to know, even after I'm gone, that my love will always feed their souls. And that choosing pickle juice is never a mistake."

Those words would be how I'd end the piece, along with the video of their high fives once they tasted the chili, followed by a group hug.

There were tears in my eyes when I heard, "Mama?"

Glancing over my shoulder, I saw Connor stepping off the bottom stair with Tucker in his arms. Tucker was still dressed in his pajamas—a short-sleeve-shirt-and-short set printed with dinosaurs—and had his stuffed cow in a headlock, its limp body dangling from his elbow. Poor little suffocated cow.

"She'll be back soon," Connor said, giving me a nod of acknowledgment.

I wiped my eyes and pulled out my earbuds. I saved my work and closed my laptop and set it on the coffee table next to two of Mama's many flower arrangements. "Good morning."

"Morning. Sorry—we didn't mean to interrupt." He motioned with his square chin to my laptop.

"I was just about done anyway." A few finishing touches and the video would be ready to upload. "Hi there, Tucker. Did you sleep well?"

He shook his head, then buried it in Connor's chest.

Despite what Leala had said, I was starting to take my nephew's rebuffs personally, especially since he'd warmed straight off to Iona and Teddy. He'd yet to meet Bree, who'd gone straight upstairs last night after dinner, and not a single one of us blamed her for wanting some quiet time.

From the coaster on the table I grabbed my mug and brought it with me into the kitchen. “Can I pour you some coffee?” I asked Connor as I refilled my mug, hoping the fourth cup would be the charm that would shake off my sluggishness.

Connor pressed his lips together, holding in a yawn, then said, “That would be great. Thanks. And don’t let Tucker fool you. He slept well. Only woke up once, which is pretty normal. He resettled quickly.”

It probably wasn’t all that normal for a dog’s barking to have woken him up—one who’d barked only because Mama had slammed the bathroom door—but life at a bed-and-breakfast wasn’t exactly normal.

Mama hadn’t said another word to me after returning to bed. She simply slipped on her night mask and turned off the light. It wasn’t long before her soft snores were filling the popcorn-scented air. She’d still been snoring when I crept out of the room earlier, and I hoped she would sleep late. Despite all her claims about her heart being fine, it was healing, and healing took time.

Uncle Camp, who was normally awake before the crack of dawn, was sleeping in, and I’d yet to hear anything from Iona’s room as well, but it was early yet. Most guests didn’t usually come down until they were ready for breakfast.

I grabbed an empty mug and filled it. “Room for cream?”

“No thanks. I take it black.”

It was just one more thing I probably should’ve known about him. After all, he’d been part of the family for eight years, not counting the two years he and Leala had dated before getting married. I slid the mug over to him. “How about Tucker?”

“He prefers cold mocha coffee. Don’t you, bud?” Tucker groaned into Connor’s chest. “What? Oh, that’s right. Hold the coffee.”

I smiled. “Chocolate milk?”

“Yeah. I’ll get it, though, once he’s a little more fully awake; otherwise, it’ll likely be shaken all over the floor.” He took a sip of coffee and turned his attention outside. As he watched the yoga lesson on the dock, the hard lines of his face softened. “The coffee’s good. Nice and strong. Thanks.”

His hair stood up every which way, even though it was damp—any attempts at taming it before coming downstairs had obviously failed. He had on a pair of sweats and a tee and tennis shoes, and it was odd to see him not dressed in his usual business attire. I liked casual Connor, I decided. He seemed less . . . stuffy.

Or maybe I was just finally seeing *him* for the first time.

"You're welcome. I was just going to put out the starters if you're hungry. There are raspberry Danish, cinnamon muffins, and fruit cups. Breakfast today is crepes, banana or strawberry, or your choice of eggs and sausage, but it's not being served until eight."

Blue eyes widened. "Impressive menu."

"I actually forgot how much I like to cook for a big group. The kitchen . . . soothes me."

"Probably need a lot of that this weekend."

I grinned. "That goes without saying."

This was the most Connor and I had ever spoken, as stilted as it was, and it didn't come without a good measure of guilt. I used a tea towel to wipe down the already clean countertop, and said, "Connor, I need to tell you how sorry I am for the way I've treated you in the past. Really sorry. I—"

"Sadie, you don't have to—"

"No, I do. I was jealous that Leala was spending all her time with you and not me. It felt like I lost my best friend, and I took out that grief on you. I was an absolute brat. I hope that—" Oh Lord, why were apologies so hard? "I hope that we can start over?"

He looked into his coffee for a moment before turning his gaze on me. "Yeah. I'd like that."

Maybe there was something to what Mama had said last night about how talking heals. Apologizing now barely made up for ten years of bad behavior, but it was a start. And sometimes a fresh start was all that was needed.

"Good." I smiled, then bustled about, setting the starters I'd made last night onto the ceramic trays.

Tucker, I noticed, was watching me out of the corner of his eye. When he realized I saw him, he hid his face again.

"Hey, Tucker, is Moo hungry?" I held up a muffin. "A muffin for Moo?"

Tucker lifted his head again, looked between me and the cow, and nodded. Finally, a nod! "Should I cut it up for him?"

Tucker nodded again and pointed at the counter stool. "Down, Daddy, down. *Pwease.*"

"Yes, sir." Connor helped settle him onto the stool, then went to the fridge for the milk. He filled a mug with milk, stirred in a good dollop of chocolate syrup, then warmed it in the microwave before transferring the liquid into a sippy cup.

I watched the routine and laughed.

"It's ridiculous, I know, but Tucker had a terrible time when Leala stopped breastfeeding and this was the only way we could get milk into him for a while. Nowadays, he only drinks it like this in the morning, and we're slowly weaning him off the chocolate."

Even though Leala had been worried about Connor being an absent husband and father, it was obvious to me he wasn't completely checked out. Tuck wasn't trying to get away from him, and he knew exactly how his little boy liked his chocolate milk in the morning.

"Hey, whatever works." I slid the plate of dissected muffin over to Tucker and leaned down. "Does Moo want me to feed him?"

"No," Tucker said, patting his small chest. "I do."

"All right, then."

I pretended not to watch as Tucker used his thumb and index finger to pick up a bit of muffin, delicate as could be. He brought it Moo's lips, then swerved it up to his own mouth and popped it in.

Connor helped me set the rest of the peninsula, putting out plates and silverware and napkins, and it wasn't long before the morning yoga troupe was heading inside.

Leala led the way into the house, followed closely by Teddy, and finally Bree and Nigel.

"Mama! Moo muffin." Tucker clambered onto his knees on the stool to show Leala his empty plate.

"Moo ate a muffin?" she guessed. "Was it good?"

Tucker nodded dramatically. "Moh?"

"More? Sure. Why not?" She was reaching for another muffin when Tucker gasped and stood up on the stool.

Connor stepped up beside him to hold him steady. "Hey, now. Careful there. Gotta sit down, buddy."

"Owie!" Tucker pointed at Bree's face.

Although Bree's color had already been high from doing yoga, her face turned a bright red, which only served to highlight her scars even more.

"Owie! I kiss?" Tucker held out his hands, wiggling his fingers, beckoning Bree forward.

Leala tried to push his hand down. "Tucker, honey, no. I'm so sorry, Bree."

Bree froze for a moment before stepping in close to Tucker. "It's . . . okay."

Tucker reached up and held her face tenderly, each of his hands gently resting on each of her cheeks, his right hand so small it didn't even cover her whole scar. He stuck his face out and planted a noisy kiss next to her nose. "*Bettah*?"

She smiled at him, the first real smile I'd seen from her, and said, "Much better. Thank you."

"*Weycome.*" He plopped back down and picked up his sippy cup as if he kissed the boo-boos of strangers every day, all the time, no big deal.

Teddy reached for a mug. "Well, there it is. I've fallen head over heels in love with Tucker, so I don't need my wish granted this year after all. Anyone want my lantern?"

We all laughed and carried on with the morning, talking about anything and everything but especially about the cookout later today—and what we needed for it. Surrounded by the energetic chatter, I mixed crepe batter and felt at ease, truly at ease, for the first time in a long while. I couldn't help thinking that today was going to be a good day, and I tried really hard to keep my focus on that, and to not think about tomorrow when I had to pack up and leave this all behind.

"Mother," Mama said, pointing at Leala from where she sat on the big cozy armchair by the fireplace.

"Mama," Tucker replied as he sat on her lap with a strawberry in one hand and a poker chip in the other.

Moo had been tucked in for a nap on the couch, in a futile attempt by Leala to get Tucker to rest, too.

Mama tried again. "Mo-ther."

Leala sighed heavily as she dipped a paintbrush into a paper cup. She was cutting in, painting only along the baseboards, corners, and ceiling, while I rolled. She'd left her hair naturally curly today, and even though it was pulled up in a bun, every so often she'd squint at the wall and pull off a spiral strand that had stuck to the paint.

After several hours of work, we only had one wall left, but it was the largest wall, and I thanked the heavens that we'd had the foresight to buy paint that had primer in it, as it didn't look like the walls would need two coats.

Iona sat in a rocker on the back porch with her book and a big glass of sweet tea. We'd chatted earlier, and she accepted my offer to drive her back to Wetumpka tomorrow morning. Taking a rideshare home seemed a silly waste of money, considering we were both going to the same place. Literally the same place. Her small bungalow on the river.

Out on the lake Teddy, Bree, and Nigel, who was dressed in the smallest doggy life vest I'd ever seen, floated on paddleboards near the dock. Uncle Camp was washing the dock, which he had done every Sunday afternoon for as long as I could remember, and Connor had gone to the market for cookout supplies, which Leala insisted they pay for when I tried to give him my credit card. I didn't argue. If she didn't care enough to ask about the details of my career to realize I could afford some groceries, then I was going to happily let her pay for everything.

The phone rang, and Mama said, "I'll get it."

Tucker said, "No, I do."

Mama laughed. "We'll both get it."

"Okay." He nodded.

She shifted him off her lap, stood, then lifted him up onto her hip. I saw her wince before she schooled her features into a smile when she saw me looking at her. Her eyes dared me to say anything.

I bit my tongue. Mama had come downstairs this morning all light and sunshine, and I didn't want to put a damper on her good mood. She'd been over-the-moon happy when we mentioned a cookout tonight and had spent the better part of the morning planning a menu big enough to feed an army.

"Sugarberry Cottage," she sang as she answered the phone, "this is Susannah. How may I help you?"

Mama stood at the secretary desk, Tucker balanced on one hip. He looked perfectly at peace in her arms, and I wondered what rankled Leala more—his happiness at being with Mama or Mama trying to teach him to call Leala "Mother." I suspected the former.

"I see," Mama said. "I'm terribly sorry to hear that. No, no I completely understand. I was just in the hospital last week myself. Had myself a heart attack."

Leala groaned.

"Why, yes, I surely will, and I'll refund your full deposit. It will be in the mail tomorrow. You take care, too. Goodbye."

"Bye!" Tucker yelled.

Mama lowered him to the floor, then handed him a pencil and a piece of paper before she opened the reservation book and made a notation on one of the pages. "Such a shame. Mrs. Maloney had an emergency appendectomy yesterday, so they had to cancel their trip to the festival."

Tucker put the pencil and paper on the floor and ran over to Leala, gave her a hug, and said, "Luh you! I paint?"

Her gentle laugh echoed in the staircase. "Sure you can."

She handed him the paintbrush, and my jaw dropped. Perfectionist Leala had just handed a toddler a fully loaded paintbrush. I wouldn't have believed it if I hadn't seen it with my own two eyes.

"I paint!" He dabbed Leala's knee, coloring it blue.

"The wall, buddy! Paint the wall," she said with a light lilt, guiding his hand toward an area that hadn't yet been rolled. "You're so silly."

And she hadn't wiped the paint off her knee. I looked at Mama, who seemed as surprised as I was by Leala's actions.

People change, she'd told me yesterday, and though I knew it to be true, this seemed completely out of character for her, so relaxed.

But then I had to remind myself that I truly didn't know her that well anymore. There had been so much we'd kept to ourselves over the last eight years. I decided then and there that I'd make more of an effort to be close again.

"I silly." He laughed and slapped the wall with the paintbrush, leaving a series of abstract crosshatches behind.

From the corner of my eye, I watched Mama watch them, and there was something in her features, an awareness, maybe even jealousy, that I'd never seen before.

Leala said, "Let me see your hand."

Tucker held his free hand out, and she guided the paintbrush, helping him paint his own palm. "Now, let's do this." She took his hand and pushed it against the wall, then pulled it back, leaving his palm print behind. She faked shock. "What's your hand doing on the wall?"

His blue eyes grew big and round, and he laughed again as he looked between his palm and the wall. "I paint!"

"You did a good job, too. Can I have my brush back?"

It took a second of deep contemplation, but he finally handed it over.

"Thank you," she said and wiped the remaining paint off his hand off with a rag.

He gathered up his pencil and paper and went running for the back porch. "Noni! I paint. I draw!"

He'd been calling Iona "Noni" all morning and had insisted on showing her every single item he came across. She'd long since told a worried Leala to stop stressing about him being a bother, because she loved his attention.

Teddy might have serious competition for Tucker's affections.

"Don't run with a pencil," Leala called after him, and he slowed to a fast walk.

Ah, that was the Leala I knew.

Leala looked over at me. "Can you do me a favor and take a picture of that wall?"

I put the roller down and snapped a shot of the tiny blue hand. "I sent it to your email." And I also added the photo to an online album of my favorite pictures. I wanted to remember this moment always.

"Thanks, Sadie."

Mama snapped the reservation book closed, effectively turning the attention back to her. "Such a shame about the Maloneys."

"How many days were they going to stay?" I asked, concerned about Mama's sudden loss of income.

"A full week. Arriving tomorrow, leaving next Sunday." Mama stared at the closed book, deep lines creasing the skin between her eyes. "Oh well. Emergencies happen."

I said, "Mama, most of the inns and bed-and-breakfasts that I stay in keep the full deposit if the reservation is canceled within seven days of the trip."

She rolled her eyes. "I'm not like most places."

"But you are a business," Leala added.

Mama's gaze narrowed. "Yes, thank you, dear. I'm aware. Bless your heart."

With her eyes closed, Leala tilted her head upward as if praying.

On the back porch, Tucker climbed onto Iona's lap with his pencil and paper. She said, "Can you draw me a boat?"

"Noni, I see boats?" he asked excitedly and pointed outside.

"Leala Clare," Iona called out, "is it okay if I take Tucker outside to look at the boats?"

Worry slashed across Leala's face, and she swallowed hard. "Just be sure to hold his hand. He loves the water and won't be afraid to jump in."

Laughing, Iona stood and took hold of his hand. "We're quite a pair, then, because I feel the same way."

Leala didn't take her gaze off them the whole time they walked toward the dock. Uncle Camp looked up and smiled as they neared.

Mama made a production of putting the reservation book away. "Someone will call this week looking for a last-minute stay. Happens every year. A cancellation is not a big deal."

I said, "Mama, it's good policy to have a protective clause for late cancellations. You might want to think about that for future reservations. I can help you draft a notice."

"*Hmm.* Yes. I'll think about that," she said sweetly before walking out to the porch, where she poured herself a tall glass of water infused with strawberry and lemons.

By her tone, one similar to Leala's dismissals, she most certainly was not going to think about it. "It's good policy," I repeated in singsong.

"*Mm-hmm,*" she said as she sat down and put her feet up on a bench.

"I'm present within myself," Leala said under her breath, then looked at me and added, "Just one more day."

Unlike me, Leala wasn't going to have any trouble leaving this place tomorrow morning. I wouldn't be the least surprised if she already had her bag packed.

I heard an engine and peeked out to see Connor's car coming up the driveway followed by a pickup truck with LOCKHART CONSTRUCTION written on the door. Both parked along the mountain laurel hedge.

Oh my.

Mama called out, "I hope Connor remembered the charcoal. Can't have a good cookout without charcoal for the grill."

I watched as Connor reached into the open trunk and pulled

out a big bag of charcoal, hefting it over his shoulder. Will stepped up next to him and took three reusable grocery sacks from the trunk. They headed our way.

Leala glanced out the window and said, "Looks like he's got that and more."

"More? Like what?" Mama asked over her shoulder.

Leala threw a worried glance at me as she said, "Like Will Lockhart."

"I'm fine with him being here," I said in a low tone, meaning it. The ice had been broken between Will and me, and the thought of catching up with him no longer brought on any stress. If I was being completely honest with myself, I'd have to admit I was actually looking forward to it, but I certainly wasn't ready to announce it out loud.

Leala must have caught the sudden glint in my eye, because she smiled as if she knew my secret. I rolled my eyes, which made her smile widen.

Mama's feet fell off the bench with a thud. She set down her glass. "What's this now? Will's here?"

Connor sailed through the front door and said, "Look who I ran into at Lockhart's while I was picking up ice cream. I managed to talk him into helping you two finish this project."

"Oh, thank God," Leala said dramatically. "I feel like I've been painting for weeks. Hi, Will."

"Hi, Leala," Will said, then spared a tender look at me. "I'm happy to help out."

I suddenly went warm. Really warm.

"Will, honey!" Mama practically sprinted into the room. "You're so kind to help out, but surely you have better things to do on a beautiful sunny afternoon."

"No, ma'am," he said. "I'm free for the rest of the day."

"We're glad to see you, Will," I said, trying to let Mama know I was okay with him being here. "Leala had resorted to letting Tucker paint. See?" I stepped aside to show off the handprint.

"Tucker's got some talent." Will smiled. "Is he ready for a part-time job?"

Leala laughed. "Not quite yet."

Mama glanced between all of us and must've realized she was stuck between a rock and a hard place. "Well. What a savior you are! Now Sadie can help me in the kitchen, while you and LC finish this entryway. Let me take those bags so y'all can get started. You'll be done lickety-split; then you can be on your way." She practically pried the bags out of his hands.

Leala glanced at me, her eyes sparkly with mischief. "Will, if you don't have plans for tonight, we'd sure love to have you join us for a cookout. As you can see, we have plenty of food."

Apparently Mama hadn't picked up on my clue that I was fine with Will's presence, because she made a strangled noise and looked at Leala with shiny daggers in her blue eyes.

"Great minds," Connor said, smiling at Leala as he headed for the backyard. "Will already accepted my earlier invitation."

"Splendid!" Mama pivoted toward the kitchen, bags in hand. "Just splendid. The more the merrier."

Will hooked a thumb over his shoulder. "I'll get the rest of the bags."

Before Connor closed the sliding door behind him, I heard Tucker yell, "Daddy, Noni, boat!"

Tucker held Iona's hand and jumped up and down excitedly as he pointed at a sailboat in the distance. Uncle Camp had abandoned his scrub mop and was chatting with Iona, both of them with big smiles on their faces. Not too far away Bree stood on her paddleboard doing the yoga pose Leala had taught her earlier. She wobbled and fell in the water, then came up laughing, a sound I couldn't hear from so far away but wished I could.

I walked over to the front door and watched Will take four more bags of groceries from the trunk, two in each hand. It had already been a good day.

But now that Will was here, it felt like it had gotten a little bit better.

Chapter 14

Leala

"Mama!" Tucker laughed, tugging on my arms. "Moh?"

Feeling slightly queasy, I was ready to be done swinging him around and around, but I needed Mother distracted for a few more minutes. She'd been watching Sadie like a hawk all afternoon, protecting her from spending any one-on-one time with Will and effectively ruining our plan to get Buzzy over here, but right now her eyes were on Tucker and me.

"Tucker, are you hungry?" she asked from the patio table where she and Iona sat side by side, shaded by a large red umbrella. "Come sit with Meemaw. I have some watermelon, darlin'."

"Swing!" he said to her, then tugged my arms again. "Moh!"

Buzzy was waiting for Sadie to stop by his house under the guise of returning his bowls. She'd hopefully come back empty-handed but with Buzzy in tow. With Will occupied playing cornhole and Mother trying to lure Tucker away from me, this was our best chance.

"Okay. *One* more time," I said as I gave Sadie, who was standing near the grill, a subtle nod. From the corner of my eye, I saw her grab the two bowls she'd set out earlier and sneak along the back of the house toward the honeysuckle-covered arbor.

I picked up Tucker and swung him around until I got so dizzy I had to sit down on the lawn to stop the world—and my stomach—from spinning. Tucker collapsed on top of me, smelling of sunshine and smoke from the grill and pure, sweet love. I wrapped my arms around him and rolled back and forth as he giggled.

An excited shout rang out from the sand pit down by the seawall where Teddy and Bree and Will and Uncle Camp were playing an intense game of cornhole.

"And that's how it's done!" Teddy let loose with a gleeful laugh as she and Bree high-fived.

Mother had an Elvis CD playing in the background, his voice drifting out of an ancient boom box, and I took a moment to just breathe in the scent of my little boy while my stomach settled.

Except for being on the receiving end of Mother's hostility, it had been a near perfect afternoon. With Connor's and Will's help, the entryway had been finished in no time at all and looked beautiful. For having had no nap, Tucker had been downright angelic, playing for most of the afternoon with Nigel and Iona and Uncle Camp, who'd introduced Tucker to jacks. My little boy had been enthralled with the tiny spiked toys and bouncing ball.

I'd come into this weekend hoping to not lose my mind, my composure, or myself, and I was fairly proud for keeping two of the three. My composure was on its way to becoming a lost cause, due to the fact I'd grown weary of Mother trying to use Tucker to bait me.

Nigel ran up with a tennis ball in his mouth, his tail wagging, and Tucker scrambled off me. "I throw!"

I wrestled the ball from Nigel and handed it to Tucker. He reeled back and threw it as far as he could—which was approximately ten feet—then laughed as Nigel chased after it. Then he chased after Nigel, who apparently decided that being chased by Tucker was much more fun than playing catch. "Stay away from the water," I called out as I stood up, and Tucker U-turned back toward the cottage.

Connor stepped out of the house with a big platter in hand, gave me a slow smile that filled me with warmth and happiness, and then headed for the grill.

At the sound of the screen door sliding closed behind him, Mother took a quick look around. "Where's Sadie?"

Citronella candles scented the air as I sat down in the shade of the patio table and feigned ignorance. "I'm not sure."

"Perhaps she stepped inside for a moment," Iona said from her seat next to me, lifting her sweet tea and taking a slow, measured sip. She flicked me an amused glance, and I had the feeling she somehow knew what Sadie and I were up to.

Mother's gaze zipped toward Will, as if to reassure herself that Sadie was not within his arm's reach. I had never seen Mother in mama bear mode, and it was a sight to behold. It might have taken her nearly thirty years to connect to it, but I supposed it was better late than never. All that being said, however, I thought she was overdoing it. It was obvious Sadie didn't mind Will being around, and I hoped the two would find some time together to patch up the friendship that had been broken all those years ago.

"Oh, look, Susannah—there's Sadie," Iona said with a nod.

Side by side, Sadie and Buzzy were chatting animatedly as they walked under the arbor, and for a moment I thought Mother was going to fall off her chair.

"What in the world?" she muttered.

Buzzy stopped to talk with Connor, and Sadie sailed over to the table as if nothing out of the ordinary was going on. "I ran over to Buzzy's to return his bowls, and it just didn't seem right not to invite him to join us. Buzzy, come over and meet Iona."

Iona sat a bit straighter and smiled as Buzzy approached. "Ma'am," he said with a dip of his head. "Any friend of Sadie's is a friend of mine."

"Same," she replied. "Pleasure to meet you. Your raspberries are some of the finest I've ever eaten."

"I can't take all the credit. There's a little lake magic in those berries. I couldn't grow a darn thing until I moved here by the water." He set a bowl of potato salad on the table, then swung his gaze to Mother. "Susannah. You're looking well. Not everyone bounces back from a heart attack quite so prettily."

Mother sniffed as though she wasn't going to be swayed by his sweet talk, then slowly smiled. "Thank you, Buzzy. I appreciate the kindness."

I stole a look at Sadie, and she wiggled her eyebrows. This plan of ours might actually work. I hoped and prayed it did, not only because Mother had always been at her best with Buzzy, but also because I hoped to allay some of the guilt I'd been carrying around for years.

"Sadie!" Uncle Camp yelled. "Come tag me out, sugar. This old man needs a break."

Mother jumped up, nearly knocking over her chair. "Wait! I was next to play."

"You can take my place," Bree said, stepping up to the table. "I need a drink."

She wore a hat that shaded her face but had her hair pulled back in a low ponytail. That she was out here with us, smiling and playing, spoke a lot of her true nature, of wanting to be included, despite her shyness, despite her scars.

Sadie said, "Why don't you and Buzzy play, Mama? You can team up against Will and Teddy. I have a few things to finish up in the kitchen."

"Yes"—Buzzy held out a hand—"why don't we, Susannah?"

After a moment of consideration, Mother slipped her hand into his. "All right."

Sadie gave me a surreptitious thumbs-up before heading into the house. Bree plopped into the chair across from me, wiped her forehead with the back of her hand, and poured herself a glass of sweet tea from the pitcher on the table. "I think I'll stick to poker from now on. Less sweaty."

"And more profitable," Iona said with a laugh.

Bree smiled at that and it lit up her whole face. She was having fun, and it was good to see.

As Mother walked behind my chair, she leaned down and whispered to me, "Don't think I didn't see that bowl of potato salad, LC. It's your favorite, no? So strange Buzzy would have that ready to go like he did. We'll talk about this later."

Iona chuckled, and I sighed.

"What?" Bree's eyebrows jumped up. "Did you set them up? Who is he?"

"Her ex-boyfriend," I said, just as Uncle Camp reached the table.

Bree whistled.

Uncle Camp patted my shoulder. "Your mama's going to skin you alive."

"I'm aware." I smiled up at him. "And it's okay. I'm used to it."

He shook his head, then spared a sweet glance at Iona before veering off toward the grill.

"Mama!" Tucker said, racing up to the table. "I thirstyyy."

Tired, as well, if the whine in his tone was any indication. I drew him onto my lap and handed him my glass of lemonade. He took a careful sip, then sagged against me like his body was melting into mine. I raked my fingers through his damp hair and didn't even mention the *s*-word. *Sleep.* With him being so overtired, it would only make him cranky. I glanced at my watch—it was nearly six. Too early for bedtime, but he'd missed his nap and taking one now would mean he'd be up all night. Not an option. I glanced over at Connor and noticed that he was looking at his phone. Had he gotten a text message from work?

Taking a moment, I focused on my breathing and tried to tell myself not to march over there, take his phone away, and chuck it into the lake alongside mine. He tucked the phone in his pocket, then looked over at me and smiled when he saw me watching him.

Maybe it hadn't been work. Maybe he'd been checking the weather. Or the sports pages. Or the safe internal temperature for grilled hamburgers. Or . . . maybe I was delusional.

"Do you think they'll get back together?" Bree asked as she watched Mother and Buzzy toss beanbags.

"Hard to say." I pulled my attention away from Connor. "They still have feelings for each other, but sometimes love just doesn't work out."

"Relationships are like those yonder water oak trees." Iona nodded to the trees in Buzzy's yard. "Sometimes you grow apart only to grow together again. If you're willing to bend, anything is possible."

Bree looked over her shoulder. "Those trees are cool."

"Cool," Tucker echoed, then yawned.

Iona patted my hand, and I wondered if she was offering the advice for Buzzy and Mother, Connor and me, or me and Mother. Or all of us.

"Do you have kids, Iona?" Bree asked.

"Never blessed, dear. I've been widowed a long time now, but I have the comfort of living near my big extended family who constantly remind me what's important in life."

Bree stole a glance at Uncle Camp over her shoulder, then said, "Do you ever think about giving love another try?"

Ah, so I wasn't the only one who had seen the sparks between them.

Iona's gaze drifted toward Uncle Camp. "I've never given it much thought. My heart has always belonged to only one man."

"Hearts are big enough to hold lots of love," I said, hoping she'd take my hint. I was a sucker for romance and she and Uncle Camp were adorable together.

Uncle Camp caught me watching him, winked, then went into the cottage.

"I do believe you might be right, Leala," Iona said with a suddenly shy smile.

I saw Connor pull out his phone again, and I forced myself to look away, toward the trees, following with my gaze the curve of their trunks as they bowed away from each other, then curved back again, their canopies blending together as one.

I wanted to believe that Connor and I would grow together again, that my marriage could be saved. But sometimes when you bent too far, you risked breaking.

Chapter 15

Sadie

"How'd you like the mac and cheese, Bree?" Mama asked. "Did it measure up to your mother's recipe?"

Elvis crooned about jailhouses in the background as Bree said, "It's good, but my mom's recipe is extra special. It has three types of cheese, jalapeños, and bacon."

"I can confirm it's the best." Teddy leaned back into the sunshine beyond the umbrella's reach. "And you know I'm a bit of a mac and cheese specialist."

Mama said, "Shoo, that does sound tasty. I might need that recipe myself."

Tucker ran circles around the table with Nigel, and I honestly didn't know how either were on their feet after being on the go all day long. I was growing dizzy just watching them go round and round.

"He's just living his best life, isn't he, the little darlin'?" Teddy asked, watching him run. "Oh, to have that energy."

"Tucker, careful of the table corners," Leala said, wincing every time he swerved close to the edge of the table. His face was the perfect height to get a black eye from one misstep.

Mama grinned at his antics. "He's doing just fine. You worry too much, LC. Let go and live a little."

Leala's nostrils flared, and I suddenly regretted my seat choice, sandwiched between the two of them and their passive-aggressive jabs. The five of us sat at the patio table, long done eating but still chatting and enjoying the early evening. Connor and Will had volunteered to clear plates, and Uncle Camp, Iona, and Buzzy were fishing off the seawall.

"You know, LC," Mama said, her voice even, "if you warn him about every little thing, he won't listen about the big things. Pick your battles. He has to learn some things on his own. It's the way of life."

A gust of wind shook the red umbrella, hinting at changing weather. Usually, this was one of my favorite times of day, when the rush of the day was just about over and stillness slowly crept in, allowing the focus to shift to the whistling wind, the scent of the lake, and the birds singing high in the trees. The warmth of the late day sun settled around me like a hug, but acting as a buffer between Mama and Leala was ruining the moment.

Next to me Leala seethed silently, pretending she hadn't heard a word Mama had uttered. I'd take her silence over the back-and-forth bickering anytime, but I honestly didn't know how she was keeping quiet.

Teddy pushed her empty plate away and set her elbows on the table. "I wouldn't mind that mac and cheese recipe, either. Oh, oh! Sadie! You should do a video with Bree and her mac and cheese while you're here in town. That recipe should be shared with the world. I mean, that is if Bree's up for it."

Bree fidgeted, then smiled. "I think Mom would like that, but I don't know." Her gaze drifted over to me, obviously waiting for me to chime in.

While I liked the idea of filming with her for a few reasons, the fact alone that Bree was willing to be on camera with her scars was enough for me to say yes. But there were logistical issues. "I mean, I would love to, but I'm leaving tomorrow morning. There's not enough time to prep and then film . . . I'd need three, four days at least."

"But you don't have to leave tomorrow," Leala piped in, breaking her silence and rejoining the conversation.

"Sure I do. I'm driving Iona back to Wetumpka, remember? We're leaving at ten."

Leala set her glass onto the table. "Iona told me not half an hour ago that she's staying for the whole week—she took the Maloneys' room."

The wind gusted again, sending strands of my hair flying across my face. "I hadn't heard that."

"It's true." Mama nodded. "I told you someone would come along to fill that room. *Policy schmolicy*," she added under her breath.

I rolled my eyes. I was drafting that policy whether she wanted me to or not. I'd leave it on her desk. Whether she implemented it was up to her, but at least I'd know I tried.

"So you *can* stay," Leala said, her gaze locked on me.

"No, no, she *can't*," Mama interrupted. "I'm sure Sadie has other interviews lined up. She should get back on the road, where she belongs. Seeing the country. Meeting new people, tellin' their stories. And just last night I planted the seed that maybe she should travel overseas. Wouldn't that be something? *Hankerin'* from across the pond?"

Teddy faux swooned. "If you go, Sadie, take me with you! Maybe I've been looking for my true love on the wrong continent. Maybe he lives in Italy. Or France!"

"*Oh là là*!" Bree wiggled her eyebrows, and they fell against each other, laughing, unaware of—or desperately trying to ignore—the mounting tension across the table.

Leala leaned forward so she could aim the full power of her glare at Mama. "Maybe Sadie wants to stay here in Sugarberry Cove. It's *her* choice."

Mama lifted an eyebrow and turned her head oh so slightly toward me. "Sadie?"

Caught up in an emotional tug-of-war, I fidgeted. "I have no interest in traveling overseas, except maybe to sightsee one day."

Mama tsked loudly in disapproval.

"But," I continued, "I am due in Georgia on Wednesday—I was planning to drive over there Tuesday morning after staying the night in Wetumpka. Even if I left from *here* on Tuesday instead of down there, there's not enough time to film."

"Why not?" Leala asked. "Aren't your videos short?"

"A lot of prep goes into the videos," I said, trying not to lose my temper at how little regard she gave to my career. The prep was most of the work, honestly. Though the filming and editing took a good chunk of time, the footage I collected completely depended on my getting to know the people I was interviewing and asking the right questions.

"Next year, then," Teddy said, trying once again to lighten the mood.

"If you can get Sadie to come back," Leala bit out. "Tucker, the table, honey!"

"He's fine." Mama rolled her eyes. "Let him be. When does mothering become smothering, LC? If he runs into the table, he'll learn never to do it again, won't he?"

"I'd rather be cautious than careless, attentive rather than distracted, because we both know what can happen when you don't care enough to pay attention, don't we?" Leala said, her whole body rigid.

Mama narrowed her gaze, and I could practically see flames shooting out her ears. This argument was escalating to a dark, dangerous place.

Connor came out of the cottage to collect a few more plates and must've seen the look on Leala's face, because he stopped just short of the table. "Everything okay out here?"

"Just fine," Mama said sharply, throwing her napkin onto the tabletop. "Where's Will gone off to? Did he finally have his fill of us?"

I thanked the heavens she was easily distracted as Connor picked up Mama's empty plate and said, "He's inside doing dishes."

Sure enough, Will's head was visible through the window as he bent over the sink. I smiled, thinking about him waking up this morning, planning his day, and somehow ending up here doing dishes.

"Oh." Mama looked crestfallen, her shoulders sagging.

She hadn't let down her guard all day, making sure Will and I stayed apart, and clearly it was taking its toll.

"Tucker, buddy," Connor said as he also picked up Teddy's and Bree's plates like he'd been bussing tables his whole life long. "Take this inside to the kitchen, please." He handed him Teddy's plate and gave Leala an empathetic look that told me he had a fair idea of why his wife was in a temper.

With Nigel following him, Tucker carried the melamine plate as if it were made of delicate china, and waited for Connor to catch up to open the door. "Where Moo?"

"Inside sleeping. Are you ready for bed?"

"No, I not."

"Good to know," Connor said, throwing a smile at Leala over his shoulder.

Bree coughed uneasily, then leaned in. "Yoga was fun this morning, Leala. I can see why you like it. Thanks for showing us some positions."

Leala loosened up a bit. "I enjoyed the company. I'll be out there again tomorrow if you want to join me. Don't you think Sadie should join us?"

"Absolutely!" Teddy said. "Leala's a great teacher, Sadie."

"Yoga's not my thing," I said, trying to keep from looking at Will.

"Have you even tried it?" Leala asked.

"No."

Mama snorted.

"You should try it. We can move it to the lawn if the dock's the issue," Leala said.

"It's not the dock," I answered, thinking it was absolutely the dock. I didn't want to be on it. It was too close to the water, and the pull would be too strong to jump in, swim, laugh, *live*. I'd never be able to leave Sugarberry Cove again. And I had to leave. I'd worked too long, too hard on A Southern Hankerin' to abandon it now.

"Leala, have you ever done yoga on the stand-up paddleboard?" Bree asked.

Leala shook her head. "I never even thought to give it a try until I saw you doing it today."

"LC was never one to color outside of the lines," Mama said.

Leala started to come out of her chair, and I pushed her back down and yelled, "Hey, Buzzy. Mama's looking for a dance partner. What do you say?"

Mama huffed. "Sadie Way Scott, what are you doing? I most certainly am not."

Buzzy, Uncle Camp, and Iona abandoned their fishing gear and headed for the table, just as Elvis started singing "Love Me Tender." Perfect timing.

"Now look what you've done, Sadie." Mama fluffed her hair.

Buzzy pushed his glasses up his nose and swept an arm toward a wide, circular section of the flagstone patio that surrounded the fire pit, perfect as a makeshift dance floor.

Mama put her hand in his and said, "Now don't you go stepping on my toes, Buzzy Hale."

He looked affronted. "When have I ever?"

"Well, people change," Mama pointed out.

"I'm hoping so," he said in a soft voice.

Uncle Camp turned to Iona and said, "I haven't danced near enough in all my years and wouldn't mind taking a spin as well. What do you say, pretty lady?"

Color flooded her fair cheeks and she laughed, the sound bubbling up, glowing incandescently in the growing twilight. "I'd be honored, kind sir."

I smiled as she took his proffered hand, feeling hope floating again.

Bree turned to watch the pairs partner up. "This is the cutest."

Teddy grinned. "I smell magic in the air. And maybe a little love, too."

Leala stood up and rubbed her temples. "I'm going inside to take something for this headache—maybe a whole bottle of something—then I'm going to get a cocktail. A big one."

That's where Leala had gone wrong—she hadn't been drinking yet. I'd spiked my last glass of sweet tea with bourbon, right after Mama tried to give me brochures on London and talked up all the old family recipes I was bound to find in Europe.

"Oh, a cocktail sounds delightful," Teddy said, hopping up to follow Leala. "Wait for me."

I watched Buzzy and Mama, how their bodies inched closer and closer together as the song went on, and again wondered how love had split them apart when love was supposed to bring people together.

"Why don't Susannah and Leala get along?" Bree asked as she swapped seats, plunking down next to me. "They're both so nice."

I took another sip of my tea, wishing I'd added more bourbon earlier. A lot more. As I watched Mama dance, looking like she fit exactly right in Buzzy's arms, I waffled on what to say. "I think they both want something the other won't give, and that bleeds into how they treat each other. Families are complicated, aren't they?"

Lightning bugs started to flicker along the honeysuckle vines as Uncle Camp dipped Iona, and his face glowed with happiness as she laughed. I hoped they danced the night away, especially after Uncle Camp's comment about not dancing enough in life.

Bree's face wrinkled as she looked across the yard. "Definitely. I've seen it firsthand with my aunts and uncles. But I was super close to my mom." Her voice cracked. "She died a year ago."

The weight of her words hit me full force, knocking the wind out of me. I'd suspected her mama had passed away, but knowing for certain made me ache for her. Losing a parent was beyond tragic. "I'm sorry, Bree. Losing someone you love is so painful, especially a parent."

"It's like what we were all talking about yesterday—how one day you're here, then you're gone. It happened just like that. It was a normal day. Sunny. Beautiful. Mom was gardening, planting daisies, and she disturbed a nest of yellow jackets. We didn't know she was allergic. She died before she even got to the hospital. I didn't get to say goodbye."

"Oh, Bree. I am so, so sorry." I wished I could do more, say more, to ease her pain.

"It was just her and me, too. My dad left when I was just a baby and never came back. She was a teacher, my mom, and my everything. Life hasn't been the same since."

How could it be? "Nobody is the same after experiencing trauma. It changes you, shapes you into a whole different person."

She nodded knowingly. "I just wish my mom could've gotten a second chance, like you did. And Susannah and Leala. And even me."

"You?"

She tilted her face toward me. "When I found my mom lying in the grass, I was blind with panic. As I ran into the house to call 911, I ran right into the glass door, shattering it. I have lots of scars—not just this one on my face. A shard went into my chest. I didn't realize how bad it was, because I was running on adrenaline. I managed to call for help before passing out. I almost died that day, too. Some days I wish I had, but not most days," she added quickly. "I know I'm lucky to be alive. I know my mom would be happy that I'm alive. But why do some people get a second chance at life and others don't?"

I wanted to cry as I grieved a woman I'd never known and the life Bree had lost that day her mother died, because I knew she wasn't the same person she used to be—and would never be her again. "I don't know. I've been asking myself that question for years."

Bree gave me a sad smile. "I mean, at least you got pretty hair. All I got are scars."

I wanted to tell her that I considered my hair a scar as well, but she was so earnest in her compliment that I couldn't bear to shatter the image she held of me. "Scars, yes, but they tell a story of your survival. They're saying you're still here. And as Uncle Camp likes to tell me, being alive is a gift."

Her smile reached her eyes this time. "Leala said something similar, about the stories scars tell. You're lucky to have a sister."

I glanced toward the house, hoping Leala was okay. "I know I am."

As Elvis transitioned to "Don't Be Cruel" and the dancers started fast dancing with wild arm swings and jerky leg movements, Bree said, "We should get a video of this."

"Agreed." I pulled out my phone and started filming, trying not to laugh too hard in order to keep my hand steady. I filmed for a good thirty seconds before switching it off and taking a couple of still shots.

Teddy came out with a cocktail in one hand and Nigel in the other. She grinned at us, then the dance floor, before making her way to the doggy play yard.

Bree and I sat in silence for a while, just watching the show being put on for us, before she said, "Sorry to dump all that on you. About my mom, I mean. I just got to thinking about moms and it all came out."

I glanced at her, hoping she understood how much I appreciated her trust. "You didn't dump anything on me. You shared your story, your pain, and I'm glad you did."

"It does make me feel better. My aunt and uncle—I live with them now—don't like talking about my mom. They say it makes them too sad, but Aunt Teddy doesn't mind."

Lightning bugs flitted around the table. "Well, I'd really like to hear more about your mom, because if she made you, then she was pretty darn special. You know, if you're still up for it, maybe we should make a video about your mom's mac and cheese."

There was a question in her eyes. "But you're leaving."

"I'll stay till Tuesday. And we'll figure out a way to make it work. What do you say?"

She smiled. "I say let's do it. Someone has to teach y'all to make proper mac and cheese."

Laughing, I put an arm around her shoulders, giving her a side hug. "Thank goodness you're here, then."

She hooked a thumb toward the house and stood. "I think I'm going to grab some ice cream and watch Netflix for a while. All this Elvis music is making my head hurt a little."

"Ice cream sounds good to me, too. I'll head in with you." I pushed back my chair and followed her lead. "If you need ibuprofen, Leala probably knows right where it is. And be prepared for her to supervise you taking it."

She laughed as we stepped into the four season room. She quickly scooped a bowl of chocolate fudge ice cream, doused it in rainbow sprinkles, and said, "Thanks for talking with me, Sadie," before heading into the great room and toward the stairs.

"Anytime." I was going to miss her when I left again and made a mental note to stop by to see her if I ever found myself in Indiana.

Leala gave me a smile from the couch in the great room, where she sat with a cocktail in hand and Tucker's head on her thigh. He was sound asleep, Moo wrapped tightly in his arms, and I imagined that as soon as her cup was emptied she'd take him upstairs and tuck him in for the night. Will and Connor were chatting about the upcoming football season, and after having spent most of the day in the kitchen, I was happy to let them finish the cleanup on their own.

I filled a bowl with vanilla ice cream, then added peanuts, maraschino cherries, and M&M'S and stirred it all together. I topped it with homemade whipped cream and fudge sauce and sat in one of the rockers to watch the dance party.

A few minutes later, I heard someone clear his throat. Will leaned against the wall. "Mind if my dishpan hands and I join you?"

I nodded at the rocker next to mine. "Have a seat. You know, there are dish gloves in the cabinet under the sink."

"Now you tell me." He sat and stared at his water-wrinkled fingers. "I'm glad to finally get a minute alone with you." He looked at me head-on, and the party lights lent golden flecks to his eyes. "I owe you an explanation, Sadie."

Maybe it was the bourbon or maybe I just didn't have the energy to pretend not to know what he was talking about. "Yeah, you do."

"Sadie! Sadie, honey!" Mama shouted. "Could you be a dear and bring me some of that fancy water?"

I held in a groan. I'd known she'd try to interrupt us, but I hoped we'd have more time together before she had the chance. "Just a minute, Mama," I yelled back, not taking my eyes from Will.

"I'll just get it myself." Mama hustled inside, Buzzy following close behind, like he was tangled in her wake.

So intent on each other, Iona and Uncle Camp didn't seem to realize they had been left alone on the dance floor. It was as if the rest of the world had ceased to exist, and suddenly I was so very happy that Iona was staying here another week.

Mama poured herself and Buzzy some water and sat down across from me. "Whew, that dancing sure brings on a great thirst."

Buzzy cast me a wary glance as he sat, and I didn't know what to make of it. I'd been indulging my mama and her need to protect me all day, but now I really wanted to hear what Will had to say. I *needed* to hear what Will had to say. I put my ice cream bowl on the side table and turned to him. "Do you want to go for a walk?"

He nodded. "Yeah, I do."

Mama jumped to her feet. "But, Sadie, there's so much to do here still. Cleaning up, prepping for tomorrow. The dining table's not going to set itself."

"It can wait until I get back, Mama."

She squared off against me. "No, I don't think it can."

"Enough, Susannah," Buzzy said, his voice tight with barely restrained anger. He set his glass on the table and stood up. "I thought you might have changed but you haven't. Not one bit. I don't know how you sleep at night."

She poked him in the chest. "Stay out of this."

He stood firm. "I won't. I kept quiet all those years ago, and it's all but eaten me alive."

Leala approached, Connor behind her, his hands resting gently on her arms. She said, "What's going on?"

"Nothing is going on," Mama said.

Buzzy ignored her. "Your mother is trying to keep Sadie and Will apart. Isn't that right, Susannah?"

"Mind your business, Buzzy," Mama warned.

With Nigel tucked into the crook of her arm, Teddy stepped onto the porch with concern flashing in her eyes. Iona and Uncle Camp continued to dance.

Buzzy wasn't deterred. "It's not right. It's not okay. You need to let love run its course and not interfere with it again. Don't you see? You can't stop it. Love always finds a way."

"Again?" I asked. I was so confused, trying to follow what was happening.

Buzzy faced me. "The night you fell in the lake, your mother's wish was that you'd leave Sugarberry Cove, explore the world. She wished it because she knew you had fallen in love with Will and feared you'd end up marrying young and staying right here."

Stunned, my breath caught. She'd *wished* me to leave? My heart broke open, causing tears to gather in my eyes. "Mama, is that true?"

"So what if it is?" she said as defiant as ever. "Look at what you've done with your life, and it never would've happened without that wish. Look at all you've done with A Southern Hankerin'. It's a bright spot this world needs! So, no, I'm not the least bit sorry for my wish. You never would've left otherwise. You'd have stayed right here and settled down."

"You don't know that," I said, the words raw, strained.

"I surely did! I saw it in the way you looked at Will. I see it in the way you still look at him." Her gaze shifted to Will. "I adore Will, I truly do, but you have so much more to explore in this world, Sadie Way. Being tied down will only stifle your creativity. You have too much to do still. Too many stories to tell."

Suddenly dizzy, my head spinning, I could hear in my head Buzzy talking about how love had been the reason he and Mama had broken up. It hadn't been their love. It had been my love for Will.

"Oh my God," Leala murmured. "You haven't been shielding Sadie from Will this weekend because of her broken heart; you've been trying to keep them apart because you want Sadie to leave again!"

Tears clouded my vision, and I felt someone take my hand, squeeze it. Will. I looked at our entwined hands. A Will and a Way. My gaze lifted to meet his, and the compassion in his eyes made me hurt all that much more.

"Not a word out of you," Mama said to Leala. "You need to own your part in this. Getting married so young—giving Sadie ideas and almost ruining her chance to see the world, to be free."

Leala looked like she'd been slapped. "Seeing the world is what *you* want, not Sadie! *You* want to be free. Of this cottage, of responsibility, of Sadie and me!"

I felt all kinds of a fool for ever thinking Mama had been trying to protect me, my heart. A tear fell, sliding down my cheek, and suddenly it felt like I was floating underwater, the words around me distant, resonant.

"Don't you spin this around," Mama snapped. "This is about Sadie and Sadie alone."

"Exactly my point," Buzzy said, his eyes filled with exasperation.

"It's Sadie's life, Sadie's choice. It's wrong of you to use a wish against her."

Mama swung her arms around dramatically, and the water sloshed out of the glass she held. "*I'm* her mama. I know what's best for—"

Wincing, Mama abruptly stopped talking. She let out a low moan, and the glass slipped from her fingers and shattered on the porch floor. She grabbed her left shoulder and sagged lifelessly, and Buzzy caught her in his arms before she hit the ground.

Chapter 16

Leala

The scent of coffee coaxed me awake, and I rolled to see the clock on the bedside table. It was a little after six in the morning. Tucker's small body curled next to mine, his breaths even and deep. Trying not to disturb him, I slowly sat up. Across the room, the sheet covering Connor had twisted around his body, leaving his back exposed. His usually tight muscles had relaxed with sleep. He had his head half-buried under a pillow, and a floor fan stirred the hair at the nape of his neck.

I wanted nothing more than to slip in beside him, wrap my arms around him, and just *be*. I wanted to feel his warmth, his strength, and absorb it. Overriding all that, however, was my sense of responsibility. I'd promised Bree and Teddy a yoga class this morning, and though I had the feeling they'd understand if I canceled, *I* needed the class more than ever today. To center myself. To find balance and peace in all this chaos and confusion.

Connor's alarm would wake him soon enough and then he'd head home to shower and dress for work. He couldn't take another day off—his boss had made that clear when Connor had called him last night from the hospital. After being unavailable for the last three days, if Connor didn't show up today, he was told he should consider looking for another position. It had been a warning, plain and simple.

And while I didn't view Connor looking for another position as much of a threat, Connor had about come undone over the possibility of being fired. He'd worked too long, too hard, he'd said, to be walked out of the building in shame flanked by security guards.

As quietly as I could, I gathered my yoga clothes and tiptoed out of the bedroom and into the bathroom next door. I dressed quickly and brushed my teeth. As I combed my hair, pulling it up into a tight bun, I tried not to look in the mirror. There was too much sadness staring back at me, too many questions, too much *everything* swirling in the milky gray.

There was no perky motivational saying to lift my mood or

bolster my spirit. There were no words right now to bring peace to my soul. I felt lost. Adrift. Floating in a life that didn't feel like my own.

I walked past the closed door of Mother's room, then down one flight of stairs, then another. Pausing on the lower landing, I was heartened briefly by the early sunbeams shining through the clear glass of the clean window. The sun had risen. Life went on. Today was a new day.

The sunlight accented the newly painted staircase wall, and for a rush job, I had to admit it had come out pretty darn well. The trim still needed touching up, but there was time. Plenty of time now that Sadie and I would be here at the cottage for a while.

"Morning," she said from the kitchen, her voice low in deference to those still sleeping. "Coffee?"

"Please." I came down the rest of the steps, noting the folded blanket and pillow on the couch. Sadie had declined to spend the night in Mother's room without her there. "Did you sleep okay?"

Her silvery hair was swept back off her face and twisted into a long braid that had been pulled forward to hang over her right shoulder. Smudges of purplish darkness colored the skin beneath her blue, bloodshot eyes, and the pink in her cheeks told the story of too much time in the sun yesterday. "No. Did you?"

Smiling sadly, I took the mug she offered and poured in a splash of cream. The colors swirled together as I stirred. "No."

The sliding door on the back porch was opened wide, and Sadie had a few of the windows open as well. Dewy grass sparkled, and sunlight glinted off the lake, promising a beautiful summer day.

By the time we'd arrived home last night from the hospital at nearly midnight, the dining table on the porch had been set, and there had been a batch of popovers and a coffee cake on the counter along with a sweet note from Teddy, Bree, and Iona. Banding together to prep for the breakfast service had been a kind, thoughtful gesture, and I was beyond grateful, even though Mother would probably have herself yet another heart attack if she knew guests had taken over running the cottage in our absence.

Holding a mug to her lips, Sadie spoke over its curved rim. "I called the hospital earlier. Mama's stable. She's running a low-grade fever but the nurse assured me it wasn't anything to be worried about."

Stable was good. Stable was great. Stable was not *dead*.

Swallowing back a rush of emotion, I stared into my coffee cup and blinked away a sudden wash of tears. Last night when Mother had collapsed, I thought she was gone, lost forever, but there had been a pulse beating faintly. So faintly. Sadie had run for Mother's nitroglycerin pills, and I had tried simply not to fall apart. The wait for the EMTs had seemed endless, but eventually they arrived and whisked her away. I'd left Tuck in the care of Uncle Camp, and then Sadie, Connor, Buzzy, and I had rushed to the hospital. The trip had been a blur, as I fought tears and regrets the entire drive.

"I'm sure she'll be bossing the doctors around in no time flat," Sadie added on the tail end of a yawn.

Feeling like I carried the weight of the world, I sat heavily on a counter stool. Sadie had already dressed the peninsula for breakfast using Mother's favorite runner, a brilliantly colored patterned cloth printed with blue, pink, and green birds. "No doubt."

At the hospital, as Mother had waited to be wheeled away for an angiogram, she had been awake—groggy, but awake. Sadie had held one of her hands, I'd held the other, and Buzzy and Connor had hovered nervously nearby. Mother hadn't said much at all in those intense moments, except to elicit a promise from Sadie and me to keep the cottage up and running until she could do it herself.

I'd have promised her the moon at that point—and would have found a way, some way, to give it to her.

When the tech had wheeled her away, my and Sadie's *I love you*s had drifted in her wake, echoing in the sterile hallway, sounding hollow. I wasn't sure Mother even heard them, but they'd been spoken. The emergency angiogram had turned into an emergency angioplasty when the doctor determined she needed two coronary stents placed immediately. Sadie, Connor, and I had stayed until she was out of danger and housed in a private room in the cardiac care unit. Hospital recovery for the type of procedure she'd had was usually only a couple of days; it was likely Mother would be home midweek.

Buzzy had stayed with Mother, promising not to leave her side until he was convinced she'd be just fine or she threw him out, whichever came first. I was personally surprised that kicking him out hadn't been the first thing she'd done since he'd ratted her out, but she'd seemed comforted by his presence. Sadie and I were going to visit her tonight, and when we did, I wasn't sure what I was going to say or how I was going to say it.

At the first sounds of the loon's morning lament, Sadie and I rushed to the window over the kitchen sink, watching and listening in silence as she glided past the dock and out of sight. I felt like crying right along with her this morning, all my emotions floating too close to the surface.

Mother and I didn't have the best relationship, but I loved her, and when she'd collapsed last night, I couldn't bear thinking that was how we ended, with sharp jabs and biting remarks and hurt feelings. If she had died, I wouldn't have been able to forgive myself.

Yet now in the light of morning and reality and truth, I didn't know how to fix what was broken. Years and years of wounds had to be patched up, stitched together, *healed*. It seemed an insurmountable task, and I had no idea where to begin. With a heavy heart, I sat back down.

Sadie continued to stare out the window, lost in her own thoughts. After Mother's collapse, there had been no more talk about the wish Mother had made eight years ago. There had been very little talking at all as we drifted, lost in a sea of worry.

But now—now there were things that needed to be said. Things that should've been talked about a long time ago. Holding the warm mug between my hands, I swallowed back all the reasons I'd ever kept quiet and said, "It was me, Sadie. It was my wish that made you fall into the lake that night. Not Mother's. Mine. It's why I had trouble looking at your hair initially—because it was a constant reminder of how utterly selfish I had been. I didn't think of the repercussions of my wish—I just made it. Don't blame Mother. It's not her fault, even if Buzzy thinks it is. I'm so sorry."

As Sadie turned toward me, the overhead light caught on the sparkles in her hair, making it seem like tiny fairy lights had been woven into the strands. She sighed deeply. "It wasn't your wish, either. It was mine."

I shook my head. "No, stop that. It was mine. Just let me own up to it, Sadie Way."

She smiled at the usage of her full name. "You weren't the only one utterly selfish. I wished that you and Connor wouldn't get married the next day. I wanted to stop the wedding any way possible. And because I was in the hospital, you two postponed the wedding and ended up eloping. It was *my* wish that came true. I'm sorry, Leala Clare."

Her words wound through me, remarkably painless since she'd already confessed her jealousy of Connor and our relationship. I'd known then that she hadn't wanted me to marry Connor. "That wish truly doesn't surprise me. That night on the dock, I sat with Connor feeling so lost in the world, that the people I loved most were being so hateful and hurtful. I wanted you and Mama to love Connor like I did. And that night, as you kept your distance and Mother was so passive-aggressively civil, I imagined my wedding, walking down the aisle to Connor's side, with you walking ahead of me, snarling, and Mother standing with a fake, strained smile on her face, and I wished—" I took a deep breath. "I wished that you two wouldn't be at the wedding. I realized I didn't want you there. I didn't want to get married surrounded by such hate. So, you see, my wish came true, too. Because Connor and I did elope without you two there. But I never, ever, in my wildest dreams imagined my wish would cause you harm. I'm sorry, Sadie."

A tear leaked from the corner of her eye as she held my gaze, and I stood up and met her at the end of the peninsula for a hug, and it felt so natural and strange at the same time. We hadn't hugged like this in years.

"I'm so sorry that I didn't realize how hurt you were by my relationship with Connor. Looking back, I can see now that I'd distanced myself. I didn't know it then, or maybe I just didn't want to admit it. You had every right to be angry."

"Maybe not that angry," she said lightly. "Forgive me?"

"Only if you forgive me, too."

"Deal," she whispered, then pulled back and wiped her eyes. "Maybe all our wishes came true that night—yours, mine, and Mama's. A triple whammy of selfishness. All this time I've been wondering why I'd been saved, but now I wonder if it was to show us just how precious life is and to not take each other for granted—but we were all too caught up in our emotions, in our selfishness, to see it back then."

I grabbed hold of her hands and held them tightly. "We see it now."

The sadness in her gaze nearly broke me. "You and I see it now," she said softly.

She didn't need to state the obvious—that Mother didn't see it and wasn't likely to.

At the sound of footsteps above our heads she sighed. "That'll be one of your yoga students. I should get the coffee cake warming and get to work on breakfast."

"Breakfast can wait," I said. "Why don't you join us? Stretch the body, heal the mind."

For a second I thought she was going to say yes, but she shook her head, and her braid fell from her shoulder and swung loosely across her back. "Thanks all the same, but I think I need the peace that comes from the kitchen this morning more than anything at all."

"I'll stay and help. I can crack eggs fairly well."

"No, no. Go on. Stretch *your* body, heal your mind. Not all nourishment comes from food."

I hated to leave her, not when we'd just found each other again. Really found each other. But I remembered that life went on. Today was a new day. I wasn't going to lose her again. "You know where to find me."

She smiled. "Always."

The early morning breeze skimmed the lake, gently rippling the water and carrying on it a whisper of pine from trees that dotted the shoreline. Teddy walked by my side, her flip-flops smacking on the dock. Her teased hair was swept back in a claw clip, and she wore a simple outfit of white twill shorts and a black tank top. A slight cigarette scent floated around her, and I suspected she had sneaked out of the cottage to stress-smoke in the wee hours of the night.

"I didn't have the heart to wake her," Teddy said. "She was sleeping so peacefully, and peace is just what she needs right now. She has such a gentle soul. A broken but gentle soul."

Bree and Nigel were sleeping in this morning, and I didn't blame them. Sleep was where I found the most peace, especially when I dreamed of nothing at all.

At the end of the dock, I unrolled my mat. "Her spirit shows in all she does. From her manners to the way she interacts with Tucker to her sweet smile."

"Last night brought back a whole host of emotions for her."

Teddy stepped out of her flip-flops and snapped open her towel, laying it gently onto the wooden planks. "With the ambulance and all."

"I can only imagine." Sadie had told me some of Bree's history, sharing how she'd acquired her scars. It had all but shattered what was left of my already broken heart. She'd survived so much at such a young age, and it was no wonder she was so shy. Yet, she hadn't given up on life. She had opened up to Sadie and me, and her love for Teddy was obvious. It was inspiring, her determination to keep moving forward and not live in the past with all her pain.

Teddy sat down and crossed her legs at the ankles. "She's really struggled this year. Dealing with her grief, her injuries, leaving the only home she's ever known, going to a new school in a different town. My nephew and his wife were granted guardianship of Bree and have done everything they can to try to help her, but with a family of their own, which includes three little ones, it's been a lot to take on, and they've been butting heads with Bree some. Plus, it pains them to talk about what happened to Bree's mama, and so she holds a lot in, when she ought to be talking it out. It's why I offered to have Bree stay with me for the summer—so they could all get a little break. Plus, I thought a little lake magic could only help with Bree's healing, and it's done just that. Being at the lake has been good for her. She's been happy here."

"Is it being near the lake?" I asked, getting comfortable on my mat. "Or is it being with you? Have you thought about having her come live with you? Might be a better fit for her, emotionally. And maybe for you, too."

"Oh, no." She waved her hand in dismissal. "It's a nice thought but impossible. I don't want to start a family war with my nephew. Plus, Bree's not going to want to live with Old Lady Aldridge. She's eighteen. She should be with younger folk. Flying free, as your mama would say."

"Maybe she doesn't want to fly," I offered, hoping she heard me. Really heard me. Not only the words but the meaning. "Maybe Bree wants to stay right where she is, with you. You should ask her what she wants. And maybe your nephew would be agreeable. After all, you mentioned they were butting heads. Plus, she's eighteen and likely doesn't need his permission anymore."

In Alabama, the age of adulthood was nineteen, but it was

probably eighteen in Indiana where Bree was from. If so, she could likely make her own choice where she wanted to live, even though she still had a year left of high school.

Teddy's green eyes darkened as looked out over the water and took a deep breath. "My studio apartment is too small. I'm not sure I can earn enough to support the two of us. What do I know about home schooling? I'm *old*."

"Sixty is not old."

"Says the thirty-year-old."

Smiling, I said, "If it's meant to be, it'll be. Think about it."

"Oh, to have that kind of faith in life." She drew in a deep breath. "What happens if I get too attached? And then she's off to college and I'm all alone again?"

It suddenly occurred to me that Teddy might have commitment issues. If so, no wonder she'd never been able to find love. She'd probably kept pushing it away out of fear. "There's a saying from the Dalai Lama. It goes something like, *Give them roots to come back, wings to fly, reasons to stay.* But you have to be able to give them a home in your heart first of all."

"My old heart," she said on a sigh.

"Which still works," I pointed out, injecting a little of my mother's drama into my tone. "Now, come on—let's start with the mountain pose." Fitting, since she was being stubborn as a rock. We went through a series of stretches in silence before I said, "Thanks again for helping out last night."

"I wish there was more we could've done." Water slapped against the dock as she bent low. "I'm going over to the hospital later this afternoon to visit with Susannah. Maybe sneak her some bourbon."

She grinned to let me know she was joking. Or at least I hoped she was joking.

"She'll like seeing you." Not only because she loved being the center of attention, but because she loved Teddy. "You're a good friend to her."

"She's a good friend to me. You girls know a different Susannah than I do, and I wish to the heavens that you knew mine."

I wished it, too, and I hated wishes.

"She's funny and creative, bold and generous. I've leaned on her more times than I can count. Looking for true love weighs on a person over time. Just trust me on that."

"I will," I promised solemnly.

As she turned her head to look at me, the sun glinted in her eyes, and the color reminded me of the morning's dewy grass. "I hope y'all find your way back to each other."

"Thanks, Teddy. I hope so, too." I truly did. I was going to try my best to do my part.

"And you'll tell Bree and me if you want us to pack up and leave, right? I know that's not what Susannah wants, but I want to know what you want, Leala."

To ease the knot in my shoulders, I reached down and touched my toes. "I want you to stay. Sadie does, too. And Mother would check herself out of the hospital and drag you back here if you left, so it's settled. You're staying."

She laughed, a throaty, rich sound. "All right, it's settled."

When the sliding screen door squeaked, I looked back at the cottage. Apparently my squeak-proofing treatment had already worn off. Iona stepped out, and she waved before sitting down at the patio table with a mug and a book, and we waved back.

A flock of birds flew overhead, their dark bodies a stark contrast to the white clouds above them. "You ready to try the boat pose? Seems appropriate out here on the lake."

Teddy smiled. "Yep. Let's keep stretching these old bones."

And maybe, I thought, along the way, she'd stretch her heart to let someone else in, because I knew it was more than big enough.

Chapter 17

Sadie

Uncle Camp shuffled down the hallway, bleary-eyed and bedraggled. "Not used to staying up past my bedtime. Apparently this old man needs his beauty sleep," he joked as he headed for the coffeepot. Then he added, "But I'm guessin' it was a rough night for all."

"You're as handsome as ever." I pushed the jar of sorghum syrup toward him. "And last night was one I'd rather forget altogether, honestly."

He'd slept in a bit, and I was glad for it, since he'd had such a late night. Leala and Teddy were still on the dock, and Iona was out on the patio, having drifted through the kitchen a few minutes ago. Everyone else was still in bed.

"I don't be blaming you for that." His hand wobbled as he spooned the syrup into his coffee and took a sip. "No one makes coffee as good as you."

I laughed and capped the sorghum syrup, which I'd never cared too much for, preferring sugar. "You're the one who taught me."

The lines around his eyes bunched together as he smiled. "You done one-upped me somehow. Whippersnapper."

Coffee seemed such a simple drink to make. A few scoops of ground beans, some hot water, and there it was. But when Uncle Camp taught me, he made it seem as though it were the most important recipe I'd ever learn. I'd been just twelve years old.

The original recipe had come from his mama, my great-granny, and had primarily consisted of chicory grounds with a little bit of coffee thrown in, and according to him it's what had cleared the hair straight off his head. He'd told me all about how she drank it using the saucered-and-blowed method, popular way, way back, when coffee was usually boiled in a tin pot on a woodstove. She'd pour the brew from a cup into a saucer, which she then would hold to her lips to blow across it, cooling it enough to drink straight out of the saucer. To cut the bitterness, she'd add a dollop of sorghum syrup, a habit that Uncle Camp had adopted somewhere along the way.

I'd listened enrapt, because rare were the moments Uncle Camp shared personal family stories, and his were like treasures I hoarded to be brought out and oohed and aahed over when I needed something beautiful to cheer me up.

My heart full of love for him, I said, "How would you feel about doing a piece for A Southern Hankerin' about making coffee?"

Over the years I'd tweaked my great-granny's coffee recipe to fit my taste buds, since her version had been much too strong. I used three parts coffee grounds to one part chicory grounds, a blend that to me was just right but was still too strong for others—like Bree, who'd had to use a lot of sugar to sweeten it up.

He chuckled. "Everyone's got their own way of making coffee. They don't need to hear ours."

"I know, but it's not really about the recipe, is it? I think people would like learning about Great-Granny and her saucers and how you use sorghum syrup as a sweetener. It's a charming throwback, and I know my viewers will love you as much as I do." I held up praying hands and gave him the biggest smile I had. "It won't be anytime soon. Maybe in the fall."

There was a decidedly dubious look in his eyes when he spoke. "All right, Sadie Way. For you, I'll do it. Put me on your schedule."

"Thank you!" I threw my arms around him.

"Sweet-talker," he mumbled under his breath as he hugged me back then stepped away to top off his cup.

The first time I'd made coffee with him was when the idea of keeping these family stories, these food memories, had taken root. I'd always thought I'd write a book about them one day, but it wasn't until the day I'd come home from the hospital after my accident that my mind shifted to filming the stories instead. That day, Uncle Camp had served me up a bowl of corn fritters drizzled in honey—his go-to recipe when we were ill—and told me how he'd once made corn fritters for my daddy when he was little and had been down and out with chicken pox. He'd laughed and laughed as he shared how at one point Daddy had used a fritter to scratch an itch. The story had made me smile, the first in days. I'd *felt* the story. It had lifted me out of a funk, at least for a little while. And I recalled wishing I had a video camera to capture Uncle Camp's facial expressions and humorous pauses. That story had been the start of A Southern Hankerin', the seed.

After I dropped out of college, it had taken months on the

road working odd jobs to save enough to buy a decent camera. I'd started seeking out those kinds of uplifting stories, those food memories, wherever I could find them. Coworkers indulged me at first, but then word of mouth took over, and the rest was history.

If I hadn't left Sugarberry Cove, would I have done A Southern Hankerin'? I wasn't sure. Maybe. The seed had been there, after all. But it definitely wouldn't be what it was now. I wouldn't have traveled. And if Will had asked me to stay in town that day I told him of my plans to leave, I would have stayed, despite my feelings of failure and my search for purpose. Because I'd loved him.

"You doin' okay over there?" Uncle Camp asked.

I pulled puff pastry dough from the fridge, where it had been defrosting, along with red and yellow peppers, and a flat of eggs, and set it all on the prep island. Savory puff pastry tarts were on the menu this morning. "Just thinking about things I haven't considered in a long time."

"Taking a hard walk down memory lane, are you? Looking back can be painful. Too painful to even talk about sometimes."

"Yep," I agreed, reaching for a bowl.

"But sometimes, it's a beautiful walk."

I let out a sigh. "Not today."

He topped off his mug. "History shapes us, molds us, forms us. You're where you are now because of where you've been and the choices you've made. You have to ask yourself, Am I happy? Because if not, every day is a new day to start over."

Was I happy? It suddenly seemed a complicated question. "I'm not unhappy. I'm just . . ." I wrinkled my nose. I couldn't find the words for how I felt right now. There was too much spinning around, like a tornado had uprooted all my emotions. "I don't know."

The spoon clinked against the ceramic mug as he swirled it around the dark coffee. "Life's too short to not be living it exactly the way you want it. You have the power to make the changes, the choices."

"It's not that easy, Uncle Camp."

"All I'm saying, darlin', is that the decisions you make today affect your tomorrows. Choose carefully."

We chatted for a while about Mama, her condition, and when she might be home, before he glanced at the glowing clock on the microwave. "Hardware store's opening about now. I'm going to make a run over there. I thought I'd take a page from your book and touch up the paint on the front porch. Give Susannah a pretty welcome home."

The front porch desperately needed tending to. "I can help you after my morning chores."

He grinned. "I was hoping you'd offer so I didn't have to beg."

"You never have to beg. I'm right here if you need me." But the words sounded hollow to my own ears, especially since I would be leaving again soon.

"Can't say I'm disappointed you'll be staying awhile longer, even though the reason why ain't the best."

If I was being honest with myself, I wasn't disappointed, either, though I knew my delayed departure was going to make saying goodbye that much more difficult. From the hospital last night, I'd called and postponed my trip to Georgia indefinitely and canceled my hotel reservations. I couldn't leave before I was certain Mama was up and around and well cared for. I'd also taken the time to add Connor's phone number to my phone, and he'd added mine to his. I'd been oddly emotional over the exchange of numbers. It represented so much more than it appeared.

But since I was staying for a while, one thing needed to be changed around here immediately: the Wi-Fi situation. I planned to call the cable company as soon as the breakfast service was over.

Uncle Camp headed for the petty cash tin, an old cookie container, and when he opened it, he was surprised to see it stuffed full of money. "What in the blazes?"

To be exact, there was $300 in small bills in the tin. I knew, because I'd been the one to put them in there yesterday. I always kept a good amount of cash on me when I traveled, hidden away here and there in my car, my luggage, my makeup bag. Right now the cottage needed the money more than I did.

"Do you know anything about this?" he asked, tipping the tin toward me.

"No, sir. I surely don't." I took a leisurely sip of coffee.

He stared long and hard, let out a guffaw that told me he knew I was lying, and kissed my cheek on his way to the front door.

A moment later, I heard footsteps on the stairs. Connor and Tucker were heading down, and by the look of it, Tucker didn't seem too pleased with the early wakeup.

"Coffee to go?" I asked Connor.

"Thanks, Sadie. I'd really appreciate it."

I poured coffee into a paper cup, snapped a lid on it, and added a protective sleeve. I handed it to Connor and said, "Good morning, Tucker."

He turned his face ever so slightly and gave me a half smile. Progress!

"Moo?" he asked, holding him out to me.

I threw a questioning glance at Connor, who gave me a shrug.

I took Moo from Tuck's hand and held the stuffed animal up to my face. "Good morning, Moo. Would you like some warm milk?" I winced. "Do cows drink milk? Seems all kinds of wrong."

Connor laughed. "Calves do."

"That makes sense. Can you tell I didn't grow up anywhere near a farm?"

"I've got you covered," he said as he looked outside toward the end of the dock, seeming pensive, worried. Leala had told me about his job being threatened, and I felt for him.

"Moo milk!" Tuck said, his smile wide. "Sadie, Moo milk."

A happy warmth flowed through me with how he spoke my name. I grabbed the milk from the fridge, poured it into a mug, and stuck it in the microwave. "Conner, you can leave Tuck in here with me. I know you have to get going."

"Thanks," he said, "but last night Leala asked me to bring him out to her when he woke up, since he was asleep when we got back."

Mama's words about Leala having separation anxiety rang through my head, and I smiled at the accuracy, even though I understood why Leala was the way she was. I put the cap on the sippy cup, pretended to let Moo hold it, then handed both to Tucker.

"*Tank* you."

"You're welcome, Tuck. And Moo."

Connor gave me a smile before heading outside. I heard "Noni!" float through the door before it squeaked shut, and I went to the pantry to grab two onions and a dozen cherry tomatoes from their bins for the tarts. I opened the spice cabinet, and as I eyed the dried herbs that Leala had organized yesterday by alphabetical order, I wished I had fresh herbs. My gaze drifted from the bottled spices out the window, narrowing on Buzzy's yard. He had to have an herb garden.

Even though he'd given me permission to make use of his garden, I still felt a little like I was planning a great heist as I preheated the oven, grabbed the kitchen shears and a small bowl, and headed outside to forage.

I stepped onto the patio and took a deep breath of the fresh, albeit humid, air, of the lake magic, scented with pine and possibilities. Rippling water glittered and glistened. I fought the urge to sprint down the dock and dive into the water and just float. Float all my troubles away.

"It's a lovely morning, isn't it?" Iona asked, smiling at me from one of the padded Adirondack chairs, where her mug was perched on a sturdy arm.

The patio was still in shadow, the sun not quite high enough to cast its full light behind the cottage. With the bowl cradled in my arms, I stepped over to her. "It really is."

She looked out at the water. "The morning after a storm tends to be the most beautiful."

I knew she wasn't talking about the weather. "Hopefully the worst has passed."

"Damage done is damage done, but careful rebuilding can lead to something stronger than before, something that can withstand the storms."

"How do you rebuild?" I asked, suddenly unsure. My mother had wished me away from the place I loved most in the world. From the people I loved most in the world. And worse, I had gone.

"Start with the foundation, shore it up good. You'll find your way after that. You have to trust the process."

The foundation. Our family core. Mama, Leala, me.

My mind went back to the mandala, to those twisted hearts.

After all this time, was it possible to open up our hearts to each other again?

More than anything, I wished we could.

Wished it with my whole heart.

Breakfast had been served and cleaned up, a harder task than usual with Tucker under foot. Bree had kept him entertained by playing peekaboo for a while, but eventually she, Teddy, Nigel, and Iona headed for town.

Uncle Camp had returned from the hardware store and was

busy on the front porch with a sander, scuffing off loose paint from the rails. My head was spinning with all there was to be done today, but I was determined to do it quickly so I could get out there to help him.

Leala and Tuck headed upstairs to start our housekeeping chores, where I planned to join them after I made a call to the cable company to add internet service to the cottage. I popped into Mama's office to use the phone and felt only a twinge of guilt as I pretended to be her when I spoke to the cable company representative and scored an appointment tomorrow afternoon for the internet installation, a small miracle.

I couldn't imagine Mama would stay angry with me for long once she discovered what I'd done, not with her enthusiasm for my work, which I'd be sure to play up when she found out. I'd asked the rep to change the account settings to automatically withdraw monthly payments from a new checking account—mine. I would cover the entire internet *and* cable bill for its contractual obligation of a year, at which time there would have to be a conversation about whether to keep the internet or cancel it. By that point I hoped Mama would have learned to love the internet and all it could do for the business, because she needed its help if the stack of bills on her desk was any indication.

I flipped through a few of the statements to see if any other than the electric bill was overdue and found her truck payment was also late. Noise from overhead tore me away from further inspection of the stack as guilt set in that I wasn't pulling my share of the housekeeping duties.

Snatching up the phone, I quickly dialed the number on the electric bill, pressed the appropriate key specified for payments, and paid the amount in full. I did the same for the truck debt. I'd come back later to check the rest of the bills—if Leala didn't beat me to it.

I could hear a murmured conversation between Leala and Tuck as I pulled open the door, looked both ways, and tiptoed out, closing the door behind me, as if Mama were here and might catch me in the act. I rounded the corner to head upstairs and came face-to-face with Will, who was coming inside, a bucket in hand.

"Hey," he said, his brown eyes full of warmth.

I'd forgotten he'd be back this morning to continue his renovation work. Happy that I hadn't tripped when I saw him, I stuck my hands in my pockets, then pulled them out again and clasped them together. "Hi."

Awkwardness swirled around us, invisibly holding us in place. In my head, all I could hear was my mama noting the way I looked at Will, and I forced myself to maintain eye contact, though all I really wanted to do was look at my feet. I tried to ignore completely how she'd announced to him and all gathered that I loved him.

While it was true, I'd never told him so. All I wanted to do right now was melt into the flooring and roll away with my embarrassment.

"Camp sent me text messages last night, keeping me updated about Susannah's condition. I'm glad she came through her procedure without any troubles. How's she doing today?"

"She's doing well. The doctor said she should be able to come home on Wednesday, barring any unforeseen complications. Leala and I are going to see her tonight, after Connor gets off work. You know, so he can stay here with Tuck. Mama's made us promise to run the cottage while she's laid up."

I was rambling, oversharing like Mama. I stuck my hands in my pockets again and gave in to the need to look downward, away from his face, his eyes, and the strong urge to step into his arms for a long hug.

His bucket was full of tools for laying tile. Notched and smooth trowels, sponges, and some doohickey that looked like the tooth extractor Hermey used on Bumble in *Rudolph the Red-Nosed Reindeer.*

Now even my thoughts were rambling. Where was Leala when I needed her most, to save me from this mortification?

"So you're staying," he said. "That's good to know."

I glanced up. Bright spots of hope shined in his eyes, and it was impossible to look away. "I'm staying until she's strong enough to take over running the cottage again."

I didn't even want to guess how long that would take or why the hope in his eyes filled me with hope, too. Hope for what? Whatever we had was long over, but even as I said the words to myself, I knew I didn't believe them. Whatever we'd had so long ago was still there, sitting on my heart, silently waiting for me to acknowledge that it had never gone away. It had faded, perhaps, but never died. Since being near him again it had flared to life, bright and proud and wanting to be shouted to anyone who'd listen. I forced myself to tune it out.

He shifted the bucket to his other hand. "I was wanting to talk to you."

I inwardly cringed. Last night he'd wanted to give me an explanation as to why he'd cut me loose, but now that he knew I'd loved him . . . I didn't think I could sit through the conversation. The last thing I needed was for him to realize that I loved him still. Despite the heartache. Despite the desertion. The love was still there, lying dormant, waiting to be watered to come fully alive again.

"About the guest rooms," he added, easily reading me.

"Oh?" I perked up. "What about them?"

"I was thinking to hire on a few extra hands to get the job done by Thursday. That way the rooms can be rented out for the festival."

"Okay. Sounds good to me."

He held up a hand. "Before you agree, it's not covered by insurance. It'll cost extra. You might want to run the numbers by Susannah. She's been concerned about overages."

"Have there been many overages?"

"Some," he said. "The plumbing all needed updating, and tile's more expensive than the linoleum that was in there—things like that aren't budgeted by the insurance adjuster."

Bracing myself, I asked, "How're you being paid?"

"The insurance money covered almost everything up front. I've been running a tab for the overages."

A tab. Have mercy. As I thought about the bills on Mama's desk, I waged an inner battle. "How long will it take you to get the rooms done on your own, doing what you've been doing?"

"Sunday or Monday. I was cutting it close, working overtime at Susannah's request. But I missed out on most of last Friday, because Camp wanted the cottage quiet for Susannah when she came home, and then she had me take this past weekend off."

Right. So she could keep us separated.

Casting aside the churning sense of betrayal, I said, "So either we hire extra help or the rooms aren't finished for the festival."

"Right."

"Could you finish one room in time? On your own, I mean."

He studied my face, searching for something I wasn't sure he found. "Tight timeline but I think so."

I hadn't come across Mama's checkbook during my quick look at her desk, but I could only imagine how low the balance was.

While I didn't mind paying any overages from my own account, I was pushing my luck where her finances were concerned. Mama didn't like handouts. I didn't want to cause her more stress when she came home from the hospital to find a whole renovation crew had invaded her home—and then risk her getting anxious about how she was going to pay for the extra labor. She needed to stay calm, which would have been a lot to ask even before her heart had become a concern. "Focus on one room. It's better than none."

He nodded. "Then I better get to work."

I pointed upstairs. "Me, too."

We stood, unmoving, looking at each other as if not wanting to stop. Finally, I forced myself to move toward the steps, away from him, away from the past, away from wishing for things that were impossible.

Chapter 18

Leala

By five o'clock, I was ready for a three-day nap. Bone-weary exhaustion had planted me on the top step of the front porch, where I'd been painting a newel post for fifteen minutes. If anyone had noticed my lack of progress, they didn't comment. I wouldn't have been the least bit surprised if moss had started to grow on my shoes.

The brim of a bucket hat hung low over Tuck's eyes as he sat on the thick grass along the edge of the walkway. He dipped a clean paintbrush into a pail of water and swished it across the bluestone pathway, his designs wild, carefree, and temporary. He looked up and exclaimed for at least the hundredth time, "Mama, I paint!"

Fighting a yawn, I smiled. "You're doing a great job, too."

Unlike me.

I'd hit the proverbial wall just after three. Tuck had once again skipped his nap, and he'd been clingy as Sadie and I had tackled the chores throughout the house, including dusting and vacuuming all the common areas, cleaning out the fridge and pantry, taking two reservations for next month, fielding calls from neighbors offering well-wishes for Mother, accepting more deliveries of flowers, and helping Uncle Camp paint the porch.

Connor was due back at six, and then Sadie and I would head to the hospital to see Mother, which was bound to be emotionally draining. I was in desperate need of a second wind.

"Bee, I paint!" Tuck cried.

He'd started calling Bree "Bee" this morning, which was a sight better than "Owie," which he had been calling her most of yesterday. It was as if he, too, had stopped seeing her scars after getting to know her.

"Can you paint a dog?" she asked him.

She sat alongside him on the grass and had been out here with us since returning from town earlier, keeping him occupied with water painting and dandelions and bumblebees.

I had been so grateful I could've cried.

For my part, keeping Tuck entertained throughout the day had been a lesson in creativity and humility. He had helped dust rooms by plucking a feather duster and rolling his tiny self under the beds, out of reach of my hands. He'd helped clean bathrooms by unrolling toilet paper and piling it in the bathtubs. He'd helped collect laundry by emptying the linen closet of clean towels and sheets. He'd helped put fresh flowers in the guest rooms by filling vases with dirty bucket water.

At home we had a set routine, but here it was a free-for-all, and I was feeling like I was doing a lousy job as a mom since it seemed all I'd been doing was redirecting, correcting, corralling, protecting, reprimanding. It weighed on me, bogging me down.

If I needed a moment to myself at home, I could leave Tuck in the living room, propped in front of the TV to watch his favorite shows. Or on the floor to play with his favorite toys. Here, I couldn't leave him alone for a second. It was too risky with people coming and going, with no childproofing in the cottage whatsoever, and, of course, the threat of the lake, where one wrong step could lead to tragedy. He could float and kick like a pro but always had floaties or a life vest on while in our pool at home. And there were no toys here except for Uncle Camp's jacks and Moo, who was now in the washer after taking a swim in one of the toilets.

"I can!" He loaded his brush with water, splashed the stone, and watched it darken as the water absorbed. He pointed at the creation. "I do!"

Teddy had gone off to the hospital to visit Mama, and Iona was inside with a new book to read but kept popping onto the porch to check our progress and smile at Uncle Camp, which was all kinds of adorable. Sadie was painting spindles at one end of the porch, and Uncle Camp was doing the same on the other side.

"What a cute doggy," Bree said, studying the splotch of water with great intensity; then she reached out to tickle him. "He's gonna get you. Woof, woof."

Tuck fell backward, giggling.

Nigel, who'd been lounging in the shade, his belly to the sky, rolled over and looked around like he'd missed something important, and I couldn't help laughing at his befuddled expression.

Uncle Camp set his paintbrush on the rim of the can, stood, stretched, then plopped down in a rocker. He took a handkerchief from his pocket and ran it across his head, then along the back of his neck. He kicked out his legs, stretching them as far as they could go. "*My* dogs are barkin'."

"It's no wonder. You've been out here since eight this morning," Sadie said as she dragged her paintbrush down a spindle. "You should go inside, get cleaned up, take a rest, and then maybe take Iona out to dinner."

A slow smile spread and he said, "Sounds like a fine plan to me." Picking up the sweet tea pitcher from the table next to the chair, he glanced around. "There was a day I'd have had this project done by noontime."

"Only noontime? Not ten or eleven? You slacker," Sadie teased.

Humor twinkled in his eyes. "Don't be ridiculous. I'm not *Superman*. But noontime. That was doable."

"Show me another man your age that does half of what you do," Sadie said. "I dare you."

"I double-dog dare you," Bree added.

"Woof, woof!" Tuck barked, and we all laughed.

Laughing felt good. It loosened some of the tightness from my shoulders, eased some of the heaviness off my chest. "It would probably help if I didn't take twenty minutes on one post."

Uncle Camp's glass of tea dripped with condensation as he smiled at me over its rim. "You take your sweet time." His eyes twinkled. "Someone used to tell me how it was better to do a job right than have to do it over."

I smiled at him. That someone had been me.

Sadie laughed as she butt-scooted to the next spindle, then dipped her paintbrush into a paper cup half-filled with white paint. "Remember how long it would take Leala to brush her teeth in the morning? I'd be half-done with breakfast by the time she came downstairs."

"Good oral hygiene is important," I said with faux outrage as I jabbed the paintbrush in her direction. "And you can laugh, but which one of us has never had a cavity?"

She rolled her eyes. "You. *Shoot.*" She looked down at her hand.

"What?" I asked.

"Splinter." She picked at her palm.

I set my brush down and motioned her over. "Let me see."

"It's fine."

"Sadie Way."

Uncle Camp chuckled and Sadie sighed but she scooted over to me and held out her hand. I gasped. "That's got to be an inch long." The splinter had pierced deeply in her palm with only its tip sticking out. "I'm going to need tweezers."

"I'll get 'em." Uncle Camp rose slowly from the rocker. He glanced at Sadie's palm when he passed by and whistled low.

"I see?" Tuck said, stepping up next to me. He leaned in and his eyes grew big. "Owie? I kiss!"

Sadie smiled as she held out her hand. He gave it a noisy peck. "Bettah?"

"Yes!" Sadie said. "It doesn't even hurt."

"Liar," I whispered.

"Ooh." Bree peered over my shoulder. "That's deep."

"It's fine," Sadie said, even as blood began pooling on her palm. "Really. We'll pull it out, clean it up, and my hand will be good as new."

I grabbed a napkin from the table. "When was your last tetanus shot?"

"No shots!" Tuck cried.

"No, no shots for you," I said, trying to reassure him.

"None for me, either," Sadie stated. "It's a splinter, Leala."

"It can have bacteria on it. You don't know."

"Neither do you. It's going to be fine. Trust me."

"You don't know," I repeated.

Uncle Camp returned to the porch, a pair of tweezers in hand. "I wiped them down with rubbing alcohol, so they're nice and clean."

I held Sadie's palm to the light and went to work. I'd barely started before the splinter broke in half, the bottom part stuck under the skin. "I'm going to need a needle."

"Oh no." Sadie backed up. "No way."

"It needs to come out," I insisted.

"It will on its own."

I didn't let go of her hand. "Before or after you get gangrene from an infection?"

"Gangrene?" she said with a laugh I didn't appreciate.

"My mom always used an Epsom salt soak to treat splinters," Bree said. "Makes it easier to pull out."

Sadie nodded. "Let's try that. No needles."

"You girls go on inside," Uncle Camp suggested. "It's about quittin' time anyway. We can finish up tomorrow. I'll be in as soon as I put this paint away."

"I paint!" Tuck ran for his bucket.

"I can stay out here with him," Bree offered. "No problem."

"Thanks, Bree. I can't tell you how much you've helped me today."

She smiled shyly, then turned her attention back to Tuck.

Sadie had already gone into the house, and I ran to catch up with her before she hid from me. Coolness welcomed me inside the entryway, and I thanked the good Lord for air-conditioning.

Sadie dropped dramatically onto the couch, and I wondered if she realized how alike she and Mama were sometimes. She'd hate hearing it, however, so I kept the thought to myself.

In the big chair by the fireplace, Iona looked up from the book she was reading. "How's your hand, Sadie? A moment ago Camp mentioned you had a splinter the size of Louisiana stuck in it."

Sadie rolled her eyes and said, "The fuss about it is more painful, honestly."

Iona laughed lightly. "Some people are born nurturers. Best to let them fuss."

I was thinking about the odds of Sadie contracting gangrene as Iona's words registered. I was suddenly filled with light and warmth that she had seen the real me after only a couple of days. I aimed a wry glance at Sadie. "That's right. Let me fuss."

"All right." She dragged out the words as if she suffered greatly. "But only because Iona said so."

I stuck my tongue out at her, ran upstairs, found the Epsom salts, and had Sadie's hand soaking in a bucket in no time flat. Drained, I sat next to her on the couch. "Does it still hurt?"

"It never hurt," she said, her tone so laced with exasperation that I believed her.

"Then you're made of heartier stuff than I am. Remember that time I got a thorn in my finger from Buzzy's blackberry bushes?" I glanced at Iona. "Hurt like the devil. I cried when I got it, I cried when Uncle Camp pulled it out, and I cried for ten minutes after from the throbbing trauma of it all until Uncle Camp gave me an ice pop just to give my mouth something else to do."

Iona chuckled. "Sounds like quite a memorable experience."

"I remember," Sadie said. "I ran upstairs to get Mama because

I thought we were going to have to call an ambulance with how you were wailing."

I lifted a shoulder in a shrug. "It hurt."

Mother had come running. She'd taken one look at my tiny wound and told me that I was too old to be crying over thorns. She'd grumbled about now being behind on her work and stomped back up the stairs, leaving me behind with a whole lot of pain that hadn't come from my injury.

I'd never again cried over a thorn. Or when I sliced my hand on a broken glass and had needed twenty stitches. Or when I fractured my wrist falling off my bike. Or when I lost my ability to have children.

I felt a nudge on my arm. Sadie's elbow. Compassion glowed in her eyes. "Thanks for fussing."

Ah, so she had remembered Mother's reaction, too.

"Personally, I find that crying can be quite cathartic," Iona said. "It's better to let the pain out than hold it in, where it can fester and turn into something that will eat you up from the inside out."

I felt that old pain festering now, deep in my chest, and suddenly my eyes burned with tears. I hadn't had a good cry since . . . well, since that day with the thorn. I teared up plenty, because I couldn't completely shut off my emotions, but a good, sobbing cry? No. Maybe it was time. Or maybe I was just too exhausted to fight everything I'd been holding in for so long.

The front door flew open and I heard, "Noni! I paint!" as Tuck came running inside, his bare feet thudding on the floor.

Uncle Camp reached in and shut the door, and I saw Bree rolling a tarp. She was a godsend, that girl.

"You painted?" Iona said with a clap of her hands. "What a big boy you are."

He nodded as he sidled up to her to accept her hug.

Tuck's gaze fell on the bucket perched on Sadie's lap. "Owie?" he asked.

She pulled her hand from the water. "Nope. See? It's all better."

I grabbed her hand to look for myself and blinked. There was no sign of the remaining splinter and no redness. There wasn't even an abrasion. It was as if she'd never had a splinter at all. I glanced at her.

Her smile was bright. And phony. "Those Epsom salts work wonders, don't they?" she said.

I studied her closely, and she fidgeted. A ringing phone split the tightness in the air, and Sadie quickly put the bucket on the floor and pulled her phone from her pocket. "It's Connor." She answered quickly, then passed the phone to me.

"Hi." I glanced at the clock. "Shouldn't you be on your way home?"

"I'm so sorry, Leala," he said. "I'm stuck at the office. I don't think I can leave for another hour. Maybe two."

I stood up to pace but anger rooted me to where I was. "Sadie and I are supposed to go to the hospital soon. Visiting hours are over at eight."

"I know. I'm sorry. I just can't—"

"No," I said, cutting him off. "You *won't*."

His tone turned hard. "You don't understand, Leala."

"I understand just fine." I glanced down when I felt Tuck's arms wrap around my leg, and those damn tears welled up again as he looked up at me with worry in his deep blue eyes, the color an exact match to Connor's eyes. I let out a deep breath. "Be careful on your way back. Bye."

I hung up before I told him what I really wanted to say, which was to not bother coming back at all. I lifted up Tuck and turned to find Sadie and Iona giving me identical looks of sympathy.

It was almost too much to bear.

"Connor's going to be late," I announced. "An hour or two, which really means three or four."

Iona stood up. "I can watch Tucker for you tonight. You two get on to the hospital as planned."

Tuck clung to me. "I can't ask you to do that."

She gave me a smile brimming with kindness. "You didn't ask. I volunteered."

I swallowed hard.

"Uncle Camp will be here, too," Sadie pointed out.

I looked toward the front porch. "Uncle Camp's tired."

"But I'm not," Iona said. "I've had plenty of rest. I'll take care of them both. It'll be my pleasure. Don't argue now. Save your energy. You have a long night ahead of you yet."

My emotions were stretched so thin I didn't know how I was going to make it through what lay ahead, first with Mother, then with Connor. But as I looked into Iona's kind eyes, I knew I couldn't do it without help. "All right. Thank you."

"We should probably clean ourselves up a little." Sadie picked up the bucket of water and gave me a sympathetic shoulder bump as she passed by, heading toward the laundry room.

Iona stepped up next to me and patted my arm. "They're not called growing pains for nothing, dear."

I knew immediately she was referring to the water oaks and how they'd grown back together. But as I went to move Moo from the washer to the dryer, it didn't feel like Connor and I were growing together at all.

It felt like we were only growing farther apart.

Chapter 19

Sadie

"She doesn't need more flowers," I said, trailing behind Leala as she speed-walked the Landing. "She has two dozen arrangements at home already."

I'd been trying to talk sense into my sister for five minutes now, but she hadn't really been listening. She'd been quiet since Connor's phone call. Too quiet.

"Leala Clare!"

Leala abruptly stopped and faced me, lifting her sunglasses on top of her head. "What, Sadie? We need to hurry. Visiting hours aren't going to wait for us."

Wanting to groan in frustration, I held it in and repeated what I'd said only moments ago.

She crossed her arms and threw an exasperated glance toward the flower shop. "Well, she can't have what she wants. Bourbon is out. Ice cream is out. Anything deep-fried is way out. We can't show up empty-handed."

I grabbed her arm. "Let's go to the Crow's Nest. We can pick out a couple of books. Maybe a few magazines. Stuff that will also keep her busy after she gets home. They have cute gift bags and cards there, too."

"Fine. But we have to hurry. We're late as is."

She didn't say "thanks to Connor," but I heard it in her tone. We walked quickly down a set of stone stairs leading to the Lower Landing, which was a promenade that directly overlooked the lake. Dark clouds had rolled in, promising rain, and the temperature had dropped a notch. The threat hadn't seemed to deter anyone from venturing out. Restaurant patios were full of diners, and the wide walkway was chock-full of people milling about. Boats sped across the water, creating waves with their wakes.

"I'm sure if Connor could get out of work, he would." I don't know why I felt the need to defend him, but I did. "He's a high-powered attorney. There's a lot expected of him."

She didn't look my way as she said, "It wasn't supposed to be this way. He'd always wanted to join a small firm, one that respected work-life balance."

"So why didn't he?"

"The offer he received from the firm he's with was too good to pass up. It allowed us to move here to Sugarberry Cove into a fancy house with a giant yard and a fenced-in pool. Perfect for raising a big family." Her voice hardened, and she lowered her sunglasses again. "I quit my job to stay home with Tuck. We were blinded into thinking we had it all. But it all means nothing if we're not happy. And we're not happy. Neither one of us. And I don't know how to fix it. Iona thinks all we need to do is bend a little, but I'm afraid we're too brittle and are going to break."

There was a lot to sort in what she said, but one thing in particular jumped out at me—how her tone had changed when talking about quitting her job. "Do you miss working?"

She glanced at me, and I wished I could see her eyes, but they were hidden behind dark lenses as she said, "Staying home with Tuck is what I've always wanted. I don't want him raised like we were—feeling like part-time children while Mama worked herself into the ground."

Mama, not *Mother*, I noted. This topic was breaking down her walls. "That's not what I asked. Do you miss working?"

"Ah, here we are." She pushed her sunglasses atop her head again and pulled on the door to the Crow's Nest. A bell jingled a welcome, and Leala rushed inside like she couldn't get away from me—or the conversation we were having—fast enough. Inside, she immediately veered right, toward the romance section.

The scent of old paper and black cherry from the specialty candles for sale brought a wave of nostalgia. I'd spent a lot of time in the shop, but the last time I'd been in here, I'd been with Will, picking out a few books to take with me to college. It had been three weeks before my accident.

A heavyset woman hurried from the back room, her dark hair twisted high on her head and secured with a yellow pencil. She stopped dead in her tracks when she saw me.

"Hey, y'all! It's Sadie Scott!" Violet Swann declared, rushing forward, her arms wide, her teeth flashing bright against dark skin. "Good night! It's been too long, Sadie."

I smiled at her enthusiasm and stepped into the hug. At this point it was easier to accept them than try to discourage them.

"How've you been, Miss Violet? How's Max?" Her son had been two grades below me and had his mother's infectious personality, loud laugh, and love of books.

"I'm just fine, and he's just wonderful. Married now. And a daddy! Can you believe that? I know I look too young to be a grandma, but it's true. I've got myself a grandson, cute as can be. Now let me look at you." She scanned me head to toe and sighed. "I sure have missed your smiling face. I keep up with A Southern Hankerin', but it's just not the same as seeing you in person. I do so love those videos, though, so if that means you don't visit as much, I guess that's the price I've got to pay. I just wish there was a balance, do you know what I'm saying? I'd love to see you here more in Sugarberry Cove."

Tears welled at the words. Her warm welcome was a far cry from the looks and whispers I'd heard when I came back home after quitting college. I blinked away the moisture from my eyes and said, "Thanks for watching. That means a lot to me."

"Hey, y'all!" she repeated with a playful shove to my shoulder. "I seriously can't get enough. Those videos hit me right in the heart. Some days, they remind me why life's worth living."

Leala, who'd been browsing a rack of paperbacks, glanced over her shoulder, her eyebrows drawn low as she listened in.

"Oh! And I've gotten some great recipes, too. I make"—Miss Violet snapped her fingers—"what's the one woman's name who made the beignets? The one down in Eufaula?"

"Marceline?"

She snapped her fingers again. "Marceline. Those beignets are divine."

The rack squeaked and Miss Violet pivoted. "Leala Clare! I didn't see you standing there, you sweet thing. How's your darling Tucker?" Her jaw dropped and she pressed her hands to her chest. "Oh my heavens, listen to me go on. I've lost my fool head, yapping away. How's your mama doing? Heard she had some stents put in. Will she be home soon?"

I wasn't at all surprised she knew about the stents. Under its tourism, Sugarberry Cove was a small town. Everyone seemed to know everybody else's business. It was the curse but also the blessing of a tight-knit community.

"She's doing well. The doctor said she should be home on Wednesday. Leala and I are on our way to see her now at the hospital but thought she might like some books for her recovery. You know how she likes to read."

"Boy howdy, do I." Miss Violet zipped over to the romance section, gave the bookcases a quick perusal, and pulled three paperbacks from the shelves and handed them to Leala. "These here she'll enjoy."

Neither of us questioned how she knew Mama hadn't read them yet. Miss Violet had never been wrong when it came to choosing books. Leala and I found a few magazines, a word search book, and a get-well card before carrying everything up to the register. When I reached for my wallet, Leala stepped in front of me and jammed her credit card into the reader, signed the prompter, and accepted the bag Miss Violet held out.

"You girls give my best to Susannah. I know she'll be right as rain in no time flat. There's no keeping a woman like her down for long. And, Sadie, I'm just so proud of you I could bust. I knew you were destined for something glorious when you were saved by Lady Laurel, and I can't help thinking she's also proud of the person and storyteller you've become."

Stunned, I could only stare.

"What is it, darlin'?" she asked, big brown eyes rounded in concern.

"I—" I shook my head, trying to sort my thoughts. "You think I was destined to do A Southern Hankerin'? That's why I was saved?"

"Absolutely!" she said. "And I'm not the only one around here who thinks so. We all thought your storytellin' skills would have you writing books one day, but when your beautiful heart shines through the screen, it's obvious that's what you were meant to do. You keep tellin' those stories, Sadie Way. The world needs to hear them."

Had A Southern Hankerin' really been my destiny? All these years I'd been searching and the truth had been before me the whole time? I wanted to believe it—truly, I ached to believe it. But that bubble of pressure, the one deep down that hadn't eased, told me I hadn't found the answer quite yet.

Even still, my heart swelled with emotion with the thought that this town was proud of me. The shame of failure had followed me for so long now that it seemed it would always be part of me, my character, my future. But now? I felt like I'd been given a gift to treasure. The gift of letting that shame go.

Tears puddled in my eyes. "I will. Thank you, Miss Violet. For everything."

Once outside, Leala gave me an odd look as we walked toward the parking lot at the far end of the Landing. "What?" I finally asked.

"Why'd Miss Violet say you were telling stories when your channel is about sharing recipes?"

"If you'd watch, you'd know."

We took two steps before she added, "And why did she keep saying, 'Hey, y'all'? Just like that one woman at the hardware store?"

"It's how I open my videos: 'Hey, y'all, I'm Sadie Scott.'"

Leala grinned, and it wobbled before turning into a full-on laugh. "No you do not. It's so, so—"

"Effective," I supplied before she said something that would hurt my feelings. "It introduces me while also conveying my Southern theme. All in five words. It works." I didn't dare tell her about my "Hey, Y'all" line of merchandise for fear she'd laugh herself straight off the promenade and into the lake.

She looped an arm through mine and leaned against me. "If you say so."

I wanted to ask her if she thought my videos had been my purpose for living, but as she hadn't watched many, I doubted she'd have an opinion. "Maybe you should judge for yourself?"

"Mm-hmm. We'll see."

I sighed in frustration at her standard brush-off. It was getting old. "You talked about how Mama should be proud of all you've accomplished and not pick at you about your choices. Well, you've been doing the same to me. Even though my career isn't traditional, it's still meaningful. And I think you'd actually find some meaning from A Southern Hankerin' if you watched it a little more often. I put a lot of myself into my work, even though I'm sharing other people's stories and recipes."

She stopped still. "I hate when you compare me to Mother."

"Then don't act like her."

She huffed, then looked out at the lake and her features softened. "I'm sorry, Sadie. I promise I'll watch."

I tipped my head, gauging her sincerity.

"I promise," she echoed.

"All right. Then I promise I'll try to stop comparing you to Mama."

"Oh, thank God." She let out a dramatic breath, then smiled at me. "And didn't I tell you people around here missed you? Miss Violet is just one example of many. And even though she wants you back on the road, I'm still hoping you'll decide to stay. *I've* missed you, Sadie."

I leaned against her shoulder. "I've missed you, too."

And I had to admit that the longer I stayed in Sugarberry Cove, the easier it was becoming to imagine myself moving back home. For good.

Our footsteps echoed in the empty hospital hallway as we made our way to Mama's room in the cardiac care unit. Somewhere nearby, a machine beeped a loud warning and murmured voices drifted lazily from patient rooms.

For a moment I let myself go back to when I had awoken in the hospital after my accident, dazed and confused as to what had happened until Mama had explained it all to me, starting with smacking my head on a pylon, the frantic search, and the rescue by Lady Laurel.

My doctor had scoffed at the Lady Laurel part and had offered up only one theory as to how I'd survived being submerged for ten minutes: the diving reflex, which slows the heart rate and reroutes blood to the organs that needed it most. It was rare, but there were proven cases in the world. A nurse offered another theory: a miracle.

Leala pressed her hand to her mouth to cover a yawn. "We should've stopped for coffee."

"We can stop on our way home."

Home. The word wound its way around my heart and squeezed, like it was giving me a hug. We slowed as we reached Mama's room, as though neither of us truly wanted to face what was on the other side of the door, which stood open. A blue curtain had been pulled, a privacy shield from those walking by.

Leala took a deep breath and tapped on the door frame. "Hello, everyone decent?"

There was a scrape of a chair; then Buzzy appeared with a finger to his lips, the universal sign for *shh*.

He motioned us in and whispered, "She just drifted off."

Mama lay in the bed with wires sprouting above her gown, which I knew were attached to her chest, and an IV line was inserted in her left arm. Machines counted her heart rate, listed her blood pressure, body temperature, oxygen level. Her hands were resting on top of the thin white blanket, and there was a deep bruise on her right wrist, where the doctor had inserted the catheter for the angioplasty.

She looked peaceful while she slept, despite the darkness under her eyes and the sickly pallor of her skin. Her curly hair sprung about her face, as uncontrollable as ever, and seeing it as carefree and wild as usual lessened some of my distress from remembering why she was here.

"How's she been?" Leala asked, keeping her voice low.

Buzzy said, "Good. Her fever broke, and the doctor says she's still on track to go home in a couple of days. She was mighty displeased with her dinner and wasn't shy in making that displeasure known."

Mama had never been shy a day in her life. "Not surprising, since it probably wasn't deep-fried."

Buzzy smiled. "She'll be consulting with a nutritionist before she's discharged. I feel as though we should all say a prayer for the unfortunate professional assigned to her."

Leala set the gift bag on the table next to the bed before sitting next to me on a stark loveseat beneath the window, her hands clasped tightly in her lap. She hadn't looked away from Mama since we'd come in, and I could see a sheen of wetness in her eyes.

"How did you two fare, running the cottage on your own today?" Buzzy asked.

"It's still in one piece," I said. "Teddy, Bree, and Iona couldn't have been more accommodating. Leala's had the toughest day, having Tucker in tow."

Leala finally pulled her gaze from Mama. "Whoever said many hands make light work didn't have a toddler with often dirty, sticky fingers. Fortunately, I had help for part of the day," she added, explaining how Bree had jumped in to keep Tuck entertained.

Buzzy's bristly eyebrows went up. "Imagine now having two small children helping out—and no one to jump in at the spur of the moment to give a much-needed respite. Having no respite at all."

Leala's eyebrows snapped together, and her cheeks bloomed with color as her gaze shifted back to Mama, then finally, down at her clenched hands.

"That's not fair," I said softly to Buzzy.

"Maybe not," he admitted with a dip of his head. "But it's something to think about now that you know how it feels."

A rare burst of sudden anger flowed, hot and furious, and it took effort to keep my voice down. "Mama had Uncle Camp and you for respite, Buzzy, which I know she took advantage of often, so enough with that. She could've sold the cottage, found another job, an easier job. She's not a victim, though sometimes she enjoys playing one. It was her choice to stay and be a workaholic. It was her choice to miss our school plays, to not tuck us in at night, to always put guests first. Don't go rewriting history because of what's happened now. And yes, maybe she made some of those choices because she was overwhelmed, maybe even resentful of the hand life had dealt her, but it doesn't change the fact that those choices were hers. She owns them—and how they shaped us. All of us." Leala put her hand on my arm, and the tears welling in her eyes broke my heart.

"Let it go, Sadie," she pleaded. "It doesn't matter now. Mother makes her choices, and we make ours. We almost lost her. And I know I'd rather have her in my life, as imperfect as she is, than not have her at all. So I choose to let it all go. I choose to forgive, and I'll do my best to forget."

I let out a weary sigh and rubbed my eyes. "That's all easier said than done, Leala Clare. In this moment, right here and now, you need to forgive. I get that—I do. My heart is breaking seeing Mama in that bed, too. But the next time she comments on your parenting or the way you wash a window, or anything the least bit critical, all the old pain is going to come rushing back. Until Mama acknowledges the pain she's caused you, you're never going to fully heal."

"I don't want to talk about it anymore." She jumped to her feet and started for the door. "Not today. Not ever. I'm ready to go now. Visiting hours are just about up anyway. I'm leaving."

I leaped up to follow but threw a dismayed look at Buzzy before I left. He looked away, and I could only wonder what was going on in his head, making Leala feel guilty like that. As if we hadn't known that Mama worked hard. We knew. We knew better than anyone. And as I glanced at Mama before leaving the room, I couldn't help but think we'd all paid the price.

All three of us.

Chapter 20

Leala

Rain lashed the windows, and sleep was being elusive. I was wide-awake, having too much weighing on my mind, on my heart. I squinted at the bedside clock. It was a little after two in the morning. Across the room, Connor and Tuck slept in Sadie's twin bed.

Connor had wanted to talk as soon as I'd returned from the hospital with Sadie, but I pushed it off until tomorrow, too emotionally spent to deal with whatever was going on between us. As I lay in my childhood bed, I felt raw, broken, exposed, confused. My head ached as my thoughts tumbled.

Tonight for the first time ever I saw my mother. As she lay in that hospital bed, I truly saw her. I saw the woman who had emotionally checked out after the death of the man she loved. She'd thrown herself into work and put on a cheery face for her guests. For her daughters. For anyone who glanced her way. She did it to make sure her girls had a roof over their heads, food to eat, and a stable life in a loving community. She hid her pain. She killed her dreams of traveling. On the surface, it seemed the easy way out of dealing with her inner pain. Bury it. Bury it deep. But I had the feeling she suffered now more than ever, because it was like Iona had said. Pain festered, eating you up from the inside out.

Without a doubt I knew she loved us—she just didn't show it like other moms.

Thunder crackled in the distance, and the gutters rattled with the force of the water running off the roof. Tuck snuffled in his sleep, and Connor rolled over, the bed springs squeaking under his weight.

I stared at the ceiling and thought about choices. The choice Connor had made in accepting his current role. The choice I'd made in quitting my job to stay home with Tuck. He hadn't even been three months old before I started regretting my decision. I loved him with my whole heart, but there were days on end that I didn't speak to another adult other than Connor, and there were some days with his long hours that I didn't speak to him, either, except by text or email. I didn't miss my profession so much as I missed connection to other people. And I'd let it fester instead of dealing with it. Changes needed to be made. *My* changes.

I practiced my breathwork for a while until my thoughts settled, but sleep still wouldn't come. I picked up my book from the bench nightstand, thinking I'd read until I felt sleepy, then switched on the lamp. Tucker groaned and I quickly switched the light off. Reading was out.

The book, one I'd bought at the Crow's Nest, reminded me of Miss Violet and her reaction to Sadie. *Hey, y'all.* I smiled in the darkness. It seemed like an underwhelming intro to me, but Miss Violet and the woman at the hardware store seemed to love it.

In my head, I could hear Sadie saying I should watch one of the videos, and I had no reason at this point to put it off. Actually, I was more than a little curious as to why everyone gushed like they did.

I leaned up on my elbows, and on Connor's side of the bench that separated the beds, I spotted his cell phone charging. I reached over, unplugged it, and rooted in my bag for my earbuds. I pulled the covers over my head and dimmed the light on the phone as much as possible. I recalled Teddy mentioning something about AuntMama and Googled that plus "A Southern Hankerin'." The results page popped up with a link to "AuntMama's Buttermilk Scrambled Eggs." I clicked it, and a video loaded featuring Sadie's smiling face as she sat in a car parked in front of a small house. I pressed the Play button and smiled again as Sadie's voice filled my ears.

"Hey, y'all, I'm Sadie Scott, and today I'm in a suburb of Atlanta, and I have a hankerin' for some eggs. Come with me to meet Chenelle, who's going to share with us AuntMama's recipe for buttermilk scrambled eggs." She grinned and nodded to the charming cottage, its wood siding painted a deep, rich red. "Let's go in."

The screen faded to black before switching to a shot inside a quaint kitchen, well used and well loved; the granite countertops gleamed, the white cabinets were slightly distressed, their knobs burnished. A plant thrived on the windowsill above the sink, and a coffeepot perked in the background. Kitchen utensils were housed in a tall red ceramic vase, and a cookbook was open on an iron book stand. A pretty woman dressed in a white blouse and jeans stood with her hip against the counter, and her name came up on the screen. *Chenelle.*

The camera panned, showing a counter laden with a carton of eggs, a pint of buttermilk, several spice tins, a block of pepper jack cheese, a shredder, an empty glass bowl, a wire whisk, and a butter dish.

Chenelle's nails were short, neatly trimmed, and painted neon blue—a color my mother would love. Dark fingers cracked an egg against the side of a glass bowl as she said, "I was six years old, newly orphaned, when I came to live with AuntMama, who back then was just Aunt Cassia. My parents had died in a bad wreck out on I-75, and I had been lost and broken and in pain. The kind of pain that reaches into your soul and twists it so much that you knew you weren't going to come out of the grief as the same person who went in."

I swallowed hard at the gut punch of emotion from knowing a similar pain, as I'd been five when my daddy died. Immediately I was invested in this woman, her story, because my heart was involved.

Empathy flooded Sadie's gaze. "Was Aunt Cassia your mama's or your daddy's sister?" she asked as she handed Chenelle another egg.

"My daddy's older sister. She was an emergency room doctor, or, as they're called now, an emergency medicine specialist." She cracked another egg, then added two tablespoons of buttermilk to the bowl. "I didn't know then that she'd put her life on hold to take me in. She had taken a leave of absence from her work at the hospital to give me the time I needed to get settled. Here," she added, passing the bowl to Sadie. "You get this whisked together while I shred some of this pepper jack."

"How much cheese will you be using?"

"About a quarter cup or so, but you can use more or less depending on your mood. AuntMama always said some days call for more cheese than others."

Sadie cradled the bowl in the crook of her arm as she whisked. "Truer words have never been spoken. Cheese therapy has helped me many times."

I smiled thinking of all the times we'd made oozy grilled cheese sandwiches. I usually burned mine, scraping the black bits into the sink with a butter knife, but Sadie's came out perfect every time.

"Same, and I think AuntMama knew it would help me back then, too. Whenever I first came here, she'd make me these eggs, a piece of toast cut into two triangles dripping with butter, and two slices of bacon. And every day, I'd push the plate away. I had no appetite, you see. And every day she'd take the plate away, pat my shoulder, kiss the top of my head, and tell me, 'Everything will be okay—I promise you.' Her calmness, her sureness, made me believe her. I gradually did start eating again. Then AuntMama had to go back to work and the time came for me to learn how to make these eggs myself. 'Chellie,' she'd say—that was her pet name for me—'these here spices are a little like life. You put in too much, and it'll be overwhelming. Too little, and it'll be bland and boring. To get it just right takes some trial and error. Be patient with yourself. Above all, give yourself grace.'"

Sadie set the bowl on the counter, and Chenelle sprinkled cayenne pepper, black pepper, and salt into the bowl. "Wise," Sadie said. "We'd all be a little bit better off if we gave ourselves a little grace."

"She was the smartest person I ever knew." Chenelle carried the bowl to the stove, where a cast iron pan sat on a burner. With a flick of her hand on the knob, a blue flame appeared.

"How old were you when she became AuntMama and not just Aunt Cassia?"

"I was still six. First grade. My school was having a Mother's Day program, one where the moms were supposed to get dressed up, and there was going to be watered-down lemonade and cookies and singing, and I was beside myself, because there I was without a mama to invite. To this day, Mother's Day is one of the hardest holidays for me. Can you pass over that butter?"

Sadie slid the butter dish across the counter. "I think everyone can understand why."

I took a deep breath and hit the Pause button, thinking about how many times Mother had missed one of mine or Sadie's events—the concerts, the awards ceremonies, even the Mother's Day teas—always using work as an excuse. Yet, in that kitchen with Chenelle, Sadie hadn't mentioned the connection to this woman she barely knew. And I suddenly realized it was because Sadie understood this wasn't her story. It was Chenelle's. Her own pain had no place. Yet, I wondered how many other people watching this video could relate. How many had felt that pain?

How many shared this young woman's grief and in turn were now connected to her in a way some would never understand?

I hit the Play button and Chenelle said, "Aunt Cassia saw my distress and said to me, 'I know I'm not your mama, but maybe for one day, one afternoon, I can fill in as your AuntMama.' To tell you the truth, I was just relieved to have someone there so the kids wouldn't talk. Tease. And sure enough, AuntMama showed up in her scrubs, smiled the whole way through the afternoon, looking proud as can be. The name stuck after that. And through the years, she truly lived up to the mama part, giving me everything I ever needed in life, especially love."

Sadie blinked away tears. "Can't really ask for more, can you?"

"No, and I know how lucky I am to have had her." Butter bubbled in the pan and Chenelle poured in the eggs. "Two years ago, I was a senior in college when I got a call at school that AuntMama was in the hospital with breathing troubles. I rushed home and near about cried myself to death when I found out how ill she truly was. Cancer. Less than a month to live. I took a leave of absence from college and moved back home to take care of her. Whenever I first came back, every day I made her these scrambled eggs with a piece of toast cut into two triangles dripping with butter, and two slices of bacon. And at first, she ate them just fine, but the time soon came when she'd push the plate away. She had no appetite. I'd take the plate and pat her shoulder and kiss the top of her head and promise her that everything was going to be okay."

A sob stuck in my throat and I swallowed it back. Through my tears I watched as Chenelle pushed the eggs around the pan with a spatula. She glanced at Sadie and said, "Most days, I still can't believe she's really gone."

"Did you go back to school?"

She suddenly beamed, breaking through the fog of grief. "Yes, ma'am. I finished up my undergrad at Kennesaw, and I'm in my first year of medical school at MCG. One day, I hope to be a trauma surgeon. It'll be hard work, but AuntMama showed me it was possible. She showed me how *all* things are possible. Especially when you give yourself a little grace."

The scene cut to the fluffy eggs on a plate, alongside two triangles of toast and a piece of bacon. Then a digital recipe card popped up with the complete recipe for AuntMama's Buttermilk Scrambled Eggs, ending with a note that said A Southern

Hankerin' had donated $1,000 to the charity of Chenelle's choice, and I wondered briefly where in the world Sadie found the money to make a donation of that size.

I used the sheet to wipe the tears from my lashes and tried to keep my sniffling quiet as I processed what I had just watched, oddly feeling like I'd been given a gift. The gift of meeting Aunt-Mama, the gift of meeting Chenelle. Somehow, from a ten-minute video, I knew exactly the kind of women they were—smart, strong, caring, and compassionate. The kind of women I'd love to have as friends. As family.

I watched a few more videos, and all had the same heartwarming tone. The comments of each video numbered in the hundreds, and I blinked in amazement when I saw that Sadie's channel had more than three million subscribers. I smiled when I saw that she had a line of merchandise, too, primarily T-shirts and mugs with HEY, Y'ALL and I'VE GOT A HANKERIN' written on them. All proceeds from those sales, I noted, were donated to a charity dedicated to feeding children, which made the tears start again.

As I lay in bed, listening to the rain tap the roof, I was filled with such love and pride for my little sister that I was just about fit to burst. I had to admit I still didn't quite understand her career as a *creator*, but it didn't matter much. It was obvious to me that Sadie had found her calling as a storyteller. The world needed to hear these stories of life and love and loss and how food held memories, and how those memories could be passed along to comfort others.

It was clear now that as much as I loved Sadie and wanted her to stay here in Sugarberry Cove, her life's work was on the road.

And I was going to have to let her go.

Chapter 21

Sadie

I put the squeegee I'd been holding down onto the patio, pulled my phone from the back pocket of my shorts, and clicked through to my notes section. I tapped the microphone icon and said, "Cancellation policies. As cancellations greatly affect our small business, a fifty-dollar service will be charged on any cancellation. The rest of the deposit will be returned if reservation is cancelled two weeks prior to arrival. Half of the remaining deposit will be refunded with notice eight to fourteen days prior to arrival. There will be no refund of the deposit fee if cancellation is made within a week of arrival."

I read the note back to myself. It needed a heavy edit for clarity, but the bones were there to build from. I'd been dictating notes to myself all morning, creating what would eventually become Sugarberry Cottage's house rules. I understood Mama's innate hospitality warred with the need for stricter cancellation guidelines, but she was hurting only herself by not having procedures in place to protect the cottage's bottom line.

I slipped my phone back into my pocket and stole a look through the open sliding door of the guest room Will was working on. He'd shown up early this morning and had been painting since, covering the walls in creamy white paint. Even from here it was easy to see that his repair work was virtually invisible. Future guests would have no idea the lowest foot of the wallboard had been replaced around a good portion of the room. It was impressive, but he'd always been good at everything he did. His chin was bobbing in rhythm to whatever music he was listening to in his earbuds, and the muscles in his arms and back strained as he slid the roller across the wall in a W pattern.

The chin bobbing made me smile, reminding me of the time he tried to grow my appreciation of old jazz. His parents had a vintage phonograph table, and Will had taken the records from their sleeves with the care of a museum curator handling a rare piece of art. When he lowered the needle onto the record, and the first trumpet notes started, his eyes had drifted shut, and his chin had bobbed to the beat. Eventually, we danced, looking up moves online so we'd get them right, and I treasured every second I had spent in his arms. I had managed to trip over my own feet only twice, with him catching me each time I faltered.

He continued to chin bob, and it was almost as if I could hear the music in my ears, too. My love of jazz was because of him. Whether it was purely for the music or the sweet memories of that day, I wasn't entirely sure. I suspected it was both.

Will turned to dip his roller in the five-gallon paint bucket and caught me watching him. He tipped his head in question, and I raised my hand in a quick wave before picking up the squeegee and the garden hose nozzle, hoping he didn't notice me blushing.

Last night's rain had left water spots on the back porch's clean windows, and they wouldn't do after the hard work Leala and I had put in to get the panes sparkling. Spraying the windows with the hose then squeegeeing them quickly returned the shine. It took only a few minutes and was worth the extra work.

I stepped back to admire my handiwork and saw Uncle Camp and Iona in the reflection of the windows. They were wandering the backyard, choosing flowers for guest room vases. Iona held a basket, and Uncle Camp was gesturing at the roses while holding a pair of garden snippers. She smiled at him, and he grinned back, and I was suddenly taken with the notion of how watching two people fall in love felt a little bit magical.

Somewhere on the lake behind them were Bree and Teddy, who had awoken early for a yoga lesson only to find out Leala was still sleeping. They'd hid their disappointment well and decided on an early morning kayak excursion instead. They'd yet to return from their exploring, and I hoped they were having fun.

I heard a soft cough and turned to see Buzzy headed toward me from his yard, a bowl of raspberries in hand. His hair was damp and combed back, clearly fresh from a shower.

"A peace offering," he said as he neared, holding out the bowl. He wore navy blue Bermuda shorts and a short-sleeve button-down printed with cheerful flamingoes that didn't match his somber expression.

I took a deep breath and accepted the gift—I'd never been mad at him a day in my life before last night, and staying mad at him now was impossible. I set the bowl on the patio table so I could roll up the hose. "Thanks, Buzzy. Your raspberries have become a favorite in the mornings. Did Mama finally kick you out of her room?"

He smiled as I turned off the spigot and looped the hose around its holder. "Surprisingly, no."

It actually was surprising, considering the blowup the other night, not only that Mama hadn't sent him away, but that he wanted to stay with her.

Buzzy went on, saying, "I came home to shower and change. I wanted to see you and Leala before I went back. To apologize. Do you two have a moment?"

"I do, but Leala's still asleep."

Connor and Tuck had come downstairs at six thirty, and Connor had said Leala was sleeping so peacefully that he couldn't bear waking her. At seven, he still hadn't woken her—and hadn't left for work at the same time as he had yesterday. At eight, he made a phone call I couldn't hear, but I'd watched him pace the driveway while he talked, his steps military precise. When he hung up, he dragged a hand through his unruly hair, and I'd skedaddled back to the kitchen before he noticed me spying on him.

It was almost nine now and there was still no sign of Leala, and I was honestly starting to worry since it was so unlike her to oversleep. I didn't think she'd slept past nine a.m. a day in her life.

Buzzy glanced at the house with a flicker of worry, as if he, too, realized the enormity of Leala sleeping late. "I'll talk to her later, then, because I truly want you both to hear what I have to say. Throughout yesterday, Susannah had been reflecting on her life, on how difficult it's been to keep the cottage running all these years, and how that stress probably hadn't helped her heart situation. Her ruminations were weighing on my mind when you girls arrived. I want you to know that I'm aware there's more than one side to the same story and I know that none of you had it easy."

I wasn't so sure about that. I'd had it fairly easy. I hadn't experienced the overwhelming grief that came with my father's death, simply because I'd been too young. Being the younger child, I hadn't had the responsibilities Leala shouldered, either. Plus, my personality was similar to my mother's, so she tended to let my misdeeds slide, most likely seeing herself in me. But I'd been the peacemaker, the buffer between them, and that had taken its toll, because I loved them both so very much.

"Life is hard, Sadie. It's messy and full of pain and pitfalls, mistakes and regrets. But it's also full of hope and happiness and love and faith. It's kind of like my garden. It needs nurturing and tending and caring. You get out of it what you put into it." He stuffed his hands into the pockets of his shorts. "Sometimes relationships are like that, too. You get out of them what you put in."

I picked up the bowl from the table. The raspberries still glistened with morning dew. Nestling the bowl against my stomach, I studied him closely. "That's a nice sentiment, but we both know that it's not entirely true. You can lovingly water, water, water your tomato plant and next thing you know you've got root rot and your plant is on its way to the compost pile."

He offered a grim smile. "What I've been doing a lousy job of saying is that I think your mother finally sees that her bittersweet garden is a reflection of herself, and that perhaps she's reaping what she's sown these past twenty-five years."

I straightened and tightened my grip on the bowl. This whole time I thought he'd been talking about his own feelings. Or Leala's. He'd been talking about Mama's? "What has she said?"

"It's not so much what she said. It's what she heard."

It took a second for me to understand. "She was awake last night when Leala and I were there?"

He nodded. "And she was mighty quiet after you two left. The quietest I've ever seen in all the years I've known her."

I held his gaze and noticed the way his eyes glinted. "Did you know she was awake when you provoked Leala?"

He gave a sheepish grin. "I wasn't trying to provoke Leala. I was provoking you. Leala fights like your mother—with slings and barbs and silent anger. It takes a lot to get you riled up, but when you are, you always say what you mean, and you say it in a way that there's no disputing it, even if it's not always what someone wants to hear. The truth hurts. But it often heals as well."

With tears in my eyes, I set the bowl down again and threw my arms around him. He hugged me tightly. Last night, I'd wondered what had gotten into him. Now I knew. He had been trying to help heal my family and had somehow known it was an inside job. He understood that if Mama was going to listen to anyone—to actually hear what was being said and not be defensive about it—it would have to be me.

I pulled back and gently punched his arm. "You sneaky, sneaky man."

He cast a look toward the lake, which shimmered in the morning light. "Sometimes you have to do what's necessary to help people move on. Not just Leala and Susannah, but me, too. There's been too much living in the past. And I don't want to rewrite history, either. I want to learn from it. Because I want a life with your mother. I walked away from her, from love, once. I'm not doing it again."

The force of the words—and the faith in them—made me smile. "I always thought you two were meant to be."

"Thanks, Sadie Bear." He checked his watch. "I need to be gettin' to the hospital. We'll see you and Leala there tonight?"

I nodded. "Six thirty."

I watched him walk back under the arbor, then picked up the bowl of raspberries and glanced at Will once again. Buzzy's words about not living in the past and not walking away from love again were echoing in my head, along with his love-finds-a-way comment from the other night.

With those thoughts whirling, I headed into the house. The back porch had been cleaned after breakfast, and Leala's lilies sat in the middle of the dining table. Iona and Uncle Camp were still outside, drifting closer to Buzzy's yard, where I had the feeling his flower garden was about to experience some beheadings.

My eyes adjusted to the change in lighting as I walked into the kitchen, where Connor and Tuck were washing dishes.

"Boobies!" Tuck exclaimed as he scooped suds from the sink. He stood on a chair next to Connor with Moo at his feet, and looked to be having the time of his life.

I laughed and walked over to kiss the top of his head. "I hope we never forget the way he said 'bubbles' when he was two."

Connor dipped his hands into the soapy water, lifted a plate, and wiped it down with a sponge. "I'm sure we'll remind him of it each and every time we see bubbles. For the rest of his life. He'll especially love it when he's a teenager."

I glanced at Tuck's sweet face, unable to picture him in his teens. What would he be like? Would he have Connor's work ethic? Leala's perfectionism? Her nurturing heart? Connor's studiousness? There was a chance he'd have none of it, but it was a slim chance. Nearly an impossible one. For the most part, children were a reflection of their upbringing. I had Mama's love of people. Leala had her positivity. And we both had some of Mama's negative traits as well. I didn't really know my daddy, but I knew we had some of him in us, too. I was a dreamer, just like he was.

"Everything okay?" Connor asked and motioned toward the window. "With Buzzy? I saw you talking with him."

"Yeah." I smiled. "Really good, actually."

"What happened last night at the hospital? I haven't seen Leala that upset in a long time."

"I wash?" Tuck asked, picking up the sponge.

Connor handed him a fork. "Sure can."

I threw a look at the clock. It was a little past nine now and still no Leala. "It's kind of a long story, but the short of it is that I think our family can finally start healing."

"Seriously? That would be . . ." He paused to search for the right word. "A miracle. That's what that would be."

"Well, if there's any place for a miracle, it's here at the lake. They don't call it lake magic for nothing."

"Done," Tuck pronounced, handing the fork covered in suds back to Connor, who then dipped it into the basin of clean water and put it in a strainer. He handed Tuck his empty sippy cup to wash, and he quickly became distracted collecting water in the cup, then pouring it out again.

"Lake magic, miracles," Connor said. "Whatever it is, I'll take it. It's been a long time coming."

It had. It was too bad that it had taken Mama almost dying for the healing to begin.

"What's next with the cottage?" Connor asked, as he picked up a dish towel to start drying. "After dishes?"

"Guest rooms. Cleaning, dusting, vacuuming. Changing sheets. Doing the wash. Making sure the bikes are clean and tires are pumped up. The porch paint needs finishing. I need to get to the market for groceries, too." I glanced around, seeing all the little things that needed to be done, like replacing knobs, washing down cabinets, cleaning the stove and microwave, wiping the blades on the ceiling fans. The list was endless, but I was up for the challenge.

He tossed the dish towel over his shoulder. "I can do any of that. Where should I start?"

Before I could answer, Will came down the hallway and into the kitchen. There was a smear of paint on his cheek, and I clasped my hands together to resist wiping it off.

"Boobies!" Tuck said, showing Will a cupful of suds.

Will stopped dead in his tracks, and his eyes widened. His gaze darted from Tuck to me to Connor. "I don't even know what to say to that."

Connor and I looked at each other and burst out laughing. Tuck saw us laughing; then he started laughing, too.

Amusement filled Will's voice as he stepped up to the peninsula and said, "I'm guessing he's not really meaning what he's saying."

I explained Tuck's pronunciation of *bubbles*, and he laughed.

"Poor little man isn't ever going to live that one down." His gaze drifted to me, and he hooked his thumb toward the front door. "I was just going to take a quick break. Maybe go get one of those fancy iced coffees down at the Dockside. Do you want to come with me?"

I had a million reasons to say no. More than a million, possibly. But I really wanted to say yes. I glanced at Connor, who I hoped would remind me of all those things aloud, but he was grinning.

"Go ahead. Go," he said. "I've got things covered here. And Camp is right outside."

"Campy?" Tuck asked, abandoning the cup in the sink. "I see Campy?"

Connor lifted him off the chair so he could see out the window. "Right over there."

"Campy! Noni! I go?"

"All right. But don't go near the water." Connor set him down, and he grabbed Moo and ran with stiff legs onto the porch and slid open the door.

"Campy!" he yelled as he ran across the patio with Moo flopping about.

Uncle Camp bent down and held out his arms, and Tuck ran into them, happy as could be. Iona laughed and handed Tuck a rose to hold, but looked to be taking the time to point out the thorns.

I turned back to Will, saw that smudge, and could hear jazz playing in my mind. "All right, I'll go."

A slow smile spread across his face, stretching wide.

I suddenly wanted to run upstairs, give my hair a good brushing, throw on some lip gloss. *Something*. But it didn't really matter. None of that stuff had ever mattered with Will.

I went into Mama's office, where I'd been keeping my purse,

frowned at the papers I still needed to go through, grabbed my bag, then closed the door. I'd taken only a step when I heard thudding footsteps on the stairs.

"Sadie?" Leala called.

I hurried to the bottom of the staircase. "Yeah?"

She raced down the long flight of stairs and paused at the landing, looking down at me. Connor stood right behind me, and Will behind him.

"You all right?" I asked her. She looked like she had woken up, saw the clock, threw on a robe, and raced down the stairs. No stopping to get dressed. No brushing her hair. No nothing.

"Tuck?" she asked, her voice thick with emotion.

"He's outside with Uncle Camp and Iona," I said. "And Moo."

Her gaze went to Connor, and abruptly, she sat down on a step and burst into tears. Full-fledged heaving sobs that I hadn't heard out of her since she was in grade school. My heart broke into a million pieces as I watched all the walls she had put up around herself dissolve into salty teardrops.

Connor placed his hand on my shoulder as I started up the steps. "I've got this. You guys go get that coffee."

Before I even had much of a chance to think about it, Connor was up the stairs, and Leala was in his arms, looking like it was the only place in the world she wanted to be.

Drinks in hand, Will and I walked toward an empty bench that overlooked the cove. The sun filtered through the rustling trees along the promenade, dappling the pavement with dancing light. Below us, between twin lifeguard towers, people were spread out on the beach with their colorful umbrellas and folding chairs. A few people were in the water, mostly kids, splashing around. A rope of orange buoys marked the drop-off into deeper waters, where swimmers were prohibited.

A stiff breeze sent strands of my hair flying across my face as I sat and jabbed my paper straw into the iced mocha frappe. "Life's been a little heavy lately. Leala will be okay."

Will had wiped the paint off his cheek on the way over here, after I finally pointed it out to him, but a few flecks remained trapped in his beard. He sat next to me, angling his body my way. "And you, Sadie Way? Will you be okay?"

I wanted to make a joke about how he'd rhymed, but he was so serious I didn't dare. I looked out over the water, watching a sailboat with a bright-yellow sail glide across the water. "I'll be okay, too. There's actually been some healing this week, underneath that heaviness. There are still some open wounds, but I'm hoping that by the time I leave town again, they won't be nearly as painful."

Running a finger down the side of his cup, he drew a straight line in the beaded condensation. "Is one of those open wounds me?"

I thought about Leala and the wall around her heart and realized I had one around mine, too. I'd kept so many people at a distance these last eight years. It was time to do some demolition of my own.

"You cutting me out of your life without even a goodbye hurt. It took years to get over it, and maybe, just maybe, I'm still not over it completely. And then finding out my mama might have played a role in it with her wish . . ." I blew out a deep breath. "It feels like betrayal. From both of you."

His body absorbed the verbal blow with a flinch. His stared out at the lake, at the same sailboat I'd been watching moments ago. "You don't know that her wish was granted. What if your accident wasn't the result of anyone's wish? What if it was just . . . an accident?"

"I wanted to stay here in Sugarberry Cove. I was going to drop out of school and get a job and *stay*. This has always been where I'm happiest. Yet, I ended up leaving, just like my mother wished. If I hadn't left, we might've—" I cut myself off and shook my head. "I would've stayed."

In my head I could hear Mama telling me that if I wasn't going to college, then it was a good time to travel, to see what life on the road offered me in terms of happiness and figuring out why I'd been saved. She hadn't only wished me away but pushed me as well. With both hands.

Light added golden flecks to Will's brown eyes as he said, "It just seems to me that Lady Laurel, who's all about kindness, wouldn't grant a selfish wish. And that's what your mother's wish was—selfish. She wanted you to leave so she could live her life through you."

The words sank in slowly and deeply. Our wishes—mine, Mama's, and Leala's—had definitely not been kind. Not even close. "But if the wish hadn't been granted, then how to explain it coming true?"

"You made a choice to leave, Sadie. It was your choice. No one else's. Not your mother's, not Lady Laurel's. Yours."

Sagging against the back of the bench, I felt like the wind had been knocked out of me. It had always seemed like the choice to leave town had been made for me. To find my purpose in life, I had simply followed the path laid out before me, like Dorothy had followed the yellow brick road. But now I wasn't so sure. Had I simply been caught up in the snowball effect after my accident? Leaving had seemed the only option at the time, to save face, to protect myself, to seek a *reason* for the accident, to find out why I was still alive.

Yet, all these years later, I was still in the exact same head-space, wasn't I? Wanting to stay, yet feeling like I hadn't found the meaning of my life. And if I hadn't found it in eight years of being away from home, was I ever going to find it?

"The reason doesn't really matter now," he added, nudging my shoulder. "It was a long time ago."

"It matters to me." All this time I had been blaming my selfish wish for my life choices. Every time I ached to go home, I'd tell myself that I had to stay away, to find my life's calling. But I'd simply been making excuses. Excuses for the choices I continued to make every single day.

Uncle Camp's voice echoed in my head. *All I'm saying, darlin', is that the decisions you make today affect your tomorrows. Choose carefully.*

As the wind blew the sailboat out of sight, I wanted to cry. Cry for who I'd been, so caught up in needing a reason to still be alive . . . and not appreciating simply that I *was*. It shouldn't have mattered what people thought or did.

He stared at his hands, his long fingers, at the calluses that told of years of hard work. "Do you ever have nightmares about that night?"

He didn't need to specify which night. I knew. "Dreams sometimes." Of floating among all the lights, feeling at peace. "Not nightmares. Why? Do you?"

"Every once in a while. Always the same. I jump in the water to save you, and I see you. You're right there surrounded by all this beautiful silvery light, holding your hand out toward me, but

I just can't reach you, no matter how hard I swim. And then you slip away."

I swallowed over the sudden lump in my throat. He'd been one of many who'd jumped in the water after I fell off the dock. No one had been able to find me in the deep, dark murkiness. Will himself nearly had to be rescued after becoming exhausted from the effort. Uncle Camp had told me Will crumpled onto the dock and sobbed when I wasn't located quickly, and I almost cried now imagining what he went through. What they all had gone through.

My voice was tight, strained, as I said, "It was a traumatic night for a lot of us. But I'm here; I'm fine. I know you did everything you could."

He didn't seem convinced, and I had the feeling that anything I said wouldn't change his mind. It was likely a form of survivor's guilt, even though I was still alive.

"What happened to you after I left town?" I asked. "What happened to becoming a pharmacist?"

After a long pull on his drink, he wiped a droplet of condensation off his beard. "I went back to college after you left, but I fell into a dark place, and it took a long time to see the light again. I slogged my way through that first year. During the summer, I found a job as an apprentice to Old Man Beasley. Remember him?"

I nodded. He was a giant of a man with a big round belly and a hearty laugh. He owned a do-it-all handyman service that Mama had hired a few times when Uncle Camp didn't have the know-how to fix the plumbing or electricity.

Will went on, saying, "That work brought happiness back to my life, but I was committed to getting my degree. I was in my second year when I realized being a pharmacist wasn't for me. I switched my major to business and at the end of that spring semester, I went back to work with Old Man Beasley. He hired me on every summer that I was in school. It took five years to get my degree. Old Man Beasley retired about the same time I graduated. He generously gifted me his client list as a graduation present. I opened my own company and haven't looked back."

I'd barely heard what he said, too caught up on one part in particular. "Dark place? Why?"

He ran his finger down the side of the cup again. "You weren't the only one with a broken heart, Sadie. I knew you were wanting to come back to Sugarberry Cove to stay, and I was ready for it. Ready to make the leap, the big commitment." He let out a joyless laugh. "My wish that night you fell in? It was to finally work up the nerve to kiss you, because I was tired of pretending to just be your friend. I loved you. I wanted a life with you. But then you came to me after your accident, talking about needing to leave to find your greater purpose. What was I supposed to do?"

My heart pounded in my chest. *He'd loved me.* "You should've told me how you felt. I would've stayed."

He shook his head. "That's exactly why I couldn't tell you. I couldn't be the person holding you back from destiny. I had to let you go."

I recalled the day I told him I had to leave, how I'd talked up needing to find my purpose in life, mostly trying to talk myself into actually leaving. Bad choices had consequences, and I was suffering from mine. Tears pooled, and I willed them not to fall.

"Not long after you left, I realized the occasional texts and phone calls from you ended up hurting more than helping my heartache. Back then it was just too painful to be in your life when I couldn't be with you."

So instead of talking to me, telling me how he felt, he'd chosen to go to a dark place all alone. "You—" My breath caught in my throat, and I forced the words out. "You could've at least told me."

"I planned to, but it wasn't a conversation to have over text message. It had to be face-to-face. So I waited. But you never really came back. Until now. I'm sorry, Sadie. I never meant to hurt you. It's just that back then I couldn't see past my own pain to consider yours, and when I did finally recognize it, so much time had gone by that reaching out felt like an intrusion into the life you'd made for yourself." He looked deep into my eyes. "I'm sorry."

More bad choices and more snowballing. If he hadn't cut contact with me, I might've come back more often. But knowing I might run into him had scared me off. He'd hurt me so badly. We'd hurt each other. "I'm sorry, too," I said softly.

He let out a joyless laugh. "We made a real mess of things, didn't we? It's not too late to try again, Sadie Way."

Try again. All at once, I felt that dormant love for him spark to life, flame, and start blowing hot, and I forced it to cool. "I have to admit that these last few days I've started to wonder if maybe we still had something, but, Will, it's not fair of me to suggest exploring that, because I'm leaving again. Soon. My job is on the road."

Abruptly, I stood up and tossed my cup in the recycling bin nearby so he couldn't see the tears in my eyes. I supposed I'd always hoped we'd find our way back to each other, someday, somehow. But suddenly it seemed impossible, and I had to admit to myself that first loves were rarely forever loves.

I willed my voice not to shake as I added, "Thanks for the coffee. I'm going to head back to the cottage now. I'm sorry." My voice broke. "For everything."

He stood up and grabbed my hand. "Sadie Way."

I looked at our hands. Ever since the first time we'd touched in tenth grade, I'd believed we were meant to be together. A Will and a Way. I closed my eyes against the misery consuming me, and when I opened them again, his face was blurry through my tears. As he wiped a tear from my face, his callused thumb scraped against my cheek. I fought the urge to press my face against his palm, to lean into him, to stay there and never move again.

"Suggest it," he whispered. "Long-distance relationships can work." He cracked a smile. "I mean, as long as you don't stay away another eight years. We're older now and understand better that life doesn't always go the way we want. Don't we owe it to ourselves to see what could happen?"

Long-distance relationships had never worked for me before now, but the plea in his voice was swaying me. I closed my eyes again, trying to sort through all my feelings. The guilt, the regrets, the love.

"Look," he said, "you don't have to answer just now. Think on it, okay?"

With a curt nod, he let go of my hand and we headed back to the cottage.

As much as I had wanted to say yes to him, to give it a try, the last thing I wanted was to hurt him. Again.

Chapter 22

Leala

I barely even noticed Sadie and Will walking out the front door. I was too caught up in myself, in the flood of emotions that had overcome me, knocking me off my feet, tipping my world sideways.

Everything had felt so wrong when I woke up. The bright sunshine streaming in the window, the pillow, the room itself. Then I saw that Connor and Tuck were gone, noted the time, and panicked. Why hadn't Connor woken me up before he left for work?

Connor held me close, letting me sob into his chest. His hand rubbed my back, and he kept saying, "It's okay, Leala Clare. Let it out."

It.

Everything I'd been holding in forever. All the small hurts. The life-altering sorrows. The rejections. The fears. The regrets. Oh Lord, the regrets.

I let it pour out of me until there was nothing left but a hollow ache waiting to be filled again.

Connor kissed the top of my head, leaving his lips against my hair. "I'm sorry I didn't wake you up. You looked so serene that I couldn't bring myself to do it. I couldn't pass up giving you another hour or two of peace. Another day of troubles and worries could wait awhile."

"It was nice of you." I wiped my eyes and nose with the hem of my nightshirt and took a shuddering breath. "I just . . . wasn't expecting it." My eyes welled again, trying to think of the last time Connor had let me sleep in. Not that I'd ever slept too late, but I'd read or watch TV in bed.

My birthday, last December. That had been the last time. Work had slowly taken over his life, his time, and there had been little left to spare for luxuries like sleeping in—for him or me. "Aren't you late for work?"

Not meeting my eye, he stood and offered me a hand. "Do you want some coffee? We can talk out on the back porch so you can keep an eye on Tucker."

Concerned by his demeanor, I took his hand and we went down the steps and into the kitchen. He poured me a cup of coffee, stirred in a splash of cream, and handed me the mug. On the back porch, I breathed in the lily-scented air as I sat in a rocker. On the back lawn, Tuck was holding a basket of flowers that also had Moo hanging out of it. I smiled despite my mood.

"I woke up early this morning to draft my resignation letter," Connor said.

Shocked, I nearly spilled the coffee and set the mug on the side table. "You did?"

"I'd been trying to come up with ways I could keep my job somehow, cut back my hours, take on another role within the company—something. But yesterday made it crystal clear that nothing was going to change if I stayed with the firm, except that I was going to lose you. And if it's a choice between my job and you, I'll always choose you, Leala."

I swiped away the tear on my cheek. For some reason I wasn't as happy as I thought I'd be. I never wanted it to be a choice. "I'm sorry. I know how hard you've worked."

"Don't apologize. This weekend's really made me see how I've lost myself. Everything I've ever stood for. Everything I've ever wanted."

"I don't think you're totally lost," I said with a small shrug. "Just . . . taking the scenic route. Fortunately, it seems like it might be a loop. One that has circled back to me and Tucker."

He glanced at me. "I love you, you know."

"I know." The stupid tears welled up again. "I love you, too, and I can't tell you how good it is to have you back. Well, after your two weeks is up, because I'm sure the firm is going to get every billable minute they can out of you."

And if there was anything I knew about Connor, it was that he'd given two weeks' notice. In that time, he'd dot every *i*, cross every *t*, and make sure that whoever took over his role was well prepared.

"Actually, when I called in this morning to say I was going to be late, I got pushback about it. So I quit right then. Effective immediately."

My jaw dropped. "No way."

At my expression, he laughed. "It didn't hurt as much as I thought it would. Truthfully, it felt pretty good."

I launched myself at him, landing in his lap. I swung my legs over the arms of the rocker and snuggled in. He wrapped his arms around me and held me close and said, "I want to take a little time. Just us, as a family."

I was already looking forward to it. "Done. Then what?"

"When I was at Lockhart's the other day, I noticed there was an office for rent above the store. I'd like to check it out. Might be time to hang out my own shingle."

If all the struggles of the past year had led to this decision, this moment of him rediscovering what he'd always dreamed of, then maybe they had been worth it. "It's definitely time."

He pulled back so he could look at me. "It means using a big chunk of our savings, cutting back some. It's . . . a risk."

I swallowed over the sudden lump of fear in my throat. The fear of the unknown terrified me, but our marriage wasn't going to last if we didn't take a big leap of faith. "I hate risks, Connor, but I believe in you. And I can go back to work."

Clouds drifted into his blue eyes. "I don't want you to have to do that. I know how much it means to you to stay home with Tucker."

I swallowed hard. "I don't mind. Really."

He tipped his head to study me more closely, obviously sensing there was more to the statement than I'd meant to share.

I pressed on before he could question me about it. "I'm sure my old job will take me back—they said they'd always leave the door open for me to return."

Something twisted painfully in me as I spoke, at the thought of an hour in the car each day, business suits, my small office with its one window that overlooked the parking lot, of being away from Tucker all day long. Which didn't make sense since I *wanted* to go back.

"Let's hold off on that for now," he finally said, still looking at me with a question in his eyes. "We'll make this work somehow. And I'll be home more to help. Everything is going to be different. I promise. I'm going to be a better dad and a better husband."

I opened my mouth to argue about the job situation, but that pain in my stomach and the look of hope in his eyes stopped me. I'd give his way a try before I made any big decisions. It could be he was absolutely right, and that I'd be perfectly happy once he was home more.

Ignoring the feeling that I was somehow hurting myself, I cuddled in close. My gaze drifted to the water oaks, and I smiled.

Connor and I had bent, but we hadn't broken.

Hours later, the sun shined weakly through feathery clouds, and the lake whispered, beckoning with its gentle pulse against the seawall. It was the perfect afternoon for a swim. The housework had been done, Connor was helping Uncle Camp finish the porch paint, and the rest of us—Teddy, Bree, Iona, Sadie, Tuck, Nigel, and I—had all found our way onto the back patio, having come together one by one throughout the day. The red umbrella had gone up, and we'd covered the table with snacks and drinks. It felt a bit like an extended coffee hour with friends, indulgent during the middle of a workday, but one much welcomed after the emotional ups and downs of these last few days.

Tucker had invented a new game, one where I threw the tennis ball and he and Nigel raced to see who could retrieve it first. So far, Nigel was in the lead. Far in the lead. As in, Tuck hadn't won once in dozens of attempts. Yet, he laughed each time, literally rolling with it at certain points, which served as an important reminder that sometimes winning wasn't everything.

"It's hotter than a tenth ring of hell out here," Teddy said, though she didn't budge from her lounge chair that was positioned in direct sunlight. She wore a turquoise-colored tankini, and her face was lifted to the sun. Her bronze skin glistened.

If I hadn't seen her apply sunscreen, I wouldn't have believed she had. She proclaimed she'd never had a sunburn in her life, that she was tan year-round, and that her dermatologist had said she had no sun damage any other sixty-year-old woman didn't have. Mother's words the other day about having suspected Teddy was Lady Laurel hovered in my thoughts, and I suddenly wondered if it was possible after all. Maybe Lady Laurel masqueraded as a sun goddess once a year, but then I remembered the drummer story and dismissed the thought.

"Come on, now." Iona looked up from her book. "It's at least the eleventh."

Even she had abandoned her signature cardigan and sat in a white sleeveless blouse. Her peaches-and-cream skin hung loosely on her arms, lined with shallow wrinkles and dotted with playful freckles.

"Twelfth," Sadie said as she scribbled in a notebook. She had been jotting notes for close to a half hour as she interviewed Bree ahead of the mac and cheese video they planned to shoot on Sunday.

"How many rings are there?" Bree asked.

I laughed. "Nine. And none of them have to do with heat."

Sadie smiled. "I mean, it's still hell, right?"

"Suppose so." I threw the ball again for Tuck and Nigel, making sure to keep my aim away from the water. The pair went running, and I imagined that both would sleep quite well tonight.

"Is Bree a nickname or your full name?" Sadie scanned her notes, as though looking to see if she'd already asked the question.

Earlier she'd returned from her outing with Will looking drawn and unhappy, and when I asked what had happened between them, all she had said was, "Choices." I hadn't pushed, giving her time to mull it all over, but tonight I'd pull out some pints of ice cream and see if I could get her to talk.

"It's a nickname for Aubrey," Bree answered. "The same name as my dad. He left my mom when I was only two, and she said she had trouble calling me by his name after that so she shortened it to Bree."

Sadie's pensive gaze shifted to me, just as I realized that Mother had started calling me LC not long after my father, Leland Clark Scott, had passed away. I'd been named for him and had always been proud to share the connection. For me, it was a constant reminder that he was still with me. For Mother, I now suspected my name was a constant reminder that he was gone.

"I don't blame her." Bree nibbled on a cookie. "I probably would've done the same thing. Bree works fine, but I kind of love when Tucker calls me 'Bee.' I could get used to that real quick."

I heard a loud splash and panicked for a moment until I realized it had just been a carp breaching the surface of the water, as they liked to do for seemingly no reason at all other than to scare the living daylights out of anxious moms. Tuck followed Nigel around the yard, both slowing down in the heat of the day.

Iona peered at the water. "Fish are jumping."

"Don't blame them," Teddy chimed in. "A little splish-splash sounds good right about now. Anyone up for a swim?"

Tuck ran up to the table, his cheeks red from exertion. "I swim!"

"That's two of us," Teddy said. "Any other takers?"

"I could do with a dip," Iona conceded. "If no one minds that I do it in my shorts and blouse. I didn't pack a swimsuit."

"If it weren't the middle of the day, I'd say go au naturel. Live a little," Teddy said. "Heck, who cares if it's the middle of the day. Go for it."

Iona laughed. "The scandal! I think I'll do my living with clothes on, but I appreciate the encouragement."

"I'm in." Bree scooted back her chair. "We can finish later, right, Sadie?"

She flipped closed the notebook. "Yep."

Bree pivoted to me. "Are you swimming, too, Leala? We can pull out the paddleboards and do a little yoga. *Om.*"

I could use a little om right about now—and cooling off. Standing, I picked up Tuck, his body hot and sticky against mine. "I'm game. Shall we meet back here in five minutes?"

Everyone agreed, and with that, almost everyone scattered. I faced Sadie, who hadn't budged. "How about you?"

She looked at the water. "I don't think so."

"It's hot," I said. "The-twelfth-ring-of-hell hot."

"It's cool inside. Air-conditioning and all."

"Will's inside."

She glanced at the lake again. "Maybe I'll dip my toes in."

I left her sitting in the shade, staring at the water, while I ran inside with Tuck. We stopped on the front porch to tell Uncle Camp and Connor our plans, then changed into our bathing suits.

We were back outside in no time flat. Bree and Teddy were already freeing the paddleboards from the rack, Iona was floating blissfully on a pool noodle, and Sadie still hadn't moved from the patio table, where she was now scrolling through her phone. "You haven't changed your mind, have you?"

"Not yet."

I smiled and tightened the straps on Tuck's life vest. "Good."

She set her phone down on the notebook and glanced at me. "I still reserve the right to change my mind at any time, though."

"Sadie, the lake misses you. Can't you hear it? *Sadie, Sadie,*" I whispered in a gruff voice. "*Where have you been? I've been so lonely without you.*"

The corner of her mouth twitched. "The lake needs to see a doctor about that frog in its throat."

"You know you've missed it, too. Go show it some love."

"Now you're pushing your luck."

I grinned. "It's worth a little pushing if it gets you in the water. I'll shove you in if I have to."

Her gaze narrowed. "You wouldn't dare."

I grinned back, thinking I probably would if she hadn't once fallen off that dock.

"Hey, Leala!" Bree shouted, her arm motioning me forward like it was the blade of a windmill. "Come quick. You have to see this!"

"I want see!" Tuck said, running ahead of me, stiff legged, always eager for a good show-and-tell.

Curious, I hurried toward the dock, and when I heard Sadie fall in step behind me, I let out a sigh of relief. "What is it?"

Bree's eyes were wide with excitement. "It was sitting right there, plain as day."

Nothing could have prepared me for seeing my cell phone sitting on the corner of the dock, as if I'd set it down and forgotten it. I picked it up and turned it on, and it worked. It worked perfectly. "Thank you, Lady Laurel!" I called out loudly, my voice carrying far and wide.

Bree's voice was filled with wonder. "I wouldn't have believed it if I hadn't seen it."

"Lake magic," Sadie said, standing next to me with a big smile.

I gave her a nudge with my elbow. "*Sadie, Sadie*," I said again in that gruff whisper. "*You know you want to jump in*."

She laughed and cast a longing glance at the water. Finally, she said, "All right, all right. But only if you go with me." She held her hand out to me, palm up.

I gave my phone to Bree, met Sadie's gaze, and put my hand in hers. Our fingers wrapped together just like when we were little girls and would skip along the sidewalk, all our problems forgotten behind us.

Wearing matching smiles, we jumped.

As we resurfaced, I laughed with pure joy when I saw her huge grin and the light that shone brightly in her eyes. I'd never seen Sadie more alive.

Chapter 23

Sadie

The tile saw echoed through the cottage as I walked down the stairs. I'd showered and changed after my impromptu swim. The feel of the water, as if I were one with it, had brought me so much joy.

The saw silenced, and I fought the urge to go down the hall and tell Will that I was willing to give a relationship a try. My heart was all in. But my mind was stuck on his dark place, and how I never wanted to be the source of his pain ever again.

Leala was still upstairs, trying to convince Tucker to nap while Connor had gone to his office to clean out his desk. Iona, Bree, Nigel, and Teddy had biked into town for a late lunch, and I was debating which project to work on while I waited for the internet installer to show up.

The floral scent was becoming overwhelming in the great room, and I was considering sharing Mama's flowers with people at the hospital tonight. I doubted she would notice a few missing arrangements—or mind sharing if she did find out. She was usually the first person to donate to a good cause.

Uncle Camp was in the kitchen rooting around in the fridge, and I grabbed a glass from the cabinet and filled it with ice, then water from the fridge dispenser. "Did you hear what happened with Leala's phone?"

He set sandwich fixings on the counter. "Surely did. Lady Laurel must be in an especially giving mood this week. Bodes well for the lantern festival."

There were splatters of white paint on his blue shirt, a smudge of dirt near his nose, and crumbs in his beard, and my heart swelled with my love for him. I pulled a plate from the cabinet and handed it to him. "Are you going to set any wishes afloat this year?"

He spread horseradish onto his bread, then added roast beef and cheddar cheese. "I believe I will."

I gave him a knowing smile. "Your wish wouldn't have anything to do with a certain fair-haired guest, would it?"

"Nigel?" he asked, after taking a big bite of his sandwich. "Nah. Though I have grown mighty fond of the little imp."

I laughed. "You know who I mean."

"Suppose I do, and I suppose I'm not sayin' one way or another. And what about you?" He jerked his head toward the end of the hall. "Is your wish going to be about a certain contractor?"

It had been eight years since I'd made a wish, and honestly I never thought I'd ever make another. But now . . . I wasn't so sure. "Do you think a long-distance relationship can work?"

He thought about it for a fair bit before saying, "I think if two people are committed to making a relationship work, it'll work. Near or far."

I set my glass on the counter. "I'd be on the road a lot."

"You could cut back some."

"I'd have to get a place here in town."

"You still have a room upstairs that ain't going no place."

"I hurt him when I left before. What if I do it again?"

"What if you don't? What do you have to lose? Either of you?"

I slid my glass back and forth between my hands. I'd already lost so much these past eight years, more than I'd ever imagined.

"All I'm sayin', Sadie, is that given a chance at love, take it. It'd be a fool who walks away, and last I checked, you ain't no fool. Anymore."

I shot him a wry look and he chuckled. And even though he'd called me out for my foolishness, I couldn't stop myself from walking around the counter and giving him a hug. "Thanks, Uncle Camp."

"Anytime, darlin'." He motioned with his head again toward the hallway. "Go on with you. Let yourself be happy."

Let myself be happy.

Yesterday, I'd told Uncle Camp that I hadn't been unhappy. Yet . . . now I realized I had been. So lost in it I'd been helpless to see it. I hadn't felt real joy in years until jumping into the water earlier with Leala. I wanted more of it, that happiness. And to get it, I had to be willing to take a risk. "All right. I'm going."

He raised his glass in a mock toast, and I smiled weakly.

A window at the end of the hall let in the afternoon light, and it soaked into the pine floors, making them look golden. The door to the room Will was working in stood ajar, and I slowly pushed it open.

His back was to me as he worked on the bathroom floor, setting tile after tile in a neat row. I leaned against the doorjamb, watching him until he noticed me. He pulled out his earbuds and tucked them into his pocket as he stood up. As he searched my face, he began to smile.

So did I.

Finally, I said, "Can I suggest we explore the possible chance that we might possibly still have something worth—"

With two steps, he was in front of me, his hands reaching for my face to cup it gently between two rough palms. I was still smiling as he kissed me, a kiss I'd been waiting for since I was fifteen years old. Because I'd suspected even then that if our hands fit together so perfectly, our mouths would, too.

I hadn't been wrong.

My reunion with Will had been briefer than I'd have liked, thanks to the arrival of a laptop I'd ordered online for Mama, followed by the internet installer, who came armed with cables, router, and modem. All of which were now housed in Mama's office.

I sat in Mama's wobbly desk chair, wondering how she got any work done when constantly checking her balance; then after a quick glance around, I realized she probably didn't work in here often.

This room was so unlike her. There weren't any bright pops of color, no patterned fabrics, no personality. The curtains were sheer white, though they'd grayed from neglect. The beige walls offered no brightness; even the desk itself was a clunky, old solid oak beast scarred from use that had to have been a hand-me-down for Mama to have kept it this long.

The only things in this space that spoke of Mama were the utter and complete lack of organization and the dust-covered framed photos on the filing cabinet, which I suspected had been placed there to remind Mama that she was in her office, not a prison, even though it felt a little like a jail cell. I didn't understand why she hadn't changed up the décor in all these years.

I'd cleared a small space on the desk and was working on the laptop setup when Leala popped her head in the office doorway. "I finally got Tucker to nap. And I just saw Uncle Camp. Anything you need to share with me? About Will?" She made kissy noises.

As I hadn't told Uncle Camp about the kiss, I could only imagine she'd deduced what had happened by the goofy smile on my face. "Nope, nothing to tell."

"Liar, liar." She grinned, then pulled a kitchen stool into the room and sat down. "I'm happy for you, Sadie. It's been a long time coming."

It was nice to see Leala happy, too. She'd been floating since late this morning, buoyed by the news of Connor's resignation and the changes they were committed to making to their marriage. Yet, I knew she harbored a secret longing to go back to work, and I worried she was setting herself up for disappointment again if she didn't bring it out into the open. I leaned back in the chair, almost fell over, and put a catalog under the short leg to keep the chair steady. "You never said if you told Connor that you wanted to go back to work."

She picked up a picture frame from the filing cabinet, wiped the dust from the glass, and smiled. "I remember when this was taken. You were just learning to walk." She turned the frame my way. It was a photo of our family having a picnic on the back lawn, with Leala chasing after me and Mama and Daddy laughing from a blanket nearby. "I never realized how much Tucker looks like you at that age. You look a lot like Daddy."

"Tuck probably will, too," I said.

She smiled. "I hope so. I kind of like the idea of Daddy living on through him, even if it's in a small way."

"Leala Clare."

"Sadie Way," she echoed in the same dull tone.

"You're avoiding talking about the job."

She sighed. "You think you'd take a hint."

The laptop whirred quietly, the only noise in an otherwise silent house. "It's not a big deal to want to go back to work."

Running a finger over the faces in the photo, she said, "It is when my whole life I wanted nothing more than to stay home with my children. I know how lucky I am to have this opportunity at all. There are so many moms out there who have to work just to put food on the table. I'm being ungrateful."

"It's okay to want to change, Leala. It's okay to change. What would you tell a working mom if she wanted to quit her job to stay home?"

"If that's where her heart is leading her, then to do it if she can."

"Then why are you arguing with where your heart is leading you? Is it because of Mama?"

Leala set the frame back on the filing cabinet, turning it just so. "I don't know. Maybe? I'm kind of lost right now, trying to figure out who I am."

"You are who you've always been. Kindhearted, loving, loyal, brave, nurturing, stubborn, slightly controlling, and always having to be right."

She tipped her head and reached for the electric bill on the desk. "I liked the first part better. And I should probably call about this bill, get it paid. I'm thinking it's not high on Mother's priority list."

"I checked already," I said. "It's been paid." What Leala didn't know wouldn't hurt her any.

Pale eyebrows shot upward. "Really? That's a relief. Maybe she's not as bad off as we think."

Reaching across the desk, I handed her the whole stack of papers, minus the bill for the truck loan. "You might want to check the rest, though."

"She really needs a better organizing system. There's stuff in here from last fall."

Agreed. Mama's priorities certainly didn't revolve around filing.

As Leala sorted through the letters, the laptop finished cycling through its startup. I almost did a happy dance when it connected to the Wi-Fi. I typed in the password—LakeMagic—and clicked through to Google to create an email for Mama and for the cottage. A website was next on my list of to-dos, but that was going to take a little time.

"I'm really hoping Mama won't disown me when she finds out what I've done," I said as I logged off. "Leala? What is it?"

Deep lines creased her forehead as she stared at the paper she was reading. She turned the paper to face me. DEPARTMENT OF THE TREASURY—INTERNAL REVENUE SERVICE was printed at the top. "It's a federal tax lien, Sadie."

"What's that mean?" I asked, coming around the desk.

"It means Mother owes back taxes. Nearly forty-three thousand dollars in back taxes. And if they're not paid, the IRS can eventually force the sale of the cottage to recoup the money." With a renewed fervor, she dug through the rest of the pile. "I don't see any evidence that she's set up any kind of payment plan."

Stunned, I sat on the edge of the desk and barely registered the noise of the front door opening and muted voices in the entryway. "When was the letter sent?"

"Last month, but she had to have received a warning before this letter arrived. Why didn't she call Connor straight away? This is in his field of law. He could've helped sort it all out."

Mama was proud and stubborn, yes, but not asking for Connor's help was taking those traits to the next level. "I don't know, but what can she do now? And how on earth does she owe that much?"

"It doesn't say why. If paying it off in a lump sum isn't possible, then setting up a payment plan will be necessary. I hate the thought of her having yet another monthly bill, especially since being delinquent carries such dire consequences. Connor and I were going to use our savings for him to start his own firm, but I think we can stretch a bit and make a contribution to help pay this down."

The door squeaked as it was pushed fully open, and I nearly fell over at the sight of Mama standing in the doorway in a loose shift dress and sandals. Her cheeks were rosy and her curls corkscrewed every which way.

"Surprise, girls! I was sprung early." She snatched the lien notice from Leala's hand and added, "I appreciate the offer of a contribution, Leala Clare, but I won't take your money. Or yours, either, Sadie. I got myself into this fine mess, and I'll get myself out."

Chapter 24

Leala

The next morning, blazing orange and red hues tinted the far reaches of the lake where the light touched first, the colors warning of another storm brewing. I sat cross-legged on my yoga mat at the end of the dock, listening to the birdsong and the frogs. I'd arrived early enough to see the loon floating by crying, her sleek body leaving gradually fading ripples in the water as the lake absorbed her sorrow.

I drew in a deep breath and closed my eyes, trying to find peace within myself. I'd had another restless night, worried about Mother, worried about money, worried about everything.

After Mother had taken Sadie and me to task for going through her mail, she had retired to her room for the night but had a steady stream of visitors stopping in. Sadie and I watched a *House Hunters International* marathon with her, and any time either of us started talking about anything other than what was happening on the show, she shushed us.

"There's time enough for reality tomorrow," she'd admonished.

How she could simply ignore her troubles amazed me, because I worried mine to death. It seemed every time I had one worry under control, another popped up. My fingernails were ravaged, and I was starting to get bald patches at my temples. There wasn't enough yoga in the world to soothe my anxieties.

When I heard footsteps on the dock, I expected to see Teddy or Bree and was stunned to see it was Mother and Sadie making their way toward me, steaming mugs in hand and towels draped over their shoulders. Both smelled of citronella and were dressed in loose shorts and T-shirts and wore no shoes. Sadie handed me a cup of coffee and then set hers on the dock. She took one towel and spread it out, then the other. And in no time at all, we were sitting side by side, Mother in the middle, looking out over the calm lake.

With them here next to me, I felt a sense of peace, despite the fact that I couldn't remember the last time I'd been comfortable being this close to my mother.

"I can get real used to this yoga of yours, Leala Clare. I can see why you enjoy it," Mother said with a teasing lilt, finally breaking the silence.

A headband held back her hair, but a few curls had sprung loose over her forehead. She truly looked none the worse for her heart adventures, except for some bruising on her arm and dark circles under her eyes.

It hadn't escaped my notice that she'd been using my full name since she'd returned home from the hospital, and it was beyond my comprehension why I suddenly missed her calling me LC.

"Relaxing, isn't it?" I sipped the coffee. Sadie had made it just the way I liked it.

"I always thought dusk was my favorite time on the lake, but I might have to reconsider," Sadie said as she stretched her legs. "There's a stillness to the early morning I appreciate, as if it's gathering its energy, readying itself for what the day holds."

Mother patted her leg. "That's a real pretty picture you painted, Sadie Way."

I glanced over at my sister. "There's definitely a reason you're the storyteller in the family."

"Hey, now," Mother protested. "I tell stories. Lots of stories. I have stories for days. Years even."

Again there was a lilt to her tone when I'd been expecting defensiveness. It caught me off guard, but I reminded myself to try to embrace the changes in her rather than be wary of them. Sadie had shared with me what Buzzy had said of Mother, the reaping and sowing of it all, and I had to admit I'd been cynical . . . yet optimistic. Hopeful, even. But I also knew that she wasn't the only one who needed to change. I had to be less reactive and defensive as well. I glanced at the water oaks. It wasn't only one tree that had bent—but both. "I know, Mama. You should take a page out of Sadie's book and think about filming your stories to share them with a bigger audience."

Her eyes widened when I called her mama; then her chin dipped as she tried to hide a smile. "Maybe I will." She fluffed her curls. "I'm quite photogenic, and viewers will love my accent, especially if I play it up a little, make it seem like *I ain't got a lick of sense*, then reel them in with my wit and charm."

Clearly, some things probably would never change where my

mother was concerned, but that was okay. She was who she was, and I loved her, flaws and all.

"I'm not a storyteller. I don't tell the stories," Sadie said, eyeing us both like she didn't know who we were anymore. "I share the stories. There's a difference."

"Barely," I said. "I saw the way you questioned Bree yesterday. Your questions will guide the story she tells your audience."

Sadie took a sip of her coffee, then grinned. "I should get *story guider* printed on a mug."

"Merch!" Mama exclaimed. "I do so love me some merch."

I could only shake my head at that. "You're a storyteller, Sadie Way. Always have been, always will be. A Southern Hankerin' might not have you putting pen to paper, but it wouldn't be the same without your heart, your voice. That's a storyteller, plain and simple."

"Leala Clare Keesling," Sadie said with a big smile. "Did you finally watch some of my videos?"

I rolled my eyes. "Don't go getting a big head about it. I watched a few episodes. They were nice. I liked them. Okay, I loved them."

Her hair sparkled in the morning light as she laughed, and the happy sound filled my soul.

"Perhaps I'll start a travel channel," Mama mused. "A Southern Belle in the Wild."

I bit my lip to keep from laughing. Mama was about as far from a belle as I was from a rock star. A boat idled past and its driver lifted a hand in hello. We waved back.

Sadie shifted, turning sideways to face Mama and me. "A travel channel? Does that mean you'll be taking more vacations?"

Mama ran a finger around the rim of her mug. "Not a vacation, no. Retirement. Listen, girls, I know I've gotten myself into a big hole, moneywise."

"How, by the way?" Sadie asked, interrupting, and I was glad she had, since I was curious, too.

Mama said, "When your daddy died, I inherited some stock. I never paid it much mind until I fell behind on my bills, and the roof and the dock needed replacing. Those stocks had gone up quite a bit in value over the years. Who was to know that I had to pay tax on the difference?"

Sadie and I both raised our hands. And if Connor were here, he'd probably pass flat out if he heard this conversation. Capital gains were a big deal in his firm. Lots of billable hours went to figuring out work-arounds to avoid paying the taxes.

"Shoo," Mama said with a tsk. "Well, I didn't. Not until the IRS contacted me out of the blue. I don't have that kind of money and wasn't sure where to get it. Originally, I'd been planning on wishing for an enormous pile of cash at the lantern festival, thinking Lady Laurel was my only hope. But I've been doing a lot of thinking this past week, these last few days especially. *Whew-ee*, there's something about dying that sure has a way of making you want to live, let me tell you."

I sighed. Nope, some things definitely would never change.

She went on. "You girls know this cottage was always your daddy's dream, not mine." She swallowed hard and added, "When he died, I couldn't bear to see his dream die, too. So I stayed on. I worked hard. I couldn't bring myself to change any of the décor, because it was all things your daddy and I chose together. I kept using his big old desk and that broken chair . . . A part of me thought that if I could just keep this place as he wanted it, it would be like he was still here with us."

I blinked away tears as I realized for the first time how much she had loved my father. She so rarely talked about him that it was easy to forget.

She went on, saying, "Since he's been gone, I've been living in a state of denial. I made choices I probably shouldn't have, not only for the effect they had on me, but on you two as well. I've made a lot of mistakes, and I'm sorry. Real sorry. It's high time I start letting go. Life is short. I need to start living for myself, chase my own dreams, and stop trying to live through others." She threw a meaningful glance at Sadie. "I can't unlearn all my bad habits overnight, but I'm trying to see beyond myself. I want to be better. I want us to heal."

Tears perched on Sadie's lashes as she said, "I want that, too."

"Me, too," I echoed, wanting it more than anything.

"I decided I'm not going to make any wishes this year. It's past time to make my own wishes come true. I'm calling a realtor first thing Monday morning. I'm going to sell the cottage," Mama said. "I can see now that your daddy will always be with us, cottage or no. He lives inside us. Where we go, he'll go. I'll use some of the profit to pay off the IRS and my other debts, make sure Camp has enough to get himself settled into a good place, then use the rest for my travel fund." Her shoulders shimmied and she grinned. "I'm going to see the world."

"I—But—" Sadie cut herself off and simply shook her head.

"I know it's a lot to take in," Mama said, "but it's for the best. All I ask of you girls is to stay the rest of the week here with me. Let us have one last water lantern festival together, here at the cottage. What do you say?"

I liked what I was hearing, but I realized I didn't trust it. I feared she was going to slip back into her old ways, her old habits, and I was going to end up hurt yet again. Still, after seeing her lying in that hospital bed, I was willing to give it a chance.

"I'm in," I said.

Sadie nodded slowly as if reluctant to agree.

Mama took a deep breath. "I want you to know that I heard you both at the hospital the other night. I *heard* you. I know I haven't been the best mother—now, now, don't argue," she added, even though neither Sadie nor I had said anything. "When children are little, they learn from their parents. Soak up absolutely everything. I've come to realize that when children are older, they start teaching us parents. I'm learning from you, and I promise to keep soaking it in. But I will say this. Right or wrong, you two are you *because* I was me. I'm real proud of both of you. Real proud. Now, come on—bring it on in. Give me some love. It's been a rough week, almost dying, and all."

Home.

The word loomed large in my thoughts as I lay next to Connor in our enormous California king–size bed. Muted light filtered through the window, giving the room a hazy, drowsy, dreamlike glow.

We'd come back home to collect a few more items to take to the cottage, since we'd be staying there for the rest of the week. Tucker had fallen asleep in the car during the quick drive over and had stayed asleep as Connor carried him and Moo inside to his small bed for a restful nap in a familiar place.

Connor and I had wasted no time in taking advantage of being alone. It was much-needed bonding time, of hearts, of bodies. My head rested now on his chest, and his heartbeat comforted, soothed. He ran his hand over my hair, his fingers playfully tugging on loose curls.

Home should bring a sense of warmth, of love, of safety, of happiness. Yet, when I'd walked in earlier, it was almost as if I'd walked into a hotel. A place to stay. To live for a while. But little else.

I lifted onto an elbow. "I think we should sell the house."

His eyes widened. "Where did that come from? We can afford—"

I held my hand to his lips, silencing him. "This house is too big for the three of us. And yes, it's beautiful, but it doesn't feel like home to me. It feels like I'm living in someone else's house. Remember our apartment in New Orleans? *That* felt like home."

We'd lived in that apartment for three years. We'd barely had any money. Connor had been in law school full-time, and I'd been working full-time at a small accounting firm. Yet we'd never been happier.

His gaze softened, and he took hold of my hand, twining his fingers through mine. "You mean the studio apartment that always reeked of grease because we lived above a restaurant, had roaches the size of my fist, had rusty water most of the year, and had six locks on the door?"

I conceded his memory with a smile. "It also had amazing purple walls, that enormous original window that filled the room with sunlight, the most comfortable red velvet couch that we found at a flea market, framed nature prints from street artists that reminded us of our hometowns, colorful throw pillows that doubled as seating when we had people over, and a giant corkboard that we filled with all our treasures. Ticket stubs, pictures, the piece of ribbon from my wedding bouquet. It was filled with *us*. Look around here. What do you see?"

He cast his gaze around the room, and I followed it with my own, tracking across the cool gray walls and pastel canvases that held no meaning at all other than the designer thought they complemented the room, across all the gray and cream accents and knickknacks that held no stories or memories.

"It's beautiful, yes, but it's not us," I said, sitting up fully. "It's not me, at least. I thought it was once. When we bought the place, hired the designer, agreed to it all. I wanted you to be happy, yes, and I know buying this place fulfilled something for you, but ultimately I think I agreed because I was trying really hard to be someone I wasn't. I think I was trying so hard to prove that I wasn't anything like my mother that I lost sight of who I truly was." I blinked away a tear. "I am my mother's daughter. I love color. And patterns. And cozy houses full of warmth and personality. Houses that tell a story, our story, of where we've been, how far we've come, and where we hope to go."

Connor sat up, leaned back against the headboard. "You weren't the only one trying to prove something, Leala Clare. I got so caught up in being successful, of proving my worth, that I forgot that self-worth doesn't come from a big paycheck. It was just so easy to fall into the golden handcuff trap, of keeping up with the Joneses, of earning more and spending more. I actually think my parents would be embarrassed by all this . . . excess. Of how far I was sidetracked from what's truly important."

The small box of items he'd brought back from the firm yesterday had been unquestionably contrary to the amount of time he'd put into his work. It was yet another sign to me that he'd made the right choice in leaving the company. He'd given so much of himself for such little return. Return that went beyond compensation. Recognition. Achievement. Pride. He'd been one of many small cogs that churned an enormous wheel, and I couldn't wait to see him flourish on his own.

Glancing around, he swallowed hard. "Yet, part of me doesn't want to let this house go. Letting it go somehow feels like failure."

I took hold of his hand. "It's not failure. It's *growth*. It's us finally realizing what we want out of life and that we are willing to make the hard choices to see it happen."

With a pained look, he asked, "Do you want to move back to New Orleans? Does this have to do with your mother? Are you plotting an escape?"

"My mother? No. She's . . ." I trailed off, trying to find a word to fit my feelings and couldn't. "She says she's going to travel, remember? I'm not sure I entirely believe her, about any of it. It feels too fast, too soon, like she flipped a switch."

His blue eyes darkened as he watched me talking. "I think it's a good thing she's thrown herself into changing. Will it stick?" He shrugged. "The trust will come one moment at a time as she proves she's trying."

I supposed that's all I could ask of her at this point—that she was trying.

"And what about New Orleans?" he asked. "Do you want to move back?"

"No. I just remembered how much I hated those roaches." I shuddered and he laughed, the sound washing over me, filling me with happiness.

"I'd like to stay here in Sugarberry Cove. Just in a smaller house, one that we choose for all the right reasons. One that we design ourselves and fill with all the things we love."

He ran a hand through his hair, already unruly, lifting it high. "I don't think you know what you're suggesting. I'm the one that picked out that red velvet sofa, remember? It was comfortable, yes, but undeniably hideous."

I laughed and fell against him, and he wrapped his arms around me. "I'll risk it."

And as I lay against him, I breathed a sigh of relief, grateful that these kinds of growing pains we were having now weren't nearly as painful.

Instead, they were filled with glimmers of hope.

Chapter 25

Sadie

By Friday, I'd settled into a surreal routine, almost as if I were living a double life. So far there hadn't been too many conflicts with juggling my career with being an innkeeper, but that was because now that there was Wi-Fi in the cottage, I had a couple of Southern Hankerin' episodes queued. The mac-and-cheese video I'd recorded with Bree was a sweet love letter to her mother, and would buy me another week at the cottage before I had to resume my regular travel schedule.

Clouds blocked the sun as it set, sending the night into early darkness. The storms that had lingered for the past two days had dropped the temperature, a straight-up blessing this time of year in this part of the country.

"What happens to all the lanterns after the festival?" Bree asked. Nigel pulled on his leash, wanting to sniff every person we passed on the Landing's crowded walkways.

As I glanced at Bree out of the corner of my eye, I smiled. She had grown so much over the past week, standing taller, straighter, facing the world head-on. Tonight, her hair was pulled back in a ponytail that swung freely as she walked, and since it was almost dark, she'd skipped the hat. When people did a double take, she smiled at them, disarming them immediately, and every single person smiled back.

"Come Sunday morning," I said, walking so close to Will that our arms kept bumping, "the community comes together for Operation Floatilla," I said, and then spelled out the word *float* so she'd get the play on words. "The lake will be covered with canoes, kayaks, rowboats, paddleboards, johnboats, and rafts, searching near and far for spent lanterns. It's a contest, and whoever brings in the most lanterns wins a thousand dollars, which is usually donated to next year's festival fund right then and there. There's lots of hoopla and the festival committee has a breakfast buffet set up—it's a big event all its own."

Bree, Teddy, Nigel, Will, and I had walked over here from the cottage together, but soon we would split up, with Will and me turning toward the general store and them heading out to dinner. In the distance I heard the faint wail of the loon, and tonight the sound caught on my heart and hung there like it never had before. It was just one more part of my life I was going to miss when Mama sold the cottage.

Bree said, "Sounds fun. Definitely count me in for Sugarberry Cottage's collection team this year."

"Count me in, too," Teddy added. "Usually I'm sleeping off a hango—I mean, sleeping in, but I can drag myself out for a good cause and a little hoopla."

Bree smiled at her great-aunt. "We can team up on the two-person kayak so you don't have to pay too close attention."

Teddy laughed and put her arm around Bree. "Your kindness knows no bounds. This is where we turn off—we'll see y'all back at the cottage." With a wave, they pivoted toward the stairs for the Lower Landing.

Yesterday, Mama had finally told Teddy about her decision to sell the cottage, and my heart had ached when Teddy cried at hearing the news. Mostly because I wanted to cry, too, but was trying to stay strong for Mama. Mama had tut-tutted a consolation, repeating once again that the sale was for the best.

And maybe it was, but it certainly didn't feel that way to me.

Leala had taken the news of the sale much better than I had. I didn't like the idea at all. The cottage had been in the family for generations. It was home. Plus, what about Uncle Camp? Getting kicked out without a say-so? It was his home, too, even if he didn't own it.

Yet . . . I wanted Mama to live her life, to go forward with no regrets.

In order for her to be able to do that, I had to set my feelings aside. It simply wasn't fair of me otherwise.

At least we'd had all this last week together under one roof. Mama had opted not to fill the guest room Will had finished yesterday to keep the cottage as it was now, full with only the people she loved and had come to care for.

And as for me spending more time with Will, Mama had stopped trying to keep us apart and, in fact, had encouraged us to spend more time together. She never apologized for making that selfish wish of hers, but her support now and her promise to stop living through others were enough for me. And likely all I'd ever get. Mama rarely offered apologies, and I had the feeling her apology on the dock the other day for the mistakes she'd made was the only one I was going to hear.

"What's on our list?" Will asked.

I'd been adding items to my shopping list throughout the day as I thought of *just one more thing* we might need for tomorrow night's festival celebration. "Apparently, everything under the sun. After the general store, we need to hit the market, the liquor store, the butcher, and find some party goods. We should probably get the nonperishable items first."

He nodded to the list in my hand. "Do you want to divide and conquer?"

I held his gaze, felt its heat, and was beyond glad we'd given ourselves another chance. "Nope."

Smiling, he took my hand, lacing our fingers together as we weaved through foot traffic. Soon, we sailed through the open doors of the general store. The scent of waffle cones, of butter and vanilla and cinnamon, wafted through the air, enticing me. "How about we get some ice cream first?" I suggested. "You know, to give us strength to get through this list."

He laughed. "We're supposed to meet Camp and Iona for dinner later, remember?"

I batted my eyelashes at him. "There aren't any rules about not having dessert first."

He shook his head but smiled as he turned me toward the ice cream counter. Once we had our orders, we managed to snag a table near the front window from a couple who were just leaving, and Will held my chair out for me as I sat down.

"Do you think Camp and Iona will continue to see each other after this week?" he asked, sitting across from me.

I stuck my spoon into a caramel sundae and smiled. "I think so. Uncle Camp recently told me that only a fool walks away from love. It's been so sweet watching them together this week. They've been staying up late, playing card games, dancing, and watching movies while holding hands on the sofa. It's adorable."

Will took a big swallow of his milkshake, then rubbed the spot between his eyebrows and let out a low moan. "Brain freeze."

I laughed at his comical expression. "I can barely remember what that feels like."

"No brain freeze in all these years?"

I dragged my spoon through whipped cream, leaving behind a deep groove. "No nothing in all these years. It has its benefits. Like when I fell down the stairs the other day." I smiled. "Nothing hurt but my dignity."

"Does your family still not know?" he asked.

I shook my head. "I really don't need my mother announcing to the town this particular talent of mine. You should see her talk about my hair. It's enough."

Worry creased his forehead. "Have you seen any more doctors about it?"

"No need. It's doing me more good than harm, so why bother? I don't need anyone to tell me it's all in my head."

"Do you think it's all in your head?"

I fidgeted, uncomfortable with the conversation but not wanting to dismiss it. Will wasn't being nosy—he was concerned. And if we were going to make a relationship work, then I needed to be honest. "No. But I don't think it's physiological, either. I think it's tied to the sense of purpose I feel, that I've felt ever since waking up in the hospital. That hasn't gone away, either. It's always there, kind of like a humming in the background. There's not a day that I don't ask myself why I was saved."

Pushing his shake away, he said, "Have you considered that there might not be a reason? That it was simply an act of kindness that saved you? Lady Laurel is known for her kindness."

On the surface, it seemed the logical explanation. Lady Laurel had simply rescued me, brought me back from death's door, because she was a generous being.

But under the surface, I felt that pulsing. The one that pushed me to keep looking for the true reason. "I think there's more to it. I just haven't figured out what that is quite yet."

"It's been eight years and thousands of miles you've traveled. What if you don't figure it out?"

These were questions I had asked myself a million times over, but it set me on an uncomfortable edge hearing them from him. "I'll keep looking."

He studied my face. "What if you've been looking in all the wrong places? What if the answer has been here in Sugarberry Cove this whole time?"

I glanced past him, through the window, toward the sliver of lake visible between the buildings across the street. My heartbeat kicked up a notch at the thought that he could be right. "It might be," I finally acknowledged. "Since I'll be spending more time here, maybe I'll finally get the answers I want."

Will slid his glass between his hands and asked, "How much time do you think that is? Once a month? Twice? Three times? And how long will you stay each time?"

"I don't know for sure." For some reason I didn't want to set a schedule. Not yet. I needed time to think things through. To plan. The logistics were going to take some getting used to. "First off, I need to check with Leala, to see if she's okay with me crashing at her house while I'm in town."

Just the other day Uncle Camp had told me I'd always have a room at the cottage, and the memory alone sent my spirits plummeting. I had to remind myself that Mama believed the sale of the cottage was for the best.

"You know, you can always stay with me," he said, watching me carefully.

My cheeks heated and I smiled. "I'll keep that option in mind."

He smiled, too. "I hope you do, Sadie Way."

Love finds a way, Buzzy had said of Will and me last weekend. And I certainly hoped it to be true, because right now I was worried that the pressure inside me to find my purpose would eventually force me to drift away again. Far away.

Why had I been saved?

I wasn't sure, but one thing had become clear. If I was going to stay in Sugarberry Cove, I needed an anchor to keep me in place. And suddenly I had an idea of where to find one.

Chapter 26

Leala

The night of the water lantern festival arrived with a gentle breeze. Bistro lights had been strung tree to tree, tiki torches had been lit, flames danced in the fire pit. For the end of August, it was a cool seventy-degree evening with low humidity, and it felt somehow like Lady Laurel had provided the pleasant weather as a gift to those who had gathered to cast their wishes afloat.

All around the patio table, lantern shades were being decorated. Tradition was that three sides of the lantern were decorated with drawings or messages or anything the heart desired. The fourth panel was reserved for the wish, which was written with invisible ink so no one else could see what you wanted most of all.

The launch of the lanterns wasn't for another hour yet, at full dark, but already the lake was dotted with boats, their lights flickering on the water and twinkling in the dusky light. Music pulsated near and far, as many parties were underway along the shoreline and on boats, and oddly the differing melodies worked together rather than competed.

For our gathering, Mama had enlisted Buzzy's help in creating a special playlist of songs that included any kind of mention of light or wishes. Ranging from "Light My Fire" by the Doors to "Freight Train" by Alan Jackson, it was an eclectic compilation that matched Mama's personality perfectly.

"You should buy Buzzy's house, Leala Clare," Mama said as she spread pimento cheese on a cracker and waved a fly away from her plate. She had decorated her three lantern shades with a mandala pattern, all the hearts open. True to her word, she hadn't written out a wish, but instead on that panel had used a marker to color a big heart with her and Buzzy's initials inside of it.

"Buzzy's house is for sale?" I asked, shocked at the news.

"Not yet." He shook his head in disbelief at Mama. "I've been toying with the idea. Seems I've been bitten by the travel bug."

"Aww." Bree smiled at him and Mama as they kissed.

Sadie groaned at seeing them when she came outside with a platter of s'more fixings. "Not again."

The sparkles in Sadie's hair seemed to glitter extra brightly tonight, and hand to heart, it did look like starlight.

"Don't be jealous, Sadie," Mama said while fluffing her curls.

"Nauseous is more like it," Sadie whispered as she sat down next to me.

This reminded me of all the times we'd hop on our bikes to escape Mama and Buzzy's PDA, but I had to admit it was nice seeing Mama happy—and seeing her and Buzzy together again.

"There's room enough for Camp over there, too, in the apartment above the garage," Mama said. "And I'm sure Buzzy will give you a good deal."

Again, he looked at her with disbelief but then laughed.

"What are we talking about?" Sadie asked as she started drawing hearts and books onto a rice paper panel.

Although she always looked beautiful, there was something especially lovely about her tonight, an extra glow that made me realize she was happy. It filled my heart, and I promised myself to remember this always, but especially in the days ahead, after she hit the road again, when I'd be missing her something crazy.

"We're talking about Leala and Connor buying Buzzy's house," Bree answered. One of her lantern panels was filled with colorful flowers, and written in a small heart among them was the word *Mom*.

My gaze skipped to Tucker, who was running around with Nigel. I hoped he'd always know how much I loved him. I added his name—and Nigel's and Moo's—to my lantern and drew one big heart around them.

"Really?" Teddy had come out with a platter of cupcakes and sat down. She faced Mama and Buzzy. "So you two can travel together? It's so precious. I can barely stand it."

"Wait, hold up." Sadie put down her marker. "What's going on?"

As Bree explained, I watched Uncle Camp, who was down at the cornhole set, tossing bags with Iona, Will, and Connor. My heart hurt, thinking of Uncle Camp having to move out of the cottage, but if he moved in with us next door, it might not feel like such a huge uprooting to him. "Buzzy, if you're serious, I'll need to talk to Connor about it."

Buzzy glanced at Mama. "I'm serious."

Mama grinned.

Tucker ran up to me, Nigel hot on his heels, and said, "Mama, throw ball?"

I smiled at him, at his messy hair and chocolate-covered mouth and the joy in his eyes. He'd actually taken a good nap earlier, which was nothing short of a blessing since we planned to let him stay up past his bedtime, to see the floating lanterns. I took the ball, tossing it toward Buzzy's yard. The pair dashed off after it, Tucker laughing the whole way. My gaze shifted to the entwined water oaks, then to Buzzy's house, which suddenly felt a whole lot like home.

"Speaking of buying homes," Sadie said. "I've been thinking long and hard about it, and I want to buy the cottage from you, Mama."

I nearly slipped off my chair. "What? Wait. How? What?" I was so confused. Surely Sadie was joking.

Mama said, "I told you, Sadie, I don't want your money. The cottage will sell just fine on its own. Don't you worry about me."

Determination glinted in Sadie's eyes as she leaned forward and put her elbows on the table. "It's time I found a home base for my travels instead of living on the road or as a guest in someone else's house. The cottage will be my anchor. I can give you more than a fair price. I know the business pretty well, and I love the business, so why *not* the cottage?"

I shook my head at my sister. "No. Uh-uh. You'll throw yourself into running the place, and your career will suffer." Now that I knew the scope of her work and understood why so many people embraced her so wholeheartedly, I couldn't let that happen. Miss Violet had been right the other day: the world needed Sadie's stories.

"I'll keep doing A Southern Hankerin'," Sadie said. "I don't know *how* quite yet, but I'll find a way to make it work."

I kept shaking my head. "Something's going to suffer if you pull yourself in too many directions. Besides, what about the money? Where are you going to get it? I can't imagine you'd be able to get the kind of mortgage this place will need."

Mama laughed loudly. "What makes you think Sadie doesn't have money?"

I shrugged. "Where would she get it? A Southern Hankerin' is free to watch, isn't it?"

"Oh, child," Teddy said, sipping a cocktail. "Those videos are monetized. All those ads that pop up on the screen? Each one viewed is money in the bank for Sadie here."

"Plus," Bree added, "I've been watching a lot of Sadie's videos since I got here, and she does brand deals sometimes—like once, she did one for a Crock-Pot. Oh, and there was one for a special kind of flour. That's extra money, kind of like someone being paid to do a commercial."

I looked at Sadie. "How much money?"

Her eyes twinkled. "Contractually I'm not allowed to answer that question."

Bree had pulled out her phone. "There's a public website that lists how much people earn from YouTube and other platforms. It's not completely accurate, but it's close."

"How do you know all this?" I asked her in awe.

She shrugged. "I thought everyone knew. Here, look."

Bree handed over the phone. On the screen was a website that had Sadie's channel listed along with a grade—an A—and average earnings per month and per year. If this site was accurate, Sadie was on track to earn a little more than a million dollars this year alone. My jaw dropped. "Holy hell, Sadie. And you let me buy the paint?"

She laughed. "You insisted, remember?"

Stunned, I handed the phone back to Bree, then faced Sadie. I pulled my shoulders back, lifted my chin, and was prepared to go to battle if I had to. "Well, having money doesn't change anything. You shouldn't buy the cottage."

"Now, now," Mama said. "Maybe we should think this through a bit."

"The lake magic's done gone crazy," I said, reaching for the pitcher of margaritas. "Mama and I have switched places. It's Freaky Friday around here."

Mama laughed, and Sadie said, "Maybe it's just *you* that's gone crazy. I can make the cottage a home. It's time I dropped an anchor and stopped drifting."

It certainly felt like I suddenly lost my mind. All these years I wanted Sadie to come back, and here I was pushing her away. "You'd be buying it for all the wrong reasons. Just like Mama kept it for all the wrong reasons."

"Hey, now," Mama said.

Buzzy held up his hands. "This is a conversation better left for tomorrow. It'll give you all some time to think it through. Tonight is all about celebrating, right?"

"Right," Sadie and I mumbled at the same time.

Tucker ran up to Bree. "Bee, throw ball?" He tossed the ball in her lap. She picked it up, then stood. "How about Bee throw *you*?" She reached for him, and he squealed and took off. She gave chase as Nigel barked.

"Now, who's ready to have some wishes come true tonight?" Buzzy asked, rubbing his hands together as he reached for his pen.

Mama shook her head. "I said no wishes this year, and I meant it."

Sadie picked up her marker and started drawing books again. "I'm out."

I hadn't made a wish in eight years, but I was tempted to tonight. Just to make sure Sadie saw reason. But no—if I'd learned anything this past week, it was to not force my wishes on anyone else. But maybe I'd wish for something generic. Peace on earth. Happiness. Good health. My gaze shifted to Connor. That he'd find happiness in his new business.

"I'm out, too," Teddy said, licking frosting off her fingers.

Sadie's head jerked upward. "What about true love, Teddy?"

Teddy smiled as she watched Bree run around, chasing after Tucker. "I think I already found it. It's been here all along, and I was just too blind to see it, thinking love had to be a certain way to be real or true. I've never been happier than I have been since Bree's been staying with me, and it was a real eye-opener that I don't need romantic love to be happy. I sure do love that girl and want the world for her. I'm going to ask her if she wants to move in with me. I'm a poor substitute for her mama, but I'm sure going to give her my best effort."

Tears came to my eyes. "Oh, Teddy. You're her AuntMama."

"Don't you go crying," Teddy said, "or you'll get me crying, and I didn't spend ten minutes gluing on these lashes for them to be wept right off my face. And I can only dream to be AuntMama's equal, but she gave me the strength to give this a try. Now, y'all, cross your fingers Bree says yes."

We all crossed our fingers—on both hands—and I noticed I wasn't the only one with tears in my eyes. Sadie's tears were dripping down her face, and she quickly wiped them away when Bree approached.

Winded, Bree dropped into her seat and took a sip of her Coke. "What?" she asked when we all stared at her, each of us wearing a goofy smile.

"Nothing." Mama grinned. "Nothing at all."

"O-kay," she said, shooting a what's-going-on look at Teddy, who patted her arm.

"We were just talking about Susannah's heart and whether it's strong enough to hold up during lovemaking."

I choked on my margarita, coughing and sputtering.

"Now I understand the weird looks," Bree said, nodding.

Mama burst out laughing, and Buzzy jumped out of his chair, his face bright red. "I think I need to go check on . . . something." He ran quickly for the cornhole game.

Sadie slapped my back and said, "Come on, now, Teddy, there are children present."

"I'm eighteen," Bree protested, taking offense.

"I was talking about Leala and me," Sadie answered, her voice rising dramatically. "There are some things we don't need to imagine . . . or discuss."

This was true. So very true.

Tucker ran up, put his hands on my cheeks, and said, "Mama, okay? I kiss?" Leaning in, he kissed my cheek. "Bettah?"

I nodded and swiped tears from my eyes. "Yep! Thank you. Whew. Good thing you were here."

He spotted the ball on the other side of the table. "I throw!"

"Keep it away from the fire," I said and held my breath, waiting for my mother to comment snidely, intimating that I was overreacting.

Mama nodded. "You mind your mama. That fire is hot."

"Hot," Tucker repeated, bringing his arm back and slinging it upward. The ball hung in the air for a few seconds before landing ten feet in front of him. Nigel grabbed it and took off.

"Ni-gel!" Tucker yelled, giving chase.

I slid a look at my mother and found her smiling at me. Perhaps Connor was right. Trust would come one moment at a time.

"Are we still doing yoga on the dock tomorrow?" Bree asked. "Or going straight into lantern collecting?"

"Floatilla doesn't start until nine, so I'm up for yoga if y'all are," I said.

There was murmured agreement all 'round the table, including Mama, which made me wonder if she'd show up with coffee in hand again and no desire to move from her seated position.

"Have you ever thought about teaching yoga, Leala?" Bree asked. "Like, for real? You're really good at it."

"I do enjoy it," I said, shrugging, "but if I do go back to work, I'll go back to my old job. Plus, I'm not qualified to teach a real class."

"She's only qualified to teach us misfits," Teddy said with a smile.

Sadie tipped her head, studying me. "What's it take to get qualified, Leala?"

I glanced at Connor to find him looking my way. He smiled, and I melted a little. "I don't know, honestly. I've never looked into it."

"Maybe you should," Sadie said, giving me a nudge with her elbow. "It shows how much you love it."

Mama nudged me from the other side. "That's a fact."

Out of nowhere, I wanted to look into it. I wanted it more than anything. But it didn't make sense. None at all, not when I had an accounting degree.

Yet . . .

My gaze fell to my lantern, and I suddenly realized exactly what I wanted to wish for. And I hoped more than anything that it would come true.

Chapter 27

Sadie

Will held a stick over the fire pit, a marshmallow speared on its end. "Leala told me that you're thinking about buying the cottage."

I glanced at my sister, who still sat at the patio table, this time with Connor at her side, their heads tilted together as Leala gestured toward Buzzy's house and absently threw the ball for Tuck and Nigel. "Leala has a big mouth."

In the kitchen window, framed in the light of the kitchen, it was easy to see Uncle Camp and Iona standing at the sink, doing dishes of all things, laughing at a joke only they knew. I suspected offering to do an early cleanup had been a ploy to get some time alone together. Maybe if all the stars aligned, Uncle Camp would have the perfect place to move to. Maybe in finding love, he'd find a new home, too, one not too far away in Wetumpka.

Fireworks popped from the area of the cove, and a burst of light brightened the darkening sky. Teddy and Bree had taken a shaking Nigel into the house when the fireworks had started to get him settled with some sort of special coat that helped calm his nerves. Tuck had been upset at first at losing his playmate, but he'd collected Moo and continued to play, now throwing the ball to himself in between asking Leala to toss it to him.

"Was it a secret?" Will asked.

I leaned back in the Adirondack chair and watched the lights of the fireworks float back down to earth, fading as they fell. "No. It's just that I wanted to tell you myself."

He turned the stick, toasting the marshmallow on the other side. "Leala also mentioned that she doesn't think it's a good idea."

"And you?" I turned my head to look at him. "What do you think of me buying the cottage?"

He pulled his stick out of the fire. "Depends on your reasoning, Sadie Way. If it's for any reason other than your whole heart is invested in owning a B and B, then don't do it. And I'll remind you again that the offer to live with me is still open."

My heart was doing funny things as he looked at me. "I actually do love running the B and B."

"As much as I'd love to have you here all the time, what about your work?"

"I love my job, too, and the people I meet on the road." Leala's voice echoed in my head, about how my work would suffer if I bought the cottage. "There has to be a way to do both."

Light from another exploding firework sparkled in his eyes. "Well, as you know, where there's a will, there's a way. I'll help you any way I can." He leaned over and kissed me.

When he pulled back, I said, "That's the kind of help I can get used to."

His smile stretched wide. "More of that where it came from." He sandwiched the marshmallow and a square of chocolate between two halves of a graham cracker, then handed the s'more to me.

Mama and Buzzy were carrying all the lanterns down to the dock, readying them to set afloat. They were laughing as they walked, and suddenly I wanted to find my lantern and make a wish after all—that they'd always remember how much they loved each other. Because knowing Mama, she was going to try his patience a time or two or twelve. Love would help them through the hard times.

Will stood up. "I'm going to get more marshmallows. Need anything?"

"No, I'm good. Really good. Thanks."

As he walked away, Tucker came barreling toward me, running after the ball that he'd just flung into the air.

"Sadie! I throwed!" He looked up, trying to track the ball's location with poor Moo flopping about helplessly in the crook of his arm. As I tracked his progress, my heart went straight into my throat. He was running straight toward the fire pit without realizing it.

"Tucker, stop!" I shouted, dropping the s'more as I jumped up. I took two big steps and leaped forward. Just as he tripped on the stone ring around the fire, falling toward the flames, I surged forward and caught him. I curled his body upward against mine, away from the heat. In my momentum, I had no place to put my foot down but in the pit itself, and flames hugged my leg as I pushed off again. I landed hard on the lawn on the other side of the pit, tucked, and rolled, keeping Tucker close to my chest, wrapped in my arms. My heart pounded, my body shook, and my leg was searing hot as I rolled to a stop.

"Tucker!" Leala screamed, the sound shattering the peaceful night, breaking it into small pieces. I barely noticed everyone running toward us as I stared at the sky, the glittery stars, trying to catch my breath.

A second later, Will was on his knees by my side, beating everyone by mere seconds. I sat up and glanced at my right leg, the skin red and raw and blistered, and let out a soundless cry at the sight. Will opened his mouth, and I grabbed his arm. "Don't yell."

He'd been about to call for help, for an ambulance, for something. "Sadie, your leg . . ." He quickly took off my shoes, tossed them aside. The sole of my right tennis shoe had melted.

"It doesn't hurt," I said. "Look. See? It's already healing."

The red was fading, the skin turning pink. In another minute it would look like it had never been touched by the heat at all.

"Tucker!" Leala shouted as she stumbled forward.

A muffled "Mama!" came from my arms, and I slowly opened them. Tuck rolled out onto the grass and laughed. "Sadie fly!"

Leala knelt down and scooped him up, squeezing him tightly, and I noticed she was shaking, too. Connor wrapped his arms around them both.

Tears sprang to my eyes at the anguish on Leala's face, the sheer terror. It only took an instant for life to change forever.

Will had tears in his eyes, too, as he helped me stand up. He yelled, "Sadie's fine! Tuck's fine. Everyone's fine!"

I heard mumbles about magic and miracles as Mama and Buzzy rapidly approached.

"Dear Lord, child!" Mama shouted when she finally made it to my side. "Why not give me another heart attack? What's one more this week?" she added dramatically as she edged Will out of the way to look me up and down. Satisfied, she wrapped her arms around me, holding me close, much like Leala was holding Tucker. "Thank God you're both okay. Thank God you were here! And to think you wouldn't have been if *I* hadn't asked you to stay the whole weekend. Lord-a-mercy! These festivals are going to be the death of me one day. I *swanee*!"

I could only smile at Mama's theatrics. I didn't know how she'd reacted the night I'd been pulled from the lake, but I suspected it was something quite similar. She was trying to change her ways, yes, but I fully believed some things she could never change—they were as much a part of her as her curly hair.

She abruptly let go of me, kissed Tuck's head, and patted Leala's shoulder. Then she clapped her hands as she headed back to the patio. "Everyone's okay! Everyone's all right! That's quite enough excitement for the night. Let's finish gettin' these lanterns to the dock! It's about that time to set them loose—and let's put this fire out, shall we? Buzzy? Grab the hose, sugar! *Whew-ee.* I need a drink."

Tucker squirmed in Leala's arms. "I fly! Again?"

"No!" we all shouted.

With a pout, he lifted his hands up in question and asked, "Where Moo?"

Moo. *Oh no.* I glanced at the fire pit and saw the poor stuffed animal lying in the flames, a shadowy lump amid the crackling logs. I swallowed hard and fought the urge to sob, instantly grieving Tucker's beloved friend. Will pulled me into a hug, and I pushed my face against his chest, unable to hold back the tears.

"Maybe he's taking a nap inside," Connor said quickly, his voice thick as he covered up the sad truth.

"We find Moo?" Tuck asked, oblivious to his loss.

His grief would come when Moo wasn't found, but for now I was grateful for him to hold on to his innocence for a while longer.

"Yeah, let's go look," Connor suggested, taking Tucker from Leala's arms and giving her a bleak look.

There were tears in her eyes as she stared at the fire, the flickering orange flames reflected in the moisture. She looked traumatized, as if all the would-haves and could-haves and what-ifs were racing through her head.

I knew those questions well and knew little good would come from dwelling on them.

Buzzy had pulled out the hose and started dousing the remaining flames in the fire pit, and I doubted it would be lit again anytime soon.

Leala suddenly turned and came toward me. Will released me in time for Leala to fling her arms around my shoulders. I hugged her back and felt her body quaking with the fear, the relief. She didn't say anything—and she didn't have to. I could feel it all in the way she clung to me.

When she finally let go, she picked up the tennis ball in the grass and chucked it as far as she could into the water, and it landed with an angry splash. Then she turned and strode toward the house, never having said a single word.

Will took hold of my hands, turning them over to look at the palms and then my forearms as if still unbelieving that I wasn't hurt. "Thank God you and Tuck are okay, Sadie Way. I don't know how you caught him in time. It really was like you were flying."

I didn't know how I'd done it, either. Adrenaline, maybe. Or maybe there *had* been a little lake magic at work. It all seemed a little fuzzy at the moment.

He said, "For a second there, I flashed back to eight years ago when you fell in the lake, to the panic, to the overwhelming fear and the sudden wish of *please*—please be okay."

My skin tingled strangely as Mama's voice echoed in my head, talking about these water lantern festivals being the death of her. What were the odds of Tuck and me having near-death—or, at the very least, life-altering—accidents on the night of the festival? Or that he'd have his at the first festival I'd been to since my accident? And that I'd be the one to save him from harm?

It suddenly didn't seem coincidental at all. It seemed like it had all been set up on purpose. I was supposed to have been here, to experience it. To *live* it. To learn from it. I glanced at the lake, instantly knowing there had been a whole lot of lake magic at work tonight.

Had the purpose I'd been searching for all along been to eventually save Tuck? I didn't think so—I still felt the pulsing pressure inside me, but it was fainter. I was so close to understanding . . . so close yet I couldn't fully grasp it. My heart pounded, my skin tingled, and my thoughts swirled, round and round, caught in a storm I didn't yet understand.

I swayed and Will put his arm around me. "Whoa, I've got you."

"I'm okay. Just a little woozy."

He tightened his grip on me rather than releasing me. "It's probably the adrenaline wearing off."

"Yeah," I answered absently, looking again at the lake. Feeling it pulsing in me. Reminding me that I was alive.

I am alive.

The tingles intensified.

"Let's get you a drink," he said. "Come on. Do you want me to carry you? I will."

The humor in his voice shook me out of my headspace. "I dare you."

He laughed, and my mood lifted, the gloom chased away by the light in his eyes. In one fell swoop, he lifted me up into his arms. "I might not put you down."

My body was pressed against his chest, and my legs hung over his left arm. "All right by me." I smiled. "Plus, I'm less likely to trip over my own feet this way. No need to take another header into the lake tonight."

He shook his head. "Don't even joke."

"Hey ho," Teddy exclaimed as she came out of the house and saw us. "Is there a sign-up sheet for this kind of transport? Because if so, I need a pencil. That's my kind of rideshare."

Bree followed closely behind her. "Sign me up, too, please."

Will laughed but didn't put me down as fireworks continued to burst above us.

Mama came out of the house with a cocktail in hand and shook her head at us, but there was a smile on her face. Before she could say anything that was sure to embarrass me, an air horn echoed across the lake, and she bellowed, "It's time!"

Leala and Connor emerged from the house, still looking shell-shocked. Tuck came out holding Uncle Camp's hand and asking every few seconds where Moo was. Uncle Camp winked at me as he passed, and Iona gave me a pat on the shoulder and a "Well done, Sadie," that made me teary again. Mama must've told them what had happened.

We all headed down to the water, Will not putting me down until we reached the dock. And even then, he held my hand as we all lit the candles inside our lanterns and gathered in a semicircle, facing the heart of the lake.

Mama stepped forward, lifted her lantern, took a deep, shuddering breath, and said, "Here's to good health, safe travels, the power of love, and the gift of life." Then she knelt on the dock, gently put the lantern in the water, and gave it a gentle shove. She watched it float away for a moment before stepping back in place.

I tracked the lantern, bobbing gently, its candle throwing a gentle glow on the water. A swell of emotion built in me, making my chest ache, my throat tighten, my nose sting.

Buzzy stepped forward, picked up his lantern, and said, "Here's to love always finding a way."

Teddy went next. She held hers low, balanced on the palms of her hands. "Here's to never being too old to realize the meaning of true love."

Uncle Camp went next, shuffling forward to pick up his lantern, which was mostly undecorated except for a bunch of squiggly lines, and I realized he'd probably had some help from Tuck. I hoped that whatever he'd written on his wish panel in invisible ink would come true. "Here's to life, love, and new beginnings."

Connor walked forward. He looked at his lantern, decorated with words that made no sense to me, like *red velvet sofa* and *roaches*, but on one panel was a set of coordinates. I knew exactly what those were and what they meant.

He said, "Here's to knowing when to let go and when to hold on. Now and forever."

"I do!" Tuck yelled, running forward with his hands outstretched. Connor held him tightly as they set the lantern in the water and gave it a shove.

The anguish in Leala's features had faded some as she watched her husband and little boy, the lines of her face softening with love. Tears blurred my eyes. I wanted to hug everyone here and not let go. Not for a good, long time.

Bree went next. She cleared her throat and lifted her lantern. "Here's to making the most out of second chances and fresh starts." Then she grinned. "I'm moving to Alabama to live with Teddy!"

There was a sudden rush of hugs and kisses, and happiness bloomed in the air, shooting high like the dazzling fireworks. It chased away the lingering traces of the earlier trauma.

Leala tucked a stray curl behind her ear and held her lantern gingerly. "Here's to strong hearts, strong minds, strong women, and the people who love us, flaws and all."

"Hear, hear," Buzzy said, and everyone laughed.

Will went next. He held the lantern high, and the light fell across his face. "Here's to the healing power of love."

Mama said it was talking that healed, but she was not entirely correct. It was love. It always had been the best healer, and it always would be, and I was grateful to have an abundance of it in my life.

Iona walked to the edge of the dock, adjusted her sweater, and picked up her lantern. "May we always live life to the fullest. Take the trip, take the chance, make the change. Dance. Forgive. Laugh. Always love. Be the light."

I stepped forward, unsure how to put into words what I was feeling as I watched the lanterns bob. My emotions were high, on the brink of full collapse. I'd forgotten for a while, especially eight years ago, how this festival was more about love than wishes. But I felt that love tonight. I felt its full force. I picked up my lantern, glanced over the drawings of books and hearts and music notes, past the phrase *A Will and a Way*, and a badly drawn picture of Leala and me and Mama, then to the candle, flickering in the night, reminding me of a time when I was floating peacefully under the water, watching orbs of light swirl around me. Just beyond the dock all the other lanterns had drifted together, one big pod, their light as a whole much stronger than those that floated alone.

I tried to keep my voice steady as I said, "Where there is dark, there is light; where there is light, there is life; where there is life, there is love; where there is love, there *is* healing. May we never forget how lucky we are to be here together."

A round of cheers went up as I set my lantern afloat, and as soon as I stood up, we fell into a group hug. Will and I stayed behind on the dock as everyone else started back toward the patio, to the cocktails, to the music. It was a celebration, after all.

Will had his arm around me as we watched the pod of lanterns drift away, bound together with love and wishes and hopes and dreams.

"Did you make a wish?" I asked.

"Didn't need to," he said. "All my wishes have already come true."

Sighing happily, I leaned against him and tried to keep the tears from falling from my eyes. Happy tears this time.

"Hey, you okay?" he asked, tipping up my chin to see the whole of my face.

"Yeah," I said, looking out again at the floating lanterns. "I'm just really happy to be alive."

The stars dotted the night sky as I crept outside, sliding the door slowly behind me so it wouldn't squeak. It was a little past two in the morning, and I'd yet to sleep.

I'd been staring at the living room ceiling, lost in my thoughts of life and love and light and darkness. But it had been the tingling sensations that had forced me to get up and go outside.

The tingles buzzed along my skin, up my arms, down my legs, along my fingers and toes. The sensation reminded me of the days when my foot would fall asleep, that feeling of numbness mixed with pins and needles as the nerve endings woke up from a deep sleep.

All this time I suspected my pain tolerance was an indication, a reminder, that part of me had died the night I'd fallen into the lake—but I'd been wrong. I realized now, with these tingles, that the lack of pain was because I'd been numb.

Numb to life.

When I first woke up in the hospital, I'd been so overwhelmed with what had happened, with my new look, with everyone around me acting so strangely, that I'd never processed what a gift I'd been given.

For eight years, I had been alive but not living. I followed the road wherever it took me, going with the flow. I never formed lasting attachments. I drifted. Lost. Restless. Hiding. Denying myself love. In a way, I was my mother. I'd been living life through others and their stories.

Now, as I finally embraced being alive, my numbness was fading, and my body, my soul, was finally coming back to life. When I stepped on a rock and pain shot through my foot, I laughed, simply because I could feel the pain. I was alive. I wanted to dance, to sing, to shout, but I had something important to do first.

Stars twinkled in the inky sky, and in the distance an owl hooted as I quickly made my way to the end of the dock. A gentle breeze blew as I sat cross-legged and just breathed in the night. Lanterns bobbed in the water, dancing in the current. I dipped my fingers in the water, swirling them around in the shape of a heart.

"Thank you, Lady Laurel," I said, my voice carrying on the breeze. "Thank you for saving me. I'm sorry it took me so long to say so. I've been . . . numb. I wouldn't be here without you, wouldn't know Tuck, wouldn't know how much I truly love my family and Will. Wouldn't know that second chances are a gift, and that I don't need a reason for it. I just need to be thankful because I'm still here. So, thank you, for giving me the gift of life."

I heard the squeak of the sliding screen door and turned to see Uncle Camp shuffling toward me. I stood up and met him halfway.

He said, "I got up to get a drink and saw you out here. Thought I'd make sure you were okay."

I looked out over the lake. "More than okay." He gave me a strange look, and I added, "I was just thanking Lady Laurel for saving my life. It took me a long time to realize I'd never done so."

He scratched his beard, then pulled me into a side hug. "Life can be hard, Sadie. Full of twists and turns, pain and heartache, and things that make you question whether life's worth living. But in all my years—and there've been a lot of 'em, mind you—I can tell you that for every hard day, there's an easy one. For every tear, there's a laugh, and that love is the patch for every broken heart. Being alive's a blessing that shouldn't be taken for granted. Some people go their whole lives without appreciating it. Eight years is nothing. A drop in the bucket. The point is you did realize it. Eventually."

I leaned into him, his love. "All it took was coming home . . . and a little lake magic."

He pressed a kiss against my temple, and I smiled as his beard scraped my newly sensitive skin, enjoying the fact that I could feel the whisper of pain caused by his bristly whiskers.

As Uncle Camp and I stepped off the dock onto the grass, a spark of light from the fire pit made me stop in my tracks. "Did you see that? The light in the fire pit?"

"A flare-up?" he asked.

"No. It was a white light." I headed that way and gasped when I saw Moo and the ball Leala had thrown into the lake sitting on one of the Adirondack chairs as if just waiting for someone to come along to play.

Uncle Camp laughed at the sight. "Seems Lady Laurel doesn't want Tuck to stop playing ball with his favorite friend."

"And living his best life," I said, echoing Teddy as tears blurred my vision. I picked up the cow, who looked none the worse for wear for his fiery adventures, and hugged it much like Tucker would have. "He's going to be so happy. Thank you, Lady Laurel!"

Uncle Camp looked out at the lake with such love and affection as he said, "May we always have a touch of lake magic in our lives." He glanced at me. "No matter where we are."

It was his way of saying he supported me no matter what I chose to do or where I chose to live, but right now, there was absolutely no place I'd rather be than exactly where I was.

Chapter 28

Sadie

For having had so little sleep, I awoke early enough on Sunday morning to join Leala and Mama on the dock for an early coffee and to see the loon float past. We'd raised our mugs in a toast to her and her kindnesses as she went by, swimming in and out of the lanterns.

When Leala had seen Moo, she'd burst into tears and had run upstairs to put him in Tucker's arms so it was the first thing her little boy would see when he woke up. The tears were another indication that she still wasn't herself this morning after last night's near tragedy, but I had the feeling it would take some time for her to heal from what could have been.

I'd left her and Mama out on the dock and had come back to the kitchen to work on a batch of cinnamon rolls, which took forever to make but were absolutely worth the trouble. I'd come inside to find Iona sitting at the peninsula with a cup of coffee and said, "You should've joined us outside."

She smiled. "Some things shouldn't be interrupted. That was prime bonding time."

It had been bonding time, and I had to admit I was going to miss it once the weekend was over. "Better late than never."

"Isn't that the truth?" she said.

I lifted the tea towel off the bowl of dough, which had been rising for an hour, and I was happy to see that it had doubled in size. I needed to get the dough rolled, filled, and cut for their second rise before the rest of the yoga crew woke up since, in the warm fuzziness of last night's lantern launch, I'd promised I'd join them for their morning sun salutation. We had all promised, every last one of us, except Will, who'd gone home before the promises were made. I had half a mind to call him to have him join us, but he'd be here soon enough. We were teaming up to collect lanterns later on.

Iona topped off her mug. "From what I've pieced together over the last week, being here last night, for the festival, was quite a big deal for you."

I cleaned a section of countertop, sprinkled some flour on it, and scooped the dough from the bowl. "It seems silly now that I stayed away so long."

"Why did you?"

It was a hard question, one with several answers. "Guilt, mostly. I thought it was my wish that caused my accident. It was a selfish wish, one that set me down a path of constantly trying to prove myself, my worth. I cut myself off from everyone in an effort to figure out why I'd been saved."

I'd been surprised when I woke up this morning to feel a familiar pulsing within me, that push and pull that reminded me so much of the water lapping against the seawall. The pulsing that constantly had me looking for why I'd been saved. I'd been so taken aback to feel it that I'd pinched myself just to see if I could still feel pain.

I could.

It took me a while to puzzle out that my numbness was tied only to my gratitude for being alive and had no connection to why I'd been saved like I'd always suspected. "I still don't quite know why I was saved, but whatever the reason, I'm grateful I was."

She smiled. "A grateful heart is a beautiful sight to see. You're positively beaming today."

"I have a lot to be thankful for."

"Indeed." She stirred sugar into her mug. "Do you regret leaving Sugarberry Cove all those years ago? Seems to me you've learned a lot about yourself, and others, during that time."

I pushed the roller across the dough. "I regret some of it but not all. I wouldn't be who I am today if not for the choices I made in the past. I wouldn't have met all the wonderful people who've shared their beautiful stories with me. But I wish I'd made more of an effort to come back home, instead of cutting myself off completely. I hurt so many people by doing that. Mostly myself."

"A painful lesson."

The wooden rolling pin squeaked as it rolled across the dough, stretching it, shaping it. "But I learned from that lesson. I won't do it again. I'm staying put. I don't know quite how I'm going to juggle two full-time jobs, but right here and now it doesn't matter. All that matters is that I'm home for good."

"I'm glad to hear it, Sadie. I've seen how happy you are here."

She lifted an eyebrow. "Perhaps your quandary isn't so much a question of juggling but balancing."

"What do you mean?"

She took a sip of coffee, and as she set her cup back down on the countertop, I noticed an empty mug next to her hand along with a small pot of sorghum syrup. I held back a smile as I imagined her having Uncle Camp's coffee ready for him when he woke up.

Tomorrow morning, she'd be checking out of the cottage, and Uncle Camp had volunteered to drive her home. I hoped that the two of them had a long, meaningful talk during that ride.

"It's rather like Leala's yoga," she said. "When you first learn to balance on one leg, there's a need for support. Find your support, Sadie, and you'll find your balance."

A bark echoed, and footsteps sounded above our heads. The pipes squeaked. Everyone would be down soon. I hurriedly finished rolling the dough, thinking about balance and support. Balance and support. How did I find it? Where did I find it?

Iona's gaze drifted toward the lake, and she said, "Now, tell me—did you really think Lady Laurel would grant a selfish wish?"

I couldn't help but smile at her wry tone. "I thought so for a long time." I told her of my wish, Leala's, and even my mother's, and how Will was the first one to point out the obvious. That Lady Laurel wouldn't grant those wishes. "But there's still no explaining why all the wishes came true."

"Did they come true?" she asked. "Or did your accident simply set forth a series of events that made it seem that way? From what I've gathered from talking with Teddy and Camp and Susannah and Will and Leala and Connor, only one wish was granted that long-ago night."

I grabbed the bowl of cinnamon topping I'd made earlier, a mix of butter, brown sugar, vanilla, and cinnamon that smelled heavenly, and started sprinkling it over the dough. "Which one?"

"The wish that you be found alive. It was their only plea while they searched for you in the water, half wish, half prayer."

Suddenly choked with tears, I put the bowl down and said, "But that wasn't a wish written on any of the lanterns. It couldn't have been. The lanterns had already been launched when I fell in the lake."

I was reminded suddenly of what Will had said last night.

For a second there, I flashed back to eight years ago when you fell in the lake, to the panic, to the overwhelming fear and the sudden wish of please—*please be okay.*

Iona lifted a slim shoulder. "Who's to say their whispers didn't carry through the air and land on the lanterns floating nearby? That might explain your hair, as well. The light from all those wishes, those wishes so pure of heart that they sparkled like life itself, was used to bring you back to them." She smiled. "And, Sadie, perhaps if you stopped looking for the meaning to life, you'd realize that there is no meaning other than to live a *meaningful* life. Love your life." She winked and rose from her stool. "Or at least those are my theories—take them for what you will."

As I watched her walk outside to join Mama and Leala on the dock, goose bumps rose on my arms, the pulsing inside me faded, and I wondered why those theories sounded like nothing but the absolute truth.

Leala

Lanterns floated by the edge of the dock, caught in the lake current that pulled them along, and every single one that passed by seemed to have either a heart or the word *love* written on it.

Love truly did make the world go round.

Yet it wasn't enough to protect those we loved the most in the world.

"Accidents happen, baby girl," Mama said to me as if she had been reading my mind. "It doesn't matter how loving, caring, or careful you are. They happen, and we have to learn how to deal with them. Don't ruin today by dwelling on a bad yesterday."

It had been decades since she called me baby girl, and a few days ago it would've rankled, but now . . . now it felt a little like a hug.

"Sometimes we deal by denial," she said. " Sometimes we fake our way along, and sometimes we simply accept what's happened and try to find the grace to carry on."

I bit my thumbnail, then dropped my hand into my lap. "I thought . . . I thought all this time if I warned him and protected him and loved him more than life itself, that he'd always be safe. And then last night happened, and in that moment of seeing him about to fall into the fire, there was nothing I could do. It was the absolutely worst feeling in the world, to know there was no way I could stop him from being hurt . . . or killed."

"I know, darlin', I know."

I took a deep breath. "I blamed you, you know. When Daddy died, I mean. I thought for sure there was something you could've done to save him, but there wasn't, was there? Because accidents happen." He hadn't fallen because she wasn't holding the ladder. He'd fallen because his foot had slipped off a rung.

She gave a mirthless laugh. "I knew. But what *you* never knew was that I blamed myself, too. If only I'd insisted on hiring a professional roofer, or bought him a new pair of tennis shoes with better traction, or been standing directly beneath him so maybe I could've caught him. I've been through it all a million times. It's like a bad dream that never ends. It fades sometimes, but something always comes along there to remind me. Looking back on it, I think that instead of just addressing it, I took some of my guilt out on you, because you constantly reminded me of it, with your comments, your name, even your eyes, so like your daddy's. I'm real sorry for that."

I pulled a loose hair off my shirt and set it free in the breeze. If only it were so easy to let go of years of pain, let the wind carry it far away.

Mama went on, saying, "I lived in fear of another accident taking away you or Sadie until I started driving myself crazy and had to stop or lose my mind completely. I disconnected, which I didn't think was hurting anyone, but it was. It hurt you. And Sadie. And ultimately Buzzy, too. I should've gone to a counselor or a therapist, but it's always easy to see that kind of thing only when you've come through the other side. Sometimes distance has a funny way of making you see things a whole lot clearer."

My eyes filled with tears as she finally opened up after all this time. "I'm sorry, too, Mama. I'm so ashamed that I ever blamed you for Daddy's death."

"Hush now," she said. "We all coped the best we knew how."

I smiled, but it felt starched, pained. "We need better coping skills."

She cupped my face with her hand. "You're already one step ahead of me, Leala Clare, with your yoga. When you almost died giving birth, you found yoga. You didn't keep everything bottled up or buried, like I did. You let it out. You let it out so you could heal."

Stretch the body, heal the mind. "I didn't know how much it helped me until this past week."

"I wasn't just blowing smoke the other day when I said I'm learning from you girls. You're teaching me new ways to cope, too, with your yoga lessons. One day I might just be able to do a handstand—wouldn't that be something?"

"Mama, I hate to tell you this, but you're not really doing yoga by sitting here and drinking coffee. Meditation, maybe. But yoga?" I shook my head.

"Well, *shoo*. That's a bubble buster. But you can teach me the proper way, right? Once you get your certification?"

"Mama, I don't—"

She reached down and pulled a piece of paper out of her pocket. "I went on that there internet last night and found this. It's a yoga studio in Birmingham that offers classes for certification. Classes start soon, and there are still spots open."

I stared at the name of the school on the paper and the phone number Mama had written down, and my heart beat a little faster. "It doesn't make sense for me to do this. I have an accounting degree."

Teaching yoga wasn't a nine-to-five job with a steady paycheck, yet I'd never wanted something so badly in my life. And suddenly I heard Sadie's voice in my head, telling me how her job wasn't traditional but it was meaningful. Meaningful meant everything when it came to happiness.

"You've always gone after what you wanted and achieved it, Leala Clare. You never let anyone or anything stop you. I've always been a little jealous of that, if I'm being honest. I was never that brave. So why stop now? What do you truly want? Because every day you get a choice to start over, begin again. And, by the way, if money's an issue in your decision, I'd be pleased to make a contribution toward your tuition if you're needing financial assistance. I love you, darlin', and I want you to be happy."

Her admission of jealousy also explained a lot about her behavior toward me over the years, and I realized how hard it had to have been for her to confess it, her pride being what it was. My heart suddenly softened as I considered how *her* choices had shaped her—then and now. I smiled through my tears and threw my arms around her. "I love you, too, Mama. I need to talk to Connor about it first, but then I'll call about enrollment. I promise."

She hugged me tighter, and whispered, "Then now is probably

a good time to let you know that I can't be providin' any tuition assistance until I sell the cottage."

I laughed. "We'll be fine, but thank for the offer, Mama."

"I'm real proud of you, Leala Clare."

Tears spilled over at hearing the words I'd longed to hear my whole life long. "You can call me LC if you want. I kind of miss it."

Pulling away, she laughed and said, "Well, don't you even dare think about going back to Mother." She shuddered.

The screen door squeaked, and I wiped my eyes and saw Iona coming toward us, then a moment later heard another squeak and Connor and Tucker stepped out.

Tucker spotted me and yelled, "Mama! Moo! Found Moo! Moo!" He raised the stuffed animal in the air, shaking it by its neck, and raced forward, nearly falling over his own feet.

"Slow down!" Mama and I said at the same time.

Then we leaned against each other and laughed.

In no time at all, everyone had gathered together on the dock except Uncle Camp.

Mama stood up. "I'll go rouse the sleepyhead. I've got to use the little ladies' room, anyhow."

Sadie and Bree were chatting up a storm about Bree moving to Alabama, while Teddy looked like she wanted a couple of aspirin and a weeklong nap. Tuck was regaling Buzzy and Iona with a story about Moo flying.

Connor leaned into me and said, "Looked like you and your mom were having a good talk out here."

I smiled. "Really good." I took a breath. "Hey, what do you think about me teaching yoga? Professionally, I mean. I'd have to get my certification . . ."

He took a beat before answering, letting it all sink in before he smiled. "You'll be an amazing teacher."

I threw my arms around him and kissed him. Teddy let out a catcall and Sadie yelled, "Get a room."

We were all laughing when Mama came back out of the house, rushing forward much the way Tucker had earlier, nearly tripping on her feet. But it wasn't excitement on her face—it was shock and sorrow.

She hiccupped, holding back tears. "It's Camp . . ."

Chapter 29

Sadie

The morning's events sat heavy on us all, weighing us down with its grief. Shoulders drooped. Chins dipped downward. Tears fell freely. My chest ached so badly it was hard to take a deep breath.

Uncle Camp was gone, having drifted off forever in his sleep.

In my head, I could hear his voice. *I'm a lucky man.*

Maybe so, but we were all luckier for having had him in our lives. His love, his care, his everything. I pulled my legs up on the chair and wrapped my arms around them, wanting to curl into myself, away from the pain.

The police had been notified, the coroner summoned, and Uncle Camp's body had been taken to the local funeral home. It had been a hellacious flurry of activity, and there was still more to do, funeral arrangements to be made.

Well into the afternoon now, we sat stunned, this family of mine, including the family of my heart. The only one missing was Iona, who had put away an empty coffee cup and pot of sorghum syrup and retired to her room a few hours ago, her face wet with tears, her broken heart visible for all to see.

Teddy flitted about the kitchen, making coffee, making tea, making anything to keep herself busy. She went from fridge to cabinet to island like she'd been doing it her whole life, seemingly as comfortable here in the cottage's kitchen as she was in her own.

Bree played jacks with Tucker on the floor, and even he was subdued, as if sensing the monumental shift to his world but not fully understanding it. Every once in a while, he'd stop what he was doing and pet Nigel's head, who'd return the love with a lick to his hand.

Mama sat on the sofa, silent for once, and the quiet said more than her words ever had. Buzzy was next to her, his arm around her shoulders, and she leaned into him, as if needing the support. Needing him.

I'd always known her to be so strong, resilient—a rock. But

her weakness had been revealed. Her grief had cracked that rock open, highlighting a soft spot inside, a heart that bled its sorrow.

Earlier I'd called Will and told him what had happened and declined his offer to come over since the house had been full of emergency personnel. Now I regretted that choice, wishing he were here to lean on.

Leala and Connor sat on the other sofa, and Leala met my gaze with moisture in her eyes. "Should we check on Iona?"

"I'll bring her some tea," Teddy said, already setting a tray. "And see if she's hungry since she hasn't eaten all day."

I glanced at the clock. It was almost four, and none of us had eaten much as grief had stolen our appetites. I rested my chin on my knees, hating this downtime but not sure what else to do. I wanted to be busy, to *do* something, to not just sit here soaking in my misery, lost in my memories, trying to recall every moment I'd shared with Uncle Camp throughout the years. It was impossible to remember them all. There'd been too many.

Nigel lifted his head as Teddy climbed the stairs, tray in hand, and I wished that I'd been the one to bring it upstairs, to give comfort to Iona, and to receive it as well. She'd worked her way into my heart this past week, with her wisdom and advice, and I was going to miss her when she finally went back to Wetumpka for good. And now I wondered when that would be. Would she stay for Uncle Camp's funeral? After all, she had worked her way into his heart, too.

A moment later, Teddy raced down the stairs. "Iona's not in her room. There's money on the bed and a note saying she was going home and thanking y'all for everything."

I set my feet on the floor and perched on the edge of my chair. "I didn't see her leave. Did anyone see her leave?" No one, it seemed, had.

I pulled out my phone and called Iona's number. A recorded message responded, telling me that the number I had dialed wasn't valid. I called again and received the same message. "This is strange."

"I'm worried," Mama said. "This is unlike her."

Leala stood. "I'll ask around the neighborhood, see if anyone saw her."

I jumped up. "I'll drive down to her house. If she took a ride-share, she's likely already home." I ran for my purse, my keys, and was out the door and on the road before anyone could stop me.

I'd planned to call with updates but realized soon after driving away that I'd left my phone on the cushion of the wingback, and I hadn't wanted to waste any time by going back for it. Iona's address was in my car's GPS memory, so I sped southward, toward the small bungalow overlooking the Coosa River.

A little less than an hour and a half later, as jazz played loudly on the radio to drown out my thoughts, I entered Wetumpka's city limits and forced myself to slow down as I followed the route through the town and over the bridge to Iona's house. When I pulled into the driveway, I stared in shock at the bungalow that stood before me, and then double-and triple-checked that I had the correct address.

It was the same.

Except it wasn't.

Throwing open the door, I stepped out onto the gravel driveway that had been paved only last week. The bungalow that sat before me was filthy and boarded up, nearly covered in vines, and the porch roof had collapsed at some point in time.

I heard a bark and looked over to see a neighbor watering the lawn, her dog keeping a wary eye on me. I crossed the lot, now devoid of the green grass I'd seen last week. My steps were hesitant, unsure on the cracked, dusty earth. "Excuse me, ma'am?"

An older woman, in her seventies at the very least, flipped the nozzle on her hose and wiped her hands on her pants. "Hello! Don't get many visitors out this way. Are you lost, dear?"

I shook my head and pointed at the house. "Do you know what happened to the woman who lived there?"

"Oh heavens. She died some years back. Forty years, fifty? A terrible tragedy while she was on her honeymoon. Eventually, her husband up and moved north, leaving this place behind to rot. If you're looking to buy the land, the county records office is the best place for you to start."

My heart started beating harder, faster. "Thanks," I said, playing along so I didn't seem like a crazy woman. "I think I'm going to poke around a bit first."

"Do be careful. That place has been abandoned some time now. No tellin' what you'll find."

"Thank you kindly."

I walked back toward the house, toward the side door I had gone in and out of not that long ago, and the river rapids splashed in the background as if urging me on. The door stood ajar. Taking a deep breath, I nudged it fully open. The house was empty, a mere shell with trees growing through the walls and the earth visible through the floor. My gaze shifted to the kitchen, and I froze, my breath catching in my throat. Amid the dirt, the dust, the decay, the fridge gleamed bright white, the same as it had nearly two weeks ago, but gone were all the photos and most of the magnets. All that remained was a single postcard held in place by a round, black magnet.

Watching my step, I moved toward the fridge, and my eyes began filling with tears when the image on the postcard came into view. It was a lake scene, with SUGARBERRY COVE written in swirling letters across the bottom. At the top was printed WISH YOU WERE HERE.

I reached for the card, tugging it free, and was surprised to see a yellowed piece of paper fall free from behind it. I bent to pick the scrap off the dirty floor and brought it toward the light to read the faded lettering.

As the words sank in, I started sobbing my heart out right there in the kitchen. I only pulled myself together and ran for the car when I realized I didn't have much time to get home before the sun set—because suddenly I knew exactly where I'd find Iona.

❧

I sped back to Sugarberry Cove, the lines on the roadway blurring, and the jazz had done little to hold my thoughts at bay, my hope.

By the time I parked in the driveway, my heart was near to pounding straight out of my chest. Teddy jumped off the sofa when I came running in the front door.

"Holy hell, Sadie! We were about to send the police after you. No one could reach you."

"I forgot my phone." I went to the bottom of the stairs and yelled upward. "Mama! Leala! Hurry!"

"What's going on?" Teddy asked. "Did you find Iona?"

I grabbed her hands. "I'll tell you all about it in a minute. Help me gather everyone together. We need to hurry."

"All right, anything! But Buzzy went home to shower. Connor, Bree, and Tuck took Nigel for a walk. Leala's out back. I'll get Susannah." She ran up the stairs.

I hated that some of them were going to miss this, but we couldn't wait until they returned. I tossed my purse on the sofa and went flying out the back door.

As soon as I stepped outside, the scent of the lake hit me full force, twisting something deep within me, something that recognized this place as home. *Home is where your heart is.* I'd never been able to find another town with enough heart to suit me, because my heart had always been here, waiting for me to return. And with that thought, I suddenly had an idea on how to balance my job with the B and B, because I knew I couldn't do it alone.

"Sadie!" Leala jumped up. "Did you find her?"

"Kind of. Come on, come on!" I held out my hand to her.

She took one look at it and slipped her hand in mine.

Mama and Teddy came running out of the house. Mama said, "Sadie! Good Lord, what's going on? Did you find Iona?"

"I did. Hurry!" I cast a look toward the horizon. The sun had started to sink. "We're going to miss them."

"*Them?* Them who?" Mama asked, trotting after Leala and me as we ran for the dock.

I scanned the water, then sat down, finally taking a deep breath. Leala sat next to me, and Mama next to her. Winded, Teddy plopped on the other side of me. We'd once again formed a small semicircle. "It'll be anytime now," I said.

Mama breathed heavily. "Sadie, I love you, darlin', but I think you've done lost your mind with the grief of it all."

I knew I looked crazy. Sounded it, too. But then I glanced at the clipping and postcard in my hand and joy welled up, brimming in my eyes. The postcard with two loons swimming together in the lake. "Just wait. Iona's with Uncle Camp. Or he's with Iona. Either way. Look! There!" I pointed to the water.

Two loons came into view, their graceful black and white bodies gliding through the water, their necks bumping against each other as they hooted softly, reconnecting, reminiscing.

Leala gasped as the pair made their way past us, pausing for a long moment in front of the dock before carrying on, swimming toward the cove. I snuffled, trying to hold in the tears that had gathered in my eyes, and I felt an arm go around me. Teddy.

I leaned into her and handed Mama the yellowed clipping I'd found. It was an old marriage announcement from a newspaper.

Mr. and Mrs. George Meaks
announce the wedding of their daughter
Fiona Alice
to
Mr. Whitman Camp Scott
on Saturday, the twenty-first of June,
Nineteen hundred and sixty-nine
Wetumpka, Alabama

I explained what I found when I'd gotten to Iona's house, how a neighbor told me the woman who lived there had died decades ago, and how the postcard had led me to where we were right now.

"Hot dang!" Mama cried. "Fiona Meaks, Iona Teakes. They're one and the same, aren't they?"

I nodded, so sure of it no one would ever be able to tell me otherwise.

Leala covered her mouth and pointed at the clipping, then at the birds floating out of view. "Iona, *Fiona*, is the lady of the lake? She's our . . . *aunt*?"

"Oh my heavens!" Teddy exclaimed. "So it is true that she can walk among us. Bree is never going to believe this."

"I didn't know Uncle Camp's real name was Whitman," Leala said, taking the clipping out of Mama's hand.

"I knew his real name was Whitman, but I had no idea Camp had been married," Mama added. "He'd never said. I'm not sure your daddy even knew, since this marriage happened when he was just a little kid, and those Scotts were always so tight-lipped about tragedies."

Leala slid her a wry look, and I read it perfectly. This from a woman who barely spoke about Daddy's death.

Mama glanced at us as if knowing what we were thinking and simply smiled.

The truth was that there was a lot Uncle Camp had never shared with us, and I realized it was probably the source of the somberness I'd always sensed within him. His young bride had died shortly after they married. It was a situation too tragic to comprehend.

"She's been waiting for him all this time," I said. "Waiting and calling for him, to let him know she was still here."

He had to have known she was the lonely loon, and it was no wonder why he'd decided to stay here at the cottage all those years ago. I smiled through my tears, recalling how he always claimed that he'd found happiness here, among the only family he had left. Which, unbeknownst to us, had included the love of his life.

I ran my finger across the pair of birds on the postcard, hoping they both knew how much *I* loved them. It was only then that I flipped over the postcard and saw that there was writing on the back.

You're welcome, Sadie.

Chapter 30

Sadie

The loons never returned.

When I was home, I still looked for them, even though I knew they were gone. However, sometimes, in the still of the morning or the peaceful hush of twilight, I swore I could hear them calling to each other, their hooting playful and light, and it always filled me with joy. The joy of knowing that love never died.

On the desk, my cell phone buzzed, and I checked the message. It was from Mama, to both Leala and me.

Just landed in Spain. No rain on the plane!

Which was followed by a dozen emojis and #SeeWhatIDidThere. She was an emoji fanatic, a hashtag lunatic, and I had become extremely grateful for all the years she had been unplugged. I couldn't help smiling as I typed back about hurricanes in Hartford, like the song in *My Fair Lady*, but then deleted it and sent her back six emojis. She didn't like to be outshone on the emoji front.

She and Buzzy had been traveling since I officially bought the cottage in October, but they promised to be back for Christmas, just over a week from now.

I swiveled to look at the painting on the wall. It was the mandala canvas that used to hang in Mama's room. I stared at the three twisted hearts in the center and fought the urge to paint over them, opening them, just like Mama, Leala, and I had opened our hearts to each other. Leaving them as they were on the canvas was a good reminder not to rewrite history but to learn from it as Buzzy had once said.

My gaze went to a framed photo that sat on the built-in bookcase Will had installed in the small office. It was a wedding photo of Uncle Camp and Fiona that I found in a lockbox while going through his things.

He'd been a soldier in uniform at the time, and she'd been in a gingham dress, nipped in tight at the waist. It looked to be at a picnic, and I would have bet my last dollar that the plate in Uncle Camp's hand held ambrosia salad.

Iona—Fiona—was the lady of the lake. My great-aunt. Once we put all the pieces together, Leala shared how once, Iona had mentioned never having children but that she had the comfort of living near a big extended family who constantly reminded her of what was important in life.

She'd been talking about us.

I still wondered to this day if in his final days Uncle Camp had somehow known Iona was his Fiona, especially with the way he'd been taken with her straight off. I rather hoped so. During these past few months I'd come to believe that Fiona had somehow known Uncle Camp's death was near, and that's why she'd suddenly decided to make a personal appearance in our lives. First, by reaching out to me about doing a piece on the ambrosia salad. And then by showing up here at the cottage to spread her love and kindness to help heal our family before we faced yet another tragedy. It was the only thing that made sense to me about the timing of all that had happened.

My gaze wandered to the postcard I'd found on the fridge in Wetumpka, sandwiched in a frame made of two pieces of glass so both sides were visible, and as always, I couldn't help thinking about the last conversation I'd had with Iona before she disappeared from our lives.

The light from all those wishes, those wishes so pure of heart that they sparkled like life itself, was used to bring you back to them.

I'd drowned on a summer night a little more than eight years ago in Lake Laurel, at just eighteen years old. But I'd been saved. Brought back to life. Brought back to a *new* life. To a new normal. All these years later, I was finally figuring out who this new Sadie Way Scott was exactly. And I had finally learned why I had been saved.

I'd been saved by the wishes of the people who loved me most in the world so I could learn to live a meaningful life. Learn to love life.

Blinking away tears, I turned back to my computer screen. I wasn't sure why Uncle Camp had never told us of his pretty bride who'd drowned in the lake, and I wondered if it had something to do with wanting to keep his ties to lake magic a secret or if some memories were simply too painful to share. I'd never know, but

I was grateful for the time I'd had with both of them, the lessons they'd taught me. The love they'd given me. And knowing they were together again had lessened the weight of my grief.

There were footsteps in the hall, and I smiled when Will appeared in the doorway, dressed in jeans and a tight long-sleeve T-shirt. "What time are we leaving for the thing tonight?"

I stood and walked over to him, unable to resist the pull. I looped my arms around his neck, and his hands circled my waist. "I'm not sure. I need to double-check. Why?"

"A client has an emergency plumbing problem." Kissing behind my ear, he added, "I promised I'd be right over, but maybe it can wait awhile longer."

Reluctantly, I pushed away from him, but my hands lingered on his chest, and the diamond in my engagement ring glinted in the light thrown by the desk lamp. Will had asked me to marry him this past weekend, and I'd said yes. "No, no. Go. I'll text you the time of the concert. And stop looking at me like that or I'll change my mind and won't let you leave."

He continued to look at me, heat flaring in his eyes. "Don't be tempting me like that."

Laughing, I took a big step back. "Besides, I need to get back to work, too."

"The book?" he asked, eyeing my desk.

The desk that had once belonged to my father. Will had worked magic on the old oak beast, taming it to fit the room better, to fit my style. I hadn't let him sand out the scars, though, thinking of how they told the story of my daddy and his dreams.

I shook my head. "A video." But I smiled thinking about the book I'd started. I was tentatively titling it *Hey, Y'all: A Southern Hankerin' Collection of Food Memories*. My creativity was coming back, roused from its lengthy dormancy. I'd barely started the book, but I was already enjoying writing up short essays, featuring people who had great stories and food memories to share but were camera shy, like the mother of the young woman I'd met at the hardware store.

"Good luck with it. I'll see you later on." He leaned forward to give me a proper kiss and lingered. And I let him.

"Whoa-ho!" Teddy said as she came around the corner. "Did it suddenly get right hot in here or is it me?"

Will and I drew apart. He laughed and said, "Real hot," before heading for the door with a wave and a look of regret.

Teddy fanned her face with one hand and held a box against her side with the other. "You two are going to light this place on fire one day, I swear." She held the box out. "This just arrived for you. No return address. So mysterious. I'm off to the market. Do you need anything?"

I took the package out of her hands. "No, thanks. I think we're good. What time is Bree's concert again?"

"Seven. She says we're under no obligation to go." She laughed, and the loose bun on top of her head wobbled. "As if."

Balance.

I'd found it in Teddy and Bree. When I offered the job of live-in manager to Teddy, she'd thrown her arms around me and cried. Bree, too. And recently Bree had confessed that her wish on the night of the water lantern festival had been to stay in Sugarberry Cove, because it had felt like home to her, too, and that we felt like family.

It might've been the sweetest thing anyone had ever said to me.

The cottage had been closed for the whole month of October, undergoing a big remodel, top to bottom. By the time it was done, there was barely a surface untouched. Having a website with online bookings had increased our occupancy tremendously. Our big, grand relaunch had been a huge success.

After the renovations, Teddy had moved into Mama's old room and Bree into mine and Leala's. I had moved into Uncle Camp's old suite, and it wasn't long after that Will moved in with me.

Teddy had flourished as the manager of the cottage, loving the new people who came into our lives nearly every day. Bree voluntarily helped out whenever she felt she was needed, in between her schoolwork, extracurriculars, and babysitting Tucker. Nigel had become the house dog, a mascot of sorts, though he spent a lot of time next door at Leala's.

"Will and I will be at the concert," I told her. "Leala and Connor, too. We wouldn't miss it for the world."

Bree had surprised us all with her decision to enroll in the local school system for her senior year instead of homeschooling, and she was thriving. She'd joined the chorus and drama club and had made some new friends. She and Teddy had been looking at colleges, and I was already dreading the day when I would wake up and she wouldn't be here, under the same roof.

My phone dinged with an incoming message, and Teddy said, "I'll be back in a bit. Text if you need me, darlin'."

I heard the front door close and the truck start up as I set the package on my desk and picked up my phone. It was a message from Leala: In Hartford, Hereford, and Hampshire? Hurricanes hardly happen.

I couldn't help laughing. Sometimes we were more alike than either of us ever realized. Mama quickly sent a dozen laughing faces, and I sent only three. Putting down the phone again, I sat and turned my attention back to the video I'd been uploading, watching the progress bar move slowly. I'd cut my videos back to twice a month, and so far there had been no big issues with doing so. I was away from the cottage a day or two at most, then back again ready to greet new guests, though I took more of a background role in that regard while Teddy took the lead.

Instead of watching the progress of the upload, I scooped up the package and carried it into the kitchen and set it on the quartz countertop. Out of the corner of my eye, I saw Nigel trotting ahead of Leala and Tuck, who were walking through the backyard hand in hand. Moo was once again in a headlock, trapped in the bend of Tuck's elbow. That poor, beloved cow.

They'd taken to coming over in the afternoons when I was home for a quick visit, a chat, a cup of coffee, cookies, *connection* before Connor got home from work at five thirty. I adored every minute of the time we spent together.

A second later, the slider squeaked, and Tucker raced to a counter stool and climbed up. "Auntie Sadie! I have cookie?"

Leala closed the door behind her and said, "I'm surprised he doesn't call you Aunt Cookie at this point."

"Give it time." I smiled and handed him two cookies, one for him, and one for his best friend, Moo. Nigel raced through the great room and then up the stairs, no doubt looking for Bree or Teddy or perhaps smelling the adopted kitten that Bree was caring for—and hiding—until Connor could gift the sweet little baby to Leala for Christmas.

I found a box knife and slit the tape on top of the package.

"What have you got there?" Leala asked, nodding to the box,

her curls falling forward as she leaned in. Her face glowed with happiness that came from deep within, from being loved, from being fulfilled, from being herself. She and Connor had moved into Buzzy's house about the same time I had moved in here, but their renovations hadn't been nearly as all encompassing as mine—mostly new paint and converting the room above the garage into a yoga studio.

"I'm not sure. It just arrived."

Leala was loving her yoga certification classes and was hoping that by this time next year she'd be using that new studio as a home business. There were already a few people interested in taking her classes. Word of mouth was powerful in a small town.

Tucker chomped his cookies while happily playing with the set of jacks I kept on the counter for his visits, and Nigel returned to inhale any dropped crumbs. One day I'd tell Tucker all about the man who'd owned those jacks before him.

"Did I see Will leave a few minutes ago?" Leala asked. "He'll be back for the concert, right?"

I smiled. Some things she could never change, either. Like worrying. "An emergency call. He promised he'll be there tonight."

She took a cookie from the plate. "Good. I don't want Bree to think we don't care."

Her gaze drifted around the room, so different in appearance from when Mama had lived here but still very much the same. Old memories lingered like ghosts, reminding us of the many things Mama had missed out on. We weren't going to make the same mistakes.

Inside the larger box was a smaller one, wrapped in sleek black and white ribbon dotted with white orbs. I pulled the ribbon free and lifted the lid to find two teacups nestled in a sea of tissue paper. My heart fluttered. I'd seen cups like these before, at a small cottage in Wetumpka, hanging from hooks near an old-fashioned oven. One cup said MR., the other MRS., but these were both in perfect condition.

"Oh, it's an engagement present! These look vintage. Who sent them?" Leala asked, digging through the box, looking for a card.

She wouldn't find one in there, but it didn't matter. I knew exactly where these had come from. "They're from a couple of old lovebirds, delivered by way of a little lake magic."

Excerpt from *Hey Y'all: A Southern Hankerin' Collection of Food Memories*

Coffee

He took his story to the grave. Some walks down memory lane, he'd told me once, are too painful to talk about. He was my great-uncle Camp, my daddy's uncle, who came to live with my family to help fulfill a dream and ended up staying, teaching us all the true meaning of unconditional love.

He's also the one who taught me that every recipe has a story. That every person has a story. That every person *is* a story. He has a story, too. A good one. One we learned only after he died.

I was twelve years old when he showed me how to make coffee the way my great-granny had taught him, which included a whole lot of chicory and very little coffee. She drank it from a saucer and sweetened it with sorghum syrup to cut the chicory's bitterness. It was a sweet habit Uncle Camp adopted as a young boy and continued long after I tweaked the recipe to include a whole lot of coffee and very little chicory.

Life hasn't been quite the same without him here. I'll tell his story for him one day, because he also once told me that some walks down memory lane can be beautiful. Since he's been gone, I've taken to drinking my coffee with sorghum syrup. It makes me feel like he's still here with me. And I swear, sometimes, in the heart of the quiet mornings, I can hear him reminding me that it's okay to grieve, that it's okay to miss him, that it's only because of the bitter that you fully appreciate the sweet.

ACKNOWLEDGMENTS

Every once in a while I turn to social media for help with naming people or places in my books. For *The Lights of Sugarberry Cove,* I asked for suggestions in naming Sugarberry's town center. Thanks go to Christa Y., whose suggestion of *promenade* combined with Jan L.'s offering of *landing* turned into Sugarberry Landing, which has an upper and lower promenade. And also to Sandy G., whose suggestion of Peddlar's Lane spurred the creation of Hawker Street. Although I didn't use my father's suggestion of Crow's Nest for a street name, I did use it for a shop—thanks, Dad.

I am thankful to Fred W. for humbly sharing the details of his own "cardiac situation," which helped me with the finer details of Susannah's issues, though she was much, much more dramatic in her retelling. May your big heart continue to heal and strengthen.

Thank you to Jessica Faust and BookEnds, who work tirelessly to get my books into the hands of readers across the world. I'm so grateful for Kristin Sevick, who knows just when to rein me in or let me run free—thank you for your encouragement and wise edits. Thank you to everyone at Forge for working so hard behind the scenes to make my books the best they can possibly be. And thank you to the team at Macmillan Audio for an amazing job on the production of the audio book—and for finding the talented narrators who bring my characters to life.

And, as always, I'm extremely thankful to my family, who inspire me daily. Much love to you.